LIKE
Fire
WE
Burn

AYLA DADE

sourcebooks
casablanca

Originally published as *Like Fire We Burn* (Winter Dreams #2) by Ayla Dade, © 2022 by Penguin Verlag, a division of Penguin Random House Verlagsgruppe GmbH, München, Germany. Translated from German by Alexander Booth.

Published by Sourcebooks Casablanca, an imprint of Sourcebooks
1935 Brookdale RD, Naperville, IL 60563-2773
(630) 961-3900
sourcebooks.com

Originally published as *Like Fire We Burn* (Winter Dreams #2) in 2022 in Germany by Penguin Verlag, an imprint of Penguin Random House Verlagsgruppe. This edition issued based on the paperback edition published in 2022 in Germany by Penguin Verlag, an imprint of Penguin Random House Verlagsgruppe.

Cataloging-in-Publication Data is on file with the Library of Congress.

Printed and bound in the United States of America.
VP 10 9 8 7 6 5 4 3 2 1

To all the girls with their heads in the clouds

Back then, you and me, we were so much,
you remember?

We were autumn kisses and winter light,
and there was love in your eyes every time
you laughed with joy, every time I said
we're more than what
others claim to be,
happy souled, empty as clouds

We were the fire burning in our hearts,
pure and indestructible, no one could put it out,
hot caresses on my skin,
I still feel them
deep inside

Every breath of ours was poetry,
the moon in your eyes, shining
onto my skin with every glance, grazing my lips,
showing me that what we had,
you and me,
was not of this world

Back then, you and me, we were so much,
you remember?

1
Some Memories Never Leave

Aria

The first thing I see are the Rockies.

It's always been this way. Every time I'd get out of bed and look out the window. Every time I'd leave the house. The Rockies were there.

And the first thing I think of, here, back home, back in Aspen, is Wyatt.

Wyatt Lopez. *The* Wyatt who broke my heart.

I could leave it at that, but it'd be a lie. He didn't just break it— that isn't remotely comparable with what he really did.

If I were forced to say what happened, I'd have to cover my ears and turn off my head because I'd still be able to hear it. Because whenever I think about it, it happens all over again. And to be honest, I don't want to think about it, ever, not at all.

And yet, I do. I mean, come on, not to do so would be inhuman.

Wyatt Lopez was everything. And I'm not just saying that because it's tearing me apart and I miss him, but because that's how things *were*. We were obsessed with each other. Not in some screwed up, toxic way, but hungry for love, both of us, and that, to be honest, is the most beautiful thing in the world. I mean, of course it is, unconditional love squared; it doesn't get any better than that. And that is precisely why it hurt so *much*, so goddamn much, when he decided to stick his pole into Gwendolyn, as if she were me, as if—*oops*—it just happened, no big deal, totally normal, just some kind of mix-up.

Memories can be *so* screwed up when they're not the good ones.

I took off because I couldn't think anymore, couldn't feel, because I cracked under the weight of too many feelings and rage and *Wyatt*.

And then there was the video. That video of *my* Wyatt with his broad upper body and his muscular arms in that dark room. I can see him stumbling and knocking a vase off the nightstand. I see it exploding on the ground, and then I see him falling somehow or other onto the bed, onto that bed with the reindeer linen and a view of the moon-bathed Aspen Highlands, bright and clear and far too beautiful for the moment. Then I see her, Gwendolyn, who must be thinking she's me, lying in that bed and spreading her legs, and then—*oops*—she ruins my life. *He* ruins my life. And then nothing's left; all I feel is pain and hate and sadness and rage and love. What a load of shit. Why love, *why, why, why*?

And now I'm back again. *Back to the roots*. The doors of Aspen County Airport open. I take a deep breath of ice-cold air and bury my hands into the lined pockets of my parka. Rub my tired eyes. Getting sleep on a red-eye flight is just impossible.

It's been almost a year since I was last here. It was just over Christmas, but those two weeks were enough to make me spend the next ten months trying to get Wyatt's face out of my head. His features are just far too beautiful, what with that little space between his incisors, those little dimples in his cheeks, and that haircut of his, wild and fuzzy on top, short on the sides, perfect every day, even though something like that's just not possible.

It didn't work. His face is there. Right there in front of me. It's been two years, but he's there all the time, even though he's not.

That's wild.

"Aria!"

I turn away from the imposing dimensions of Snowmass Mountain and look to my right.

William is leaning against his sky-blue Ford pickup. He pushes off and spreads his arms into a huge hug. That's William. Aspen's administration guy. Aspen's nuttiest inhabitant with the biggest heart you could imagine. And he loves hugs. What he'd really love to do is hug the whole wide world. He always says this planet's too lonely. That the world needs love and those who are ready to give it. *How right he is*, I think, before thinking of Wyatt again, *Goddamn, when is this going to stop?*

I smile. "Hey, Will." His mustache scratches my cheek as he wraps his arms around me. He smells just like he did before. Antiques and horses.

He lets go and puts my suitcase and bag in the back. "I wanted to come with the carriage."

"I'd have liked that."

"I know." He goes to the passenger-side door and opens it for me. "But I'm afraid the highway would've scared the horses."

"I bet."

It takes William three tries to get his truck going. The motor growls to a start, and the radio springs to life with some country song or other. That's Aspen for you. Everything seems peaceful. A massive mountain range and, right in the middle of it, little house upon little house upon little house with people who all know one another. If this was a film, we'd all be wearing old-school clothes and dancing around our bell tower with country tunes in the background because everything is beautiful, everything is homey (so long as you don't go any deeper into the sounds of certain folks' hearts).

We leave the airport and take the highway downtown.

"Your mother's happy to see you."

"I'm happy, too."

Mom's got rheumatism. Over the last few months it's gotten worse, but she kept it a secret because she knew that I'd immediately toss everything overboard and come home. Because that's how I am, always worried, far too selfless, and full of love, even though Wyatt did his best to destroy everything inside me.

But I'm Aria. I am *nice*. I am *good*. That's why I'm here. I don't care about my heart. But I care about my mom. And, well, to be honest, I've spent the last two years hoping someone would call and say they needed me so that I could come back home. I would never have admitted it to myself on my own. I would never have been able to say, *Hey, Aria, let's be honest, you don't even want to be at Brown. You'd rather be back at home. You want to go on morning hikes and become one with the Aspen Highlands, want to see the footprints of little birds in the snow, and want to watch Wyatt from a distance and imagine how things would be if he had never cheated on you.*

What a nice thought. *If he'd never cheated on you.* Today we'd still be what we used to think we were.

"I don't understand why you don't want to work at the stables, Aria." William turns on his blinker and takes the exit. "The job would be perfect for you."

"Your horses *hate* me, Will."

"They don't hate you. They're just wary."

"Last winter Sally tried to bite my arm off."

"Don't take it personally. She was really agitated back then."

"You should stop putting her on a diet all the time. She becomes a danger to the public. Really, that animal is a real T. rex."

He sighs. "I'm afraid she's going into menopause."

"A tragedy. She's going to trample all of Aspen. I told you back then already. 'This egg doesn't look all that good; don't let it hatch.'"

William laughs. "It's nice to have you back again, Aria."

I smile, sink deeper into my fake-fur hoodie, and imagine hearing these words from someone other than William. Imagine hearing them come from a man who, two years ago, placed his mouth upon lips that weren't mine. An awful thought. Awful. I don't want to think about it, but I do.

Masochistic, right?

"You can let me out here, Will."

"Nonsense. You don't want to lug your suitcase halfway through town."

"It's just a couple of minutes on foot."

"Yeah, that's what I said. Halfway through town."

I roll my eyes but smile. "Then drop my things off for me at home, okay? I've missed Aspen. I need it right now."

"Roger that. But be careful with the T. rex. It could come after you."

"Gotcha."

William pulls over and lets me out. My brown Doc Martens sink into a pile of leaves next to the bell tower. I can hardly wait for fall to give way to winter. Aspen is simply magical in the winter.

Making my way through the streets, I can't help but think about how *different* Providence is. A big state capital, everybody anonymous. No one says hello to anyone. Everyone is just rushing about, their eyes filled with stress and the fear of missing out, of not managing to do something, of going down somehow, anxious about everyone and everything.

Things are different here. Aspen is a tourist hot spot, but it's small. Everyone knows one another. I could tell you everything about my neighbor Patricia's life, with dates and all, and she's almost ninety. Things happen, and everyone finds out about them. Things happen that will never be forgotten.

I stop in front of the corner building with *Kate's Diner* written on it. It's still early, just before seven. The baby-blue sky is streaked with pink and little cotton candy-like clouds. The sound of blinds going up in the windows of Woody's Supermarket fills the windless air. In Kate's Diner there's a line of people on their way to work who've stopped in for coffee. The wind picks up and rustles the leaves before blowing them past me, on the other side of the street, looking in through the windows. Kate is whirling about behind the counter, her flower-patterned apron wrapped around her waist, hurrying from one coffee machine to the other and placing the coffee cups into the hands of her daughter, who passes them on to their customers.

Gwendolyn. I hesitate to use her nickname, *Gwen*, because that would mean I like her, and I don't. Not anymore. In the past, maybe, yeah, back then she was my bestie who'd laugh when Wyatt and I would stick popcorn in our noses and see who could blow them farther, but not any longer; now everything's different. She's the reason my heart doesn't work anymore. She and Wyatt, they broke it. Just like that. You don't just go around breaking hearts. They're precious, and you don't destroy precious things.

Gwendolyn looks up as she hands a customer their cup. She smiles and says something, probably wishing them a nice day. Why not? Some people can still have those. Nice days, I mean. As they turn away and she greets the next customer, her eyes flit over the person's shoulder and outside.

She sees me. She sees me, and her smile disappears. I don't look away. I want to know what she thinks. I want to know whether she regrets what she did. She needs to look at me and feel like shit, damn it.

But there is nothing there that I can recognize from a distance. No movement. I am reluctant to admit that Gwendolyn is just like me. She's a master of hiding her emotions. A perfect poker face.

I wish I could hate her. Sadly, I'm just not made that way. Objectively speaking, I can understand. If I were her and someone like Wyatt showed interest in me, I probably wouldn't be able to resist, either. I don't think any woman could. Refuse Wyatt, I mean. He's got that way, that particular charm you simply can't refuse. I mean, everything about him is stylish and adventuresome, special, new somehow, even years later, and a little bit mischievous. I'm sure he shone for her. He was forbidden fruit, and she took a bite.

Gwendolyn turns away as Kate sticks yet another cup of coffee in front of her nose.

I move on. The bells begin to chime, announcing the hour. Two guests are coming out of our wood-paneled B&B. The man is pulling on a blue beanie as his wife points to Kate's in the distance. They trot past me, and I manage to put my palm on the door before it can shut.

Back home. For the first time without a return ticket waiting to be used. I'm back. And I'm staying.

It smells of wood. Of pancakes and maple syrup. And the trusty old leathery smell of the worn L-shaped sofas in the corner of the parlor by the brick fireplace where there's a fire going.

I close the door. It's empty here, but in the eating area on the other side of the stone arch, I can see guests at their little tables. Eating breakfast with happy faces and with peaceful hearts. Because that's what our B&B is like. It makes you feel at home.

My steps are swallowed up by the oriental rug. Mom doesn't notice me as I make my way through the arch. She's standing at the breakfast buffet trying to decide which crocheted flower coaster to put under the cherry jam.

"The orange one," I say, smiling. "You won't get the spots out of the white one. We've done that number already."

My mother spins around. The glass of jam bumps against the bowl with the fruit salad and clangs through the air.

Rheumatism has changed my mom over the last two years. The cortisone has made her puffy, and the stress has given her wrinkles, but I don't see that right now. Right now she's beaming, and all I can think is, *My God, how beautiful she is, how beautiful.*

"Come here, dear." She puts the jam down—onto the orange coaster, naturally—and presses me close. Her dependable smell of rosewater mixed with maple syrup gives me back some of my childhood—it's like I'm five again. Mom ruffles my hair, and I hug her tighter before she lets go once more.

"Breakfast?"

I nod. "Caffeine. I need caffeine. And a bagel."

"I bought you your cream cheese. Chives and onion."

"They don't have that out in Providence," I say, as Mom and I sit down at the small, previously set table by the fire. This is something I really love about our house. There's a crackling fire almost everywhere you look. "I went to every supermarket you can think of. Every. Single. One. Mom, do you know how many supermarkets there are out there? A lot. And I mean everywhere. I was like a dog looking for a bone. At some point, I was simply known as the cream cheese girl."

Mom pours us each a cup of coffee. Our "no-point" cups. A colorful mix of the weirdest designs. We go looking for them at flea markets and thrift stores. It's our thing somehow. Today I've got one that says, YOU STINK. It's my favorite.

"I told you not to do that. Rhode Island isn't Aspen, Aria. They tick differently. They don't find cream cheese girls as cool as we do."

"Yeah. I didn't want to believe it, but it's true."

The toaster spits out our bagels. Mom moves to get up, but I recognize the pain in her face and stand up before she does.

"Don't get up." When I get back from the buffet, I can see Mom spreading her fingers with a groan. With a sinking feeling in my stomach, I sit back down and push a bagel onto her plate. "How bad is it? Really. And don't give me any excuses. I'm your daughter. Tell me how you're doing. And tell me the truth, please, because everything else is just bullshit, okay?"

For a long time she just looks at me. I recognize the reflective look in her eyes because I have the exact same ones. She can't fool me. Mom's weighing whether to tell me the truth or not, but seeing my ironlike gaze, she folds.

She sighs. "Not so good. But I can deal with it, Aria. It's nothing you should worry about."

"We'll figure it out. I'm going to help you."

Mom's hands look stiff as she takes hold of her cup and brings it to her lips. The sight tugs at my heartstrings. And not in a pleasant way.

When my mother notices, she puts her cup back down and bows her head. "Aria, dear. *I'm doing fine.* You need to concentrate on your studies. At twenty, you're too young to spend your time helping someone else and let life pass you by."

"I'm concentrating on my studies. I can help you all the same."

My mother takes a sip of her coffee before casting me a questioning glance. "I still haven't understood how this whole transfer thing works."

A couple comes into the eating area with a little girl. Six at the most, with two pigtails. Cute. My lips form a soft smile when I see the young girl's eyes shining as she hurries over to the chocolate spread.

"It wasn't as complicated as you think."

The girl tugs at her father's arm and points to the chocolate cream. I turn and look into my mother's far-too-tired eyes. "I submitted an application, and my request for a transfer to Aspen University was granted."

Mom leans back in her wooden chair with a creak and looks at me skeptically. "What's with your internship in Seattle?"

"I turned it down."

"*Turned it down?* You didn't tell me that, Aria!" Her glance is reproachful.

I shrug and nibble at my bagel.

"Have you found a spot in Aspen already?"

Her question goes straight to my gut. I start to feel queasy. Suddenly the cream cheese doesn't taste so good. "No. There's time."

She sighs. "Aria."

"I'm gonna find a spot, Mom."

"It's about your future."

"Yeah. And as I said…" The last bit of bagel disappears into my mouth as I polish off my coffee and stand up. "You don't need to worry about that at all. I'll take care of it. I'm Aria, in case you forgot. Aria, the one who takes care of everything. Aria, the one who's got everything under control. No problem, Mom."

She smiles as I plant a kiss on the crown of her head, but she doesn't look too convinced. No wonder. I've never been "Aria, the one who's got everything under control." Mom knows that better than anyone.

I silently clean off the table, and every time I come back to take something into the kitchen, her bright eyes study me warily and anxiously.

"It's all good," I say when I'm done. "You'll see."

What a lie. Strangely enough, lying is always easiest when it has to do with easing other people's concerns, even though you're screaming and crying and a real mess inside. But I couldn't tell her that. I mean, I could, but it would be *so dumb* to weigh her down when she's doing so badly. I'm not going to do that.

Then I leave the eating area. I smile warmly at the family in the living room, hurry past, and make my way up the massive wooden stairway. Every step creaks. My fingers run along the lacquered banister, feeling the knots. I'm so familiar with every one of them that I know exactly where they are. Upstairs, I automatically turn my head toward the right end of the hall. When I was young, I'd sit on the cushioned bench in front of the window for hours, watching the people outside. I let my eyes move across the walls. They look the same as always. Half paneled in white, the other half covered with baby-blue, flowered wallpaper. The heavy wooden chest of drawers is still there, too, between the doors to the guest bedrooms, and the only thing that's changed with the two massive brass chandeliers above my head are the lightbulbs. How familiar this place is! And how good that feels. I go down the hall, a melancholy smile on my face, and on through the connecting door on the left that leads to our living area.

This hallway is no different from the guest hallway—it's the same one, just separated by the dividing wall we had built. At the end of the hall, there's a wooden ladder of thick tree trunk struts going up to the attic. And that attic is my room.

My room.

It looks the same as it did two years ago, before I left Aspen. Paisley lived here for a little while. She's a figure skater who moved here last year. At that time, she was a bit lost; she'd run away from her trainer in Minneapolis and ended up finding herself in Aspen. I love her. *Everyone* loves her. Paisley is… She's like Aspen. When you're with her, you feel at peace.

I grin as my glance sweeps across the room. Either she painstakingly tried not to move a single thing, or Mom put everything back just like it was so that I'd feel at home. I can imagine both.

The walls run straight down; the window is located on the straight triangular wall that overlooks the street. In elementary school I was the coolest because I told everyone I lived in a triangle.

This room is the dream come true for any girl who's into the cozy Christmas vibe. String lights wrapped around the roof beams. Walls of rustic wood. There's a big wardrobe against one wall, an ancient desk that I never use, and two chests of drawers. My eyes wander over to the white sofa beneath the double window. There's still that gold garland with a Christmas star over the curtains that I put up some years back. I didn't feel like taking it back down later on. I just like it.

It's strange being back here. Not just for a period of time, but *back*. Back in Aspen. Back in my room. What a mindfuck. This is where everything comes together. All the good memories, but the bad ones, too.

I sink down onto my feathery bed. I couldn't do that in my dorm room at Brown; the bed was as hard as a block of cement. All my savings, thousands of dollars for a bed of rock. Nice, huh?

My dad made this one. I was fourteen, and my legs had grown so long that they hung half a foot over the end of my kiddie bed. I had to curl up in the fetal position to fit. Thinking about it is just bizarre.

That was around the time I got together with Wyatt. We were both still totally green behind the ears, so in love that we could hardly look at each other without blushing. One Saturday morning, Dad decided to test Wyatt's bonafides as an artisan. He took him up to Red Mountain, chopped down a tree, and, over the course of a single day, made this bed with him. After that, as far as he was concerned, Wyatt was part of the family. Or, well, at least until the day my dad decided to take off to the Hamptons with a tanned tourist and was never heard from again.

With a loud sigh, I fall back onto the patchwork quilt and raise my arm to brush the string lights out of my face. They're hanging all the way across the room. Originally, they were affixed to the wooden beam above me, but over time some of the tape lost its grip and they started to droop. I look through the skylight right above my head. We had it put in later because, when I was a kid, I always talked about wanting to be able to count the stars before going to sleep. At the moment, morning clouds are wafting across the horizon, dyeing the sky pink. I close my eyes.

This room belongs to me. I lived in this triangle for years. It's mine, but I feel estranged somehow. I feel like I don't know who I am anymore.

In Aspen, I was Wyatt's Aria. In Providence, I was the sports medicine student, a melancholic Aria who never went out and missed the snow-covered mountains, missed weird William, the town halls, the tourists, the hikes, tracks through the snow, screaming kids on skates, and waffles with hot cherries in front of the fire during snowstorms.

And now I'm back, but I'm not Wyatt's Aria anymore. And I'm not the Aria going to Brown either, spending her days feeling lonely.
Who am I?
Ladies and gentlemen, I have no idea.

2

Growing Distance between Us

WYATT

"PAY ATTENTION, MAN. PAY ATTENTION. IF YOU DO THAT, I'm gonna kill you, and—okay, wow, you are such a fucking *asshat*."

The remote slips out of my hand and onto the rug as I lift my arm off the cushion and let it fall back down. I sit up, grab my Coke off the table, and take a gulp. My hockey team's playing on TV. The Aspen Snowdogs versus the Seattle Kraken. The first NHL game of the season, and I'm not there.

I don't want to think about it. I don't want to remember what caused me to be sitting here now, unable to play, because every thought about it is a blinking red self-destruct button telling me what a dirty piece of shit I am. All the same, two-thirds of the time there's been nothing else in my head because I've been having to watch this really terrible hockey player named Gray fuck up my position as a forward. He just scored a goal but with a high stick. *A high stick.* That's against the rules. He's got to sit it out on the bench for two minutes, but on his way, he gets cut off by one of our forwards, and, man, that dude is *pissed*.

The front door opens. My sister Camila puts her keys down on the chest in the hall and walks in with two paper bags. She looks over at the TV with a furrowed brow while slipping out of her butt-ugly UGGs. I don't understand why anyone would want to wear those things when slippers from Target look just the same but cost only ten bucks.

"Why's Paxton going after the new forward?"

The neck of the Coke bottle fizzes as I put it back on the table. "He's not the new forward. He's a temporary replacement."

"Whatever."

I take the paper bags out of her hands and peer inside. Chicken wings from the ski hut.

"It's not whatever. *New* would mean that I'm out. *Temporary replacement* means that I'm coming back."

My sister rolls her eyes and sits down on her cushioned seat in the bay window. "Fine. Why is Paxton going after the *temporary forward who will only be there until King Wyatt reclaims his throne?*"

She mutters something under her breath in Portuguese, too fast for me to catch, but it sounds like trouble wrapped in cinnamon. I hand her one of the bags. Camila slides out of her coat, drapes it over the back of her chair, and grabs the bag with greedy eyes. She's still wearing her work outfit, a long wool skirt emblazoned with the ski hut logo. Also, socks with little sardinhas on them—those tiny Portuguese fish she says bring good luck.

"He made a goal that doesn't count. He high-sticked it."

"That was dumb. Get on with it and kick his ass, Paxton," she says before biting into a wing. She cackles, then turns to me and says, "Avô would have called that a chicken dance."

"Is your first shift going to be canceled tomorrow?"

Meanwhile, the ref has stepped in, and Gray has reached the bench. Camila bends forward and picks the wool blanket off the sofa. I wince. She always does stuff like that. Her room is a disaster zone. Torn notebooks, snack wrappers, open soda cans. I avoid that part of the house and keep the hallway window open. It's not enough, but I don't want to go in there. Well, she's a teenager.

"No," she says, without looking at me. She stares at the TV. "You wanted to talk to Dan about getting earlier shifts during the week."

"*You* wanted me to talk to Dan, Wy." My sister casts me an accusatory glance, which doesn't quite land, what with half a chicken wing sticking out of her mouth. "I told you: I take the shifts that bring more tips."

I can only think of one thing. *RAGE, RAGE, RAGE.* If I don't stop to hold my breath and count to ten, I'm going to get loud, and I don't want to get loud because that just makes Camila bitchy and disappear into her cave where I think something could start growing legs and walking out on its own... Okay, maybe that's a bit much, but, as I said, she's a careless teenager.

I don't want her to be alone. And I don't want to be alone, either. So I stand up, go into the kitchen, calm down, and come back into the living room carrying wet wipes.

"Mila," I say, handing her a wipe, which she reluctantly accepts. "This is your final year in high school. Old Clearwater said that you have to really make an effort in a few classes. You've got your SATs coming up. Your results will dictate which college you can go to. You want to go to college, don't you?"

My sister ignores me. She's good at that, always has been, as if I was nothing but air. She nibbles on her chicken wing and draws in sharply when our right forward lets the other team's forward slip past. "Body check, Caden, body check! *Meu Deus!* What do you have muscles for?"

"Mila."

She gives an annoyed sigh. "Should I quit, Wy? No problem. Gladly. Then I'll have enough time to spend bent over my books memorizing all that stuff. The only thing is, it'll be a bit tough by candlelight and no internet."

"What?"

"You're not playing, so you're not making any money. Mom and

Dad left us the house, but with hardly anything to cover our bills. We've got to pay for stuff. Electricity. Internet. Groceries."

Like always, whenever one of us mentions our parents, things immediately get heavy. Our dad died when we were little. Avalanche. Two years ago, Mom followed him. Cervical cancer. I remember the day like it was yesterday. Camila was trying to make caldo verde that day—half broth, half disaster. The memory still makes me feel so… empty and lost. Every day.

"You're seventeen, Camila. You're not responsible for taking care of us. Tell Dan you're quitting. I'll get a job."

"Ai, que saco," she mutters, rubbing her temple.

"I am not a pain in the ass, sis."

Camila snorts. "You are, because otherwise how could you even think I can just quit?"

"I'll find a solution."

"Sure. During the day you'll concentrate on your PT, and at night you'll go swing a hammer somewhere with your broken arm. I totally forgot about your superpowers, Wy."

"I'll ask Knox if he can lend us something."

Camila tosses the gnawed wing into the paper bag and looks at me. From her eyes I can tell that she understands just *how much* her education means to me. She knows that it goes against all my pride to ask my best friend for money.

Her face grows softer. "Neither of us wants that. I'll talk with Dan about the shifts, okay?"

"Pinky promise?"

My sister smiles. "Pinky promise." She holds out her little finger to me, and I need that little finger so bad right now, I don't even need a second to grab it with my own. She looks at me, and her smile disappears.

"What?"

Camila leans back and pushes the paper bag off her lap. "I've got to tell you something."

I *hate* that sentence. Really. Absolutely hate it and have ever since Camila began to speak. I almost get a heart attack every time; I am so afraid of something terrible happening to my little sister.

"If you've got a boyfriend, I don't want to know. That possibility simply does not exist in my head. Never will. If you bring him home, I'm going to ghost him. I'll ignore him and try to walk right through him, get him up against the wall body check–style and…"

"Aria's back, Wy."

I sink into ice water. All the way up to the top of my head. Everything in me freezes. My blood is below zero. Am I still alive? No idea. It is so cold, holy *shit*, is it cold.

"What do you mean?" I mumble.

Camila begins playing with the leaves of the hanging plant above her head and looks out the window. The pane reflects her face. When she exhales, the glass fogs.

"She came back to help Ruth out with the B&B."

"You're lying." No idea why I say that. She doesn't lie. I know that Camila would never screw around when it comes to Aria. Aria is my sore spot, my open wound that no one is allowed to touch, or I'll lose my shit, and Camila knows it.

My throat is dry, my heart pounding. "Since when?"

"This morning."

"Did she come alone?"

Frowning, Camila turns away from the window, her light-brown wavy hair brushing her shoulder blades. "How else?"

Sunk into my thoughts I stare at the label of my Coke bottle before I start to pick at it with my fingernail. After Aria left Aspen, I asked Knox to let me use his Instagram account to be able to see her profile. She'd blocked me. I investigated every single person that had liked her photos and meticulously followed her stories—I mean, really self-destructively, my pulse racing the whole time. Something could pop up, a second champagne glass or a male-looking finger. Or she could just go for a walk, but I'd ask myself if maybe there was someone next to her that I couldn't see. I had those thoughts non-stop. It was disgusting, really; I just destroyed myself. But I couldn't stop, and the thing was I'd always get that heart-pounding adrenaline rush whenever she uploaded a new photo. I'd get dizzy, and that'd make it tough for me to recognize the photo. *You see, Wyatt, this is torture, pure torture, and you deserve it,* I'd think. But then the image would solidify, and it'd just be something normal, like a picture of a sunset or her Starbucks cup or whatever. One time there was even a smiley face on the wall.

But there was never any other guy. Not that I would've noticed, of course. I mean, sorry, but Instagram isn't real life, and she could've done whatever she wanted without me finding out 2,000 miles away. Anyway, not a day goes by that I don't think about her being with someone else, and I have to stop what I'm doing and catch my breath.

"She's here alone," Camila says. "And she's here to stay."

She's here to stay. Que merda, that's heavy. I feel like I'm standing next to myself. The living room is just a fuzzy screen. I think I'm vibrating, and that's kind of mad. I mean, what kind of person starts *vibrating* when they hear that their ex-girlfriend is back in town?

"But she's studying at Brown," I say, as I can't believe that all this is really happening. I need confirmation. "Aria… Aria can't simply *stay here.*"

"She changed schools." Camila stretches, and her hand knocks into the plant pot when she stands. "I'm hitting the sack. Just wanted you to know before you run into her somewhere."

I nod, completely in a trance. *Holy shit.*

My sister runs a hand across my shoulder as she walks past and gives me a wan smile. "Don't expect anything from her, Wyatt. Things between you two are over. Okay?"

"Sure. It's all good. Clean your room."

"Hmm. Another hopeless case."

I throw the paper bag with the chicken bones after her. She

avoids it, laughing, leaving the bag simply lying on the floor. Then she disappears upstairs.

With a sigh, I sink back against the cushions and run my right hand across my face. My left arm is hanging limply off my side. Ever since the accident, I've hardly been able to use it. My muscles simply aren't playing along. Whenever I try to lift it, it only makes it to my chin, or, well, sometimes it does, and that's already saying something. But then it sometimes goes up to the start of my neck and a bit farther up my neck, and I flinch in pain. It happened a little bit after the transfer period, when the Snowdogs bought me. I think life wanted to take me down a few notches. Pick me way up and then slam me into the ground for what Aria had to go through thanks to me. Life simply laughed and said, *Happy birthday, Wyatt, buddy, this is your life now; get used to it.*

I'm not getting used to it. I hear voices. Sometimes they sound like Aria laughing and laughing, and then they sound like Aria crying and crying. That's my new normal; I know that already. But ever since that day last summer, it's been a whole lot more than that. There are things I can no longer forget. I can't sleep, and when I can, I usually wake up every hour, screaming and bathed in sweat. It's awesome, let me tell you.

And so, no, I'm not getting used to it. Definitely not.

I take another gulp of my Coke and watch our goalie, Samuel, manage to stop the puck with a painful-looking contortion. The puck smashes against the side and skids off. The audience goes wild, and the commentator talks about what exceptional talent the Snowdogs have. But I hardly catch any of it because all I can think is, *Aria's back. Aria's back. Aria's back.*

"Fuck it." I put my Coke down onto the table and get myself together.

Just today. Just this one time because she's back.

It takes a while for me to get the jacket over my useless arm. I can't drive, so I have to walk,

The path to the start of Buttermilk Mountain and on to downtown seems endless. It's dark; all that's here is the pale glow of the streetlamps with their lonely cones of light. The winter season hasn't started yet, so the streets are empty. The wind is blowing leaves across the street. At the bell tower I stop and sit down on one of the benches; my heart is beating so quickly I look at my Apple Watch. My pulse is way over a hundred. Thinking of Aria is the most terrifying and yet most wonderful feeling I know. It's always been this way. I love order. Aria was the only person who could regularly cause me to experience chaos inside.

I'm tense. I bite my lower lip and focus on the massive clock up there in the tower as if it could tell me which way to go. As if it knew how my life would turn out.

"What are you doing here?"

I turn. Knox is standing next to the bench, two paper bags from Kate's Diner in his hand. Looking into my face, he frowns. "Shit, you look wiped. Everything okay, man?"

"Aria's back."

"Yeah." His face takes on a sympathetic expression. "I ran into her a little while ago. I was going to call you a bit later on."

"Camila told me."

Knox looks up at the bell tower, then to the B&B on the other side of the street. He runs a hand through his brown hair, holds his breath, and then slowly lets it back out. "Wyatt, what are you doing here?"

I shrug.

"Go home." When I don't respond, he sits down and offers me one of the paper bags. "Sandwich?"

I shake my head. "Camila brought chicken wings."

"Good. Paisley would've wrung my neck. She already texted me earlier this afternoon saying that she *absolutely* had to have an avocado sandwich from Kate's after training. And these here were the last ones." He stretches out his legs and with the tip of his boots plays with a yellowish-brown maple leaf. "You see the game?"

"Not all of it."

"How'd it go?"

"The forward sucks."

"Of course he does." Knox laughs. "There's only one Wyatt Lopez."

The door to the diner across the street opens. The figure skaters Levi and Aaron come out. Just like Knox's girlfriend Paisley, they're at iSkate. Seeing me and Knox, they raise their hands. I nod in return, and they disappear.

Knox pats me on the back and stands up. "Let it go, Wyatt. You'll be back on the ice in no time. Your life will continue." He lets out a quick, soft laugh. "Hard to believe I'm the one saying that, but it's true. I'm the best example, right?"

I lean back, turn my baseball hat around backward, and stick my right hand into my coat pocket. I'd love to just snort and tell him that I don't want it to continue. Not without Aria. I mean, I gave it a go, and things just suck without her. We were together for six years, grew up together, and, no joke, I have no idea how adulting works without her.

But I don't tell him that. I won't tell anyone that. And so I smile instead. "Tell Paisley I said hey."

"I will. See you."

"See you."

He looks at me as if he knew what I was thinking. And, to be honest, I think he does. Knox and I know each other. Maybe even better than we know ourselves.

He pats me on the back a second time before disappearing across the street and getting into his Range Rover.

I lean back and look into the sky. It's dark blue and studded with stars that are so bright my heart should be glowing. But it's not. Only Aria can make that happen because only Aria can cast away the dark. Aria always shined enough for the two of us, but then I took the light away and left her alone and empty.

God, do I feel bad. I ruined that precious person, and now here I am, sitting on a bench in front of her house as if I have the right to.

I should go before she sees me, and the sight of me alone rips her heart back out. I'm a fucking bastard who didn't deserve her. Knox is right. I should go. And so I get up and start to turn, but at that very moment, Ruth's Mitsubishi pulls up in front of the B&B, and I see her immediately. Aria, at the driver's wheel, her mouth slightly open, turning off the engine. I don't move a millimeter. My body is paralyzed.

Her lips are the first thing I notice. Curvy and full, with that particular heart shape I know like the back of my hand, having traced it with my finger one hundred thousand times. At least. The tip of her dark ponytail brushing her hips. Getting out of the car, I see that she's wearing a gray-brown hoodie with a pair of yoga pants.

She doesn't see me. She opens the trunk and pulls out several wooden boxes of fruit. I want to help. I want to take the boxes out of her hands and carry them inside. I want to do everything for her and want to tell her that I'm a piece of shit that didn't deserve her—if she just gives me one more chance, I'll be there. I'll be everything.

Instead, I just stand there with my useless arm and watch her stack the boxes up to her chin and wobble across the street.

I hadn't thought seeing someone would hurt so bad and, at the same time, be such a relief. I hadn't thought love could really grow stronger though the person had been away for years. And I hadn't thought a person could hate themselves as much as I hate myself right now.

I can't do it. I can't just sit here watching her and *not* do anything!

Before I even notice what I'm up to, I'm on my feet and halfway across the road.

"Aria."

Her shoulders flinch. The boxes fall to the ground with a crash, spilling apples across the asphalt. She ignores me. As if she hadn't heard me at all, she crouches down and begins to pick them up. But she can't trick me. In the meantime, I'm standing right in front of her, my white Nikes right next to her trembling fingers with their chipped nails. My right knee gives a slight pop as I bend down to help her pick it all up. Her lips are a thin line as she does her best not to pay any attention to me. But then I reach for the same apple she does to brush her fingers. Our touch sets off an emotional avalanche inside; it electrifies me, makes me feel *alive*, and I see that it's the same for Aria. I can see it in her wide-open eyes, the petrified look on her face. She can't pretend I'm not here anymore.

But she immediately collects herself. "Leave me alone, Wyatt." She energetically tosses the last apple into the wooden box, places it on top of the other two, and stands up.

"I wrote you letters," I say. "Did you ever get them?"

"Yeah," she replies curtly. Her ponytail whips from her right hip to her left as she makes her way across the street.

Completely on autopilot, my body starts to follow her. "You never answered."

"Why should I?"

"Did you read them?"

For some wonderful, not entirely discernible reason, Aria stops and turns to face me. Her cheeks are dotted red, like they always are whenever she's angry. "No, Wyatt, I didn't. I threw them away. Every single one, because nothing you could have written would've changed a thing. There is nothing in the world you could say to make up for what you did, *okay?*"

She didn't read them. The realization turns me to stone. Of course I didn't expect her to write back or call and say, *Hey, Wy, it's all good, dumb shit. Things didn't go well. I'm coming back home and will be there tomorrow. Pick me up. Kisses. See you.* But I figured she would've at least *read* what I'd written. Understood why what happened happened and simply needed time, *a lot of time*, to work through it all.

But that's not the way things turned out. I feel myself starting to panic. For *two long years* she's thought I hurt her *on purpose*. For two years she's learned to hate me with a vengeance. I shut my eyes but quickly open them back up, afraid that Aria won't be there. I exhale in a shudder. "Aria, *please* listen to me. What you saw in that video must have caused you the worst, most nauseating pain—I *know* that. And I can't even imagine what it must have been like for you, what strength you needed to handle it. Because I don't think I could've done it. I probably would've died or something, no idea, and I'm sorry, merda, I am so *fucking sorry!* I wish I could feel what you must have felt instead, just to take that pain away from you, but I can't. What I *can* do is tell you *why* it happened and ask you to please, *please* listen." I quickly gasp for air in order to continue. "Back at that party, that thing between Gwen and me, I…"

"Stop!" Her face is a mask of pain, as if the tiniest reminder would be too painful to handle. She takes a step back. "Stop. I didn't want to hear it last year after the Christmas dinner, and I don't want to hear it now."

"But *Aria*…" I sound like I'm begging, every syllable accompanied by panic and doubt. "Please, then you'll understand why…"

"I will never understand why, Wyatt." She's holding onto the edges of the fruit boxes so tightly her knuckles turn white. "Whatever your reasons were…or maybe I would understand, but, whatever, I would never be able to forgive you because I saw it, okay, I *saw* you cheat on me, and I *can't* suppress those images."

"But I didn't…"

"I came here because Mom needs me and not to start back up where I stopped. It's taken me two years, seven hundred and forty-two days to be exact, to learn to go on somehow. And because I'm back here now, I won't allow this whole struggle to be for nothing; I have no interest in starting all over again. I don't want to know your reasons, Wyatt; they won't change anything, they'll just drag me back into the past and make me suffer all over again. And I don't want that. I just *can't*."

"But if you knew what happened, maybe that would change everything; maybe we could even be what we were once, you and me together and…"

"Wyatt." The corners of Aria's mouth warp, and her chin begins to tremble. The solid wall of her face collapses, and all that's left is a visible pain that I can't describe. "You and me, the thing with us, please, let it go, let *me* go—because if you keep holding on…" She swallows. "I won't make it."

My throat closes up. I can't breathe. Suddenly I see that hell isn't a place beneath the ground. It's right here. Dark feelings, hot pain.

"But…" My voice breaks. Here I am standing on the street next to the B&B, in front of me the face of my ex-girlfriend, trying not to cry and at the same time not to suffocate. "But *I love you*, Aria."

There, I can see she feels it, too, hell, and it's grabbed hold of her heart with burning red hands. Her expression reflects my excruciating feelings.

"I love you, too, Wyatt. And always will. It's just, well, that doesn't change anything, does it?"

There's nothing I can say to that. I mean, I can't because she doesn't want to hear what I have to say. And I don't know which pain is bigger: the fact that it's over or being unsure whether something could change if she'd only let me explain.

I will never find out.

Aria turns and leaves. She disappears behind the door that, in reality, is just a door, two inches of beechwood, nothing more. But it feels like a whole lot more. Like a crevasse without any bridge, with her on the other side and me over here. And between us a nothingness that can't be overcome.

3

Love Will Mean Some Falling, and She's Afraid of Heights

ARIA

I REALLY NEED TO BE FINISHING UP THE ORDERING LISTS for the B&B. And pronto. The deadline for the next delivery is almost past. On top of all that, I need to wash and iron all the bed linens. But I hate ironing, seriously, I *hate* it. All those creased lines, they never disappear, so who cares?

Yeah, so I went for a hike. I couldn't help it. The morning sun was shining all fall-like through a crack in my curtains right into my sleepy face. Getting up to look out the window, I saw the mountains towering into the sky, wild and free and wonderful. They were calling my name, and all I could think was that that's exactly how I want to be. That wild and that free. Maybe they can show me how it all works.

I grabbed an apple turnover from Patricia's Pastry Shop and was off—wearing Mom's hiking boots, which are two sizes too big for me. But that's how I roll. I don't fit. Not with Wyatt. Not at Brown. Not in Mom's shoes.

The air smells of moss and the bitter scent of wood. Chestnuts and leaves. I find myself in the middle of a yellow sea of light made of aspen trees. I love it. They bloom in October, showing the colors they've hidden all year long. We're all a bit like that. A touch of October in our hearts.

The earth muffles my steps, and after a few feet I hear the gurgling of a stream. Licking the stones on its way downhill, the water is surrounded by colorful wildflowers and moss. I take a photo with my phone and save it in my photo folder for special moments.

The path is steep. Coming from downtown, it follows the stony mountains over a thousand feet up. Normally the Ute Trail is really popular with tourists, but in the early morning or late evening there's hardly a soul. In the past, I'd often go jogging here. The stillness in the mountains is special. It's almost as if I could hear the whispering of the leaves in the gentle breeze, hear what they had to say about life. Whenever I come here, I just feel different. As if I'd simply left my problems at home. Pressed Stop. *See you later, dark thoughts. Not today.*

After a little while, the ground turns rocky. The tiny chunks crunch beneath the soles of my boots. Continuing upward, the crisp air cools my sweaty forehead. My breath begins to grow heavy, and my legs start to burn. I haven't been on this path in two years, and, back in Providence, I only went jogging twice. I bet now even William has more stamina than me.

But once I start on the last bit, I know it's been worth it. For this moment. This second. It's got to do with this first glimpse, this bounce of the soul that only comes when you stumble into a completely magical moment.

I stand on the boulder, completely still. My shoulders rise and fall to the rhythm of my breathing while my eyes sweep across the outcrop, taking in every single inch, confirming that everything is just like it was back then.

My feet carry me to the tree that will be ours forever and ever and a little bit longer, too. Wyatt's and mine. That's how often we came here. *That often.* Every chance we had. My birthday. His birthday. Christmases. Holidays neither of us celebrate. Any excuse to be here and to believe that every second was special, to believe that *we* were special, our love and everything in between we didn't have any words for because it was all just too meaningful. That's what things were like between us. Wyatt was Wyatt, and he was the most valuable thing my heart had to offer.

When my pet canary Utah took off, Wyatt came up here to this outcrop and hung a swing off the tree. No big deal, just two strong cords and a piece of wood. But he showed it to me and said that I shouldn't have any pet birds at all, Utah was free, and all I had to do was swing as high as I could, and I'd be able to fly and be just as free as she was.

The swing's still here. The wind blows my hair out of my face when I sit down on the wood. Slowly, almost cautiously, I grab the ropes and let my feet glide across the stony ground. At first, I swing really slowly, back and forth, back and forth, but then I begin to swing more quickly, higher and higher, so high that I fly out over the end of the outcrop and all of Aspen spreads out beneath me. Downtown, all the paths into the mountains, Silver Lake, and everything below me from over one thousand feet in the air.

I'm not afraid of falling because I've been falling for a long time now.

4

The Hardest Thing I'll Ever Do Is Walk Away Still Loving You

ARIA

A CLOUD OF FEATHERS DRIFTS THROUGH THE ROOM WHEN I shake out the pillow. They hover for a few seconds, then come to rest on the wooden floor. I palm the blanket of the king-sized bed flat, throw the coverlet over the top, and place a piece of Aspen's famous nougat chocolate on the pillow. I'm right about to go to the bathroom when the bedroom door swings open—right against my forehead.

For a moment I can't see. I stagger, stretch my hand out, and try to balance myself on the rustic sideboard by the wall.

"Oh, shit. Did I hurt you?"

"Yeah." I have to blink a few times before the stars disappear and a big, beautiful female being with fox-red hair, freckles, glacier-like eyes, and a cashmere coat appears before me.

Harper. My bestie since we were young and the most misunderstood person in Aspen. She can seem off-putting and arrogant if you don't know it's just her way of protecting herself. Harper is so afraid of friendships! She thinks everyone's deceptive. And I think that, over the two years I've been gone, her venomous behavior toward others has only grown more intense—because I know that she just hung around on her own the whole time I was away. Mom told me.

"Good," she says, her little purse hanging off the crook of her arm. "Then you know how I felt when I was forced to find out you were back when I was *at training*."

I sigh. "Sorry, Harp. Really. I wanted to write, but it all came together so quickly, and by that point I was already sitting on the plane."

"It's all good. 'Oh, hey, I'm Aria. I just got up and was hit by a flash of inspiration. I'm going to go back home. And with a snap of my fingers, I'm already on the plane. And—oh! Man, all I did was blink, and here I am already! Wild.'" She snorts. "I found out *at training*. Is what that means clear to you?"

I sigh again, walk past her to the bathroom, and spray the toilet with cleaning agent. "Yeah. You heard Gwendolyn and the others talking about it and felt like you'd been duped."

Harper leans her shoulder against the doorframe. "You better not think you can score points with that crap now. Au contraire. You *knew* I'd find out about it there and didn't call me *all the same*."

"Harp, come on." Frowning, I wipe the toilet clean, toss the rag back into the bucket, and stand up. "Yesterday there was just too much going on. I got here and everything was…"

"Wyatt," she says. "Everything was Wyatt."

I want to protest. So I raise my pink rubber-gloved hands but have to consider what to say. When nothing comes to mind, I let them sink back down. "Yeah." Capitulating, I exhale. "Everything was Wyatt."

For a moment Harper eyes me before pushing past, sitting down on the toilet seat, and watching me spray the sink. "Did you see him?"

I swallow. "Yeah. Yesterday."

"Were you okay?"

"No."

She twists her mouth. "You've got to forget all that, Aria. It's been ages. Wyatt was with other women while you were away. A lot of them. It's all over between you two."

Got it. Wow, the world's still spinning, but without me. That's how Harper rolls. She tells the truth. She always has, and that's actually what I like about her best. But at the moment it feels like she's filleting my chest with a knife. Beautiful little slices, real slow with those clean cuts that *really* hurt. I take a sharp breath. The biting smell of the cleaning agent burns my lungs, and all I can think is, *God, don't breathe in too deep, pulmonary fibrosis, pulmonary fibrosis.*

Harper leans her head back, pressing her red hair against the white tiles. "I'm sorry, A. I wish it were different. You didn't deserve that."

Feigning indifference, I wrinkle my nose and act like the conversation never happened. Maybe my head will believe it. Maybe I can prevent it from stealing my sleep later by supplying me with images of Wyatt and other ladies. But my head is a whirling mess, and I don't think that someone like me can pull something like that off.

"I'm almost done," I say, wiping the faucet before polishing it with a microfiber cloth. "Are we going to go to the town hall?"

Harper arches one of her perfectly tweezed brows. "You want to go to the town hall?"

"Yeah."

"Wyatt will be there."

"I don't care."

She laughs. "Yes, you do."

I go into the hallway, take fresh hand towels off the cart, and shuffle back into the bathroom. "Wyatt took away enough from me. It's time for me to start reclaiming my life." I put the hand towels in the cabinet beneath the sink, pull off the rubber gloves, and grab the cleaning bucket. "Are you coming?"

Harper grins. "You can't believe how happy I am to have you back."

Everyone says that. And I believe them. Everyone but him. Maybe I should start being happy with that.

"Change of plans, Harp. I'm not going. I'm going to turn around right here and scale the highest point of the Aspen Highlands and go back down on the back of some skier if need be, but I'M. NOT. GOING. IN. THERE."

My best friend's grip grows tighter. She pulls me farther in the direction of the huge barn that at some point or another William chose for the town halls. "And just a minute ago you were so brave. No use arguing, A. If we don't go, we're going to get a warning, and William will force us to prepare a PowerPoint presentation on how to make Aspen more attractive for the next one. You know that's how he makes those who skip his town halls pay. Do you really want to go around decorating storm drains with artificial flowers, Aria? Do you? Not me. Storm drains should remain storm drains. So, come on."

"I feel sick. We're too late. Everyone's going to stare at us."

Harper takes my statement with a skeptical side-eye. "You mean *Wyatt's* going to stare at you."

My silence is confirmation enough. She rolls her eyes. "Don't worry. He won't. He's far too much of a pussy."

As the door to the barn opens, my heart is pounding so loud that I don't even notice the scratching sound the hinges make on the wood. All I can think is, *I don't want to see him. I want to see him. I don't want to see him. I want to see him.*

I *don't want* to see him because I *do*.

We're met by stuffy air. Heads turn. One after the other. The domino effect. I wonder if Wyatt is one of them, but I don't think so because he was never the type for this kind of prodding and participation. Wyatt does his own thing.

There's William on his podium above all the bales of hay. Well, his rain barrel. A rotten, battered, old rain barrel sawed in half, both its sides patched together with hot glue. It is covered by a crooked wood panel that wobbles dangerously whenever William shifts his weight. Man, his throne is so ugly! So ugly, and yet it's his pride and joy.

"Harper! Once again, too late." He raises his index finger threateningly.

Harper spreads her arms wide in a bewildered gesture. "And Aria?"

"Shh," I hiss. "Don't say my name!"

"You're not invisible, you know."

"But when you say my name, it makes me present."

"Your huge hat makes you present, Aria. Take that thing off. Everyone knows it's you hiding underneath it anyway."

"I don't want to."

"Aria?" William puts on his monocle. I don't know why he does that. He's got a pair of normal glasses. They're hanging on a chain around his neck, but every single time he pulls out that old monocle. "Why are you wearing that hippie stuff?"

"Oh!" I hear Kate's voice ring out from somewhere in the middle of the audience. "Is that from Target, Aria?"

No. Not my name. No, no, no.

Will rolls his eyes. "I don't think Target carries hippie hats, Kate."

"They do!" Spirit Susan, our spiritually tinged dance teacher, waves her violet-colored silk stole to draw attention to herself. "In the costume section, next to the athlete's foot ointments."

I'm starting to feel hot. Hotter than hot. I'm burning. My ex-boyfriend's somewhere in this barn, staring at me and my hat with his unbelievably warm honey-colored eyes and thinking of athlete's foot. A nervous wreck, I start balling my fists and shifting my weight from one leg to the other. "Harp, if you don't find a pair of empty seats immediately, I'm going to croak, really, just like that, right here."

"There are a couple over there," she says calmly, grabbing my hand and dragging me past the various rows. Then she stops in her tracks. "Nope. Won't work."

"What?" I break out in a sweat. "You can't be serious. Keep going, Harp!"

William hisses angrily. "Harper, you *always* interrupt my town halls!"

She uneasily bites her lower lip. Everyone is looking at us. And I mean *everyone*. And one of those pairs of eyes belongs to Wyatt. "We can't sit there, A. Knox is there."

Okay, that spells trouble for Harper. I get it. Last year something happened between Knox and her, and my best friend, who never had feelings for anyone, who never let anyone but me get closer than six feet, suddenly started video calling me, her eyes full of stars, telling me far too many things I never wanted to know about Knox. It lasted weeks—until he ditched her. That's how Knox used to roll. Until Paisley, that is.

I force myself to scan the barn and beg my mind to automatically block out Wyatt's face if it happens to appear. Thankfully, it works.

"Harp, *please*. Those are the only seats that are free. *Please*."

Harper grinds her teeth and makes a move to simply walk back out of the town hall, but seeing my desperate expression beneath my huge, even *more* desperate-looking hippie hat, she lets out a loyal sigh. "Great. *Great*. But you're sitting next to him."

"No problem. Come on." I lower my eyes and focus on the notches in the wood, one, two, three, seventeen, until we've squeezed our way through the rows and, relieved, I fall into the chair.

"Your hat just poked me in the eye, Aria."

I blink. Next to me Knox is rubbing his face while Paisley leans past him and gives me a wide smile. "Hi!"

I return her smile. "Hi."

Knox sighs. "*Hi*, they say. Simply *Hi*, as I sit here and my eyesight fades."

"Sorry, but the hat is crucial."

"Things were so nice without you."

"I missed you, too, Knox."

"Shh." Harper's eyes flash, but she doesn't look at him. From the corner of my eye, I can see her moving about uncomfortably on her bale of hay. "I'm missing Aspen's Happy Halloween Highlights for this year."

Knox tilts his head. "I bet there's going to be pumpkin carving."

"Never," I say. "We had that two years ago. Will does something new every year."

"Maybe he'll dress the horses up," Paisley murmurs. "Sally will terrorize the whole town."

"Sally terrorizes the whole town even *without* a costume," Harper counters and immediately bites her lips.

William spreads his arms. "It's time to announce this year's Halloween Highlight! Jack, would you be so kind…"

In the front row, Knox's father looks up from his phone. "What?"

"The highlight," William hisses and points at something sitting in a rusty wheelbarrow and covered by a horse blanket.

Jack seems confused. "What about it?"

"Roll it over!"

"Oh. Sure." He gets up, walks to the wheelbarrow, and pushes it over to William's throne.

"It's not even ten feet, why doesn't he do it himself?" Paisley asks.

Knox squeezes her knee. "Let him have his moment, babe."

"What moment is that?"

I lean over. "You see that? In William's face?"

She frowns. "No. What?"

"That's his epic Katniss Everdeen look. The one she's got when she does that whole fire thing."

"Fire thing?"

I lift my chin. "*If we burn, you burn with us!*"

At that very moment Will interrupts his speech while trying to swat a fly buzzing around his head and my declaration of war echoes through the entire barn.

A few people laugh. Dan, the owner of the ski hut up in the Highlands, whistles through his teeth and calls out, "Grab your torches, friends!"

Will frowns. "I'm worried about you, Aria. First, your hat, now this. Is something wrong?"

"All good, Will." With a grin Harper crosses her legs and bounces her Burberry ankle boots against the bales of hay. "Aria was just expressing her frustration with general injustice. You know how it is. Feminism."

"Ah." Will nods tentatively. "Yes, well…"

Paisley looks past Knox to us, stifling a grin. "What's with this Katniss look you're talking about?"

Knox's eyes light up with amusement. "When he puts that one on, he's having a moment. You've got to let him have it, or he'll explode."

"You've seen that happen before?"

"Pretty often," Harper says. "And it ain't good. I cleaned The Old-Timer for three days of my own free will after ruining his 'Look, the third reindeer of mine is missing its stomach' moment."

"The Christmas reindeer," Paisley says. "They're real important to him."

I nod. "Yeah. Oh, heads-up, he's pulling off the blanket!"

The barn goes dead quiet. Every pair of eyes is on the triangular horse blanket. The air is charged, and William reveals…

A pumpkin. A jack-o'-lantern, to be precise. But not a good one. No, a slimy one that's collapsed into itself, with hollowed-out eyes allowing me to see its orangey innards. It's *really* not attractive. And it stinks. It must be rotten already.

I clock the room and see the same disgusted expression on everyone else's face. William is the only one beaming.

"Will…" Pastry Shop Patricia clears her throat. "Good God, Will. What the hell *is* that?"

William looks from her to the pumpkin and back. "A pumpkin, Pat."

"I can see that. But what do you plan to do with it?"

Apparently, that was the wrong thing to say. William puts his hands on his hips, puffs out his chest, and lifts his chin. "I grew this here pumpkin well past season so that it would get this big! I've been keeping it in shape for this very moment for months. I'm lucky that it worked out so well and I could be part of Halloween Highlight."

Silence. Someone coughs. Somewhere a child begins to cry.

"This thing is supposed to be the *highlight* of downtown Aspen? *Are you mad*, Will?"

I don't catch the answer because I'm overcome by a crushing tinnitus, followed by a racing heart and sweat. That was Wyatt's voice. Wyatt. I mean, I'm not dumb. I knew that he was here, somewhere real close. But hearing his voice sets me spinning off into an endless abyss.

Am I allowed to get up? Get up and just walk out? Is that okay? I feel a bit woozy, but I should give it a go. One foot after the other. No big deal, right?

"Aria." Soft, cool fingers take hold of my wrist. I feel a ring. Harper. The ring was her grandmother's. I'm not really here, but I know that my best friend is holding onto me. "What are you up to?"

"Escaping," I mumble.

"Sit down, A. Seriously. You'll stick out much more if you—stop it, stop hitting me, shit, come on… WHY DO YOU ALWAYS DO THAT?"

I've bitten Harper's hand, and her yell has made its way throughout the entire barn, and now I'm running away because I have to. I BIT HER, and WYATT SPOKE.

The former doesn't matter. It's just an excuse to suggest that I'm not running away from my ex. Which is actually kind of dumb, because I know it anyway, but that's how feelings go. They sneak in, pretending to be beautiful, only to turn really ugly at some point and rob you of rational thought.

My feet stumble forward, and then the impossible happens: I tumble over a pair of white Nikes and land with my knees on hard clay soil. Pain shoots up my legs. I'm sure I've broken something, my legs or my heart, or maybe both. And, oh my God, where's my hat? Okay, time to just keep still right here on the ground and shake my hair into my face.

Everything's under control, really; it's all totally cool until two index fingers part my bangs and present me with the most beautiful face in the history of humanity.

"Did you hurt yourself?"

No. That was you.

"I don't want to see you. Let go of my hair, Wyatt."

He doesn't. He just looks at me. Everyone is, actually, but for me it's just Wyatt. And then he laughs. Just like he used to. Before the thing with Gwendolyn. Loud and a little wild. His husky voice is warm somehow and drives straight into my heart, where it was at home for years but where it no longer lives, though it likes to think it does, which is why it keeps on knocking to be let inside.

I'm getting even dizzier. I've got to have a concussion.

"Stop laughing. Take your fingers out of my hair, Wyatt. Immediately."

I can smell his aftershave. It's the same one as before. That crisp Alaska scent with mint and lemon and something else, wood or pine or something. But it's not really the aftershave; it's *him*. Everything's just like before. And I don't want that. It hurts so bad. He should stop, but he's not. And I feel like he's undoing me a second time just sitting there *laughing and laughing and laughing,* and I can't. I just can't do it anymore. My throat closes shut.

I take a swing and bat his hands out of my face, those goddamn hands that Gwendolyn touched after he'd promised me they were just for me.

His laugh dies out. And so does my heart.

"Don't ever touch me again, Wyatt."

As I get back onto my feet and leave the barn, it's deadly quiet, and I'm fairly certain that everyone is watching me go.

Everyone but him.

5

Pain Makes People Change

WYATT

"LOPEZ!" THE DOOR TO THE CHANGING ROOMS SHUTS behind the Aspen Snowdogs' right forward as Paxton shoulders his hockey bag and points at me. "You back, man?"

"Nope." I slap Paxton's outstretched hand and shake my head as he nods to the drinks machine.

Shrugging, he pulls out a Red Bull and leans a shoulder against the machine. "Tell me," he says, taking a gulp and winking at our team psychologist as she walks past with a reserved grin. He's the only one who would do something like that. I mean, dude, it's the *team psychologist.*

"What are you doing here?"

"PT."

"Oh, right. The whole program."

Yeah. The whole program. Paxton's eyes dart to my left arm while taking another gulp of his energy drink. He doesn't say anything, and every second that passes makes me feel worse. There's a lot unsaid between us—things he doesn't want to say and questions I don't want to answer.

What happened?

I heard some things. Are they true?

Is it all your fault, man?

I take a deep breath and bury my hands in my hockey jacket. "Gray really played like shit yesterday, huh?"

"Is that *a joke?*" Paxton downs the rest of his drink, crushes the can, and tosses it over my head into the trash. "That dude's a catastrophe! No idea how Coach Jefferson could accept him. Xander almost let loose on him after the game in the locker room. No shit. If Owen and Caden hadn't held him back, he would've torn the dude's teeth out in response to that shit out on the ice."

I laugh. "Did he stay for the party?"

"Nope. Didn't dare. You've got to get better, Wyatt, for real. Without you, we can forget this season."

"It won't be much longer now." What a fucking liar I am. As if I had any idea how long it was still going to take. I haven't made any improvements in months. And for months now my little sister has been working on top of going to school so that we can pay the bills. For *months* I've hated myself more than ever.

"Right on." Paxton pushes off from the drinks machine, straightens his big hockey jacket, and runs a hand through his hair.

Female readers of *Sports Illustrated* elected Paxton the Aspen Snowdogs hottest player. My sister's got a thing for him. She didn't tell me, but I know because at some point or another I just couldn't take it anymore and cleaned up that room of hers. She'd scribbled his name next to a bunch of little hearts and flowers in her spiral notebook, probably when spacing out in class or whatever. I had no idea she did that kind of thing. Drew little hearts and flowers, I mean. She's usually so cold and just done with the world, goes to any and every party and drinks, drinks, drinks to forget. She often looks so destroyed that I overlook the little girl who's still there inside wanting to draw little hearts instead of letting dudes stick dollar bills into her underwear and waking up in the hospital after getting her stomach pumped.

I wish I could help her somehow, but I can't even help myself. So, come on, let's be real, what can I do? The truth is, I'm no model whatsoever. I'm just shit. The dude who cheated on his girlfriend. The guy who showed his little sister how to booze.

The dude who ruins lives.

"So, Lopez." Paxton is punching his open palm in a steady rhythm. "Day after tomorrow there's a press conference. You going to be there?"

"Of course."

"They want to talk about your state of health." He says this with a look as if he's weighing whether I'm up to it. Which confirms that he knows what happened back in early summer.

"No big deal, right? I'll be there."

"Solid. Then see you there. Hit it."

"Yo. See you."

He lifts his arm to pat my shoulder before catching himself—my muscles are in the shitter—and deciding to snap his fingers and point at me instead.

I hear his footsteps move down the hall. A few seconds later, I hear the backdoor of the training center shut. I close my eyes, take a deep breath, and make my way upstairs to the PT rooms. I've been here so often over the last few months that my feet know the way by heart. Straight through the lobby, past reception, through the doors to the stairwell, and up to the second floor, where everything smells like baby cream, cleaning agents, and foam couches.

My physical therapist is just picking yoga mats up off the floor and putting foam rollers back onto the shelf when I walk in. He's my sixth therapist in three months. Soon I'll have gone through every one of our physical therapists—and then? If things continue like they have till now, will they kick me out? I can picture the press conference where they'll say, "Wyatt Lopez is no longer treatable. He's no longer a member of the Aspen Snowdogs. Forget him."

I knock on the door. The lanky, blond therapist dude turns

around and smiles. "Oh, hey, Wyatt. I'm Mike. You can go ahead and shut the door."

My soles squeak on the shiny gray linoleum, and my heart begins to beat more quickly. I hate it here. I don't want to admit it, but I am so afraid of the next few hours that I can hardly breathe. Like a kind of panic attack or something. I've heard about those. Regardless, it sucks. I can feel beads of sweat forming on my neck. I can feel them in my collar and sliding down my back. My fingers are trembling, but Mike is still smiling, and I wonder, *How can he do that? How can he smile as if this was all easy? As if this was something fun we were doing, so much fun that we can laugh through all of it,* easy peasy?

He sits down on the edge of the massage table, swinging his legs back and forth. Really cool.

"How you doing?"

What a question, really. Ha ha, nice one, dude. I could puke.

"Good."

He points at my arm. "My colleague Jeanette said that things just didn't seem to want to work out between the two of you."

I nod.

"Why not?"

"No idea."

Mike's quiet for a few seconds, then he sighs. "If you want to get back out on the ice, you're going to have to trust me."

Now I'm the one who almost has to laugh. Trust. Right. As if trusting people were that easy. What's he thinking? Nothing, probably. Mike's probably one of those guys who has had the same girlfriend for ten years and nothing ever goes wrong. He goes home every day at five, the two have dinner, watch a series, and then have sex, and that's that, and the next day's exactly the same. There's never any reason not to trust anyone, never any reason to feel bad. That's Mike, I bet.

"She says you cramped up and broke things off."

I shrug. "Could be."

Mike tilts his head and tugs at his training pants. "We're not going to get very far like this, Wyatt."

I hold his stare. I don't like him with his five-o'-clock-time-to-go-home-dinner-TV-sex life.

"With all due respect, Mike, you're my *physio*therapist, not my therapist. The Snowdogs are paying you to take care of my muscles. I'm not going to lie down and tell you what's going on in my head, dig?"

Mike looks at me exactly like I thought he would. Like I'm an arrogant piece of shit, but I don't care. I am just so done. I have no interest in politeness just to be liked. I say what I think, and if people find me arrogant, whatever, I just don't care.

"Nice." It sounds bitter. Mike stands up and points to the table. "Sit down here with your back to me and let your arm hang down, relaxed."

I spend the next two minutes pulling off my sweater. It's stressful, and that frustrates me. I just want to be able to function again. I want my life back.

Mike rubs his hands with oil and follows me with a reproachful glance. I sit down. My body is flowing with electricity. Or it feels that way at least. Everything is prickling with fear about what's about to happen.

But maybe not, I think. *Maybe today will work out.*

Maybe, maybe, maybe.

"I read your file," Mike says. He comes up next to me and drives a finger into my spine to get me to sit up straight. "According to examinations, you had a tear in the levator scapulae muscle, which elevates your shoulder blade. That tear also put the neighboring muscle groups under tension, and the reason why you can no longer use your arm properly is probably due to the pain from the trigger points, which is radiating outward."

"Yeah." *Please put me back together. Please.*

"That's the first thing I'm going to look at. Don't be alarmed; my hands are cold."

"No problem." *My heart is, too.*

When he traces the affected muscles, I feel an intense pain from my fingertips all the way up through my head. But I'm familiar with that already. That's not why I'm squinting. Pressing my teeth together. Holding my breath.

I'm waiting. Waiting for the moment that will make this impossible. My recovery. I'm waiting for it to come and waiting for it not to come.

Mike lasts longer than all the other therapists did. He manages to stroke my muscles for three whole minutes while I feel like my skull is going to explode with the pain. Three minutes of hope. Three minutes in which I believe I may actually recover—until my pulse begins to race and all I can think is, *Fuck, it's happening again. Why?*

I'm starting to grow dizzy. My fingers are tingling. From this point on, Mike is far away, real far away, and I can't feel his hands. It's like I'm no longer in the treatment room.

It's like I'd *never been here at all.*

A bloodcurdling scream rings in my ears. For a second I think I'm going deaf; really, everything's gone. And then I smell smoke— smoke and something metallic, like iron.

I stick my hand out and grab something damp. I can feel something sticky on my skin. I realize that it's blood before I see it, and my head is empty, nothing there but the word BLOOD. BLOOD, BLOOD, BLOOD.

I can't move. I'm stuck. This is the worst part. This hopelessness is spreading throughout my body, cutting me to pieces, ruthlessly taking me apart, and destroying whatever's left.

I could have helped. I could have helped if my body hadn't failed. The thought fills every inch of my head until I think it's going to burst. But it doesn't, and everything starts to grow even louder. I can't handle it, but I don't have any choice.

I COULD HAVE HELPED.

But I didn't because I couldn't move. Because I was too weak. Because I ruin lives.

It's my fault, everything's my fault, and I've got to relive that over and over. The smells are so present that I just want to escape, but I can't because I'm stuck. Everything's so loud I just want to put the world on mute. And the pain is worse than anything I've ever felt.

The moment lasts a cold, dark eternity. By the time the images start to fade and a large anatomy poster begins to take shape in front of me, my body is bathed in sweat. It's blurry, moving here and there, half there and half gone, nothing completely real.

My skull is pulsating. Only vaguely do I perceive that Mike's a few feet away from me, rubbing his chest with his fingers and staring at me.

"You punched me," he says, but his words just fly past.

I vomit onto the floor, a gray-brown sticky puddle that looks like my life. My body is so slack that it's hard to sit, so I pull up my legs and move into the fetal position. I feel *really ugly, really pitiful.* Breathing slowly, I turn my head and press my nose into the table paper just to smell something other than smoke and blood, guilt and hate. The paper grows damp. Maybe it's my sweat. Maybe it's tears. No idea.

A few minutes go by before I hear Mike offering me a cup of water. Somehow that brings me to my senses. My limbs are as heavy as lead as I sit up, and I feel feverish. It takes so much effort that I have to pant, and using my voice takes all the strength I can muster. And I say the exact same thing I said to the five therapists who came before Mike.

"I'm stopping treatment. We don't need to make any more appointments. I'm…" I wipe my nose. "I'm sorry."

Mike frowns. "Wyatt…"

He doesn't get any farther because before he can even form the next syllable, I'm past him and out the door.

Ten seconds. I give myself ten seconds to lean back, focus my eyes on the ceiling, and catch my breath through rattling teeth. Then I kick the door backward and leave the training center with the bitter thought that I'm going to have to get used to the idea that I may never get back out on the ice and play hockey again.

It's the second worst thought I've ever had. The second worst I've ever had to admit.

The worst was when I realized that Aria had left me and would not be coming back.

But now she is back, though she's not with me because I fucked things up big time. And there's no getting around that.

I take the bus back downtown and think about what to do. About what my future is going to look like. Is there any kind of professional field I'm actually interested in? I've never actually thought about it. Things were always clear. NHL hockey. Period.

Maybe I could study sports medicine, like Aria. And if we ever get along again, at some point we could open an office together and…

Yeah, right. *As if.* We're not going to get along. She's done with me. Aria Moore loved me with every fiber of her heart, but now that's over. Things change, Wyatt. Deal with it.

I've almost made it to the bell tower when I see Camila. I'm so confused that I stop in my tracks.

It's eleven in the morning. My sister should be at school, explaining to old Clearwater what vectors are and all that shit. I watch her for a moment to see which way she'll go. When it's clear that she's heading for the designer stores, I move in behind her and follow her all the way to Dolce & Gabbana.

What the fuck is she *doing* here?

The streets are so full of tourists I almost have to get right in front of the shop windows to see her. And I really wish I wasn't, for when the saleswoman shows *my little sister* a red and a black set of underwear, I feel like I'm in the wrong film. It gets worse when Camila nods at the red and follows the woman to the register. We just have enough money for groceries, utilities, and those ridiculously expensive vacuum-cleaning bags, and *she's buying underwear at Dolce & Gabbana?*

I wait until she's out of the shop with the ivory-colored bag in her hand. She doesn't notice me and walks right on past.

"You're going to turn around and bring that right back, Mila."

My sister stops. "What are you doing here, Wyatt?"

"Are you serious?"

"I…"

"You have one chance to try and explain this. What the hell? Why aren't you at school?"

"Free period."

"Bullshit. Right now you've got math with old Clearwater. She's *always* there."

My sister bites her lower lip, and then I know I'm right. She only does that when she's nervous.

"I don't get it. We can hardly cover our bills, but you're out here shopping *at the designer stores?*"

"Meu Deus." Mila lifts her chin. "It's my money, Wyatt. I earned it, no? I can do whatever I want with it."

That hurts, and she knows it. She knows how to hurt me. I'd love to freak out and yell at her, but she's my little sister and our parents are dead. I'm not just her brother but her father, too, somehow, and losing my shit would just make everything worse.

I close my eyes, take a deep breath, and swallow my rage. "You know I'd let you spend your money on whatever the hell you wanted if we weren't in this situation. Come on, return those things."

"No, pai!"

I am not her dad, but she knows exactly how to piss me off.

"Camila, please. As soon as my arm starts to work again, I'll be back out on the ice and getting paid. I'll buy you ten of these sets if you want. I'll buy you anything, really, but not right now. Right now we've got to stick to a budget."

My sister crosses her arms. The bag wiggles back and forth. "I did the calculations, Wyatt. With my tips from the ski hut and my regular salary from last month, we'll make October no problem. I can afford this, okay?"

"But you don't need it. Why do you want that kind of underwear? I bought you some not all that long ago."

"From Target! You brought me cotton panties from Target!"

"Yeah, exactly." I don't understand the problem. "You said you needed some new underwear, so I brought you some."

Her face turns bright red. Then she throws her arms into the air, snorts, and simply walks off.

I follow her. "Hello? What's your problem?"

She looks straight ahead. "I'm not going to talk about my underwear with my brother. Now leave me alone."

"I won't. You should be at school and busy with algebra."

Camila stops so abruptly that I only notice once I'm five feet past her. I turn around to see her glaring at me.

"Fodasse, Wy, take care of your own shit!"

"I'm trying. You're at the top of my list."

"All I did was buy myself a pair of underwear!"

"Yeah, exactly. Underwear for a couple hundred dollars."

"A couple hundred dollars that *I* saved from the money that *I* earned because you're unable to work."

It feels like she's dumped a bucket of ice over my head. My lungs feel numb. Somewhere in my chest there's pain; it might be my heart. Which is why I say something I shouldn't and that I immediately regret as soon as the words leave my mouth.

"Mom and Dad would be disappointed in you."

Camila gasps. Her shoulders jerk like I've hit her. Well, I guess I did, not physically, but emotionally, and that's worse because now there's a huge crater in my chest constantly reminding me of it.

The little bag dangles weakly in her tiny hand, and suddenly I feel such immense pity for her that I want to cry. Here's my little sister with something that she bought and that she was happy about until I came and ruined it.

Just like I always do.

The skin around Camila's eyes flushes. Her chin trembles. I want to hug her, but before I can, she says the worst thing she could. And I deserve it, even worse, in fact.

"I understand why Aria left you. I understand her, and, maldito, thank God she did, Wyatt. Thank *God*. If she'd stayed with you, she'd have gone to shit. Because you make *everyone* go to shit. And you know what? If Aria ever spoke to you again, it would just be to say that you turn everyone and everything to shit."

Then she turns and leaves.

I lose myself in the crowd of people walking past. I'm not gone, and yet I'm not really here, either. And in this strange state of limbo, I finally stop thinking about helping myself and start thinking about what I can do to bring a smile back to my sister's face instead.

6

Somewhere Between Hello and Goodbye, There Was Love

ARIA

"HIGHER. NO, TOO HIGH. A BIT MORE TO THE LEFT, more, more, a little bit more—stop! Too far."

I sigh. "Forget it. My arm's about to fall off. We'll leave it as is."

Harper crosses her arms and raises an eyebrow. "The lights are screwy."

"No one will notice." The ladder's wobbling dangerously as I make my way back down.

"*I'm* noticing."

I roll my eyes, stick the roll of tape into my pocket, and fold the ladder back up. "You're abnormal. The whole lounge is made out of string lights. Wherever you look, Harper, there are lights. No one's going to notice that number eighty-three up there is off."

Harper shrugs and follows me to the storage closet. "If you say so. Where's your mom?"

"At the doctor's."

"Still?"

"Yeah. She's having one of her episodes."

Earlier this morning my mother could hardly get out of bed. My heart bled as I watched her force one leg after the other, bit by bit, across the mattress while grabbing hold of the metal rods along the sides. She didn't want any help. Every time I tried, she pushed me away because she's too proud. I hate that. She's not doing well, and when my mom's not doing well, I feel like shit. But I understand because I'm just as proud as she is.

"How's she getting back?"

I close the door to the storage closet and walk over to the big wooden cabinet beneath the TV to look for the board games. "William's bringing her. You know where Xtreme Activity is? I could've sworn it was here with the others."

"A kid set it on fire."

"What?!"

"At games night last year. An aggressive kid who couldn't stand to lose. He totally lost his mind and threw the whole game along with the box into the fireplace. One guest filmed it with their phone. You can find it on YouTube if you look for 'Weird guy goes weirder in Aspen.' You want to see it?"

I frown. "No. That was my favorite game."

Harper grabs the lighter off the mantelpiece and starts stacking wood and trying to get it lit. "You just shouldn't have left."

"You know why I left, Harp." I pull Monopoly, Taboo, Scrabble, and Twister out of the cabinet and put them down on the big table before making my way back toward Harper. "Stop holding that against me all the time."

My best friend doesn't look at me. She messes around with the fireplace poker instead. The flames are glittering in her eyes, but that often happens, even when there's nothing on fire.

"You hurt me."

Warmth seeps through my veins. Harp rarely shows her feelings. Her parents are cold, and she grew up the same way. No hugs, no nice words, hardly any moments of comfort, and no tears...ever. Ever since we were kids, Harp has avoided being at home as best she can. She practically grew up with us. The B&B is as much her childhood home as mine. Mom is closer to her than her own mother is.

I sit down on the crocheted jute pouf, take the poker from her hand, and put it back in its place. As she still refuses to look at me, I take her hands.

She finally manages to turn toward me, and I see so much anger, sadness, and vulnerability in her delicate features that my throat closes up and I almost start to cry.

"I'm sorry, Harp. Really. I am *so* sorry for taking off without saying a word. For not being there for you when Jake died. Sure, we talked on the phone, but I should have been there physically. I know that your fathers worked together and that, being a good friend, Jake was always an anchor for you. And I'm sorry for not answering so many of your calls and that I only sent you the occasional email when I was really doing badly. I didn't want to have to think about Wyatt. Didn't want to be asked about him. I have no idea how I can make it up to you, and I know that you needed me. But, you know, I also needed myself; I needed myself *so bad*, Harp. But that doesn't mean I didn't think about you. Whenever I saw someone in the cafeteria mix ketchup and mayo, you immediately came to mind. And whenever one of my roommates used mousse, I'd think of how you'd wrinkle your nose and say, 'Use Curl & Shine from Shea Moisture if you want your curls to look good, sweetheart.' I didn't forget you, Harp. I never would. But I forgot how to laugh and how to live and tried to learn that again by starting over. All on my own, you know?"

She gives a long, deep sigh. "Sure, A. I get that. But I missed you." She presses my hands. "You're the only family I've ever had, and then *you were simply gone.*"

I feel a burning pressure growing behind my eyelids. "I know."

"And I hate Wyatt for that. I hate what he did to you. I hate that he's the reason you had to go."

"Maybe you can teach me how to manage that."

Harper looks confused. "Manage what?"

I smile sadly. "Hating Wyatt."

She lets go of my fingers, stands up, and runs her hands down her French braids. "I'm afraid you're never going to be able to. It's like you're being self-destructive."

"Seems like it."

"When's Will getting here with your mom?"

"Any minute now." I get up, too, and look at my phone. "Oh, Knox is outside. I'm supposed to help him with the pumpkins."

Harper's eyes grow big. "*Knox?*"

"He comes to games night every year."

"Not last year he didn't."

I stick my phone back into my pants and shoot her a compassionate look. "I'm friends with him and Paisley. Knox likes you. He always has. But sometimes things just don't work out feelings-wise like we want. Sometimes they just work out differently because they're supposed to."

"Yeah. But…" She fidgets from one leg to the other, looks to the door, and then back at me. "It's so humiliating, Aria. I mean, he slept with me even though he knew it was just that, while I…while I projected so much onto it. I mean, I never would've thought he'd pull the same shit with me that he did with all the others because I didn't think he'd just toss all our years of friendship away like that."

From outside I hear him honk several times. It's deafening. Then his voice drifts through the window. "Get out here and help me with this mountain of pumpkins, Aria Moore. I'm not schlepping them in by myself!"

With a sigh, I tuck a strand of my best friend's red hair behind her ear. "He was in a terrible hole back then. I don't think he was thinking at all. You know how Knox was. And you know that he's sorry. He told you that, right?"

Harper purses her lips. "Yeah."

"Then try to forgive him. Try to accept that he wasn't the right guy for you. Wish him luck with Paisley."

"It's not like I don't wish that for him, A. It's that I'm *ashamed*."

"You don't need to be. There's nothing you can do about feelings." Knox honks again. I take a deep breath and cast Harper a questioning glance. "So?"

She rolls her eyes. "Okay. But only because I have no interest in staying at home tonight."

"You can be proud of yourself."

Another eye roll, but I know that she is. Proud of herself. This is a big step for Harper.

Opening the front door, I see Paisley wobbling across the street, a pumpkin under each arm. She's put her hair into a side braid so that her ears are sticking out rather noticeably. "These are some monster pumpkins! Huge, mutated monster pumpkins, and when we cut them open, little animals are going to come crawling out."

The wind brushes my face and sneaks under the collar of my sweater as I walk over to the trunk of Knox's Range Rover. Knox is leaning against his car, arms folded, staring at us. "What's wrong with you? Get moving, Winterbottom."

"Nope. I'm here to see how you all manage on your own."

Paisley looks over her shoulder at me. "Call the ambulance, Aria."

"What?"

"Knox is going to need it when this pumpkin hits his head."

I laugh. Knox widens his arms and puts on a shocked face. "Et tu, Brute?"

Paisley rolls her eyes and looks at me. "Ever since his seminar on psychic manipulation in the Roman Empire, he's been dropping *Julius Caesar* quotes."

"Knox *is* Julius Caesar," I reply.

Her giggles waft over to us before she disappears into the house. Knox grins. He drags four of the huge pumpkins out of the car and looks like the happiest guy in the world.

"You deserved that, Knox. For real."

He looks up. "What do you mean?"

"Being happy. It's the only thing your mom ever wanted."

Knox's eyes rest on me for a moment before scurrying to the door, as if he could see through it to Paisley. Then his face darkens. "Can I be honest a sec, Aria?"

"Huh?"

"I didn't believe that was even possible anymore."

"Can I be honest for a sec, Knox?"

He tilts his head.

"None of us did. But we didn't stop hoping. That's the real point, I think."

For a second he doesn't react. Then he smiles and nods toward the B&B. "Come on. Let's get to carving these pumpkins, Moore."

I have no idea how it happened; I was only gone for two minutes, but the entire B&B looks like a battlefield. The wooden floor is teeming with pumpkin-covered newspaper. Paisley is digging into her pumpkin as if looking for diamonds, while Harper is just sitting next to her, looking a little overwhelmed, a Swiss Army knife in one hand, her own pumpkin in the other. She doesn't like to get dirty.

Paisley knows that, but she just keeps talking at her incessantly. "Halloween just comes once a year. Once a year. Come on. You can wash your hands afterward. Now carve a face. I want to see what you come up with!"

"I can't carve," Harper says. I get the feeling she's only interacting because Knox has just stepped inside. Paisley and Harp aren't the best of friends, but they slowly seem to be becoming okay with each other.

Knox puts his pumpkin on the side table, sits down next to Paisley, and pulls out his pocketknife.

"Everyone can carve."

"Not me." The only sign of how hard this is for Harper is that her ears have turned red. "I'm the type of person who sticks their knife into the pumpkin and ends up knifing their own arm."

We laugh, and for a while we talk about everything under the sun. About Will's terrible pumpkin, which is indeed next to the bell tower already. About Knox's studies. About my time at Brown. Wyatt's name hovers in the air, a taut band ready to snap because we all know that's the reason I left, and we are just waiting for his name to come up. I mean, he's already here, unstated, in between every syllable I expend regarding my studies and Rhode Island.

But no one mentions him. No one says things like, "It's sooo sad" or "You were sooo cute together," because every one of us knows that words like that are like lashes, and lashes hurt.

We talk and talk and talk, and the radio's playing a song by One Direction. I love that Harper has bits of pumpkin on her jeans and is *laughing* anyway. She's laughing at the face Paisley's carved because Paisley can't carve, and when I say that, I mean she *really* can't carve; everything's just caved in on itself, and all that's left of the face is a big, slimy hole.

As we're putting our mutant pumpkins out on the porch, William's pickup comes down the street. He parks on the other side of the road, opens the door for Mom, and offers her his arm. The sky is darkening, and the light from the streetlamps lights up their tired faces. Nevertheless, she puts on a smile when she sees us, and all I can think is how strong my mom is.

"I like the first one," she says and, deeply impressed, points at Paisley's ugly jack-o'-lantern. "That there is art."

"That there's just a mess," Harper says.

Knox puts his arm around Paisley and pulls her close. "My girlfriend. She's multi-talented."

"Speaking of art," William says as we make our way inside, closing the door behind himself and helping Mom out of her jacket. "Have you all seen *my* jack-o'-lantern? It's next to the bell tower."

Harper and I exchange a glance. Paisley pretends to scratch a spot on her pants.

Only Knox nods thoughtfully. "Never seen anything better, Will. Never seen anything better."

Will looks happy as a clam.

"Okay, people," I clap. "We gonna play Monopoly?"

"But this year I'm the dog," Knox says as we sit down on the sofa.

Paisley pushes away his hand as he reaches for hers. "I want to be the dog!"

"No way." He puts his arm around her and moves to grab the figure. "I've never been the dog. Wyatt always was, and now it's the first game night without him, and I can—oh." His eyes dart over to me. "Sorry, A."

I swallow. "No problem."

Out of the corner of my eye, I see Mom cast me a worried glance while William busily arranges a group of pillows behind her head.

Couldn't "Weird guy goes weirder in Aspen" have burned Monopoly instead?

Knox purses his lips and puts the piece back in the box. "Fine. No one gets to be the dog. Give me the hat, Harper."

Will bends over the table. "I'm the wheelbarrow!"

Harp hands it to him. "That fits you, Will, really."

"Why?"

"It just does," I say. "If you weren't a person, you'd be a wheelbarrow."

Paisley hands out the money. "I think so, too. Why are there smileys on some of the bills, Aria?"

My eyes rush to the piece of paper in her hand. Wyatt drew all those smileys on the bills because he was always convinced that Knox and I were stealing from him.

Knox and I look at each other. His expression is sympathetic. Mine is doubtful.

"No idea."

Knox doesn't correct me. Maybe he'll tell her later, but right now he doesn't want his best friend to become a topic. And I'm thankful to him for that. "So, we want to play or what?"

Monopoly was always a thing between us. Every year we'd swear never to play again, and every year we'd do it anyway. Then it'd get loud, and everyone would compete for the streets, train stations, and hotels as if it was the last thing we had left to do to be happy. And suddenly we didn't recognize one another anymore and were happy to see someone else land in jail and would lose our shit when we didn't win the pot of gold.

And that's exactly how it goes today, too. After two hours of battling it out, William's thrown his tie into the fire, Harp has bitten off two fingernails, my hair's on end, Knox's face is a deep red, and Paisley looks positively distraught. Mom's asleep.

We decide to call it quits, afraid that on this rainy October night something really bad could happen. Really, right when Knox was about to win, Will's and my glances made it clear that we were planning to make him disappear in the Aspen Highlands. It was Paisley's idea to stop. I think she was getting scared. She's still got to get used to how we do things here in Aspen.

I hear William lean over my mom and ask her quietly whether she needs anything. His voice sounds strange. Different. Warm and soft somehow. I don't know this side of him, and, to be honest, it's a bit weird. Mom grumbles something, which must be a "no," for shortly thereafter Will says goodbye.

"I've got to go to bed. My acid-base balance, you know?" At the door he turns to Knox. "Do me a favor and have another look at my pumpkin, would you? I've got a hunch he isn't feeling too well."

"It's a pumpkin," Paisley says.

Will looks confused. "I know. Why are you telling me that?"

"Well, I mean, pumpkins can't feel, and, umm…" The look on Will's face makes her uncomfortable. His eyelid begins to twitch—a bad sign, a really bad sign. Paisley sighs. "Doesn't matter. Goodnight, Will."

"We'll go see him on our way back home," Knox says.

Only then does Will seem happy, and he leaves.

Harper slips into her cashmere coat. "I've got to get going, too. Tomorrow's training is earlier than usual."

Paisley sighs frustratedly. "Getting ready for championships. The time of year Polina becomes a tyrant."

Knox gets up, too, and grabs his car keys off the dining table. "And I've got exams. So, see you later, A." He pats me on the back and ruffles my hair. "It's cool that you're back."

I say goodbye to everyone with a smile, close the door, and lean back against the wood. My smile dies. For a while all I do is stare at the floor and lose myself in the notches until my mother's voice tears me out of my trance.

"Come here, Aria."

I look up. Mom rolls to the side to make room on the squeaky old sofa, patting her hand on the space next to Hershey, our gray cat. Everything is quiet except for the crackling of the fire.

"I thought you were asleep."

"I was." She holds up the wool blanket. I slip in next to her, snuggle my head up against her chest, and enjoy the way she smells, which has always reminded me of maple syrup. Hershey stretches out, moves his heavy body, and curls up on my stomach.

Mom kisses the top of my head. "But you woke me up."

"I was quiet."

"Your thoughts were screaming through the house."

I sigh. "Was it that obvious?"

"Since that thing with the smileys, yeah."

"What should I do, Mom? I can't cope. He's everywhere."

She starts kneading my back. It's something she used to do when I was little that helped chase off all the dark clouds.

"Of course he's everywhere. We live in a small town, and he's filling up all your heart."

"But I don't want it to be like that."

"Yes, you do, dear. You do. You just don't *want* to want it."

"Isn't that the same thing?"

"Oh, no. Not in the least."

Although the fire's going strong and I'm beneath the wool blanket, a cold shiver shoots through me.

Mom begins to move her fingers up and down the baby hair on my neck. "If you want him to disappear, then you have to leave him behind."

"I was gone for two years. *Two years.* I left Wyatt behind a long time ago."

My mother laughs. Her breath brushes my forehead. "You weren't ever really gone. Physically, maybe. But not with your heart. It's just as stuck on that Portuguese hockey player with the cute gap in his teeth as it was back when you were in eighth grade and he sent you those singing trolls for Valentine's Day."

"They were love elves."

Well, in truth, it was the custodian and those two cafeteria ladies who smoked two packs of Camel Lights out behind the dumpsters every day and had voices like sandpaper. But it was cute all the same.

"Exactly. That was the day the boy won your heart. And he's still got it. If you want it back, grab your Bic and draw a line."

"I did!"

Mom snorts. "In pencil."

"Oh, come on." I kick the blanket off and stand up. Hershey protests by arching his back and disappearing. "You're starting to piss me off."

My mother raises an eyebrow. "Because I'm telling you what you already know?"

"No. Because you… Because…"

Her brow makes it all the way to her hairline. "Because I'm right and you don't want to admit it?"

Heat shoots up my neck. "No. Because you're making me think of him when I want to forget!"

"You think about him every second; it doesn't matter what anyone else is talking about. Whenever I ask you if you've gone shopping already and you say, *Yeah*, your thoughts are *Wyatt, Wyatt, Wyatt*. Whenever I ask you if the guestrooms are ready and you say, *Yeah*, your thoughts are *Wyatt, Wyatt, Wyatt*. Whenever I ask you…"

"Enough already! Give it a rest, Mom! Just stop. I know all that. I… I just don't want to hear it, okay?"

Mom sits up, her face tensing in pain. But a few seconds later she is looking at me with compassion. "Don't you think it's something you should hear, sweetheart? Don't you think it's something you should confront?"

I ball my hands into fists, dig my nails into my palms, and grit my teeth. My heart begins to race. Wyatt was always good at that. Making my heart race, I mean.

"I should confront the fact that I need to prepare the guests' breakfast. I've got to tell Patricia that we need some pumpkin bread and get everything ready for the first reservations, too."

Mom's shoulders sink. It looks like the topic's not yet closed for her, but then her lips form a tired smile. "Okay, Aria. You still aren't ready."

No. I'm not. I can't even think of his name without breaking out in goose bumps. I can't think of anything to do with him, not that long scar on his hand from the wild coyote bite, not his faded baseball hats, or the feeling of his wide shoulders pressing against me. Shit, I can't even drive by his house on the way to Target. I make a fifteen-minute detour instead and take the unlit backways to the left, past Buttermilk Mountain, left, left, left, because taking a right always means Wyatt.

I really *should* be over it already, but I'm not, and that just eats me alive every day, and, yeah, the thought that I haven't managed to do a damn thing without him in two years and that my heart is still so hung up on him scares the shit out of me. I mean, what about in another ten, twenty, or thirty years? What if my heart stays hung up on him *forever* and can no longer figure out how to get back home?

7

I Am the Designer of My Own Catastrophe

WYATT

OCTOBER TWENTY-FIFTH. THE THIRD SUNDAY OF THE month. Our traditional pumpkin-carving-and-games night. Knox, Gwen, Harper, Aria, and I started in elementary school and just kept on going, but at some point, everything changed. Knox's mom died, and he developed that ice-skating phobia of his because she'd been a figure skater and had died making a jump. He stopped coming because he didn't want to hang around Harp and Gwen anymore, who were also figure skaters. So, after that, it was just the four of us.

Until I made the biggest mistake of my life without even being able to remember it.

Aria took off. There were no more game nights. There wasn't anything anymore. My life sucked; it still does, and I wish I was five years old again, going to school with my dalmatian backpack.

The neon light above me is flickering. I'm sitting in Kate's with my head against the window, waiting on my fries. Camila's got to work, and it was depressingly quiet and empty at home. I had to be around people to drown out the voices in my head. They're still there, but at least the jukebox here plays good tunes, people are talking, and I can pretend I'm not alone.

"Hey." It's Gwen. She's woven ribbons into her braids and decorated them with little golden rings. The black bandanna around her wrist brushes my fingers as she pushes the plate onto the table. "Sorry that I'm the one bringing them over. Mom had to go around the corner."

"No problem."

I want to start eating, but Gwen doesn't leave; she just keeps on standing there, next to my table, staring at my fries.

"You want some?"

She blinks. "What?"

"My fries. You want some?"

"No."

"It looks like you do."

"Why would I?"

"Because you're staring at them."

"No, I…" She sighs. "Can we talk, Wyatt?"

Her words form a stone in my stomach. A huge, sharp, painful stone.

I don't have anything against Gwen. What happened between us wasn't her fault, really. I didn't know what the hell was going on, and, according to others, I was giving her clear signals. It's not her fault, but ever since then I haven't been able to look at her, and I can't stop making her responsible for everything because that's just the way I am. And maybe that's uncool, maybe that makes *me* uncool, but that's the way it is, and sometimes you just can't change things.

"I don't think that's a good idea, Gwen."

She kneads her hands. "Yeah, I thought the same thing at first, too. But, to be real honest, Wyatt? That's bullshit. We've been friends all our lives. It was a mistake. A big, *fucked-up* mistake. But do we have to avoid each other because of it? Aren't we old enough to be able to talk about it and let it go? There is so much hate and misunderstanding in the world, *so damn much*. Let's not add to it."

For a few seconds I just dip my fry into my ketchup without

saying a word. I know she's right. We're grown up and should put this behind us. But just her standing here next to me makes me feel bad. It's like contact with her was forbidden or something.

At the thought I immediately look out the window to make sure no one is watching us. The streetlights have come on and are illuminating the ugly-ass pumpkin on the other side of the street. A couple of tourists stop to stare at the bits of mold before shaking their heads and moving on. Other than them, I don't see anyone I know.

"Don't worry. They're over at Aria's."

"What?"

"Knox, Paisley, and Harper are over at Aria's. Today is the twenty-fifth. Pumpkin-carving-and-games night. Don't you remember?"

"They're over at Aria's and didn't invite us?"

"Umm." She looks at me for a second, then she sits down in the red upholstered booth and leans forward, her eyes narrowed into slits. "You cheated on Aria with me, Wyatt. Why on earth would she invite us?"

"No idea. She shouldn't. Of course she shouldn't. But, you know, all the same…"

"I know." Gwen sighs and leans back. She grabs the ends of her hair and observes them. "Strange feeling, huh?"

"Hmm."

My eyes wander past her to the jukebox, which is playing some Coldplay song or other. The red-yellow colors start to blur. I toss one fry after the other into my mouth and grow more and more frustrated.

Gwen is tapping her foot on the tiles in a steady rhythm. I can't stand it. It's driving me mad. "Stop."

She looks at me questioningly. "What?"

"That thing you're doing with your foot."

"Sorry."

Sighing, I drop the fries back onto the plate and run a hand across my face. "Gwen, you're right. Treating you like this isn't fair. But…"

"It's okay." She stretches out her hand. At first I think she's lost it and is moving to grab me, and I swear my heart stops. I grow so panicky I'm about to jump up and run out when I see her begin to trace the patterns on the tabletop and realize that *I'm* the one who has completely lost it.

Goddamn, Wyatt. Chill out, my man.

Gwen looks at her fingers. I can hear the wheels turning in her head as she considers what to say. Eventually, she pulls her hand back and pulls the sleeves of her sweater over her fingertips. She's nervous. That's how we are; that's how life is. It makes us nervous because we don't know how things are supposed to go on after what it did to us.

"Wyatt, I'm sorry. I'm sorry Aria took off because of me. Ever since then, not a day has gone by that I don't blame myself. I mean, if it hadn't been for me... No idea. Maybe you all'd have kids or something."

I laugh out loud. "We would *definitely* not have kids already, Gwen."

She shrugs. "Maybe not. But you'd definitely be living together and ordering pizza at Don Giovanni's in the evenings before playing *Mario Kart* on your Switch and going to bed far too late because you're so happy and..."

"Stop." I force myself to smile so Gwen doesn't feel snubbed. But it's tough because what she's saying is true, so damn true, and that just makes everything worse. Que merda, I'm such a mess, and then I hear something like that, and all I want to do is puke and go to sleep so that I don't have to hear anything else.

I push away my plate. Man, I don't feel good. "I mean... Yeah, Gwen. Maybe it'd be like that. But thinking about what things would be like if nothing had happened between the two of us doesn't help you or me a single bit. Something *did* happen. And that's my fault." I try to catch her eyes. They're big, sad pieces of caramel. "Mine alone, okay?"

She nods. Gwen doesn't believe me; that much I know. I don't think she wants to keep on talking about it, either. The whole thing just depresses us.

"Can we leave it behind us?" Her voice is soft. Almost like she doesn't trust herself to ask me. I mean, it's a big deal. You can hardly leave something like that behind you.

I lean back and take a deep breath. "We can stop avoiding each other. I mean, you're right. We're grown-ups. What happened happened, and it sucks. But treating each other like shit won't change that. That won't bring Aria back."

A weak smile appears on Gwen's face. "I'd like that, Wyatt."

"Yeah." I sound relieved but a bit tired, too, a bit tired from life. "Me, too. You were always a good friend. This all just never should have happened."

For a moment she scratches the tabletop with her nail. "I never had the chance to tell you how sorry I am about your mom."

I nod. "Thanks, Gwen."

"And about Aria."

"Let's not talk about her anymore."

Gwen looks up. Her gaze rests on me for what feels like an eternity. "You still love her, right?"

What a question. I pull off my hat and put it back on, backward. "Of course I love her. I broke her heart, then she broke mine, and then things were simply over. We've never really talked about it, never sat down and said, 'Okay, we had our time. Now it's over. Let's move on.' It was just over from one day to the next. After six years. Just like that." My words are so harsh that Gwen flinches. "Do you know how it all went down with my mom, Gwen?"

"No," she whispers.

The bell above the door rings as a couple comes in. They are laughing and talking about the pumpkin outside. I watch them for a second. Watch their caresses, and I am jealous of what they have because I had it, too, and I want it back. My eyes rest on the guy's smile as he offers his girl a chair. Then I quickly turn away.

Gwen, wide-eyed, is waiting for me to go on.

I take another deep breath. "I'd just gotten home from the hospital. The doctors said it was fine for me to go. Mom still had some time. At least a week. I'd stroked her hand as she lay there, just skin and bones. Tubes everywhere. You know what she told me?"

"What?"

"'Take care of your sister, Wyatt. Make sure she's okay, and, above all, make sure that you're okay. Be good to Aria so that I know she'll take care of your heart when I can't anymore.'"

Gwen's face completely loses its color. "God. Wyatt, I…"

"That was her request. Her *only one*. I promised her. And it was the last thing she ever said to me. That night I got a call from the hospital. It was all over."

Gwen's lips are trembling. The skin on her chin creases, and her eyes grow damp. "That's awful, Wyatt."

"Aria wanted to be there for me," I say. Now that I'm starting to talk about it, I can't stop. I hadn't thought it would be like this, but letting everything out after holding it in for so long really is a relief. "She came by every day. Cooked. Took care of Camila. Did her homework with her. Took care of the calls I simply couldn't take care of. She called the funeral home and got everything together while I just sat there on the sofa, not speaking to anyone. Two weeks after the funeral, an old friend from the minor leagues came over. Jared. He was on his way to Knox's birthday party but wanted to stop by beforehand to give me his condolences. At that second something shot through me; I have no idea what, but it was unreal. Somehow I just *knew* that Jared had drugs on him. I mean, it was *Jared*, and he *always* had something when he was on his way to a party. So I asked, and he gave me some Molly. I was totally gone. I mean, wow, was I fucked up. We went to Knox's party. I took some more, then started drinking on top of it. I remember that, at some point, all I could see were intense colors, everything was completely distorted, and then everything just went black. The next day Aria was gone. She was gone, and I had absolutely no idea what had happened before Knox showed me a video someone had sent him."

Tears are falling down Gwen's face. "Of you and me."

"Of me and you."

"Wyatt, I had no idea…" Her hand is shaking as she puts her fingers to her lips and looks at me. Her voice breaks. "I was drunk, too, you know, and I… I have no idea how I should describe this. I was completely outside of myself." She casts a quick glance at the neighboring table where her mother's taking an order and pauses. Eventually Kate smiles at the customer, clicks her pen closed, and hurries back into the kitchen. "It was…"

"Give it a rest, Gwen." My voice is soft. I didn't know I was still capable of such a tone.

She shakes her head. Her braids swing from one shoulder to the other before she puts her elbows on the table and buries her head in her hands.

I reach out and stroke the back of her hands. "Hey, give it a rest. It's not your fault. You didn't have any idea what was going on."

Gwen raises her eyes. "But I could have asked. I shouldn't have just accepted everything!"

"But that's life, right? Everyone does things that later on they think should have gone differently. Really, Gwen. You were just in the wrong place at the wrong time. I can't tell you what was going on with me that night, but I'm sure that, if it hadn't been you, it would've been someone else."

Gwen stares at the table. Her lips are swollen from crying. "Maybe that would've been better."

At that moment the door to the diner opens again. The sound of the bell echoes through the room. I look up, and suddenly my entire body freezes and grows numb.

It's Aria. She takes a small step forward, then stops, staring at me in disbelief. It feels like a million seconds go by. I'm unable to get enough of her, and every one of our shared memories floods my head—until I realize *why* she hasn't moved an inch.

My hand is still on top of Gwen's; my fingers are still stroking her skin.

The realization hits me like an electric shock. I jerk back into the upholstered back so quickly that I knock the breath out of myself.

The last time I had an asthma attack was when I was a kid, but I swear this feels like the same thing. My ex-girlfriend's bright green eyes seem to have set my synapses aflame. I'm ninety-five percent electricity. Four percent panic. One percent spoiled hope that's still there because my heart is just too loving.

It's like our souls are completely naked. We both know it, and we both want to hide it, but we can't because there are powers that are stronger than us. The power between us is one of them. Always was.

Gwen's head spins around. She sees Aria, gasps, and jumps up. "Aria, I swear, this was just…"

The sound of Gwen's voice breaks Aria out of her trance. She blinks and looks at Gwen for a second before abruptly turning and going to the counter. Kate is just pushing a cookie into a bag and handing it to a guest. Then she turns to Aria, and I feel like I'm in a movie that's so bizarre it's got to be a dream. Someone wake me up. Someone punch me, please!

"Aria, sweetheart." Kate's eyes dart to me, then to her daughter, then back to my ex. "What can I do for you?"

"Coffee," Aria stammers, her voice breathless and choppy, her cheeks flushed. That always happened when everything was too much. "Our delivery didn't come today. An accident out on the highway, apparently, and, well, it's Sunday. Woody's and Target are closed so…" She takes a deep breath. "I desperately need coffee. For tomorrow. Breakfast. Guests. I… Coffee."

Kate isn't dumb. She knows what's up. Over and over her eyes drift over Aria's shoulders to us, and every time I feel smaller and dirtier and just want to sink into the ground and never come back up.

"Of course, sweetie. What do you need? Arabica? Robusta? Decaf?"

"Everything."

How she says it.

Everything.

Me, too, Aria. Me, too.

Kate goes to get the coffee and comes back with three bags. She smiles sympathetically as she hands them over. "You need anything else, sweetie?"

Aria takes the bags, shakes her head, and mumbles a quick *thanks.* Her hair is covering her face as she turns and marches past us. Of course she doesn't look at me again. Of course she doesn't.

The door closes. How could all the guests just go on sitting at their tables and eating and laughing and not catch on *at all* to what just happened? I mean, that was sick; it was earth-shattering, but nobody cares.

My eyes meet Kate's. She makes an effort to seem apologetic because Kate's cool and has nothing but love for everyone in Aspen, but all the same, her words hit me. "Wyatt, I think it'd be better if you go."

Because I hurt Aria. Because I hurt her daughter. Because I hurt everyone. Camila was right. I just turn everyone and everything into shit. That's how I roll.

And so I nod, peel myself out of the little booth by the window, and disappear into the cool evening air, that air that's so magical— but not for me.

8

Heartbroken and Homesick, Because You Were Both My Heart and My Home

ARIA

"MR. BENSON, I KNOW THAT IT'S FRUSTRATING, AND I really am *terribly* sorry. But you simply are not in our reservation book."

His voice grows louder. I have to move the phone away from my ear as he shouts, and his voice, it's so *intimidating*! Awful. I'd love to give him all the rooms in the house just to not have to listen to him anymore.

"I made my reservation five months ago! *Five months!* I was counting on it. Do you know what kind of light this puts your B&B in? I'm going to leave a review online. I am going to…"

"Mr. Benson, please calm down. Over the last few months there have been a few, umm, personal issues here at our B&B. The manager and owner is really struggling with her health. It was not our intention to let your reservation slip through the cracks."

"Well, then do something about it!"

With a sigh I twirl the phone cord between my fingers and use my other hand to go through the reservations again. No chance. We're all booked out.

"Hello? You still there?"

I close my eyes and run a hand across my forehead. "Yes, I'm here. May I call you back, Mr. Benson?"

He snorts. "You're just trying to get rid of me. I know how women do things. First you say you're going to call back, and then you'll simply be not available."

"We're a B&B, Mr. Benson. We can't simply disappear. And I'd appreciate you not being sexist."

"Sorry?"

"Men use excuses, too. I don't like hearing women being degraded."

Mr. Benson mumbles some kind of apology, accepts my offer to call him back, and hangs up. Exasperated, I put the phone back on its cradle, stretch my arms, and lean back my head.

"You doing yoga? What are you doing with your head?"

I wheel around. Mom is sitting in her chair next to the fireplace, sipping her coffee out of one of our flea-market mugs. Due to her rheumatism, her fingers have grown stiff and swollen. I immediately see she's having trouble holding onto the handle. She's using our Daniel mug, the one labeled *DANIEL, LISTEN TO YOUR GRANDFATHER* on the side. It's funny. It's like we know Daniel somehow.

"No. I'm just tired."

"Why?" She puts her coffee down on the side table, pulls her hair tie off her wrist, and tries to put her hair up in a bun. "Didn't you sleep okay?"

After the third try, I stand up, take the hair tie out of her hand, and help her. "So-so."

Mom pats her bun and sighs. "Aria, maybe you should talk with him. Just to be done with it once and for all."

"No."

"Daniel would want you to."

"I don't want to see him."

"Who? Daniel?"

"You're funny."

"You all live in a small town. You're always going to run into him."

"But as long as I have anything to do with it, I'm going to avoid him."

"You all…"

"No, Mom. Just no, okay?"

Her lips are a thin line. She wants to say something, I know that much, but she doesn't. Instead she just flares her nostrils and nods.

"Fine. And now I don't want to hear his name anymore."

"Fine."

The door opens, and William comes in. October fills the room with the smell of leaves and chestnuts.

Will's movements seem stiff somehow; I think he's got a new jacket. That bothers me because, as long as I can remember, every fall William's always worn the same old gray trench coat. It's faded and looks kind of vintage-y, with spots and patches. I wasn't aware of just how much it fit him until now, seeing him in his new biker's jacket that *doesn't suit him at all.*

"*Will.* What *is* that?"

"A jacket, Aria."

"A *leather* jacket?"

His cheeks turn red. "Fake leather. I wanted, umm, to look snazzier."

"*Snazzier?*"

"Yeah. Cooler. Like the young folks out there. The hipsters."

"Oh my God, Will."

He clears his throat. "Ruth, shall we?"

"Yeah," Mom says and stands up.

"Where are you all going?"

William looks at me quizzically. "To the naturopath. You made an appointment for her there, Aria. You did, right?"

"Oh, yeah. Yeah, I did. Thanks for taking her."

Shit, Aria. Your mom is the reason you're back in Aspen. Pay attention to her! What's wrong with you?

"See you, dear." Mom slips the purse over her shoulder and kisses me on the cheek. "Remember to go shopping for the Halloween party."

"Yeah, sure. It's on my list. Right after I finish up the rooms for our evening guests."

My mother scrutinizes me. "You sure you're going to manage?"

I smile. "Of course, Mom. Don't worry about it."

"I'm always worried."

"I know. But my grades are fantastic. I'll manage it all."

She doesn't believe me. I can see it in her eyes. And she's right. My mother knows me, and, to be honest, back at Brown my grades had already kind of gone down the tubes after it became clear to me that I needed to get back to Aspen. And I haven't been to any lectures here yet. Everything's kind of overwhelming at the moment, though I wouldn't have any problems if Wyatt wasn't all over the place.

I quickly banish the thought, put on a smile, and nudge the two toward the door. "We'll see each other later. Will, make sure Mom allows the guy to do his thing. If you notice her pretending that everything's great, tell him that she's lying."

"I'd never do something like that," she counters.

I open the door and make a sweeping motion with my hand. "Another fat one, Mom. If Daniel only knew!"

She laughs. My eyes dart to Will, and I raise my eyebrows, my silent plea for him to *really* pay attention. He gives a brief nod, and his beard—which, as of late, he has been letting grow longer and longer—brushes his leather jacket. He likes that. I think he finds it really cool. Snazzy, this new-and-improved Will. *Snazzy.*

I spend the rest of the morning getting the rooms in shape. I put in my earbuds and listen to Taylor Swift at full blast while making the beds and cleaning the bathroom. Afterward, I spend about half an hour on the phone trying to understand what's going on with the delivery.

Eventually I put the phone back down, fish my to-do list out of my back pocket, and scribble *Grocery shopping for the week* beneath *Halloween preparations*. I hover with the tip of the pen over the paper for a second, then add, *Catch up on all the lectures you've missed*. A second later, *Forget Wyatt*.

With a sigh, I lean back against the wall and stare at my wrinkled list. "How on earth am I supposed to manage all of this?" I mumble, then close my eyes and begin to tap my head against the wall in a steady rhythm. "How on earth will I manage all of this when he is *all* I can think about?"

"Man, Aria."

I flinch and open my eyes.

Knox is standing in front of me, his leather university bag slung over his shoulder. He's wearing a gray Wellensteyn coat and brown Doc Martens, the same ones I've got. Knox looks so incredibly student-like, it's funny. It's hard to believe that he was once a sensational snowboard star who almost always left the house in sportswear.

"You're talking to yourself."

"Just sometimes."

"Every day, I bet."

I run a tired hand across my face. "Why are you here?"

Knox walks through the stone arch into the other side of the eating area. The quiet is interrupted only by the sound of the coffee machine grinding beans. A few seconds later, Knox reappears with a cup in his hand, sits down in the leather chair by the fire, and crosses his legs. "My laptop is fried."

"Buy a new one."

"I did. But it's not showing up till next week. Do you have one?"

"Of course I have a laptop."

"Can I have it?"

"Huh? No."

Knox slurps his foam. "Why not? You don't need it."

"Of course I need it. I'm still going to classes."

"Oh, right." Another slurp. "Totally forgot. You're always hanging around here at home."

I wink at him. "Because I've got to help Mom out, idiot."

"I know." Now his voice sounds softer. He leans his head back and looks at me. His eyes are even greener than mine. In the past, people often thought we were brother and sister. Back when everything was simple and our biggest problem was whether we'd get together to play hide-and-seek. "Let's be honest, A... Why didn't you ever talk to Wyatt about what happened?"

"Because it's pointless."

"What if you're wrong?"

"I'm not." I push off the wall, walk over, and sit down across from him on the arm of the couch. "I don't care *why* he did what he did. Wyatt changed after being discovered and bought out of the NCAA right after his first year of college. He lost his head. Parties here, booze there. It was clear that sooner or later other girls would enter the picture. That's how hockey stars are. They don't stay together with their high school sweethearts."

Knox grinds his jaw. "Can I tell you what really happened?"

"I saw the video myself, Knox. I *know* what happened. In detail and full color."

"But if you..."

"Stop defending him!" He falls silent when I spring up from the couch and interrupt. "He's your best friend, and you would say anything to help him. I get it. But he fucked up, okay? And, yeah, maybe it's hard for me, maybe I'm not over it, but I will be, not today, not tomorrow, but at some point. But if I start thinking about how things were, about what happened, then I'm starting all over, and that's why I just don't want to know. So, drop it, Knox, really. I want to move forward, and I can't do that when he's all over the place without actually being here."

We stare at each other for at least three breaths before Knox exhales and raises his arms, defeated. "Fine, Moore. You win. Do I get your laptop now?"

"If you help me go shopping, you can borrow it until next week."

Knox runs a hand through his hair as he stands up. "Of course. Halloween stuff?"

"And groceries for the guests. The delivery didn't come." I take my jacket from the wardrobe. "You coming?"

"Yep. Hey, Aria, are you going to be that dude with the ripped-out eyes again?"

"No."

We step out into the cool autumn air. Knox presses the button on his transponder, and we get into his Range Rover. "Then what?"

"Dunno. Was thinking about being a moldy jack-o'-lantern."

He grins. "You beast. Aspen can't handle two of those."

"What about you?"

"A pair of underwear."

I stare at him. "For real?"

"A pair of cardboard underwear. It'll cover my whole body, and just my arms, legs, and head will be sticking out. It'll be badass."

"You are sooo weird, Knox."

"Says the weird lady who talks to herself."

I laugh, but it dies when I realize that Knox isn't taking the back roads to Target, and I see my ex's house for the first time in years. The house where I spent most of my childhood. The white porch with its now rusty iron swing really looks *abandoned*, as if no one lives there anymore. The house where his mom took me in her arms when my dad disappeared to the Hamptons, and I didn't want to talk about it with my own mother. The house where Wyatt and I had our first movie nights. Where at some point our early kisses grew quicker, hotter, and all we wanted was *more, more, more* than could ever be enough.

"Hey, Aria." Knox points at the fir trees at the start of Buttermilk Mountain. "You remember that night we saw those two wolves?"

I follow his eyes and smile quietly. "We were thirteen, yeah."

"In winter," Knox replies. "It was so fucking cold."

"You stuffed your hands into your pockets and put them between your legs."

"And you threw your chewing gum onto the ground. You said the wolves would eat it and their mouths would get stuck shut."

"After that, I never wanted to see your hands again."

"I washed them."

"I don't believe you."

"No, really," he laughs. "Not right away. But two days later."

"You're disgusting."

"Man, come on. Of course I washed them."

My lips form a small smile as we pass the forest, and I lose myself in the dark. "In the end, they simply took off, the wolves."

"Yeah. No reason to hang around when they know that something's pointless, right?"

I look at Knox. He's got his eyes on the road. But I know what he means. And I also know he wanted to distract me until we passed Wyatt's house.

"Thanks."

Knox doesn't respond. He just smiles. Maybe I can do that again, too, at some point.

Smile.

9

I Try, but I Fall, Close My Mind, Turn It Off

WYATT

THE PRESS CONFERENCE IS TAKING PLACE IN ONE OF THE mega-modern rooms on the top floor of the training center. Rounded walls of glass that look right out onto Snowmass Mountain, its tips kissing the sky. A whole horde of journalists has already arrived. They're all making their final preparations, sitting around on the extravagant lounge chairs, which, as far as I'm concerned, are way too expensive for this kind of conference room. A few are messing around with their cameras, and others are scribbling onto their clipboards—questions they don't want to forget, probably. It'd be terrible for them not to figure out what was going on with the Lopez kid. I'd like to tell them, "*Hey, you all see that? Yeah, exactly, that's my private life,*" but all they'd do was laugh.

There are a lot of us on the team, but today they're just interviewing those who are regularly sent out on the ice—well, and me. Because the press conference is supposed to inform the journalists as to when the Aspen Snowdogs' rookie NHL talent, who'd been bought over the summer, can finally get out there. They all think I can't do a thing, and that, secretly, I'm supposed to get transferred so that no one finds out that I'm the biggest mistake the team ever made. I'm sure Aria thinks so, too. That I'm the biggest mistake of her life, I mean. Suddenly my throat closes up, my pulse starts to race, and I wonder why I'm always the one who gunks up the machine.

To distract myself, I let my eyes wander over the crowd.

Stay cool, Wyatt. Just breathe slowly from your stomach, and then everything'll be cool.

My crap replacement forward is here, too. Gray. How he made it to the big leagues is a mystery. Next to me, Owen, our left forward, is bouncing his leg. He's the youngest, just turned eighteen, and he gets the shits whenever there are people hovering about with cameras. In the fifteen minutes we've been sitting here, he's gone to the toilet three times, and I *know* he's got to go again because he keeps lifting up his ass like he wants to stand up but doesn't trust himself.

"Owen," I whisper. "Stay here, man."

"I'm shitting myself."

"We're about to start."

Samuel, our goalie, is on his other side. He lowers his head so that he can halfway see Owen's face and raises an eyebrow. "Give us a heads-up before you explode. I've got a date afterward."

At that moment the door opens and Coach Jefferson strides in, followed by our spokesperson, Carl. They sit down at the other end of the table, on either side of Xander. Carl looks at Paxton, who's sitting in the middle and, as captain, is supposed to take the questions. He nods at Carl to get started.

"Ladies and gentlemen, colleagues, we decided to hold this press conference today to answer all the questions you have regarding our new forward, Wyatt Lopez. We want to allow you the opportunity to ask questions, and we'll do our best to answer them. As always, we ask you to handle this knowledge in a collegial and responsible manner. It would be a shame to see slander or gossip show up in the headlines over the next few days, when we all know that there isn't any truth to any of it. We'll take your questions now."

The room fills with flashes along with the collective sound of cameras clicking away. And then we're off.

"Why has Lopez still not been used?"

"Are the rumors that he's been traded again true?"

"What's with his injury? How did it happen?"

"Does he have a girlfriend?"

"He always looks so sad. Why? What's up?"

Normally I'm self-confident and quick on my toes. I'm usually the one to get the last word. It's tough for me not to have an answer ready. But this is screwing me up. Hearing these questions is like getting knifed, over and over. It's not enough to just get me in the stomach; nope, it's got to hurt, and with every stab I've got to think about things I don't want to remember. I just want to be *out of here*, even if that makes me a wuss.

I close my eyes and take a deep breath. Paxton clears his throat, and I know that I've got to say something. I open my eyes and catch Paxton raising his massive arm to point at a journalist in the first row who's been shouting his questions the whole time, a dude with a long forehead and thinning hair, even a bit receding, now that I look a little more closely.

"You were drafted during the last transfer period. That was months ago. When are you going to play?"

If only I knew.

"Umm." Out of the corner of my eye, I see Carl's eyes turn into slits. We had three meetings to prepare me for this conference, two of them with a professional speaker. He compared filler words to big old pimples. No shit. He said they keep coming back, and no one wants them.

I exhale, and my shaky breath brushes the microphone. "It won't be long now."

Weak sauce. You can see it on everyone's faces. Several journalists roll their eyes and make no effort to hide how pissed off they are, having expected a lot more, a real highlight. I should open my mouth and say something that knocks their socks off, makes them go *DAY-AMN*, but, well, surprise, that's me. I'm a disappointment, even for journalists.

Paxton casts me a glance. I nod, and he points to the next journalist. A woman this time, blond bob, cat-eye glasses with deep shadows underneath, totally overworked. She looks like one of those people who wants a career at all costs, so she works when others work and works when others sleep, too. She adjusts her glasses, sits up, and starts tapping her pencil against her notebook. "According to rumors, your ex-girlfriend is back in Aspen. You're said to have cheated on her. Is that true?"

For a moment I'm so stunned, I can't answer. I mean, what the hell? Is she fucking with me? I start to open my lips to say just that when Paxon interrupts. He seems to be able to read my expression.

"Our players' private lives aren't what this press conference is about."

An exaggerated smile appears on her lips. She clucks her tongue, strangely satisfied with my reaction. Her hand literally flies across the paper. It distracts me so much that I don't catch Paxton pointing to yet another person.

"Is it true that the Snowdogs are thinking of sending Lopez back to the minors?"

As if. What a fucking question. I actually have to snicker and hold back a laugh. I cast a glance at Caden, our right forward, to share it with him—*Can you believe this asshole thinks I'm going to be sent back down, Caden?*—but he's not laughing. He's staring into the glass of water he's clutching in his hands. My glance wanders to Xander, but he's messing with the buttons of his shirt and ignores me.

This is turning into the disaster of the century. Why the fuck are the guys on my team acting like this dude hit the mark?

And then it dawns on me. This guy must have gotten some kind of secret info that wasn't supposed to come out today. And this info was something everyone else on the team must have been aware of. Everyone but me.

I look over at Carl, but he's a chickenshit and won't look at me. He's looking at the ceiling instead, thinking about how beautiful it is, I'm sure, *so white and minimal*, simply irresistible. Coach Jefferson alone returns my glance. And he looks exactly like how I feel. Devoured and puked up again. He was my coach back in high school. Just for a few weeks, before I made it to the NHL. It's thanks to him that I got my spot. He's the one who suggested me to the Snowdogs' head, Zayne Callahan. And now he's looking at me all tortured and shit, like he really was sorry, like he would trade places with me if he could so I wouldn't have to go through what I'm going through, but that's bullshit. People always say that, but it's something they'd never do.

What they really mean is just, "Too bad Wyatt's broken." My arm, not my head. They have no idea my head is *way* more broken.

But me? I'd be sorry, really. I'd be sorry for me, for my sister, and for Mom and Dad, who are up there somewhere, floating over those cotton candy–like clouds and proud of the only thing they can be proud of as far as their son's concerned. I'd be sorry for my past, for my hope, that one percent of hope that's held up because who knows why. I'd be sorry for everything I ever believed in, everything I ever fought for.

And I'd be sorry for Aria, who always said that I'd make it all the way to the top and that she'd always believe in me. But here, now, I'd destroy that last little bit of belief, whatever image she still had of me. And then I'd be gone, right? There'd be nothing left *at all* of the Wyatt she once loved. I can't let that happen. I mean, if I did, then that'd be the end of the last little flame that's still inside me.

And what would be left?

"No one's trading me." My reply is quick, anxiety and panic in every syllable; my lips even brush the mic and fill the room with a screech of feedback. Everyone makes a collective face before—after an uncomfortable two seconds—they register what I've just said. A few sit up, then a volley of voices rings out.

"Are you sure?"

"What makes you think so?"

"That's not what we've heard."

Panic.

Carl's eyes are almost popping out of his head. Sure. Everything that's being said here will show up somewhere or other. So if I say that the Snowdogs aren't going to trade me, although that seems exactly to be the plan, that doesn't make them look too good.

Only then does it really hit me.

The Aspen Snowdogs intend to trade me. Que merda. They really want to get rid of me. It's not uncommon for this kind of news to be kept from the players, who end up finding out through others or the press. It's ice hockey, and everyone just thinks, *Cool, great sport.* They think everyone's there out of passion and that everyone who supports the team is the same. But, truth is, a hockey team's big business. All they care about is money. Just like with so many things in life. Not being upfront about that kind of thing with the players isn't unrealistic, but it's still a disgrace. And I never—I mean, under no circumstances—*ever* thought I'd be involved in something like this.

Carl opens his mouth to speak. But I can't let him do that because I know, I *know*, when those words leave his lips, there'll be no turning back.

The *Titanic* is going down. I'm Jack. Carl is Rose. I go for the mic. It's the door we're swimming with, and, sorry, Carl, sorry, Rose, but I need this door because I want to *live.*

"I'm playing," I say firmly.

Everyone is staring at me. Every single pair of eyes in the room is hanging on my every word.

I can feel sweat beginning to bead on my neck and race down my back. "Next weekend. Home game. Against Boston. I… Umm… I will be there. Out on the ice."

Man, whatever I just did was the dumbest goddamn thing I could think of. Shit, I can't even lift my water glass without wincing.

The team's looking at me like I've lost my mind or something. Carl looks like he is on the edge of a breakdown. His eyelids are trembling. But Coach Jefferson looks proud. He's a bit like me. A bit off, I think. That's why I like him. The light reflecting off his half-bald head is blazing as he nods and smiles, nods and smiles, as if I actually did something right when all I feel is that I'm a *total ass*.

Suddenly the silence ends like my bomb had only just exploded. The journalists jump up and start yelling over one another, all the cameras trained on me, thousands of questions, and then a thousand more, and all that's in my head is fear. Next to me, Owen can't take it anymore. It's all too much. He's been farting the whole time; it's awful. His face is deep red, but no one seems to notice because they're all looking at me.

"Paxton," I say softly, as I just can't pretend right now. "I've got to get out of here."

My teammate creases his blond eyebrows, and his forehead breaks into so many wrinkles, it's like they're overlapping. "Funny," he hisses. "You're so funny, Lopez. It's not like we're in the middle of a fucking *press conference* or anything!"

"You can't just go," Samuel mumbles. His voice is deep and warm and reminds me of Samuel Jackson, which is funny because they even have the same name. "Are you aware of what kind of shit you just dropped, man?"

"I don't give a fuck." I stand up. The legs of my chair screech across the polished floor. I push past Owen without a word. Carl moves to grab my arm but stops when he sees that I'm at my limit and casts me a threatening glance instead. *Don't even think of leaving,* it says. *Don't even think of going, kid. I'm going to murder you.*

But I leave anyway. What do I care about Carl and the look on his face?

Camila is waiting for me in the parking lot. She's sitting at the wheel of her car scrolling TikTok when I get in.

"That went quick," she says, putting her phone to the side and starting the engine. "How'd it go?"

"Like a prison break."

"What?"

"I fucked up, Mila."

"Porra." My sister rolls her eyes while putting the car in reverse. "You're constantly fucking up, Wy."

I put on my seatbelt. "Yeah. But this time it was bad."

"It's always bad."

I lean my head back and massage my temples. "They want to kick me off the team."

"*What?*"

"Yeah. So when the reporters asked, I said that I'd be playing next weekend."

"*WHAT?*"

"I know, Fodasse, Camila. Fodasse! What should I do now?"

"Umm." She turns onto the main road and blinks her eyes. Several times. "Clarify? Say you're sorry? Say that you're doing better but that you're not ready yet?"

"No can do. I've got to do this."

"Oh, right, of course, you mean to tell me HOW?" Camila's voice grows shrill. Her fingers are clutching the wheel. I'm quite sure she's imagining it's my neck right now. The woman is terrifying. If she wasn't my sister, I'd be afraid of her. "What's wrong with you, Wyatt? Seriously, what's *wrong* with you?"

"No idea! Maybe I'm just trying to make everything okay?"

"*To make everything okay?*" She steps on the gas, and we shoot down the highway. "*You still all right there upstairs?* You can't play!"

"Well, I mean, *in theory*, I can. Practically, on the other hand…"

Camila makes a frustrated sound, hammers her head four times against the headrest, and takes the downtown exit. "What do you want to do, Wy?"

I look out the window and think. Houses rush past. Jack-o'-lanterns out front. Jack-o'-lanterns out in front of *Aria's*. Kids in costumes trick-or-treating.

"Oh my God, hold up," I say.

Camila looks at me. "What? Why?"

"Stop."

"I can't stop here. This is William's no-parking zone."

"*Meu Deus*, Camila, it doesn't exist! He simply made that shit up. Hit the brakes!"

"I don't want to. William scares me."

"STOP THE GODDAMN CAR!"

She stops. I turn around in my seat and look through the rear windshield at the other side of the street. The B&B has been decorated with fake spiderwebs, a fake zombie, and fake blood. It's all over the windows. The walls. The ground. Even on the trash cans. There are strobe lights hanging off the gutters, moving and throwing their light over the street, together with the sound of thunder. The door is open. Aaron and Levi are standing on each side dressed as Tweedledee and Tweedledum from *Alice in Wonderland*. They let a few costumed kids inside, and when they turn to the side for a second, I catch a glimpse of the interior. I get butterflies because it's just like it was in the past. All I'd have to do was get out of the car and cross the street, and Aria would be waiting for me. Maybe in that costume with the missing eyes again. I liked that one. She looked really tough and kept on saying odd shit, stuff she'd never say otherwise out of fear of looking uncool. We'd kiss, and I wouldn't care *how* strange her costume was; she could always turn me on, make my heart beat quicker; I didn't need booze—love alone did the trick. She'd touch me, and I'd be drunk. She'd kiss me, and I'd be even drunker. She'd say my name, softly, as if it was something precious and she had to be careful not to break it. But now everything's broken.

"Halloween," I say to myself. "Today is Halloween."

"No shit, Sherlock, for real? I wouldn't have figured that one out."

"The B&B's throwing a Halloween party."

Camila's expression grows more sympathetic. "Like every year, Wy."

"Yeah. But Aria was gone. Now she's back, and suddenly it's all like it was."

My sister puts her hand on my shoulder. It's soft. "*Nothing's* like it was, Wy. You and Aria are no longer together." That's something I don't want to hear because it's awful, just awful.

Camila sighs. "It'd be a better idea to think about what you plan to do about what you said back there, I mean…"

"Drive to the costume shop."

"*What?*"

"I need a costume."

"Huh? Oh. No, Wyatt, simply no."

"Yep."

"Wy, you can't be…"

"You can't stop me. If you don't drive, I'm going to get out and run."

Her eyes dig into mine. I hold her glance until she finally nods and heaves a sigh; she understands that this is what I'm doing.

"Well, fantastic. *Great.* But I'm coming with you to this party, Wyatt. I'm coming with you because I am certain that something's gonna happen that shouldn't, and that pisses me off. You feel me?"

"Yeah."

My sister makes a sound somewhere between a groan and a growl. A little like a frustrated guinea pig.

She takes off and heads left, past William's movie theater, The Old-Timer, past Don Giovanni's Pizza, toward the costume shop.

"Why can't I simply *not* be interested in your life?"

I tug at her earlobes. Her helix piercing moves along. "Because you love me. You'd never admit it, but that's okay, because I love you, too, Mila, and I'd never admit that, either."

She rolls her eyes again but smiles faintly this time.

It disappears as soon as we stop in front of the store, which is decorated with clowns and bats. Now she looks concerned. Concerned and afraid.

"This isn't a good idea, Wy."

"I know." I take off my seatbelt and open the door, my stomach full of butterflies again. "Let's do this."

10

Watching Scars Turn into Butterflies

ARIA

"DIDN'T YOU MEAN TO GO AS A PUMPKIN?"
Paisley appears next to me. The light makes her face shine in different colors. Red eyes, green throat. She takes a falafel off a plate that has been decorated with ketchup to look like blood.

"Yeah," I reply, reaching for one of the red cups to pour myself a pumpkin punch. "But James from the costume shop didn't have any more. To be honest, I think he got rid of a bunch of them because no one here in town can take looking at the rotting one downtown any longer."

"Probably. But your makeup is cool."

"Thanks. I come from the Land of the Dead. In that *Coco* movie, you know? Have you seen it?"

"Yeah. Knox has made me watch every movie Disney's ever made. Every single one. Even *The Fox and the Hound.*"

"Oh, that's rough."

"I cried my eyes out, you know? How can Widow Tweed just leave the fox at that game reserve?"

"Poor Tod."

"You can say that again." Paisley runs a hand down her side

braid and plays with the hair tie. She's Elsa, of course, because Knox loves all things Disney and Paisley's a figure skater. "Great party, Aria. Nice one."

"Harper and Mom helped out." The punch is so tasty that I down half the cup in one go. It hasn't always been like this. Six years ago the punch still tasted awful; I just about gagged every time, but everyone drank it all the same. No idea why, but somehow it just belonged to our Halloween party. Over the years, we've perfected the recipe. Now it tastes just like it's been taken out of a fantasy world.

"Umm, Aria," Paisley says as I polish off the rest. She raises an eyebrow. "There's booze in this, right?"

"Yep." I pour another cup. "Why?"

"You want to do yourself in or something?"

"No." *Yeah.* "You want some?"

"No, thanks." Paisley smiles and nods at the Diet Coke in her hands. "I've got training in the morning."

"On the weekend?"

She shrugs. "In preparation for the competition."

"Ah, gotcha. Where's Knox?"

"Over there." She points to a wide carton in the shape of under-wear that's having a hard time squeezing across the dance floor. Paisley's eyes glow while looking at him; it's like he was a Greek god. Of course. I get it. A box of underwear like that *is* kind of enchanting.

"He really did it," I say. "What a freak."

We watch Knox battle his way through the dancing crowd. Before making it to us, he manages to bump into at least four people. One of them loses their balance. Now there's a lobster on the ground. Knox tries to help it up, but it's a bit like two T. rexes trying to hug each other. Lobsters and underwear don't really fit.

"Hey," he says once he reaches us and puts his arm around Paisley. "What are you drinking there?"

"Pumpkin punch."

"The awful one?"

"The good one."

"Cool." Knox grabs a full cup out of my hand. Rolling my eyes, I pour a new one. The bass booms through the parlor, making the floor vibrate. Pouring the punch, I manage to get some on my hand. It's sticky, so I lick it off. But looking up, I realize that I'm unsettling the lobster somehow, as it's looking at me, back still to the floor, the crowd all around, *staring*, and now it's unnerving *me*. I slowly close my mouth. It keeps on staring. Or so it seems to be. They're just two little black buttons, but they're trained on me while whoever's in there keeps on flailing about like a lost bug of some kind; it's creepy.

"Don't look," I say. "But it seems like the lobster's got a thing for me."

Naturally, they immediately look over. Knox in his underwear and Paisley with a lovely spin in her amazing dress. Rather discreet.

"Weird," Paisley says. "Look at its claws, how they just keep wiggling back and forth."

"I think it's unsettling," Knox says. "And I'm a pair of underwear."

"If you think *that's* odd," I hear Harper say from behind me before she puts her chin on my shoulder. "Then check out who's over there next to the fireplace. Camila."

"Oh my God," I answer. "You're right."

Paisley furrows her brow. "She's not even dressed up."

My heart starts to pound. "Is Wyatt…"

"No," Harper replies immediately. "I looked everywhere after I saw her."

A strange feeling shoots through me, something like a mix of disappointment and relief. But I don't generally like mixes of anything beyond this pumpkin punch here. They mess with your head, and my head is bad enough already on its own.

I turn away with a sigh. "She's not responsible for what Wyatt did. I'm happy she's here."

Knox is observing Camila with narrowed eyes. He seems strangely still, as if considering what piece of the puzzle here doesn't fit.

Paisley flicks him in the side. "Wanna get going? We've got to be up early."

"*You've* got to be up early," he corrects her before stretching and treating us to a big old yawn. "*I'm* a student. I can sleep in."

"You're a bum."

His eyes go wide, and he raises his arms above his carton. "Did you just call me a *bum*, Aria?"

"Yeah." The corner of my mouth twitches. "You bum."

"Now I know why I didn't miss you, A. Cool, I'm out of here."

I start to panic. "You can't go."

"Why not?"

"Your underwear's blocking the lobster's view. If you go, you're leaving me at its mercy!"

Knox grins. He leans forward—well, as far as his costume allows him to—looks deep into my eyes, and says, "That's. What. You. Get. For. Calling. Me. A. Bum."

Harper wipes a fleck of white that I applied too thickly off my face. "I've got to go, too, A. It's almost one. I'm tired out from all the dancing, and iSkate won't show any pity."

"Okay. Take off and let me sink. I'll remember this."

"Well, look on the bright side. You won't notice once you're sunk," Knox says. "You'll already be dead."

Harper shudders. "Such a horrible word. Don't say that."

"Dead."

Paisley punches her boyfriend's shoulder, then turns to me to wave goodbye. "O, Captain, my Captain!"

"You're my girlfriend, Pais. You can't be cool to people who call me a bum."

She casts him a sympathetic glance. "But you *are* a bum. Sometimes." Knox pretends to lunge at her, but Paisley slips away and laughs. "But I love you anyway! I love you anyway!"

They take off, and now I'm on my own with all these strangers in my house, Camila, and the weird lobster. Meanwhile, he's no longer on the ground. Maybe he's snuck up to my bedroom and will watch me throughout the night with his black-button eyes while wallowing on my carpet.

I slowly make my way to the buffet, grab a few of the vegetarian pigs in a blanket, and do my best to ignore Camila as the DJ puts on a tune by David Guetta.

"Hi."

Oh my God. The lobster! Right next to me. A guy. I am so startled that I bump into the makeshift chips table with my butt. But somehow the lobster manages to stop everything from tumbling onto the floor at the last minute with one of his pincers.

My heart is hammering against my ribs, but that's mainly because of the punch. If it had spilled, I'd have been devastated. "You startled me."

"I can't understand you!"

"YOU STARTLED ME."

"SORRY." The three little legs on his abdomen cause the table to wobble a second time as he halfway turns to the right and points to the other side of the arch with one of his pincers. "WANNA GO OVER THERE?"

Oh, shit. The lobster's a serial killer. Totally. He wants to skin me alive with his claws. But there are a lot of people around, even the son of Aspen's sheriff, who's dressed as a sheriff himself. Ha ha. The lobster won't pull it off. So I shrug, pour myself another punch, and put myself in mortal danger. It's quite a feat, what with the strobe light and all. I can hardly see the floor and have got to make sure I don't step on his tail.

We sit down on the floor in the corner by the bookshelf, the lobster somewhat sideways due to his tail and me on my knees. He doesn't look all that comfortable, but he doesn't seem to care.

"I noticed you because of your…umm…costume."

"I'm Coco," I grin.

"You know Día de los Muertos isn't Halloween, right?"

I blink. "Isn't it, like Halloween?"

"Not even close."

"Oops. Now I feel bad."

"Sorry. Didn't mean that. To make you feel better, I really love your, umm, dress. It suits you."

"Oh." I look down and don't feel anything but sadness. To be honest, I've never liked wearing dresses. Yoga pants are my thing. Yoga pants and hoodies. Or oversized wool sweaters. I dig the slob look, essentially. But when James told me about the missing pumpkin costumes, I had to improvise. I googled "quick costume, light, not ugly," and came across this *Coco* thing without knowing the movie is about Día de los Muertos. But she wore a skirt, so I thought, *Okay, come on, Aria, nothing to lose. You're in the process of trying to find yourself, so put on a skirt; maybe it'll help.*

The only dress in my wardrobe is the one I wore to prom. The dress I wore when I was voted prom queen—next to Wyatt. He loved seeing me wear it, seeing me dance in it. He loved it when the lace tore as we kissed, sitting in his car, as we touched and got hotter and hotter, and my skin began to flush from all our kisses and caresses. And he loved taking it off me later that night once we were back at his house in his dark oakwood bed with the creaky frame.

"Thanks." My throat is dry even though I've been downing punch all along. "I'd give you a compliment, too, but your costume is freaky. On top of it all, what's with your voice? You sound like Darth Vader."

"Goes with the costume."

"What does Darth Vader have to do with a lobster?"

"Well, if you want to know the truth, he is one."

"A lobster?"

"Yeah."

"Then Anakin Skywalker's a crustacean."

"Exactly."

"Ditch the lobster head. Then we can talk like normal people, and maybe I won't think you're a serial killer anymore."

"Nah." Simply *nah*. As if that's something he could just say. Just like that.

"Umm. Okay. You know, I really have no interest in talking with a lobster today, so…"

As I move to stand up, the lobster wiggles his claws and blocks my way. "Hey, no, wait, sorry. So, I'd love to show you my face, but I feel like that would ruin the magic somehow."

"You're messing with me, right?"

"No."

I blink. His oddly deep voice doesn't make the whole thing any better. "No idea what your idea of magic is, but lobsters aren't really my thing."

"That's not what I meant." He stretches out a claw to push back into place a book that was about to tumble onto my head. That was considerate. Maybe I'll just marry him and get used to the black-button eyes. *Well, Aria, when all else goes to shit, you'll still have the lobster.*

"I mean, it's cool to just be nobody for a while. Not you and not me. For a night, just Coco and the lobster."

Uh oh. Red light. *This dude's not all there, Aria. Take off, far away, where no one can find you, and, above all, you can make your god-awful homework disappear.*

I ignore the voice.

"In some weird-ass way I like that," I say, sticking out my hand to shake the lobster's claw. "Does that just go for the way we look or for our names, too?"

"As you want."

"Hmm. A name would be good. Would temper the serial killer vibe a tad."

"Cool. Well, so, I'm…Paxton. My name's Paxton."

I smile. "Cool, Paxton. I'm Aria."

"Aria," he repeats, real slow, with a low tone in his voice as if he wanted to let the sound melt in his mouth. "I'd love to get to know you a hundred times just to hear you introduce yourself over and over."

"That's a bit cringe."

"Sorry."

"So, umm, you from Aspen? Everyone knows everyone else here."

He leans back against the bookshelf, tucks his tail beneath his legs, and sits so that he can cross his legs. "Yep. Born and raised." His eyes wander to the hem of my dress. The black-button eyes come to rest on the torn piece that extends to the black fabric. "Your dress is torn."

Just four little words, right? But more somehow, tugging at my memories the way they are.

"Yeah."

"How'd that happen?"

He asks it like it would be of interest to him, but for some reason, that doesn't feel right. There's something in his tone, something I can't quite put my finger on. There's something in his voice, some-thing sad and raw, but at the same time warm and *homey* somehow. I break out in goose bumps. I don't know what to think. I mean, come on, I'm talking to a lobster here!

My lips move to say something but stop. I don't want to talk about Wyatt. I'm just getting to know someone here and really, really want to try to do this right. In the end, I don't care if something comes of it or not, but I really want to try; that's the first step in moving forward.

"No idea," I say tersely. "At some party or other, probably. Those things happen, right?"

It takes the chorus and half a verse from Snoop Dogg's "Young, Wild & Free" for him to answer.

"Yeah. Those things happen, Aria."

God. It's just not *possible* for the sound of my name to trigger such a feeling in me. Especially in this Darth Vader voice. I mean, come on. While I'm thinking about it, Lobster Boy suddenly strips off one of his claws. Underneath it he's wearing red satin gloves. I don't know why, but it's weird. With an agonizingly slow movement, his fingertips graze my temple. I hold my breath. My body is all nerves as he tucks a loose strand of hair back up into my bun. And leaves his hand there. He simply leaves it there, right on my head, before moving his palm down to the edge of my jaw. His thumb moves gently across my skin. Delicate, hardly perceptible, and at the same time so intense that it burns. I'm on fire.

"Aria," he says so softly that I can barely hear it here in our dark corner, but I do, and my body reacts. I start to get hot, then cold, then hot again. The way he says my name makes me want everything, and that's normal; I mean, I don't know him. I don't even know what he really looks like. But if he looks at all like the way he's making me feel, then that'll be enough forever and always. "I've got to get going, but meeting you was the most beautiful thing that's happened to me in years."

"I… Wait, what? Already?"

He stands up. "I've got to go."

"Can we see each other again?"

Okay. Paisley was right. Too much pumpkin punch. Definitely too much pumpkin punch. This feels like a movie set in some other woman's life that I'm lucky enough to be in once.

Lobster Boy picks his claw up off the floor and shakes his head. "Not for a while, I think."

Oh my God! He doesn't want to see me again! At first he couldn't stop gawking, and now he's had enough. This is so typical of my life! No, this *definitely* has to be my own movie. But I don't want it to end already, so don't give up.

"We could text each other," I say, standing up and showing him my phone. "If you give me your number?"

Lobster Boy hesitates. He keeps looking around the room as if there was something that might either keep him from going or force him to disappear the very next second. But then he grabs the phone out of my hand and types in his number. "If you still want to in the morning, then text me. But if not, well…" He reaches his hand out to caress my face one more time. The red satin shimmers in the light of the strobe. His touch makes me feel like I'm everything. As elegant as silk, as precious as diamonds. Simply *everything.* "This will be our last moment, and I will love it *forever* but accept that that is what it was."

Holy crap is that bizarre.

"Okay," I whisper. His hand slides off my face. He turns and disappears within the crowd. I watch him go until his lobster tail is no longer visible, then wonder whether what's wrong with me.

Well, wrong or not, this was the liveliest, most intense, and most *heart*warming thing I've felt since that gray day two years ago.

And, to be honest? For that, I'm happy to be wrong.

11

I Didn't Mean to Ruin Everything

WYATT

MY EAR IS VIBRATING. SUDDENLY WILLIAM'S THERE, IN MY dream, sticking my head into his rotting jack-o'-lantern, and for some reason it's vibrating. Right when it's about to explode, I realize it's some new way of killing people. The pumpkin will explode, and with it my head. William will be my executioner. All my friends, together with everyone else in Aspen, are standing around him, watching. Aria is bouncing around with pom-poms and cheering the pumpkin on. Then it explodes, and I wake up.

I'm in bed, my breathing heavy. At first, I get the shock of my life because my ear is still vibrating, and for a second I think it wasn't a dream. I feel like I'm stuck in an endless loop, but then I realize it's just my phone.

The blanket slides off my naked upper body as I roll onto my stomach and grumble into my pillow. But the vibrations won't let up, so I blindly reach for my phone, press the green button, and put it on speaker so I don't have to move.

"What?" I mumble without knowing who's calling.

"Wyatt." It's Knox. Judging by the sounds in the background, he's eating. The spoon clinks against the ceramic bowl. "Please tell me you weren't the lobster yesterday."

Grinning, I roll onto my back and fold my hands behind my head. "I have no idea what you're talking about, man."

"What the fuck was going through your head?"

"Huh? I just told you it wasn't me."

"You and I both know that it was you hiding in that freaky costume, Wy."

I snort. "Says the dude who showed up as a pair of underwear. What gave me away?"

"Mila. And the way you stared at Aria. Only you are that batshit."

My grin keeps getting wider. I stretch out, rub the edges of my pillow between my thumb and forefinger, and let the previous night go through my head. "She talked to me, Knox."

"Shit, Wy, come on. Can't you just leave it alone?"

"No. Not as long as I don't get to explain to her what really went down back then."

Knox keeps on chewing away. "I tried to tell her. She doesn't want to hear it, man. The video was enough."

"She doesn't want to hear it from *you*. But if I get the opportunity to clear everything up, then maybe I'll finally get through to her."

Knox sighs. "Fine, your secret's safe with me. That goes for Paisley, too, as I'm pretty sure she wouldn't tell Aria. But you've got to promise me something in return, Wy."

"Shoot."

"Don't hurt her again."

"You fucking with me?" I ball my hand into a fist around the corner of the pillow. All of a sudden, I'm filled with rage. "I *never* meant to hurt her. And I didn't do it consciously, either. For six long years I grabbed stars out of the sky for her and had no intention of ever stopping!"

"Chill, dude." Through the phone I can hear Knox putting his bowl in the sink. "I know she was the one and…"

"Is."

"What?"

"She *is* the one."

"Yeah, that's what I meant. And I also know that you were completely gone that night, didn't have any idea what you were doing, and don't remember a thing."

"Thank God I don't."

"I just want to say, Wy, if you want her back, you've got to *promise* me that something like that never happens again. No drugs at any après-ski or hockey parties, and no more puck bunnies."

"You know that I haven't taken anything or had anything to drink since…last summer."

"Yeah, Wyatt, of course. And I also know what Aria means to you. I just want your word. Or else I'm going to go see her right goddamn now and tell her that you were the fucking lobster."

"You have my word, Knox. I *swear* that I'll treat Aria like a queen."

"Good." He groans briefly, probably bending forward or something, and then there's a rustling. "You didn't mention that your arm was better."

"My arm's fucked." I release my fingers from the pillow and run them through my hair. I edge to the side of the bed in my boxers and tug a pair of socks over my feet. "What made you come up with that?"

"There's an article here in the *Times*. It says that you're going to be playing next weekend, but I thought that…"

"Caralho! They printed that shit that fast?"

"What do you mean?"

I moan in frustration as I stand up and grab a shirt out of my closet. "There was a press conference yesterday, and it turns out the Snowdogs want to give me the boot. So I said that I'd be playing."

From Knox's end all I hear is his steady breathing before a longer exhale. "You're not going to be able to pull that off, man."

"Nooo, really?" My voice is muffled as I pull on my Snowdogs hoodie. "One sec. My phone's been blowing up with texts." I look at my display. Seeing our spokesperson's name, Carl, I suck in my breath.

> Come to the training center.
> Right away.
> Zayne Callahan wants to talk with you.
> He'll only be here till eight, and he *really* wants to talk
> with you, so I suggest you move your ass, Lopez.

The last text came ten minutes later.

> And bring me a soy latte, will you?

I close my eyes, take a deep breath, and put my phone back to my ear. "Sorry, Knox, I've got to split. I think there's a problem. The big guy wants to see me."

"Shit. Well, I mean, he can't just kick you off like that, can he? What's your agent got to say?"

I grab my hat off the dresser, put it on backward, and bound down the stairs. "He wants to wring my neck, too. No idea what's going on right now. I'll call later, bro."

"Word. Do it."

In the kitchen I do my best to be quiet because it's just a little past seven and Camila is still asleep. First I make myself a coffee, then one for her, like every morning. I'm about to put it on the table when the front door suddenly opens. It's such a shock that I actually duck behind the island. If it's a burglar or something, I should run back upstairs and get my hockey stick. But no, it's my little sister sneaking in on tiptoe.

There is *so* much makeup on her face that I barely recognize her, and underneath her jacket I catch the hem of a miniskirt. She looks beautiful, but tired, so damn tired beneath all those layers of makeup. It's hard to believe what I'm seeing, so I just stand stock-still in the doorway to the hall.

As Camila takes the first stair, I awake from my stupor, but I don't know if that's a good thing because I'm pissed and sad and overwhelmed.

"Where were you?"

She winces. Her hand slides off the rail, and she presses her back against the wall while her eyes dig into mine.

"Wyatt. I thought you were still asleep."

"Funny. I was thinking the same thing about you."

She bites her lower lip. Her dark-red lipstick smears. As she takes a breath, I realize that she has no idea how to talk her way out of this.

"How long has this been going on? How long have you been sneaking into the house in the morning and acting as if you've just gotten up when you come down to breakfast?"

She purses her lips. Camila won't say anything; I know that much. She never does. Instead, she crosses her arms just like always when she wants to erect a wall. "Just today. I wanted to go to another party yesterday."

"Sure. As if, Mila."

"It's simply got nothing to do with you, Wyatt!"

I want to slam my palm against the doorframe, but I force myself to stand still.

"I'm responsible for you," I say, trying to keep my voice calm. "Do you think I want someone to show up and put you in a girl's home because I failed to notice that my underage sister was hanging around clubs all night before going to school in the morning?"

"Well, I'm *still* going to school! And my grades are still good! So why are you concerned?"

"For you, damn it! Camila, I am worried about you because

I love you and want things to go well for you. You missed that somehow?"

She sticks out her chin. "I'm good."

"Apparently not. Take a look at yourself, Mila. Sure, you're beautiful, you're always beautiful, but I can't even recognize you. I'm just worried."

Her eyes fill with tears, but she holds them back. Tears of rage, I know that much. She always cries when she's furious. Her face distorted, she grabs her bag and pulls out her wallet. It's still the pale pink *Hello Kitty* one I gave her for Christmas when she was thirteen. Her cheeks are starting to turn red as her chin trembles, and she pulls out a clump of bills. "I'm doing this for us!" She tosses the money at my feet. "You think I like going to school without having slept, and then going to Dan later on at the ski hut, and then attempting to do my homework before going back out again?"

"Where, Mila? Where have you been going? What the hell have you been *up to*?"

"You know what I've been doing, Wy."

"Stripping."

"Dancing."

"You dance around, half-naked, at parties. That's stripping."

"No, it's dancing! I don't take off my clothes for anyone!"

"I know that that's what you do, Mila. You did that in the past already, and..."

"The past isn't today!" Her glance is firm. "Just because in the past we did things that we aren't proud of doesn't mean that they stay that way forever. People *change*, Wy. And it's fun, okay? I'm passionate about dancing. Dancing is... But ever since Mom and Dad..." She raises her arms in a desperate gesture, her eyes shimmering.

As angry as I am, the look on her face makes it all disappear. Standing there, her mascara running, her lipstick pale, tears in her eyes, porra, all I can see is my hurt little sister.

"Listen..." I say. "I don't want to say that stripping is not okay.

It's a job, and if you like it, fine. But do it when you're twenty-one. You're still in high school, Mila. You're not even *allowed* in those clubs."

She stares at me, still mad.

I sigh. "I don't want the authorities to say I'm unfit to take care of you."

I move to take her in my arms, but she pushes me away.

"No, leave me alone, Wyatt. Just leave me alone."

"Mila, please. I'm sorry. I'll sort everything out and even get some office job or other, or…"

"You've been trying that for months, Wyatt, and haven't achieved a thing!"

My heart starts to feel heavy. "Then I'll find another way. I'm going over to the training center, and I'm going to play next weekend. I don't care how tough it's going to be. And then I'll get my money, and you can stop having to do all this stuff at long last. Promise."

For a second there's a glimmer of battered hope in her eyes, but then it's gone again.

"Stop constantly promising shit you can't deliver." With that, she turns and stomps up the stairs.

For a few minutes I can't move. I feel like absolute shit. It's only when Camila comes back down without any makeup on and with her backpack that my muscles remember how to function. I follow her down the hall.

"I'm sorry, Mila. Really. You were truly beautiful with that makeup. I'm a dumbass. Take the coffee I made for you at least, and…"

"Vaza!" She opens the door and steps outside. Then she pauses, and it looks like she might be coming to her senses to make peace, as it just plain sucks to leave things like this. Or maybe she wants her coffee.

But all she does is turn around and throw her wallet at me. "I don't want this anymore. I'm going to buy a new one."

My sister knows just how to hurt me and manages it a little bit more every time. I close my eyes, rub a hand across my face, and for a moment enjoy the fresh air coming through the open door. Leaves are rustling over the street, and the world sounds peaceful. But when I open my eyes and watch my sister get into the car with teary eyes, there is not a single ounce of peace within me.

I'm a dad even though I don't have any children. I have a daughter even though I'm not a dad. And I have no idea what to do to make it better. Everything within me wants to be there for Camila, wants to know that she's safe, and wants to take away whatever's bothering her. But nothing I do seems to work. It dawns on me that all this time I've been preoccupied with myself, with my own fucking feelings, and I haven't paid attention to my little sister at all. Is it possible to sink any deeper? I mean, can I possibly feel any shittier? It's no goddamn surprise that *she* feels like shit when I'm not there for her. She's a teenager without any parents, for God's sake. I've got to start taking care of her. I've got to start taking myself out of the frame here and putting her in the foreground.

Across the street, Jocelyn is raking leaves. She's always been old. My first memory of her is her handing Camila and me strawberry ice cream from the ice cream van. I was seven, and Jocelyn looked just as old then as she does now.

She waves and gives me a wrinkly smile. She always tells me how strong I am and that she admires me. *"You're a good kid, Wyatt. You're doing things right. Your folks would be proud of you."*

No, Jocelyn. No, they wouldn't. They'd hate me for everything I've done. They'd hate me for letting their daughter down.

All the same, I give her a quarter smile in return. She seems happy enough with that and turns away. The wind is cold and eats into my dry skin. I take my phone out of my pocket and check the time. Just about seven-thirty. I call a cab, get in, and give the driver the address. His watery eyes keep flitting back to the rearview mirror, and every time I look up and notice, he quickly looks back at the road.

Pulling up at the training center, he clears his throat and says, "That'll be seventeen dollars. And, umm, best of luck this weekend, Mr. Lopez."

"Thanks." *I need it.* I give him a twenty and open the door. "All good." To be honest, I could use the change for detergent, bread, or shampoo, but, come on, how bad would *that* look? I can see it now: "Wyatt Lopez, the Aspen Snowdogs' forward, doesn't even tip his taxi driver!"

The NHL building is huge. It's made up of six rectangular blocks and an immense outdoor area. When I was still playing in the minors, I'd often stand right here, right in front of the entrance, my eyes closed, imagining being a part of the whole thing.

And now I *am*, but it sure doesn't feel like it. It's like I'm dangling with one leg over a cliff, in constant fear of falling.

Since coming here to sign my contract, so much has changed. Every time I had to go up to the second floor for PT, I'd get a knot in my stomach. Meanwhile, that knot has grown huge, and it's smothered any feeling of happiness I'd associated with the building.

At the reception desk, I lift my team ID and walk silently past. The digital faces of my team grin at me from the support beams in the lobby. Even *I'm* there. How was I ever able to do that? Smile and mean it. The doors to the elevator close while I'm staring at my photo. I was so proud when that shot was taken. It was the first day I was allowed to put on the green Aspen Snowdogs jersey. I can see the white twelve on my shoulder sticking out. Right. I'm not going without a fight. I don't care how bad my arm's doing; I'm going to play. I will give it my all. I did not *bust my fucking ass* my whole life long to make it to the NHL just to lose it all again thanks to a temporary injury.

The doors open again and deposit me into the tenth-floor hallway. The big dudes' floor. None of us ever finds out what happens up here. This is where decisions are made, money flows, and power is at play.

Carl is standing behind the highly polished reception counter. The crystal chandelier is lighting up his face and pitilessly bringing every wrinkle to light. He's talking with the secretary, his back to me, his ass leaning against the tabletop.

I rap my knuckles on the counter. "Hey."

Carl turns around. "Oh, Lopez." He looks at my hands. "Where's my soy latte?"

"I'm a hockey player, Carl, not your assistant."

His eyes dart to the secretary, and his ears flush red.

"Remember that in the future," I hiss.

Carl purses his lips but doesn't respond. He seems to have realized he can't pull that shit with me.

"Come on." He walks out from behind the counter and down the hall. "Zayne's waiting."

He says his name like he was a god whose feet we needed to lick or something. But what Carl doesn't seem to get is that, without us players, Zayne would be nothing but a businessman without a hockey team.

Carl stops in front of a glass office the size of an indoor amusement park and knocks on the glass door. Zayne's behind his desk, making a call. Seeing us, he waves us inside and hangs up.

I sit down in front of him in a designer chair. The window on the right gives a direct, pretty impressive view of the Rockies.

"Okay, Wyatt." He turns his chair halfway to the left and puts his black-and-gold Armani sneakers up on his desk. I'm jealous, I admit, and decide to buy myself the exact same ones if my NHL salary ever makes its way to my bank account. "What are we going to do with you?"

I shrug. "Let me play."

His gray eyes zip to my right arm, then back to my face. "We both know that you're in no shape to play."

"We don't," I reply.

A half-amused, half-annoyed smile appears on Zayne's face.

"Would you like me to read you every single report I have on your condition? Don't make that kind of face. Did you think I wouldn't inform myself?"

Yep.

Sighing I put one leg over the other and bend forward. "My muscles aren't in the best shape, I'll give you that. But I can play. Let me prove it to you."

Zayne cocks an eyebrow. "And risk ending up last in the league?"

"I could show you today, out on the ice, at the exhibition game."

"That wouldn't be a good idea," Carl blurts out. He takes a quick step forward and waves his arms, as if he actually had some influence. "The press is going to be there today. Journalists. Bloggers. Fans. If Lopez screws up out there…"

"I'm here, thanks. Don't refer to me in the third person when I'm sitting right next to you, Carl."

Our spokesperson gnashes his teeth, but Zayne looks strangely amused.

"Well then, Wyatt, the exhibition game begins in," he looks at his smartwatch, "ninety minutes. Get changed and join the others. They're warming up downstairs."

My heart skips a beat. I wasn't expecting this. In ninety minutes my feet will be back out on the ice for the first time in months. I can feel my stomach beginning to tingle, partly out of excitement, partly out of happiness. But the happiness wins out.

"Got it." I push back my chair and am happy to see Carl looking so pissed off. "My jersey is…?"

"I'll have someone bring it to your locker. Skates, too. What size?"

"Eleven."

"Right." Zayne tilts his head. "I bought you based on your performance assessments. They convinced me. You've got talent, I know that. Don't make me regret my decision, Lopez."

"The ice is my life," I reply firmly. "You'll see."

12

He Always Had That Vibe, the Kind You Could Get Lost in, and I Guess I Did

ARIA

MY BEST FRIEND'S JAW DROPS. AS LONG AS I'VE KNOWN her, that's happened a total of maybe five times. *Maybe.* And I've known her all my life.

Harper's hands are still wrapped in the white linen she was about to put on the bed before I dropped the bomb. "I don't believe you. You're lying."

I grin but turn so she doesn't see it and wipe the duster across the top of the desk by the window instead. "For real, Harp. You should have been there. Somehow…there was magic in the air."

"He was dressed as a lobster, A."

The dust tickles my nose. I rub the back of my hand against it but end up sneezing anyway.

"I know. But both of us know that there was a guy underneath."

"Did he reveal himself?"

"No. And don't shake the bed linen beforehand; it causes wrinkles."

My best friend leans back against the desk and rolls her eyes. "What if he's not your type whatsoever?"

"That's hard for me to imagine. And even if he wasn't, I mean, there was just such a perfect vibe between us; if anything, the way he looks is secondary."

Harper raises her eyebrows appreciatively. "That must've been one tasty lobster."

Laughing, I throw a pillow at her. "Stop. But, well, yeah. It was weird. After Wyatt, I didn't think I'd ever be interested in anyone ever again. Inside I was simply empty, you know?"

My best friend sits down on the freshly made bed and whistles. "What's his name?"

I hand her the squeegee for the window I'm spraying with glass cleaner.

"Paxton. He says he was born and raised in Aspen. But that could only mean…"

"Paxton Hilcon."

I lean against the wall and watch Harper clean the window. "Didn't he live outside of town? He always came to school on the bus."

"Yeah, but at some point he moved to his dad and stepmom's. They live close to Buttermilk Mountain, right before Silver Lake." She catches the excess water with a rag before it can drip onto the windowsill. "You know the one. The red house he was always throwing parties in back in tenth grade."

I nod. "The one with the huge, blow-up snowman at Christmas."

She makes a face as we step out of the last room and put the cleaning things back onto the cart. "He's in the NHL now. For the Aspen Snowdogs."

"*What?*"

A guest comes out of the room across the hall and shoots me a frown. I quickly offer him a polite smile and wish him a lovely Sunday in Aspen.

Once he's made his way past us and disappeared down the stairs, I spin around to Harper and grab her arm. "No *way*. That's just too much of a coincidence. Show me a picture."

"Ow. Get your nails out of my flesh, you monster."

"Sorry. I can't see it as I don't have any battery. You?"

"Yeah, one sec. Let's go downstairs. Everyone can hear us here."

I reluctantly follow her. My fingers are tingling, but two little words are enough to cool my excitement.

Hockey player.

Didn't I want to be through with all that? Maybe Paxton is different, even if I consider the chances low. Hockey players have a certain reputation...and it sure applied to Wyatt.

"Harper," I whisper as she makes her way past the fireplace and through the stone arch. Four guests are sitting at their tables enjoying a late Sunday brunch. When they see me, I smile, but it collapses as soon as they turn back to their plates. "*What are you doing?*"

Harper takes a cup and puts it under the coffee maker. "I need caffeine. Do you have any idea how tired I am? Training at iSkate is harder than ever since my folks got me this new trainer, and..."

"Show me a picture!"

"Chill, A." She casually pours sweetener into her cup, takes a spoon out of the cutlery tray, and stirs her foam. "Patience is a virtue, you know, and you..."

"Goddamn, Harp!" Her spoon flips out of the cup as I reach past her and grab her phone out of her back pocket. The spoon clatters onto the wood floor. Spots of frothy milk decorate the rustic wood. Only vaguely do I register Harper giving the guests an apologetic glance and raising her hands disarmingly.

I quickly type "Paxton Hilcon" into the search field and immediately get a thousand results. Sports articles, blog entries, videos, pics...

"Click on the picture," Harper says, so I do and land on the Aspen Snowdogs' home page. All I get is a single image of the whole team, each of them in their jerseys with their helmets under their arms.

"Here, look." Her perfectly manicured nail points at the display.

"The blond guy with the gray eyes. Just like in high school, but without zits."

The first thing that comes to my mind is, *True, and he doesn't look like Wyatt.* Followed by a feeling of relief.

The second thing that comes to my mind is, *True, and he doesn't look like Wyatt.* Followed by a feeling of disappointment.

The third thing that comes to my mind is, *The dude two people over from Paxton sure looks a hell of a lot like Wyatt.*

And then I think I've got to be hallucinating. Underneath the dude's photo is his name. "Wyatt Lopez," I croak.

The sound of his name on my tongue makes me break out in goose bumps. It's like returning to a place you loved but haven't visited in a long time and realizing that it's just as beautiful as before.

I've always liked Wyatt's last name. Back when we got to know each other, I'd lie awake at night and repeat *Lopez, Lopez, Lopez* until the name wasn't a name anymore but simply the strange sound of two syllables. Even at Brown I'd do that sometimes. I'd be there in my dorm room bed, under Mom's patchwork quilt, moonlight illuminating the smiley face my predecessor had left on the white wall (what was up with *that?*), repeating *Lopez, Lopez, Lopez.*

I finally find my voice again. "That's Wyatt, Harp."

Wrinkling her forehead, she puts down her cup and looks at the phone, then over at me. "Yeah. He's been in the NHL since the transfer period in July. The Snowdogs' owner signed him. You didn't know?"

"How would I? I was in Providence, and you all didn't say anything to me."

"Well, I mean…"

"What?"

"Well," she takes a deep breath. "Don't take this the wrong way, but you weren't exactly communicative out there, A. And whenever any one of us *did* manage to get you on the phone, we certainly wouldn't have risked mentioning Wyatt. We were happy to speak to you at all."

"That's ridiculous. You could have told me. Really. I mean, I'm happy for him. Wyatt… He deserves it. He's worked hard half his life to get there. We're not together anymore, fine, but I can still be happy for him."

For a moment Harper watches me over the rim of her cup, then she shrugs. "Enough about Wyatt; we're talking about Paxton." She puts her coffee to the side, puts her hands on my shoulders, and looks deep into my eyes. "So, you ready?"

"For what?"

"To go see him."

"I don't need to. Yesterday he said he didn't really have much time at the moment. But I'm going to text him later on this evening, and then…"

"Get dressed, Moore. We're going to go watch some hot hockey players."

"What?"

She grabs my wrist, pulls me past the guests and up the stairs, through the connecting door to our living area, and only lets go of me when I'm in front of the ladder up to my room. Once we're there, a slightly enthusiastic smile appears on her lips, and her eyes begin to shine as she opens my wardrobe to dig through my clothes. "Today's the exhibition game at the rink; it's open to the public, and we're going."

My stomach drops another floor. "Oh, but Wy…"

"He won't be there." Harp grabs a pair of overalls and a flannel shirt, which makes my heart skip yet another beat as it used to be Wyatt's, and tosses them onto the bed. "Shortly after being signed, there was an accident in Breckenridge. I don't really know the details, but ever since then, Wyatt's been on the bench."

"Oh." Hearing that Wyatt was in an accident makes me shudder. Is it normal for me to want to see him and ask whether he's okay?

I bite my lower lip and push the thought aside. *Paxton.* Today's all about Paxton.

"You sure Wyatt won't be there?"

Hmm. Guess I wasn't all that successful.

"Not a hundred percent sure, no. But at most of the other warm-up matches, I saw him in town. I mean, he was never at the rink."

I'm struggling, but the last thing I want is to continue to be influenced by Wyatt even in the future. If I don't go to the rink today, that is exactly what will happen. My first step in a new direction shouldn't be blocked by my ex. "Okay. Let's do this."

Harper claps. "Perfect. Get changed, and then I'll do your hair."

"My hair? I like my bun."

"I can't believe you're going to go out with a bun, but, fine, whatever. The better you feel, the more open you will be."

"Harper." My left pant leg catches on my ankle as I pull up the overalls. "You say that like I'm immediately going to be doing Paxton out on the ice."

Shrugging, she drops onto my bed and casts a glance at the old elementary school picture of the two of us on my nightstand. How simple life was back then, and Wyatt was just a kid with a dalmatian bag and gap-toothed smile in the back row.

"I'm going to bet that over the last two years you haven't exactly reached pleasure's peaks, so to speak."

"Ugh. Don't put it that way. That sounds like a cheap porn."

"Sooo…you ready to take Paxton's spear in your backdoor?"

"HARPER!"

She laughs. "Okay, okay. Hurry up. Training's starting soon."

The drive takes fifteen minutes. Harper sings along with every song that comes on the radio while I drum my fingers on my thighs and try to get my nerves under control.

"Relax," she says, turning into the parking lot and looking for a space. "God. I forgot how many peeps like hockey. Ah, here's one. Nope, guess not. Fucking Smartcar."

"But there's one up there."

Harper backs in. Getting out, my legs are pudding, and my stomach is a beehive. We're late, but that's why we're lucky and there's not much going on at the entrance. The girl at the front sells us two tickets and shoots me a sympathetic look—my skin color must not look all that healthy.

"Harper," I whisper as I hurry after her down the hall. "Is my face green?"

She turns. "A bit. If you talk to Paxton, try not to be standing under one of these terrible neon lights. Otherwise, it won't be noticeable at all."

"Sweet. Next Halloween we'll be the perfect team, a lobster and the Incredible Hulk."

"I think we need to go down here."

We come into a huge entrance hall where various drink stalls are set up in preparation for the onslaught during the break. Several digital advertising pillars are towering up toward the ceiling, each of them showing a different team member's face. The one of Wyatt lights up next to a drinks stand with Bud Light signs. He's grinning, a dimple to the left, a dimple to the right, beneath his arm a helmet, his shoulders puffed up thanks to the thick pads underneath his jersey. His number has been sewn on with white thread and stands out against the green fabric.

My footsteps fade as I come to a stop. Harper is already about ten feet ahead before she notices and turns around. She follows my glance, exhales, and comes back. She puts her fingers on my upper arm. "Aria." Her voice is soft. Caring. Compassionate.

"His number." I have to clear my throat to get rid of the lump. It doesn't really work.. "He chose the number twelve."

Squinting, Harper looks from me up to his picture and back. "I don't get it. Why's that important?"

Because it's all I've got left.

"We got together in December. December 12, 2012. Afterward, he changed his number from seven to twelve and said… He said…"

Harper presses my arm. "What did he say?"

I take a deep breath. It hurts to think about, but talking about it is even worse. *"That's for forever, Aria. Just like us."*

Silence, broken only by our breaths, mine choppy, hers slow.

"I'm sorry," she says eventually and sighs. "But *he* was the one who didn't want any more of *forever*, A. Don't forget that."

That's something I'll never be able to forget, Harp. Never.

"Yeah. But… He could have changed it. The number, I mean. After everything was over."

She shrugs. "Habit?"

"Maybe." My eyes bore into the digital reproduction of my ex's face. It hurts so bad; I want to scream and cry and *rage*. Why did he have to do that? Why wasn't what we had enough for him? Why did he take my heart and break it? Well, not simply break it but cut it into pieces, throw it away, and leave it behind as an empty shell? Six years tossed away just like that, in a single night, in *one single night*.

I take a deep breath, then turn away from the picture, look up, and move toward the big double doors to our left. "Come on. Let's go find seats."

Harper follows. Opening the door and stepping into the arena, I'm met by a blast of cold air. It is ear-splittingly loud. The fans are screaming; the red folding seats are completely full. Players in green jerseys are racing across the ice and playing the puck so quickly that I can hardly keep up.

"No chance!" Harper bellows. "I think we're going to have to stand!"

"I don't want to stand!" I yell back. "It's cold!"

"It's going to be cold if you sit down, too, fool. Whatever, let's go down there, by the players' entrance, behind the penalty box; it looks like there might be a few seats there."

"Fine."

To be honest, I don't think we're really allowed to be here, but at least we've got a really good view. We're right behind the plexiglass and next to the tunnel that leads to the locker rooms.

"Cool." Harper rubs her hands together and blows into her palms. "During the break they're going to come this way. Most of the time, they stop to talk with fans. And that's when you're going to snatch Paxton, got it?"

The girl next to us casts Harper a dismissive glance that says as much as, *Hands off Paxton, bitch!*

"I'll try."

Harper looks content. "Now let's pay attention to the game. I haven't been to a game in *years*. I don't even know what you're supposed to yell."

"I don't yell," I protest right as a player zips past us, skillfully avoiding a defenseman. I notice him because the way he pulls off the quick change of direction seems familiar. His *taunting* way of moving about the ice. His *self-assurance* of movement. As if he knew exactly what he could do, how to play the puck, confuse his opponents, and wear them down. As if he knew he was the best. Something's tugging at my memories, reminding me of something I buried long ago and never wanted to bring back up to the light.

But my mind is remote-controlled; it *forces* my eyes to focus and understand the player's number. All the same, the information reaches my brain in fragments.

Twelve.

Wyatt.

Wyatt's number twelve.

That's him. It's him.

Oh. My. God.

I clamp my hand over my mouth and stagger back a few steps but end up bumping into the scowler and have to stay where I am.

It's not like I haven't seen Wyatt since being back in Aspen, but this…slays me. This is like someone ramming a drill into my chest, pounding memories and emotions into my head, each and every blow causing me such violent pain that I feel sick and start to see black dots while all the shouts in the rink swell into a single noise.

Out on the ice, Wyatt symbolizes everything we were because this is exactly how things got started. Between us. Back in high school.

"Hey, Moore," he'd said, by my locker, his baseball hat on backward even though we weren't allowed to wear hats in the first place. He didn't care. Wyatt always wore them. And whenever Principal Johnson took it away from him, he'd show up the next day with a new one. Wyatt smiled at me, backpack hanging off a single shoulder, wearing his Aspen High hockey jacket. "You coming to my hockey game this weekend?"

"Why should I?" I asked, trying to play it cool, while inside I was completely done, my head a simple loop of *Lopez, Lopez, Lopez, oh my God, Lopez, Lopez, Lopez.*

"Because I want to make a bet with you. I know you like betting."

"Whatever." I closed my locker, American history books in my arm, and simply looked at him because that's what I wanted to do, look at him, madly, for hours, maybe even forever.

He laughed. "Not. At Will's last fundraiser, you bought tickets all day long even though the prize was simply a bunch of painted stones."

"That's not true."

"It is. I watched you."

"The whole time?"

He didn't even bat an eye. "The whole time."

And so I asked, "What kind of bet?" and he said, real cool, real self-confident, as if he *knew* what I was thinking, as if he *knew* that night after night I would lie in my bed staring at the ceiling, whispering *Lopez, Lopez, Lopez* until I fell asleep. "If I score a goal, I'm going to ask you out. Out there in the middle of the ice, in front of everyone. And if I don't, I'll leave you alone."

At that second my heart decided to slide into my pants. I still remember how out of breath I was even though I was simply standing there with my books in my arm.

"You could just do it now," I answered, scared shitless that he wouldn't get a goal and really *would* leave me alone. It would have been a disaster not to find any more notes in my locker saying that he liked the way my hair shone, that I had the most beautiful freckles in the world, or that he got dizzy whenever he looked at my legs because they reached all the way *up to the sky* and he was afraid of heights.

He had tilted his head and grinned, *and how*, with those dimples of his and that face that was the cause of numerous crying fits in the girls' bathrooms.

"But you could say no."

"I could do that in the rink, too."

He laughed that raw laugh of his that stole into my heart forever. "We both know you would never do that in front of all those people."

He was right.

"That's your plan?"

"That's my plan."

Then I was the one who had to grin. "Make that goal, Wyatt Lopez."

It was a relief to say his name after it had been on my lips for so many months.

He made the goal. And asked me out in front of everyone, right out there on the ice. He roared it. After that, we were together every single day.

We were Wyatt and Aria.

And now we're nothing.

He races past me, full of self-confidence, full of energy, as sure of scoring a goal as he was back then. But then he catches sight of me, grinds his skates into the ice, and comes to a stop. Just like that. He loses the puck. Just like that. He stares at me, everything like it was before, but shocked now, as if we were fourteen again. But as if this time I'd said no.

I stare back.

Just like that.

13

Maybe Your Laugh, Maybe Your Smile—Whatever It Was, It Made Me Fall Pretty Damn Hard

WYATT

ARIA'S EYES ARE BRIGHT GREEN. YOU CAN'T MISS THEM. Doesn't matter how fast I skate past; it doesn't matter how many people are standing around her. Her eyes burned themselves into my mind years ago, and seeing them now, even just a suggestion of their green, attracts my own like two magnets.

I dig my blades into the ice and stop. My shoulder objects with serious pain. For a second everything goes black and then just blurry. I grimace and gasp for air. A few seconds later my sight's back to normal. Owen gets the puck, but fuck it. She's there, in her overalls and that flannel shirt that used to be mine; her hair is in a casual bun, loose strands falling into her face to tickle her freckles, and all I can think is, *This is how everything began between us, Aria. You remember?*

Her lips form my name. The look on her face, the way she's breathing the syllables, her green eyes big and round—porra, it all just wipes me out. A sound that I can't define any farther escapes my mouth. A mixture of love, longing, and pain. No one can hear it, but a white cloud forms in the air in front of me.

A shrill sound sweeps across the ice and breaks our eye contact. Blinking, I look around. My teammates glide over to me and gather in a cluster as they trudge through the gangway door.

With the fist of my good arm, I punch Caden in the shoulder. "What just happened?"

When Caden grins, I notice blood on his mouth guard. Paxton's elbow caught him in the face. He takes his guard out, drool sticking to his hand. "I can't tell you, man. You were paralyzed by a dark-haired gal in a flannel shirt."

"Funny."

He takes off his helmet and smirks. "Owen got a goal, and now we've got a break. But, tell me, Lopez, who's the slice?"

My skates glide across the ice as, one by one, our teammates slip through the door. "Don't refer to her that way."

"Only if you tell me who she is."

Rolling my eyes, I take out my mouth guard and leave the ice. Caden steps into the locker room behind me.

"My ex."

His eyes widen. "No way."

"Why not?"

His eyes dart to Aria who is pushing her way through the crowd with Harper to reach the players.

Why is she doing that? That was never her thing.

"She's hot, dude. Why aren't you together anymore?"

Cause I fucked up.

"Long story." My tone makes it clear that I'm in no mood to talk to him about my Aria. So he just nods and turns to a bouncing fan with pink hair, who shrieks and holds out her arm with a Sharpie. This is one of the reasons why I love being a player. This openness toward the fans. Most NHL teams do their utmost to stay cut off, especially in big towns like Vancouver or New York, but here in Aspen we do things differently.

Two steps farther in, another girl bends her upper body over the railing. At first I don't realize what she's up to until I feel her fingers close around my wrist. Adrenaline floods through my body because I wasn't expecting to be touched and I don't want Aria to notice. So I snatch my hand away and stare at the girl with wide-open eyes. She looks hurt. Next to me, Xander rebukes me with a warning look, and he's right. Our fans are behind our success. Zayne drills that into every player from day one. Sighing, I wipe a hand across my face, put on a smile, and turn back to the blond. "Sorry. Was just surprised."

She takes a deep breath and gushes forth her next sentence in a single breath. "You are even hotter IRL than in your Insta photos!"

"Umm. Thanks?"

With a cute look on her face, she digs around in her bag before pulling out a Sharpie and holding it under my nose. "Can I get an autograph?"

"Of course." I take the marker and pull off the top. "Where?"

She pulls down the collar of her shirt and squeezes her breasts upward. "Here!"

Zayne wants us to be nice to our fans. Okay. I can do that. But I won't do something like this. "Nope. Sorry, but your body belongs to you."

She runs her tongue across her lips. "It can belong to you, if you want."

"No, thanks. And it shouldn't." I take hold of her wrist before turning it and leaving my name behind on her forearm. But encountering Aria's eyes right after, I know she caught every word. I wipe my hand across my sweaty neck and attempt a smile, just for her, just for us—but in a breath, she turns away.

Harper is tugging at the arm of our right winger. "Hey, Paxton." He turns around. "Hi."

"My friend *Aria* and I," she says, pointing her thumb at Aria while saying her name slowly and deliberately, "just wanted to say how good you were out there."

"Thanks. But training isn't over yet." He laughs. "Still time to screw up."

"I doubt it," Aria mumbles. She's speaking so quietly I can hardly catch what she's saying. Owen nudges me, wanting me to move on. Sorry, Owen, never ever. I'm aware that I'm standing in the way and staring at my ex, but not even the trophy could get me into the locker room right now.

With a grin, Harp puts her hands on her hips. "Unless you drank too much at a certain Halloween party."

HOLY SHIT.

That's why Aria's here. Because of *Paxton*. Her presence irritated me so much that my mind was unable to put the individual pieces of the puzzle together. For a wild moment, I even thought she was here *because of me*.

What a joke, Wyatt. What a *joke*.

Paxton leans against the plexiglass. Wrinkling his forehead, he raises a brow. "Well, actually, yesterday…"

"My shirt," I say out loud.

Harper, Paxton, and Aria look at me quizzically.

I point at Aria. "You're wearing my shirt."

She looks down. Her fingertips stroke the checked fabric. "I didn't realize that."

"That's not true. Of course you did."

Ladies and gentlemen, this is the *dumbest* goddamn diversion tactic the world has ever seen.

Aria's ears turn red. She glares at me. God, how much I've missed them, those glowing red-rage ears of hers. Every time I made her angry, it happened, and every time she could never keep it up for long because I'd grab her, bury my hands in her hair, and kiss her so intimately, so hotly, that she'd forget why she was angry, that she'd forget *how to be angry with me* in the first place. I'd pick her up, put her against the wall, and enjoy feeling her lips swell and grow warmer the longer I kissed her.

I'm on the verge of doing it again.

"You want it back?" she asks, her forehead lined, eyebrows tight. "Nice, Wyatt. *Nice*. No problem. I'll do that. Right here. Because I don't want to wear *any*thing that once belonged to you."

Her fingers are trembling with rage. She's having a bit of trouble getting her overalls free and, as a result, is becoming even more upset. Harper looks at her, concerned. I, on the other hand, have to keep myself from smiling.

Then she manages, and the straps slide off her shoulders. She tears off the shirt, throws it at my feet, and crosses her arms in front of her chest. "*There you go.*"

"*Ari*," I say, quietly, my voice quivering. "Put the shirt back on. It's cold as hell in here. You're gonna freeze."

"I don't want it. I don't want *a thing* from you."

Out of the corner of my eye, I can see Paxton looking from me to Aria and back. Suddenly he pushes back off the plexiglass and raises his arms. "All good, peeps. Something's going on here that I don't want anything to do with." Walking past me, he pats me on one of my shoulder pads. "Get moving, rookie. We want to go over a few things."

He leaves. Aside from Caden and Xander, I'm the only one still out in the corridor. The fans are calling out my name, reaching out their arms, but I only have eyes for Aria.

Harper's glaring at me now, too. "Why are you even talking to her at all? Fuck off, Lopez."

Aria purses her lips. "Harp."

"Only when she puts the shirt back on."

Harper throws her hands into the air. "Why didn't you just keep it, seeing that it's yours and all?"

My lips break into a grin. "She knew. Why did you put it on when you 'don't want anything to do with me'?"

"Harper chose it for me."

"As if you *never* objected to anything Harp wanted to do."

Aria swallows. She's fighting tears.

My body reacts automatically. "Hey." I take a step toward her and move to touch her cheek, but she flinches so violently that I pull my arm back. "All good. All good, Ari. I'm going. But please, *please* don't cry."

"That's what you're saying now, Wyatt." Her face is spotty, and her lips are trembling. "But you're the reason why. You are *always* the reason why."

"I'm sorry."

Harper balls her hands into fists and punches me in the chest. "Just go, Wyatt!"

I hesitate. But when I see how difficult it is for Aria to keep herself together, how much I am hurting her by simply standing here and looking at her, I get a grip. I pick the shirt up off the ground and move to give it to her, but she takes a step back. So I turn around and go.

As soon as I'm out of sight, I press my nose into the fabric and breathe in her perfume. It fogs my mind. That's how things go with Aria. She fogs my mind whenever she looks at me, whenever she laughs, whenever she sneaks into my heart and it begins to tickle, soft, real soft, because the most intense feelings always come softly.

Back in the player's area, I go to my locker and stuff the shirt into my bag before anyone can talk to me. Owen is lying on a bench, one of his legs dangling, the other up on the wood, tossing the puck back and forth with Caden, who is leaning against the wall. Samuel is bending over, and Paxton is laughing about something or other that Xander's showing him on his phone. Pulling my water bottle out of my bag and downing about half in one go, Paxton looks up. "Yo, Lopez. What the hell was that all about?"

"No idea," I respond curtly.

He drops onto the bench and begins kneading his thighs. "Right. That was your ex, man."

I don't say anything. While Caden keeps on casting me glances, Owen just keeps on respectfully playing with his puck.

Xander comes over and leans against my locker. "Tell us. Are we a team, or what? What was up between you two?" Xander asks. "She hook up with someone else at some point, or…"

"SHUT YOUR FUCKING MOUTH!"

Xander retreats, but, as all that's behind him is the wall, he runs into it with his back and flinches when I grab his jersey with my good hand. "Shut your fucking mouth, Xander, or I swear I'm going to fuck you up."

He raises his arms right as Samuel appears next to me and puts a hand on my bad shoulder. And pushes. Hard. I let out a tortured sound. He immediately lets go but keeps his eyes fixed on me. "Sorry. But let it go, Lopez. He got the picture."

"Yeah, sorry, man," Xander says as I let go of him, snorting. "I didn't know it was so close to you."

You have no idea.

"Just don't ever mention her name again." My eyes sweep the whole locker room, taking in every single one of my teammates. "Any one of you."

All of them nod and mumble something like "Of course," "No worries," and "Okay," and I really pray that they stick to it. Aria's scent is still in my nose, and I think I'm about to freak out because she's just outside the door, just a few feet away, and I can smell her, just like in the past, and *shit*, I'm not going to lie, that just screws me up, that just really screws me up.

Suddenly Coach Jefferson comes into the room. He claps his hands once and then leans his shoulder against the iron struts of the locker benches. "Listen up, guys. The ganging-up stuff was good, but there were a couple of things that bothered me. Xander, whenever Wyatt moves to go through the middle, you look overwhelmed. Why?"

Xander shrugs and avoids my glance. He's pissed. "No idea."

"You feel comfortable on the boards because you know how to box in your opponent and get the puck away from him. That's cool. But I get the impression that if you have to cut him off in the open lane, you have no idea how. You let him through every time."

"I'm not as quick," Xander mumbles.

Caden shakes his head. "It's got nothing to do with speed, man. You can't let him pass you in the first place. If he comes through the middle, cut him off. If he tries to pass you, maneuver and get ahead of him."

Owen laughs. "My mom runs a dance school, Xan. If you ask her real nicely, she'll show you some smooth left-right moves."

Xander pulls one of his shoes out of his locker and throws it at Owen's head. He rubs his forehead. Samuel bursts out laughing.

Jefferson snaps in my direction. "Wyatt, your puck handling was flawless. But keep an eye on the ice as a whole. I get the feeling all you play is what's in front of you, and everything beyond that is a surprise."

I lean back on the bench and raise a leg. "Could be. But I manage with the game situation all the same, Jeff."

Samuel beats Jefferson to the punch. "Of course. Otherwise you wouldn't be in the NHL. But sooner or later there's going to be a game where, thanks to you not paying attention to the formation of our rivals, we lose."

Paxton nods. "We know you're good, Lopez, but don't get complacent. Play with foresight, got it?"

"Yeah, I get it."

"Okay, good." Jefferson glances at his watch and waves us along. "It's time. We're about to change distribution. Wyatt, you're going to go with Owen to the center. Xander, Caden, Paxton, and Gray on defense." His eyes meet every player in the room. "Wy and Owen, bring the puck into the other third of the ice and pass." He looks around the substitutes, pausing on the faces that he's most likely to send out on the ice. "Pass to Lewis, Sanders, Trevor, or Blewitt."

We leave the changing room and walk down the corridor until we reach the players' entrance. The flashes of the bloggers and reporters who need our pictures for their next articles light up. My gaze automatically slides to the right. Aria and Harper are still there. Harper keeps poking my ex in the side and stretching her neck to look at Paxton, while Aria just stares out at the ice, her arms crossed. I want to put my lips on those goose-pimply arms of hers, kiss her warmly inch by inch, and feel her tremble, not with cold, but with love, before wrapping my arms around her body and holding her close so that I can feel her heartbeat and know what happiness means again. Her heart is happiness. That's it.

I don't do anything of the kind. Instead, I press my teeth together and ignore the sharp pain that's been spreading through my arm since we started warming up, attempting to paralyze it. But I've got to get through this. I can't afford to get booted. *Literally*.

I glide behind Samuel onto the ice and take up my position next to Owen on the left side of the reduced playing field. Owen looks at me and wags his fingers to suggest a route.

I shake my head and draw imaginary lines in the air. "We'll get through better this way!" I call out.

Owen nods and gives me a thumbs-up. The players set up in front of us, ready to check us and take the puck away, and then Coach Jefferson blows his whistle.

Owen skates halfway up the center line. He waits for Blewitt to attack and thrust his stick forward, then shoots the puck skillfully past him and through his legs to me. It's a quick shot, a little too diagonal. At first I think I can't get it, impossible, but I'm fast, I'm agile, and I'm a hell of a hockey player. With a deft right turn, I put my stick out and take the puck, but just as I'm about to reposition myself and push forward, I feel a sharp pain followed by a smash. Seconds pass, maybe hours; no idea. I feel dizzy, but then I blink, and then once again, three more times, and only now does it dawn on me that the bright neon lights of the rink are making it impossible to see.

I'm on my back. But it's not that bad. What's bad is the sharp, all-enveloping pain that's wandering up my arm to my shoulder and streaming into my head. If it was only the pain, I'd say, *Fuck it*, but, no, I'm starting to panic. *What's going to happen now?* I wonder every second, just like I always do when I feel this kind of pain. When the physiotherapist wants to work on me, I tuck in my proverbial tail like a dog out of the fear of having to experience what I want to forget forever. That's how memories go; they show up anytime, anywhere, especially at those moments you're least expecting them, and that's when they start tearing and scratching and pulling you apart until nothing's left.

The neon light turns into dazzling dots. I start to see black. All the sounds around me begin to fade, replaced by screams, by rattling, by a loud bang.

There's blood. Nausea. Hate. I hate myself so much because things are the way they are, and yet I should hate myself even more than I do.

Something is digging into my chest. A boring pain. Memory itself, maybe. Or maybe it's wolves digging their claws into my skin. It sure feels that way. Who knows?

Someone's pushing my hip. I have no idea in what reality it's happening, until Owen's voice makes its way through.

"Wyatt, hey, Wyatt, come on, man, everything's cool. Everything's cool. Can you hear me?"

The darkness disappears. Gold dots saturate the black until my head begins to perceive the blurry image of the present. The whole team is standing around me and looking down in concern, led by Coach Jefferson.

Great.

The audience is looking down from the stands. Flashes. The clicking of cameras echoing off the high walls.

And then there's Aria. Her green eyes boring into mine. I realize that I'm in shock and that I'm afraid, but I also feel unstable and suspicious. Her fingers are digging into Harper's upper arm as if they were looking for some kind of support.

I'm only starting to register what just happened. Xander's elbow managed to tag me during a check. In my bad arm. I fell. Then… the flashback.

Que merda!

I scramble to my feet, push Owen to the side, and make my way past Paxton and Samuel, enduring the reporters clicking away with their cameras—*click, click, click*—so that they can show the world how shitty I'm doing at my worst moment and the public can lick it up.

I elbow open the doors to the players' area and make my way down the tunnel, without looking at anyone.

I disappear into the locker room, tear my helmet off, followed by my jersey and pads. I pull my Aspen Snowdogs hoodie over my head, grab my bag, and walk out.

I'm almost in the lobby when I suddenly hear someone calling out my name. "Wyatt!" Everything in me freezes because nothing, and I mean *nothing*, would have given me the hope of ever being approached by her again.

I turn. Aria is standing there looking at me, rubbing one hand up and down her naked upper arm. She looks like she regrets being here. But here we are. An ocean of feelings between us, each on their respective side and no bridge in sight.

Shit sandwich, right? What can you do?

Nothing.

You just stare at each other and hope that a bridge will appear. But of course nothing like that will ever happen. Whatever bridges there were collapsed years ago.

Aria digs her nails into her arm. There are dark-red half-moons on white skin.

"I hate what you did to me," she says. "I hate that it cuts into my heart every time, every second that I think of you. I mean, fuck you,

Wyatt, really, *fuck you* for making me think of you fucking her every day, making me think of how I was sitting at home baking a vanilla cake even though I can't bake while *she had your fucking dick in her mouth*, and, yeah, the fact that I'm standing here is ill, simply ill, and I hate myself for it. I hate myself so fucking much for the fact that my feelings are so *obviously* disturbed, that *I'm* so clearly disturbed. But I have to do what I'm doing right now because I know that, if I don't, I'm going to die inside, and that would just make everything worse..." She catches her breath. "Are you okay, Wyatt? Is...everything okay?"

High hopes, I think. This here, her green eyes, her blotchy face, the longing she's hiding behind her rage, the sparkle in her eyes as they dart across my upper body, her tongue slowly and unconsciously moistening her lower lip—all of this belongs to my high hopes. Somewhere there's hope. Deep down inside me. If I go looking for it, maybe I'll find it.

Fuck the bridge. I'm going swimming. My footsteps echo off the walls.

"What are you doing?" she asks, softly, barely a whisper, as I come closer. "Wyatt, what are you doing? Don't come over here. Don't come over here, I'm serious. Just tell me if..."

I put my hands to her face and kiss her. Our lips touch, intensely, warmly, and longingly, as if they'd gotten lost and given a bit of their soul away every day in order to find themselves again.

These are her lips, I think. *Soft, heart-like, just for me. She's the one I love, and she always will be. It doesn't matter if she moves on; it doesn't matter if she decides she wants me again. None of that matters. She'll remain my number one, forever and always.*

Aria returns the kiss, and that's dynamite for my brain; everything explodes. All I see are colors, pure light, and there it is, that thing we call *love*.

Our caresses aren't gentle. This isn't a gentle encounter, but the satisfying of a desire, the downing of a drink after years of thirst, a free fall into a time that's long since passed, and because we know this, we do everything we can to avoid the ground.

But it's there. Right beneath us. Aria knows it. She was always the one who couldn't ignore the obvious. Her palms touch my chest as she pushes me away and denies our lips what they have been begging for forever.

Aria struggles to catch her breath, but she doesn't say anything. She just stares at me. And suddenly I can't stand her standing there, in her thin top, goosebumps across her arms.

I pull off my hoodie and pull it down over her head. Confused, she slips into its sleeves, which are far too large for her tiny arms. She disappears into my sweatshirt, and the beauty of the moment takes my breath away.

"I'm good, Aria," I mumble. "Everything's okay as long as you're here."

Before she can say anything, I turn and go, her face still in my head, those green eyes. And all I can think is that the feeling in my chest, this warmth when I feel her lips on mine, *is poetry*.

That's it.

14

Thirteen Past Two, Thinking of You

Aria

Tonight my room turned into two hundred fifty square feet of chaos.

I'm usually pretty organized. I usually make sure to pick up the socks that made their way under my bed and throw my yogurt cups into the trash.

But not today. Today everything is different. Today I'm wearing his sweatshirt and don't want to ever take it off. I don't want to shower anymore; I just want to lie in bed and pretend that everything is just like it was before.

Last night is my fantasy. And it never needs to become day again.

I've been sitting cross-legged for hours, surrounded by my notes, packs of Skittles, cans of Diet Coke, and dates. No idea why I chose dates, but they were there, and for some reason I wanted them.

I've been trying to beat all my notes on the musculoskeletal system into my brain. Actually, it's not all that difficult. It's just a lot. And I don't have time for *a lot*. Or the head.

My earbuds are playing Taylor Swift on repeat. My eyes have narrowed into tiny slits while staring at the bright screen of my iPad. It's hard for me to make out the tiny letters. I curse Knox for not having brought me back my laptop yet. And because it annoys me so much, I grab my phone, open our chat, and write exactly that.

I curse you for not having brought me back my laptop yet.

Annoyed, I toss my smartphone back onto the pillows. It slides between the cracks and sinks beneath my teddy bear. I reach for the can of baked beans that's on my nightstand, and for the next few minutes it's a steady rhythm. Baked beans, writing, dates, writing, writing, baked beans, a few Skittles in between, writing.

After two more pages, I put my pen to the side and shake my hand. With a sigh, I fall back onto my mattress. The tips of my hair tickle the carpet while my eyes wander up through the window.

Darkness. There's a storm. Pine needles scrape the glass. I close my eyes and listen. Sometimes I think the quiet is speaking to me. If I listen really hard, I can hear a whisper. My gut feeling is that, when we concentrate, when we don't focus on anything in particular and listen to what's not there, so to speak, we can hear ourselves. Because that's the thing, right? There's really no such thing as nothing. If there's someone there that we're listening to, then it's us. I mean ourselves. Our inner voice. The one that usually holds back as it's far too soft to be heard. These moments we can talk with our souls are precious. And when we're granted the privilege, when our souls come to tell us what we need to know, we should listen, and I mean *listen well*, for everything they tell us is true.

And right now mine's saying, *Wyatt.* That bugs me. It only shows up rarely, and when it does, I want more.

Today the quiet is disappointing. Today we're not buds. Maybe tomorrow.

I roll onto my stomach, stand up, and close the curtains. My limbs are heavy. I'm tired. My head is tired. From all these thoughts, from all this living.

I sluggishly make my way across the room. I dodge the dark

folder with all my Brown stuff. My guitar. A potato peeler (how'd *that* get in here?). And, last but not least, a section of string lights I wanted to untwist before I got sidetracked. It's been lying on the floor ever since. Could be my twin, with the only difference that it gives off light, and I don't.

I climb down the ladder and sneak down the hall. If I'm not careful, the boards creak. It's the middle of the night, 2:13 a.m., to be exact, and I don't want to wake Mom up.

I push the swing door open and step into our kitchen. It's small, and the ceiling slopes down to the windows, which are hung with white lace curtains. On the walls there are pictures and pans and cups and all sorts of things, a real hodgepodge, but it's just so *cozy*, I hardly know of a more comfortable place. Wyatt and I spent hundreds of hours here. We'd sit together at the wooden table in the corner, on the bench, me with my back against the wall, my legs stretched out over his, while Mom would be at the gas range, cooking caldo verde, a Portuguese soup made of cabbage, chorizo, and potatoes. Wyatt's mother, who was Portuguese, had given her the recipe. Whenever there was a good song on the radio, all three of us would sing. Beautiful memories. I wish they weren't. The more beautiful they are, the more painful.

"Hey, sweetheart."

I look up and see Mom in the warm light of the glass chandelier above us. She's stirring a pot. The heat of the flames is making her hair stand on end.

"Why are you awake?"

Orange-colored dots sprinkle the kitchen counter as my mother taps off the end of the wooden spoon against the side of the pot. "I had a nightmare," she says, puts the top on the pot, and turns toward me. Mom is wearing a pink onesie that Patricia knitted for her. I'd love to have one, too. "Vaughn won the soup cook-off tomorrow."

"*Vaughn?*" Frowning, I take the cocoa out of the cupboard and heat some almond milk in the microwave. "Why's he part of the soup cook-off?"

"He's competed before already. And because…it was a premonition," she mumbles, which is suspicious, because Mom doesn't think much of what gets mumbled. I stir the mix into my drink and raise my eyebrows. Noticing my skeptical look, she clicks her tongue and raises her arms. "*Fine.* William let it slip."

"*Will?*" I shake some mini marshmallows into my drink. At least half of them land on the long, woven runner. That's how things go with me. Whenever I try to hit the bulls-eye, things fall to the side. "He *let slip* the names of the people who signed up for the event?"

She shrugs. "No big deal, right?"

"Umm. Hello? Earth to Mom? Which part of 'he let slip who had signed up for the event' demands that kind of answer?"

My mother throws a raisin at me from a ceramic bowl that's next to the stove. One of them lands between my toes, and I accidentally crush it. Gross.

"You want some tea?" she asks.

"No. Look. I'm drinking hot chocolate."

"Oh, right."

"You're confused because William likes you."

The teapot begins to whistle. My mother flinches, but I can't say if it's because of my words or the sudden noise.

"That's nonsense, Aria."

"That's the truth and nothing but the truth. I mean…" A marshmallow melts on my tongue. I savor the moment. "*He showed you the list of participants!* That's forbidden. It's even written in the rules. I could get him in trouble."

"He wrote the rules, Aria."

"Even worse, no? He's deceiving us all. Who can we even trust anymore?"

Instead of reacting to my words, Mom just puts a teabag into her cup, which is labeled *DEAR SANTA, I CAN EXPLAIN,* and pours water over it. Her steps are heavy as she makes her way over to the table and sits down across from me. "Why don't you tell me why *you're* up."

I can't tell my mother that the B&B is taking up too much of my day and that I have to study at night. I wrap my hands around my cup and watch the floating marshmallows. "It's a full moon."

"Ah ha." Mom strokes the swollen outer surface of her hand with stiff fingers. "And does the full moon have some kind of strange power over you that I should know about?"

"What do you mean?"

"Your sweatshirt, Aria. Aspen Snowdogs?"

"Oh, that." I lean back. "It's Wyatt's."

"No kidding."

"I don't want to talk about it."

"Of course not."

"Hey, Mom?" I nudge her upper thigh with my raisin toe. "You still haven't told me anything about the naturopath."

She takes a sip of her tea and looks at me over the edge of her cup. Green eyes. Like mine. Tired and weak. Like mine. Hardly any hope left. Like mine.

"We're trying out a few natural remedies. Drops and injections that are supposed to help with my joint pain."

I pluck at a stitch on the crocheted tablecloth. "At Brown a student group a year or two ahead of me conducted a study on rheumatism. The results of those patients who consulted a naturopath were significantly better than those who had used cortisone."

My mother smiles. "We'll see."

She's losing her faith. That hurts to see. Mom was always strong-willed. Nothing could get her off track. *Nothing*, aside from this fucking illness that crept in and decided to suck the life out of her.

A copy of today's local paper is lying on the table. The large picture of a young man with red-blond hair smiles back at me.

Mom follows my glance. She pulls the paper to her and sighs. "The Frazers placed a memorial announcement. For their son."

I put my cup down and run a finger across the letters. "I'm still so sorry that I couldn't be here for the funeral. Jake was…" I shake my head. "He was simply Jake."

"Yeah." Mom puts the paper to the side with a sad look on her face, grabs her cup, and stares at her tea. "He was a good kid, through and through. He used to look after you when your dad and I would go out."

"I remember. That was a long time ago. How old was I?"

"Eight, nine. Something like that. You always played hockey here inside, and every time your father would lose his cool because you always managed to break something."

"Sounds like me."

Mom gives a faint smile. "Life is precious, Aria. A real gift. We never know how long we've got. You should enjoy every second and always do exactly what you want to do. Do what makes you happy."

"I know, Mom."

"Sometimes I think you've forgotten. Especially when it's got to do with you and Wyatt." She finishes her tea, caresses my cheek, and slowly gets up. "Don't stay up too long, sweetheart."

"I won't."

"Goodnight."

"Night."

"I love you."

"Love you more, Mom."

She puts her cup in the sink, smiles weakly at me, and leaves. Ten seconds later I hear her bedroom door close.

I pull up my legs, pull Wyatt's hoodie over them, and close my eyes.

Breathe in. Exhale only when it's time to breathe in again. And again. And once more.

Wyatt's scent. The one I smelled every time I'd wake up next to him. Every time he'd wrap his arms around me from behind when we were on the couch watching hockey on ESPN.

I don't know how long I've been sitting here, breathing in and forgetting to breathe back out. I play with the drawstrings, make a knot, and undo it again. The feeling of wearing Wyatt's hoodie is doing something to me. It's weird. Something unreal. In my head a voice is telling me that I'm not allowed. That it's destroying me.

I'm already destroyed, I think, but the voice just laughs. *Even worse*, it says. *Much, much worse.*

That's how it is between Wyatt and me. We're destroyed, both of us, and he's the one who wanted it this way.

All the same, I can't stop my nerves from pulsating when I take in his scent. I can't stop my heart from thumping when I imagine him wearing this very sweatshirt. The one that's against my skin and makes me feel like I'm touching him. Touching him without touching him. While he's touching me without touching me. It doesn't make any sense, and yet it does.

It makes sense because my dumb, dumb heart still loves him. Wild, right?

I don't know if there's any way to stop this. If it's possible for my heart to forget. I've heard that forgetting's not that easy. Some people say it doesn't work at all. And that's what I'm really afraid of. I mean, I'm sitting here pressing my nose into his hoodie in order to suck up the last little bits of scent that are still there.

I finish my hot chocolate, put my cup in the dishwasher, and sneak back up to my room.

Crashing onto my bed and digging about for my phone I manage to wrinkle all my notes. Knox has written back. And I curse you for waking me up in the middle of the night, you Gollum, you. But that isn't important anymore.

With trembling fingers I click on Paxton's name. His profile is a snow dog with a hockey stick in its mouth—the Aspen Snowdogs logo. I take a deep breath and begin to type a message.

Hi. It's Aria. It's past two in the morning, and, theoretically, I'm really, really late, but maybe you'll let me get away with it, because I'd really, really like to get to know you. My thumbs hover over the display, then I erase a "really." Sounds too desperate. Two seconds, take a deep breath. *Send.*

Hard to believe I did it. I'm proud of myself. Super-duper proud. With a slight smile, I put my phone on airplane mode and bury my face into my pillows. Between the crannies, the snarled patch of string lights shines into my eyes. *How they shine*, I think. *How they shine and show me that they can. Just like that.*

I think about Paxton and don't feel a thing. I think about Wyatt and feel everything.

I fall asleep and keep on thinking.

15
About a Wolf Who Loves the Moon

ARIA

"WHAT THE..." SOMEONE'S PINCHING MY LEG. I PULL A pillow over my head and kick. Whoever it is needs to fuck right off.

"Your room stinks like a caveman's den. When did you last— wait, are those baked beans *in the can?*" Another pinch. "And you call *me* a bum, Aria? Me?"

Blinking, I open my eyes. Knox is standing next to my bed in checked capri pants and dark-brown leather ankle boots; my laptop is in his hand, which he is using to tap against my forehead.

I reach out my arm and wave my hand through the air. "Go away."

That's the last thing on his mind. He sits down next to me instead and pushes against my shoulder until I turn over onto my back like a sack of potatoes. Then he just stares.

"What's going on?" I ask.

"Something's going on in here, that's for sure. Something weird."

"Huh?"

"Aria, you're wearing *Wyatt's hoodie.*"

With a sigh, I roll onto my side. "That doesn't mean anything."

On my nightstand I discover the rest of the lemon cake that I didn't manage to polish off last night. One of the biggest advantages of running a B&B is having pastries around whenever my head tells me I need them. Every day at coffee time, I serve up something from Patricia's Pastry Shop for the guests and usually grab the leftovers. I reach for the plate, fill my mouth with the last bit of cake, and am as happy as can be, for sugar is indeed happiness for me.

"What are you doing?" Knox asks, speechless.

"I'm eating cake."

"I can see that. But why?"

"Because someone somewhere on this earth is celebrating their birthday, and I want to celebrate along with them."

"You just woke up."

"I don't get the problem."

Outside, the bell tower is ringing. I almost swallow the wrong way. There isn't a crumb left when I put the plate back down. I quickly stand up and slip into my blue Birkenstocks. "What time is it?"

"Just about eight." Knox casts a glance at my notes, which are still strewn about my bed, most of them completely crumpled up after my having slept on them. There's whipped cream on my most important folder. Knox picks up a piece of paper with my drawing of the cervical vertebrae and their trigger points. The terms were still in my head yesterday.

Levator scapulae. Sternocleidomastoid. Musculi scaleni. Digastricus.

"You pull an all-nighter yesterday or something?"

I walk into the adjoining bathroom to change. "Yep," I call back. "But it didn't go too well." I quickly give myself a French braid and put on mascara. "Do you know if Mom's already downstairs?"

"Yeah. She made breakfast for all the guests."

"Shit. I wanted to take care of that."

"You're chaos on two legs."

"Nothing new, huh?" I toss my mascara back into my cosmetics bag and brush my teeth in double time. When I come back into my bedroom, I find Knox looking at the picture of Harper and me on the nightstand. I quickly rummage about in my drawer and pull out two mismatched socks. Winnie-the-Pooh for my left foot, a striped sock with holes for my right. My toenail is poking out. I'm happy for it. Freedom's important.

"What are you doing here?"

Knox points to my laptop. "Just so you don't wake me up again."

"Just put your phone on silent."

Instead of responding, his eyes dart to Wyatt's sweatshirt, which I throw onto my bed along with my short pajama bottoms. "Can you tell me what that's all about?"

"No."

"Aria…" There is so much of everything I don't want to hear in his tone. *Aria, be careful. Aria, you've suffered enough. Aria, leave it alone. Aria, no.*

No, no, no.

"No worries," I say. "It doesn't mean anything. Just a stupid coincidence."

Knox dramatically spreads his arms. "Oh, *right*." He palms his forehead. "How could I be so dumb? Your ex's—that is, my best friend's—sweatshirt just *happened* to be lying in your mailbox, and you just *happened* to have nothing else to wear."

"Exactly. So, Knox, take off. I've got to get to work."

"You going to the soup event later?"

I close the door to my room and walk down the hall next to him. The thick carpet swallows up our steps.

"Of course. William would hate me if I skipped out."

"You think?"

"Don't tell me you were considering not going!"

Knox groans. "Just once! As if that'd be so bad. I've been there Every. Single. Year."

"It's *William*, Knox. Of course that'd be bad. He'd still be holding it against you when you had three grown children."

"Yeah. Paisley also said we had to go."

"Then listen to your girlfriend. She's a bright girl."

I bring him to the door. Knox opens it, but before going, he leans against the frame and raises his eyebrows. "You know that in less than ten seconds I'm going to call Wyatt and ask him what's with the sweatshirt, right?"

"I know."

"And you're sticking with the stupid coincidence line?"

For a moment I drift back to yesterday. To the moment in the players' hallway when Wyatt came up to me and put his lips on mine.

For two long years I surrendered to the memories of what those moments used to feel like. But two long years couldn't prepare me for what it would feel like again. The truth is that I didn't want it to end. I didn't want it to end, and pushing him away was the toughest thing I've ever done. Letting him go didn't feel right.

I tried not to think about it anymore. I tried to convince myself that that moment never happened. But of course that's ridiculous. I mean, when something happens, it *happens*, and you know it. It's pretty simple.

It made everything more complicated. I only made it through the whole time without Wyatt by convincing myself that he didn't love me anymore. That was easier. I mean, why else would he have cheated on me?

But yesterday…

I looked into his eyes. They were full of longing and fear, of sadness and exhaustion. But most of all, heavenly desire. And yet, there was just one single question in my mind.

Why?

Wyatt Lopez, why won't you let me go?

You are the one who did this.

You are the one who destroyed everything we had.

You alone.

And now you're kissing me, with love in your eyes, with longing in your heart, as if you could just *do* that?

I take a deep breath and meet Knox's eyes. "It doesn't matter because it's over. Whatever he tells you doesn't mean anything."

He looks at me quizzically. It looks like he wants to say something. With a sigh, he puts his hand on the back of his neck and rubs his closely cropped hair, looks up at the ceiling, and closes his eyes. Then he nods. He puts a hand on my shoulder before turning around, crossing the street, and getting into his car.

I watch him go. Everything seems normal. Ridiculously normal. And that pisses me off because it's a lie. There's *nothing* normal going on here. It feels like the world is upside down. Like there are rooftops on the ground and walls in the sky. Heads walking down the street. Mouths instead of eyes, pupils instead of lips.

Wild shit. Nothing normal at all.

But the bell tower's still there. Just one street away. Tall and unchanged. Over on the corner, the neon lights of Kate's Diner are shining. And over there, Patricia, a smile on her lips and in her heart, is bringing waffles to put out on a table outside. And just one more street over, William's pulling down the shutters of his store and getting into a discussion with Vaughn, who wants to park in Will's no-parking zone.

Everything's just like it always is. The mountains are on the horizon. Aspen Highlands to the left. Buttermilk Mountain to the right. And somewhere or other, Snowmass.

Laughing people all over the place, breathing happiness through their eyes and filling their lungs with Aspen's harmonious air. I still remember what it was like when it was the same for me. I was really doing well back then.

"What are you doing?" Mom asks, coming into the kitchen.

"Looking at the world."

"Close the door, Aria. The guests are cold."

"Not happening."

"Why not?" Mom remains standing next to me, in one hand a basket of bread rolls for the German tourists, in the other a pot of fresh coffee.

"It's morning, but the moon's in the sky."

"Sometimes it's like that."

My eyes focus on the white, shimmering full moon over Aspen Highlands. "I just had a kind of theory, Mom."

"What's that?"

The wind tickles the skin of my hand.

"You ever wonder why werewolves howl at the full moon?"

My mother heaves a sigh. Her what's-with-you-we've-got-guests-to-take-care-of sigh. She's about to go, but I suddenly get the feeling that I absolutely *have to* tell her about it. It could change the world.

"No, wait. Listen. I think werewolves are in love with the moon. But it's hopeless because there are two hundred and forty thousand miles between them. They know that but suffer all the same. So they say to themselves, *Once a month. Just once a month I'm going to show everyone just how much I'm suffering.* The wolves howl because they're in love with the moon, Mom. They love the moon but can never touch it."

My mother looks at me like I've lost my mind. "You should start keeping a diary. Seriously, Aria, I'm beginning to worry."

"Wyatt's to blame for all my gray clouds."

"Wyatt's to blame for *everything*, Aria." The coffee in the pot spills over as she makes a sweeping arm movement. "Give it a rest. Stop defining yourself through him. You're more than your memories. You're an individual. And you've got to understand that. Love him, for all I care. Love him until you're one hundred twenty-seven or whatever years old. If that's what it's got to be, accept it. And if not, accept that, too. Find a base that you can deal with. And, above all, accept that you're allowed to be sad. That's normal. That's *human*. But that doesn't mean that you have to stand still." Her expression grows softer. "What have you gone through all this pain for, Aria? For *nothing?*"

My throat closes up. "I just wanted to tell you that the wolves love the moon."

"No, Aria. No, that's not what you wanted to tell me."

"You're brutally honest."

"Of course I am."

"I'm going to check on your pumpkin soup."

"You don't need to."

"But I want to."

"Don't touch my pumpkin soup. I want to win the golden ladle."

"It's not really made of gold, Mom. Will just painted a copper one."

"You live in your fantasy world, Aria. Let me keep mine."

Fair enough. I move to help her with the rolls and the coffee, but she turns away.

"You're not going to work today."

"Why not?"

"I want you to go downtown to buy yourself a diary."

"And just because you want me to, I will?"

"Yes."

"No, Mom."

"I beg you. And then go to your room and study."

"Why?"

"Because you're in school, Aria, and I never see you studying. But I *do* see the rings beneath your eyes every day."

"But…"

"I've got everything under control. Today's a good day."

My glance drifts to the moon. My thoughts drift to the moment Wyatt's lips touched mine. How he smelled. How I felt all of a sudden. Inspired. Hooked. I didn't want him to stop. And yet I was the one to break things off. Because it's just not possible. Because I just can't feel that way. Not after what happened. I feel like the wolves.

I turn and grab my jacket from the coatrack. "Okay. We'll see each other at the event."

She blushes. "I am *so* excited already."

"You're not all there, you know."

"I get it from you."

16
My Sister Is Worth a Thousand Friends

WYATT

ZAYNE CALLAHAN IS SPINNING AROUND ON HIS STOOL.
He has his fingertips together in the shape of a pyramid, and I'm
wondering if he belongs to the Illuminati. Wouldn't surprise me; I
mean, this dude is *loaded*.

"Wyatt, we're still in the middle of the transfer period."

"I know."

"You've been injured for half a year."

"Yeah."

"You haven't played a single game."

"I'm aware of that."

Zayne stops spinning. Now he looks right at me and crosses one
leg over the other, so that his ankle is resting on his knee. "I gave you
a chance yesterday. You said you could do it."

"And I can. It was…a stupid accident."

"A stupid accident," he repeats and leans back. "Lying to my face
is kind of a bold move, don't you think?"

I pull my baseball hat off and turn it around in my fingers.
Whatever hope I had left is disappearing. Everything inside me is
heavy with fog.

"Okay, yeah. But I can do it, Zayne. I'm *really good*. If it weren't for this damn injury, I'd be scoring goals every game. Sending me back to the minors just wouldn't be fair."

Zayne grunts. "That's not how things work, Lopez. Yeah, you're good, or I wouldn't have gotten you for my team. But what good are you when I can't let you play? *What good are you* when you're not scoring goals?"

My palms are full of sweat. I rub them off on my jeans. What good are people when they can't do anything? You've always got to be able to do something; that's what this life is like and always has been. When you can't do anything, you aren't worth anything. What the fuck? Right now, I really can't do shit, and I feel like a hopeless bum who still has too much hope, hope that he shouldn't have. I mean, I CAN'T DO A THING, okay?

I take a deep breath. "Just give me a little more time, Zayne. Until the deadline for the training period is up. *Please*. If I'm still useless, fine, go for it, kick my ass down a league."

The Aspen Snowdogs' owner puffs up his cheeks. His forehead breaks into creases as he stares at me. Then his shoulders slump down as he exhales and leans back his head.

"Fine, Wyatt. Until the deadline. But at our home game next weekend, you're going to be riding the bench and will only be back on the ice when you're healthy. We'll tell the press that what you said at the press conference *was* true, you were indeed supposed to play, but, *stupidly*, you broke a rib during training."

A feeling of relief floods through me. A liquid kind of bliss that seeps into my nerves.

"Thanks," I say while standing up from the mussel-shaped velvet armchair. I'm almost at the door when I turn around. "No offense, but you *really* should kick Gray off the team."

Zayne gives a bitter laugh. "You have no idea how much I'd like to, kid. Boston and Seattle have offers from me on the table for another replacement, and as soon as I've got someone else, Gray's gone. I thought he was really promising. But, well…" He smiles.

"Everyone makes mistakes, Wyatt."

Not folks like me, Zayne. Not folks like me.

This hope, man, really, it kills me. I don't know why it's there at all, but it always creeps up on me when everything's going to shit. My parents died, everything was a fucking mess, but this feeling of hope showed up to say, *"Hey, don't worry, I'm here, no big deal, things will get better."* And I was like, *Wow, okay, solid, I believe you, just a little bit maybe, but enough.* And so I drank way too much because I thought shutting everything out was better and my sense of hope would take care of the rest. It didn't. Aria took off, simply packed her shit and left, after all those years, no *see you,* no *later.* Then again, why would she? I mean, after what I did, it's not like we'd be seeing each other again that soon. And me, "That was that. For real this time." But the sense of hope came back, tickling me and purring, *"Hey, don't give up; things will work out."* While all I could think the whole time was, *NOTHING WILL EVER WORK OUT. THAT WAS IT. GOT IT?*

And now it's back. I won't be able to get rid of it. Like a nasty zit that comes back no matter how many times I pop it. I wake up in the morning, and, yep, there it is again, big and red and glowing in its glory.

But this is my last chance, and, to be honest, if I don't get my shit together, heal my arm, my head, and, essentially, my soul (which doesn't really seem all that healable), then that'll be that, over and out. And then I'll have to turn my life upside down and start all over again, from zero, or maybe zero point one six, because there's this hope in me saying, *Come on, pal, zero is zero, and zero is nothing; that won't work, come on.*

Up to the transfer deadline, I tell myself over and over. Maybe saying it over and over will help. *Up to the transfer deadline. Transfer deadline. TRANSFER DEADLINE.*

This is what it's like in my head the whole bus ride back to

Aspen because I don't have enough for an Uber. People are staring at me because they know who I am, and they're wondering why on earth I'm riding the bus. I could tell them. It'd sound something like this: "You know, actually, I should be swimming in cash, but, ha ha, I don't have a dime, and at night my sister goes to parties and comes back overflowing with Washingtons, and I have no idea why she's not a kid anymore. All the same. You know what? I'm just riding this shitty bus and looking at your fucking faces until the TRANSFER DEADLINE. And you know what else? I'm not going to make it because I'm so wiped out. Awesome, right?"

That's what it would sound like if I were to open my mouth. But I just stare back until they look away or scratch their throats or backs or butts or whatever.

Jocelyn is standing behind her white lace curtains watching me as I turn onto our street. I see her right away because her house is the first one on the block, and all that's next to it is a long, bare path leading straight into the woods, and behind the woods is Buttermilk Mountain, endlessly high and endlessly beautiful.

That's Jocelyn, always just standing at her window. It's not a big deal; that's just how she is, and to be honest, I don't really care. But the way she tilts her head and the look of pity on her face just makes me so friggin' sick. I mean, how bad can I look?

Walking through our front yard to the porch, I notice all the hellebores and pansies among the rest of the brown. It's not like it's beautiful. I mean, they're shriveled up and ugly and kind of brown, too; everything's brown, and all I can think of is how sad it is because this was Mom's passion; it's Aria's, too. They would garden together and water together and laugh, their faces full of dirt. My heart would skip a beat every time I saw them.

But nothing blooms here anymore. Now everything's dead.

Camila is sitting in the living room. Her hair is pinned up in a kind of black bun with a thick, ugly pin, but somehow it looks good on her. She's in her seat in the bay window, the one with the colorful cushions, her legs pulled up, a wool blanket over them because she's always cold, a checkered notebook on her lap, the same one with Paxton's name inside it and all those little hearts.

When I put my keys into the wooden dish on the sideboard, she looks up.

"Hey," I say, but she ignores me and just keeps on writing with her pink felt-tip pen, the one she shouldn't be using to do her homework. I've told her a hundred times. "Hey," I say again, somewhat louder.

Camila rolls her eyes.

I walk over to her and sit down on the couch. *Keeping Up with the Kardashians* is on TV. I pick up the remote and turn it off.

"I wanted to watch that."

"Can we get along?"

"No. I wanted to watch that."

"I don't care."

Camila turns toward me with a huff. Her notebook slides halfway off her knee. I catch sight of formulas and roots and letters and vectors, but no little hearts, no Paxton, and I'm relieved.

"All that shit before was fucked up, Wyatt."

"I know. But, to be honest, from your side, too." I slide toward her and take her hand. She tries to pull it away, but I don't let go. I won't let my sister go, or she'll fall way too deep, and I don't want that to happen because then she'd be like me. "I know it's hard, Mila. Especially for you. You and Mom, you all had a strong bond, like kryptonite or something, and it's obvious that you're just done, especially after Aria took off because she was all you had left. And, yeah, I was selfish; all I could think about was myself because I was drunk and doing drugs and just thought, *Who cares?* But I should've thought about things a little more, should have considered that there would be consequences to my actions and that they could affect Aria, and then maybe I would have thought about more than just me and my own heart; I would have thought about yours. I'm sorry, Camila, I'm really, really sorry."

She grows teary-eyed, but she isn't going to cry. Later in her room, maybe, but not in front of me. She's a big girl now, she's earning money, she's got to be strong, and she wants to show me that so badly. She's seventeen, damn it, *seventeen*. She should be wearing sparkly dresses and dancing in gyms with pom-poms in her hands and a smile on her face. Instead, here she is looking like she's got three lives behind her already, all of them bad.

"It's Aria's fault," she says. "She's the one who took off. Not you. She ditched me. Not you."

I press my little sister's soft fingers, just like when she was four and I was eight, and she'd be in her little bed howling, and I'd rush in to comfort her so that Mom and Dad could go on sleeping.

"She took off because I did something terrible, Mila. She would've stayed. And the fact that she took off has nothing to do with you, okay? Nothing that went down between us had anything to do with you. She still loves you, I'm sure of that. I mean, she's Aria, and you're her little Mila, the one she made bracelets for and did paint-by-numbers and baked Christmas cookies with, and that will never change."

"Even so," she says, her cheeks flecked with red, shaking her head. Her bun waggles left, right, left, right. "Even so, Wy, it doesn't matter. I couldn't go to her anymore."

"Why not?"

"Because you're no longer together."

That hurts. It sounds fake because Aria Moore and Wyatt Lopez are two names that just belong together.

"Listen, Mila. You and I are two different people. Just because the same blood is flowing through our veins doesn't mean that you've got to suffer for things I've done. I fucked up, you know? Aria left me, not you. And if there's one of us that's just got to deal with the situation, then you should at least make sure to enjoy every second that she still loves you. Because she does. There's absolutely no reason to see things otherwise."

My little sister's eyes rest on me. Her irises are the exact same color as mine. Chocolate brown. They're only a little different right around the pupils, somewhat brighter, like a golden circle.

"Okay," she whispers, but Camila isn't the type to whisper, so she clears her throat and says it again, real loud and strong, because, if anything, she wants to be strong. "Okay."

"Wow, all right, you don't have to yell."

Camila laughs.

I swear my heart starts to vibrate. This is the nicest thing I've felt in days, weeks, months, or even years—no idea. It's nice, however long it's been.

I stand up. "We going to go to this soup thing?"

"But I don't want to try any." She puts her notebook to the side and crawls out of her niche. "They're always terrible, the soups."

"You've got to try mine, though."

"You made a soup?"

There is so much surprise and disbelief in her question; it's like cooking was something superhuman.

"Yeah. I even signed up. I want to win that golden ladle."

Camila follows me into the kitchen. Or, well, no, it's more like she *slides* into the kitchen in her wool socks with the little yellow dots. "What do you want that for?"

"No idea. But I thought if I win, there'll be a sense of achievement, right? People need that. Something that gives them the feeling of not being total dipshits."

My sister gives me a half smile. "You're not a dipshit, Wyatt."

I smile back. "Thanks." Then I hurry behind the island and lift the top off my pot. Camila peeps inside, full of expectation. I mean, I've made a soup! Hardcore!

But the excitement in her face disappears once she looks inside. "What is that?"

"Good, right?"

"It looks like vomit, Wy."

"It's banana pudding."

"Banana pudding."

I nod, the ladle in my hand ready to stir it again.

"You're gonna lose."

"Why?"

"Banana pudding isn't soup."

I click my tongue. "You're taking that too literally. It's William. You remember the cook-off two years ago? That's when he…"

"Made lump-of-flour soup! That was so disgusting. He wanted us to eat it. Every one of us." She makes a face. "I almost have to choke when I think about it. For real."

I laugh. "Yeah, he was so convinced and simply didn't get that everyone had taken off because of him."

Camila blinks. Unsurprisingly, she looks a little disturbed. "Okay, Wy. I take it all back. Your banana pudding will make it."

"Banana pudding is love."

She wriggles her eyebrows, dips her finger into the pot, and licks it off before nodding. "Banana-pudding-love."

"If William knew he was going to be eating something you'd stuck your unwashed finger in, he'd tear you apart."

"How do you know I haven't washed it?"

"Because you're like this. When I come out of my room, the whole hallway smells bad because your mountain of laundry is emitting nuclear levels of old shirts. How much you want to bet that at the bottom of it you've got wet bikinis from last summer that are rotting away as we speak?"

"Could be." She dips her finger in again. "This is pretty good."

"There is a tower of old Coke cans under your bed."

"Yeah and?"

"And your bathroom, man, the drain. Look, I'm breaking out in goose bumps, see? If I think about all the hair, rust, and who-knows-what living in perfect symbiosis in your shower drain, I start to gag."

"But you're not gagging right now."

"Am, too. Inside. If you only knew."

"We going to this thing or not?"

"Yeah." I put the top back on and carry the pot out of the kitchen. "But when we get back, you're going to clean your room."

"Ain't gonna happen," she says as she slips into her god-awful UGGs, and I slip into my Timberlands. When we both straighten up at the same time, she looks over her shoulder, and her bun wobbles again, left, right, left, right. She laughs, not that lovely, long forgotten, unworldly kid's laugh that's still somewhere deep down inside her, but a real, open one.

"The rats, Wy, the rats would be disappointed."

I love my sister and always will. Sometimes more, sometimes less, but always enough to the power of two.

17

In All My Dreams, I Have Already Kissed You

ARIA

IT'S ONE OF THE COLDER NOVEMBER DAYS. NO BLUE whatsoever left in the sky; everything is gray. For the first time this year I had to dig out a scarf, hat, and gloves.

Harper is waiting for me downstairs. She's talking to Mom, who's holding her pumpkin soup under her arm. I take the last few of the creaky steps, swing myself over the railing, and land in front of them.

"I'm ready."

Harper grows wide-eyed when she sees how I'm dressed, and Mom stops mid-sentence.

"What?"

Harper points at me. "What is *that?*"

"My face."

"Aria," Mom says, her voice stunned. "When did you start wearing so much makeup?"

"What do you mean?" My heart skips a beat. "Too much?"

"That all depends," Harper mutters. "Are we going to an audition for *America's Next Top Model?* Then no. If we are, then I'll have to go back and change my clothes because I thought we were just going across the street to the cook-off."

I groan. "So it *is* too much."

"No," Mom replies. "It's just… You look so different. Your eyes look like, I don't know, a cat's, like Hershey's, and your cheeks…Suddenly they're just so lively."

Relieved, I exhale. "I looked in the mirror, you know."

"Oh, wow, breaking news." Harper tugs at my elbow and points to the door. We go out. It won't be long until the first snow. We go to the right, toward the bell tower.

"Funny, Harp. So, I looked in the mirror, and all of a sudden it seemed to me that my skin was gray somehow and that it looked unhealthy. Don't you think so? There were those deep shadows beneath my eyes and…"

Mom turns to look at me. "And you just noticed that now?"

Harper nods. "That's been your face for two years, A."

"How lovely of you two to tell me."

"We thought you knew," Harper says.

To be honest, there was no reason for me to think about it. I spent most of my free time on my concrete-like dorm bed, in intimate togetherness with the smiley on the wall, and I didn't let anyone see me. I thought I only looked foggy and gloomy on the inside, but apparently my grief had also spread to the outside.

"Whatever," I say as we cross the street. "In any event, I don't want that anymore. I think that, if I'm starting over, especially if I want to give Paxton a chance, then I've got to fight these gray clouds inside me."

Mom looks confused. "Paxton?"

"The Hilcons' son," Harper says, while rubbing her hands together before burying them in her pockets. "Man, is it cold."

"I didn't know that you and the Hilcon boy were going out." There's disappointment in her voice. "How long has that been going on?"

"We're not going out. He was at the Halloween party, and maybe we'll get to know each other. *Maybe*. If he texts back."

That's not enough for my mother. I can see it in her eyes, a curious gleam that tells me she wants to know every last detail because that's how me and Mom are; we're like the *Gilmore Girls*, we tell each other everything. But now is not the time; we've reached the square. Aspen's residents are bustling around the large meadow surrounding the tall bell tower. Some of them have gathered in a cluster to huddle around William, each with a large pot in their arms. I give my mother a look that's supposed to express something like, *Later, Mom.* She raises an eyebrow in return, which says as much as, *You'll tell me every little detail later, by the fire, with hot chocolate in our hands and cozy socks on our feet, right?* I nod. But then I notice Wyatt's eyes are resting on me as well, and I have to concentrate so that I don't screw up.

Don't trip, Aria. Chin up. He's just some dude who stole your heart, but that's okay. It doesn't matter; just keep on walking.

"I've got to go see Will." Mom briefly lifts her pot. "Register my soup."

"Good luck," I reply. "Don't disappoint Daniel."

"Never." She sticks out her tongue and walks off.

Harper looks amused. "You all are never going to give up this Daniel thing, are you?"

"Nope. He is *so* cool." I point to a beer table where, aside from Spirit Susan and Vaughn, no one else is sitting. "Should we go sit with them?"

"Okay."

As soon as we sit down, my phone starts to vibrate in my pocket. I pull it out and feel my heart grow wild, bounce against my ribs, and fall before getting up again. I push Harper and whisper, "Paxton answered."

"What'd he say?" She tries to snatch my phone out of my hands, but I'm quicker and pull it away. In so doing, however, I manage to elbow Susan in the shoulder.

I spin around. "Sorry, Sue."

She waves it off but snags her oversized carnelian ring in her orange-colored stole. She's a bit spiritual, Aspen's Susan. "Girl, please. My bones aren't going to break with any old bump."

"That'd make a good song," Vaughn says, then grabs his guitar and begins to strum. "Oh, please, my dear, what ya think 'bout me? My bones can't break, can't break, oh, but what about my heart?"

Susan bobs to the beat. "Bongos would fit, Vaughn."

"No one has bongos anymore," Harper says.

Susan sits up straight. "Wanna bet? I've got some in my trunk. Hold on a sec."

"You've got some in your trunk?" I ask. "Why?"

But Susan doesn't respond. She's already off, her orange-colored stole fluttering behind her. Vaughn takes off, too, his new song upon his lips. For a moment I just sit and watch how happy everyone seems, how happy they seem to be listening to Vaughn and standing around on the meadow during the cook-off, when Harper's voice comes through.

"He's gold, Aria."

I turn around again and see her staring at the screen of my phone, which is in her hands.

"Hey!" Annoyed, I grab it back. "Klepto!"

"Kleptomania would mean that I steal all the time."

"Yeah." I unblock my phone and glare at her. "You stole my colored marker in third grade and ten Nintendogs."

"I gave that back to you."

"Oh, and admit that it was *you* who stole all the doubles of my Twilight stickers!"

"Man, come on, you had *doubles*, you freak! When are you going to let it go?"

I point at her. "Ha! So, it *was* you!"

"Great. Yeah, it was me. And you remember that Edward sticker of yours, the glittery one that suddenly disappeared? I STOLE THAT ONE, TOO!"

"You monster!"

"Now, would you finally read the message, A.?"

With a gnashing of teeth and narrowed eyes, I turn away from Harper and look at the display.

aria—write me at two forty-one in the morning, write me at three-o-six, write me a second later or a second before, it doesn't matter, and maybe this'll sound corny, maybe a bit weird, but once you decide to get to know me, i promise you that you'll only fall into my arms once, because afterward, i'm never going to let you go again, long text, no periods, just commas, because this thing between us is going to be a story with no end

"Harp." My phone is trembling in my hand. "Harp, how can he write something like that?"

"What do you mean?"

"I totally suck compared to that, no matter how I respond."

Buttoning up her cashmere coat, my best friend frowns. "What do you mean?"

"Because I'm a Gollum. There are cans of baked beans up to the ceiling of my room. I had lemon cake for breakfast, and for days I've been running around with the same old bun on my head. How on earth is my brain going to come up with words to compete with this?"

"It doesn't have to do with competing with him, A. The dude is clearly into you and wants to make that clear as best he can. That's beautiful. Not a lot of guys would do that so openly. It's not a contest, okay? Just be yourself."

I think for a moment, then respond. That sounds like a marriage proposal.

The answer comes immediately.

Maybe it was.

Stop or I'll start being happy.

Happy because of me?

Yeah.

He's online. Typing. It says so right there, right beneath his name. Paxton typing…

And then nothing. Suddenly he's offline. This is so frustrating! I want to throw my phone into one of the nearby fire bowls that William set up for the event.

"Was that weird of me?" I ask Harper, who, naturally, has been looking over my shoulder the whole time. "I mean, could I have scared him off? He's probably thinking, *Oh God, the freak. She doesn't even know me, and she's writing about me making her happy.*"

Harper blinks. Then blinks again. Then she takes my phone out of my hand, scrolls through the chat, puts the phone back into my hand, and points at his first text. "Read that again and tell me he thinks *you're* weird."

"Hmm. Good point."

"He was a lobster, A., and you're totally into him. You both are totally wacko. I can hardly believe how much of a fit it is. He'll probably be living with you in your Gollum cave by next week, and you'll both be sharing a can of baked beans with a single spoon."

"Wouldn't that be nice?"

Her expression softens. "Put your phone away, A. He'll respond."

"Okay." I tuck it into my parka. "We want to try some soup?"

"Yep. Off to battle." With an elegant movement, Harper swings her legs over the bench and stands up. "And I'm all set should we get food poisoning." She counts her fingers. "Pepto for my stomach along with drops—natural and non—for nausea, ginger candy, fennel tea…"

"We're not going to be eating anything that just looks wrong."

"Looks wrong?"

"You know, lumpy, bad color, filled with strange pieces of who-knows-what…"

"Right. You remember when we were twelve? There was that *really* yummy soup, the one that looked really normal, and then we were in bed for almost a whole week because…"

"It turned out to be frog spawn soup. God, yeah, I remember. Who made that?"

Harp sucks in her lower lip and thinks. "Vaughn, I think."

We stroll past Costume James, who is deep in conversation with Kate. "Kate, you need to rename your nut cake if all it's made out of is almonds."

"Uh huh. And why is that?"

"Well, almonds aren't actually nuts; they're stone-fruit seeds. I renamed my Cookie Monster outfit when I learned that his name was really Sid, by the way."

"I'm not going to call my cake stone-fruit cake, James."

Harper and I make our way among all the trestle tables with their numbered soups. I look over to Vaughn, with his long hair and biker boots. Susan is walking next to him, playing her bongos, which are attached to a cord hanging around her neck.

"Vaughn's submitted a soup, too."

"Which number?"

"No idea. That's going to be tricky. Let's go find Mom; she'll know."

Harper says hi to Levi and Aaron, who wave, and then asks, "How so?"

"William told her."

Her eyes grow wide. "*What?*"

I nod. "He spilled the beans."

"Incredible."

"Right?"

We get into line behind Paisley and Knox.

"Hey," I whisper, poking Paisley in the side. "Which soup is Vaughn's?"

"No idea. Why?"

"It's poisoned," Harper says.

"Oh, no." Paisley's eyes grow large. "How do you know?"

Knox ladles himself a bowl of soup from a pot labeled "*Number Five.*" It looks normal. A fresh green. Broccoli or spinach, I imagine. "A few years back, Vaughn took out most of Aspen. Frog spawn soup."

"Yuck."

I stretch my head and look for Mom. She's standing a few feet away, next to William, rubbing her hands together, and watching every one of Aspen's residents who comes to try her soup. I raise my hand and wave to get her attention. It works. She looks over. I mouth Vaughn's name and point to the pots. She smirks and raises three fingers. I blow her a kiss and turn back to my friends with a serious face.

"Don't touch number three."

Harper and I take a bowl and inspect the various soups. Every year there are all kinds of recipes, from curious to terrible to extremely good.

"There's a pig's ear bubbling in that one," Paisley says. "Normal or weird?"

"Weird," Knox and I reply in unison. He eyes the pot warily, then looks at his girlfriend. "I wouldn't try it if I were you."

"Not even an Olympic gold would convince me." She takes a scoop of Mom's pumpkin soup. Harper does the same and takes a step to the side so that I can have a bit as well. But as I'm stepping forward, a snub-nosed, tanned profile from the neighboring pot jumps into my field of vision. Camila is ladling something into her bowl that doesn't look like soup but like a lumpy, yellow paste. She notices me watching and offers me a hesitant smile. "Hi."

"Hi." I point at the stuff in her bowl. "You sure you want to eat that?"

She follows my eyes as if she didn't know what I meant before nodding. "Yeah. It's just banana pudding."

From the corner of my eye, I notice Paisley and Knox disappear to say hello to Gwendolyn, who has just wandered over to Levi and Aaron. Seeing her makes everything in me go tense.

Harper seems undecided between staying or leaving me alone with Camila. Eventually, she points to a nearby table. "I'm going to go sit down."

I nod. It's a weird situation. The thing with Wyatt shouldn't affect the relationship I have with his sister. I mean, she's got nothing to do with the way he acts, and yet… The sight of her makes my heart ache. She looks so much like her brother, it hurts.

"Umm." Unsure of what to say, I shift my weight from one leg to the other. "You were at my party."

Camila nods. "Just for a sec."

"Cool."

"Yeah."

Right as I'm wondering what else to say, someone pokes me in the ribs from behind. I turn and look into Patricia's watery gray eyes. The skin above her thin lips wrinkles a little more each year, and she's twisted her gray curls up into two little knots. "Aria, dear. If you don't get a move on, I'm going to give you a swift kick in the behind."

I grin. "You better not, Patricia. Just last winter you were telling me how pricey your new hip was."

"My artificial hip can kiss my ass. I want soup."

"Such a sweet face, but, wow, what a tongue…" I shake my head. "So vulgar, Patricia, so vulgar."

"I'll show you vulgar if you don't let me get some of that pumpkin soup, pronto!"

Camila presses her lips together so as not to laugh. With a calming gesture, I sweep my arms and make room for Patricia to trot past me. My eyes dart back to Camila's bowl, then I turn to the banana pudding. "Right, today I want to be open. But if you poison me, you're going to be covering my ER bill, got it?"

Camila grunts. "That would require Wyatt getting back out on the ice." I flinch at the sound of his name coming from her mouth. She notices and shoots me a sympathetic look. "Sorry. It's just weird, you know? I mean, not mentioning him in front of you because... Well, you know..."

"All good." I force myself to smile, scoop some banana pudding into my bowl, and strive for the most upright posture I am capable of. "Nothing you can do about it. And, umm..." I bite my lower lip as we turn away from the soups and begin walking across the meadow. "What I've been meaning to tell you for a long time is, you can come see me whenever you want, okay? When something's bothering you, when you just want to talk, when you miss your folks, or you need a girlfriend—I'm always there for you, Mila."

She runs a fingernail along the lines of the stapled-together cardboard tray in her hands. I can see her swallowing and her nostrils quivering before she looks up. "Thanks."

I nod. With a smile I watch her turn away and go off to her friends. It's still on my lips when I turn and move toward Harper.

"Aria."

I stop. For two long seconds I'm frozen in place, bowl in my hands, Aspen all around me, everything full of life. I could keep going. Simply ignore him. I mean, why should I talk to him. *Why?* Because we kissed? Because that touch knocked down all the protective barriers I'd carefully erected over the last two years?

Maybe. But maybe because I just can't do anything else. Because my heart wants to. Because *I* want to see him, *have to* see him, his beautiful features, those gold-brown eyes, like caramelized sugar, those full lips he put on mine yesterday, setting off an explosion.

I slowly turn around. So slowly that, in the meantime, a hundred years go by. At least. And then he's standing right there, right there in front of me, with the softest, sweetest features, as if he had just found his family, his family that has been missing for decades. He's wearing a dark-blue down Tommy Hilfiger jacket, his chest quickly moving up and down.

"Thanks," he says, completely out of breath, completely off the rails even though he's not doing anything but standing in front of me. "For what you just did."

It takes me a second to realize he's referring to Camila because, looking at him, all I can think of is yesterday's kiss, his chapped hands encircling my face.

A lot of things go through my mind looking at him. I think, *How dare you speak to me, here, in front of everyone, in front of our family, because that's what Aspen is. We're all one family somehow.*

I think, *How beautiful you are. How beautiful.*

I think, *WYATT LOPEZ, YOU FUCKING ASSHOLE. You not only broke my heart, no, you tore out everything that was left so brutally because breaking my heart wasn't enough. You just accepted that I was bleeding out inside, that I was freezing inside without you, without your love, without what we had. And everything inside me just turned gray, my emotions shriveled up; we're talking bombed-out levels after all the mines you laid. Who knows how long it will take for someone to set off an explosion inside me again, and it's all because of you!*

There's no more us because you didn't want us anymore, because you drowned everything in acid and poison, because you fucked everything up, YOU ASSHOLE, and I hate you for it. I hate every memory, every feeling I associate with you. Most of all, I hate you. I hate the fact that I love you. You hear me, you idiot? I love you, and I miss you, and THIS HAS GOT TO STOP.

And what do I say?

"Yeah."

He slumps his shoulders and takes a step back, as if meaning to go, but then, suddenly, grabs my hand. My bowl hits the ground. Yellow bits of banana sprinkle the frosty grass. My mouth opens, and I gasp for breath. *Help. What's happening? Why am I accepting this?*

Why do I want this so badly? And he looks at me with his honey eyes, warm and impulsive, but then his fingers relax. He wants to let go. He wants to go.

Then all of a sudden I'm the one overreacting. Some fuse must've blown, I mean, definitely, because now I'm the one grabbing his fingers so hard he can't pull away.

WHY ARE YOU DOING THIS, ARIA, WHY? HAVE YOU COMPLETELY LOST YOUR MIND?

Wyatt is staring at me, eyes wide, his lips open, and then everything goes quickly. He pulls me to him, just a few steps (seven, to be exact), and suddenly we're behind the bell tower. Not a soul around. Everyone else is on the other side.

I push my back against the wall of the tower while in front of me there's Wyatt, breathing heavily. Ice-cold behind, blazing heat in front of me—what a moment, what a mixture, hot and cold, just like our love.

Two breaths go by, and then Wyatt steps closer. His hand lands on the wall to the left of my head, and then his face is right above mine. I recognize the shadow of his lashes on his skin. I recognize the longing in his eyes. I recognize so damn *much*, and I don't want to at all.

His lips are just a few millimeters from mine. He is *literally* taking my breath away. I can't believe this is happening, that I am letting it happen, his closeness, everything. But I just can't do anything else. I can't.

Wyatt makes a stifled sound that robs me of all my willpower. My knees grow weak, and any second I think the ground is going to disappear, and I'm going to fall, simply fall, because I'm in the middle of a high that can't possibly last any longer. I have to put a stop to this. Right now.

The words are on my lips, and I'm about to say them, to say that he has to stop, that this won't work, when he raises his other hand. Slowly, ever so slowly, as if it hurt, his fingers move down the outer edge of my jaw to my chin, and the only thing that makes it over my lips now is a faint whimper.

Our touch is as soft as a whisper, barely perceivable, and yet everything and more. My body is on fire. I am burning. Shivers are running through me, and I can barely catch my breath.

We look at each other… Six years of history together, hot blood in our veins, electrified nerves, our pulses racing. And then Wyatt kisses me. He kisses me, just like that, here and now, and all I need to do is stop this from going farther. But all I *really* do is put my palms to the back of his head and pull him closer because I need him, damn it, I *need* Wyatt Lopez.

Between two touches he lets out a sigh, as if this moment was the most beautiful and at the same time the most painful thing ever. It's all far too intense, far too blatant, for both of us, because I feel the exact same way.

This here isn't like yesterday. This here is hard and passionate and impulsive, and it feels like breathing after being underwater for too long. And yet it also feels like drowning, like that last first moment you only get to experience once, which is why you want to savor it, take it all in, and never stop.

All his weight presses against my body, and yet it's not enough. I can feel him getting aroused in exactly the right place, and if it weren't for our pants, we'd be skin to skin right now, red-hot heat, an inferno, Wyatt and me.

It's a bittersweet image, and it makes me quiver, makes me whisper his name. The sound of my voice sends a shiver through his body, which is followed by a tormented sound, and I know him so well, inside and out, that I know, I *know* it was too much for him. Too much for him to bear.

I'm right. The last touch of his lips is velvety soft, barely a breath, before he breaks away from me.

Wyatt leans his forehead against mine. Our eyes are open.

We look at each other, breathing heavily, gasping intermittently, incapable of grasping what's happening, of working through it.

When Wyatt finally speaks, his voice is hoarse and weighed down by the heaviness of the moment. "You are the most beautiful thing my heart has to offer, Aria Moore."

And then he goes. He goes, and I just keep on standing here, my soul laid bare, out of breath, my lips swollen, my heart pounding, and then it's gone, all my hope is gone, right here, right now. Because I'm positive that I will never feel anything like this with anyone but Wyatt. Because this here isn't normal. Because this here is something big, something earth-shatteringly, galactically ungraspable.

But it's just not meant to be. The hopelessness comes in waves. It floods me until nothing's left of the happiness of his touch.

18
Addicted to Hope

WYATT

It's been two weeks since the soup cook-off. The sweet taste of Aria's lips has been with me for fourteen days. Honey and cream cheese, her favorite breakfast. I am holding onto these memories because ever since the…*incident,* naturally she's been avoiding me. During the last two town halls, she sat with Harper off in the back corner, but without a hat this time at least. She probably thought I wouldn't notice her, but I notice Aria *everywhere*; it doesn't matter how well she hides.

Strangely enough, the fact that she takes off whenever she sees me doesn't bother me whatsoever. I know now that things between us were never over. The way her body reacted to my touch, the way her eyes glistened, full of life and love, the way my lips could make her tremble… Aria Moore still wants me but is doing everything not to think about it. I know her so well that I just knew, I *knew*, that not even ten minutes after our kiss, "Paxton" would get a message from her because she's just so in love with me, that it's driving her mad, and she's doing everything she can to try and forget me and my caresses.

The first text came eight minutes later. And since then, we've been texting each other. Every day. She thinks I'm someone else, but all the same I couldn't be happier because SHE'S WRITING ME, and THAT MEANS WE'RE COMMUNICATING. There's a constant grin on my face. Even Camila and Knox have asked me if I'm taking drugs again.

Fuck that. Aria's the only drug I need.

Opening my eyes this morning, I noticed it. That feeling inside me. An inner warmth spreading through my veins and making them pulse with energy.

This is happiness, I think with surprise. *I'm happy.*

A smile creeps across my lips while I stretch out my good right arm and reach for my phone. Sleep still sticking to my eyes, I blink at my screen with tired lids. Four messages. My heart makes four little jumps. Her name four times in a row.

Brownies for breaktfst, this is gonna be a good day!
breaktfst
BREAKFAST, goodness
Sorry.

Just the idea of her sitting at the table, shoving this piece of chocolate into her luscious mouth... Shit, I'm getting a hard-on. Stifling a groan, I stretch out, run a hand through my hair, and type an answer.

Only if the brownies are as sweet as you.

I know Aria loves it when I write that kind of thing. I mean, she did in the past. Every time I'd let romantic words slip, she'd purr like her cat Hershey and never stop grinning.

I'm wondering if I should rub one out in the shower after I go for a jog, like every day, thinking about Aria's lips around my dick, or if I should just give in right now.

But my plans are thwarted with a knock at the door. Camila pops her head in. "Wyatt?"

"What's up?"

"You awake?"

"Naw."

She opens the door a bit wider and tiptoes in on bare feet; she's in a Snowdogs T-shirt that's way too big. She stops in front of my bed and begins kneading her hands. "Listen…"

I'm immediately alarmed. I sit up. "What's wrong?"

In the faint light of the streetlight coming through the curtains, I can see that she's nibbling her lower lip. "Maybe you should come downstairs and see for yourself."

"No. Tell me here."

"I'm afraid."

"Camila…"

"Just come downstairs, okay?"

She turns and leaves. Watching her go, I can't help but notice how thin her legs look. Camila was always thin, for sure, but now… She doesn't look healthy. Something's not right.

I run my hand over my face before peeling myself out of my bed, pulling on a shirt and a pair of pants, and making my way downstairs.

Camila's waiting for me in the kitchen.

"So," I say, annoyed. "What am I supposed to… *Santa Maria de Deus*…"

Half of the kitchen is underwater, and the walls—*Porra!* The walls are completely soaked. Mom's flower wallpaper is peeling off, and that's just the worst, really. My heart breaks in two. The ceiling is dripping onto the island, the stovetop…

"A leak," I say, more to myself than to my sister. "A pretty strong one."

Camila's tongue darts across her lips thoughtfully while she takes it all in. She painstakingly attempts to avoid the water. "You think we can take care of this on our own?"

"No way." I walk past her through the puddles with my naked

feet and run my hand down the wall. "Pack your things. Only the most important ones. Quick. We gotta get out of here."

A look of panic shoots through her eyes. "Why?"

I stomp back, grab her hand, and pull her upstairs. "We've got all our electrical cables running behind the wall. No idea how bad the damage is, but water and electricity are definitely not a good combo."

My sister gives a stifled gasp, runs down the hall to her room, and throws everything she can into her sports bag. I do the same, and twenty minutes later we're stepping onto the Highland Express because, of course—*of course*—Camila forgot to get gas, and halfway down the road we ran out.

The ski and snowboard season has begun, so the bus is packed with everyone trying to get to Aspen Highlands. Camila clings to me as I try to keep my balance without having to rub up against anyone else. Everyone's staring at me shamelessly. At the second stop, three women get on and, as soon as they see me, they start squealing.

"That's Wyatt," the tallest of the three whispers. She's even taller than me. "Wyatt Lopez."

"Who's the girl?" the middle one hisses. Neon-pink tips of hair are peeking out from beneath her wool cap and tickling her chin. "His girlfriend?"

"He doesn't have one," the third says indignantly. She doesn't even try to lower her voice. "He cheated on his high school sweetheart. It was in *Teen Vogue*."

In *Teen Vogue*? Shit, how deep do these reporters dig?

Camila has to have noticed that my body's tensed up. She leans to the side and looks over my shoulder. Her eyes wander past the lanky guy with a red face behind us, past Belly Bernard, the Highlands' massive gondola operator who rides the bus every day, before stopping on the groupies. "Hey!" she calls out. Heads turn; every pair of eyes in the bus is now looking at Camila. "Don't know whether you noticed or not, but my brother's a human being, okay? He's got ears, even if they're big, knobby, and downright ugly. So shut it. I really have no interest in slipping on your drool."

The one with the pink tips blinks before a quick and breathless, "Can I get an autograph?" escapes her lips.

"Umm," I say, my eyes scurrying over all the people in the bus. "Now's not exactly the best time."

Camila pokes me in the side. "Don't be so nice all the time. They were just talking about you like you were a zoo animal."

The bus stops, and the three groupies start pushing their way past the others to get closer.

Belly Bernard grunts and steps in between. "You'd better get out here. I don't know how long I can hold them off. Up on the mountain, they'll probably fall all over you."

"Truth." I grab Camila's far-too-thin wrist. "Come on, quick."

Our bags keep getting caught on people as we quickly elbow our way through. But then we're out of the bus and into the Highlands' fresh winter air.

Man, is it cold, but thank God we got off one stop early. It's just a few minutes' walk over the frozen asphalt to the Winterbottoms' huge resort. And when I say huge, I mean *immense*. Knox's father is a real estate agent. Almost every resort in Aspen belongs to him. And so their villa is gigantic and looks right out onto Aspen Highlands.

The sound of our steps float through the cold air as Camila and I make our way up the curved driveway to the front door. I'm just about to ring when the door opens and we become witness to a real intimate, real passionate, and, for us, real uncomfortable kiss between my best friend and Paisley.

"Later," Paisley whispers to his lips.

KISS.

"I'm going to miss you."

KISS.

"I'm going to miss *you*."

KISS.

"What do you think, Mila? Are *we* going to miss her once we've fed her to the black bear?"

Knox and Paisley move apart. Knox bangs his head against the door. "Fuck, Lopez!" Paisley knocks her keys off the sideboard with her elbow.

"Dunno," Camila answers. "We wanna find out?"

"Man, Wy." My best friend puts a hand on my gray Abercrombie sweater. Apparently he hasn't been awake too long because his hair is sticking out all over the place. "To what do I owe this pleasure?"

"We were going to ring, but then you decided to include us in your slobber fest here."

Paisley turns red. The blotches move up her neck all the way to her ears before spreading out across her high cheekbones.

At that moment, Gwen's camo-colored Jeep pulls up. She puts down the window and sticks her head out. "*Come on*, Pais. We're running late, and Polina's going to murder me if her Olympic hope isn't out on the ice on time."

Paisley grabs her bag, flashes us a sheepish smile, and sprints over to Gwen. A few seconds later the Jeep reverses over the fastidiously manicured lawn, killing a few of its beautiful chrysanthemums, and speeds off.

Knox leans against the doorframe and stares at me, then Camila. "What's up, bro?"

"Water damage," I reply. "In our kitchen."

"Shit." He steps to the side to let us in, and we walk into the oversized living room with its wooden, rustic-looking modern furniture. "You all hungry?"

Camila shakes her head. "Just coffee for me, thanks."

Knox raises an eyebrow. "Paisley made her avocado sandwiches."

"I'll take one," I say.

Knox nods and ambles into the kitchen. He puts on some coffee while I start making calls to various workmen and the insurance people.

"They're inside and will be taking care of everything," I say eventually, and I toss my phone onto the table next to the couch. I lean back into the cushions and pinch the bridge of my nose. "The universe hates me."

Knox puts the coffee and sandwiches down in front of us and drops into the chair in front of the panoramic windows. Behind him, the white tips of Aspen Highlands kiss the sky.

"Is insurance going to cover it?"

My eyes still on the chandelier above us, I shrug. "No idea."

"Let me know if you need any money."

"Wyatt." Camila turns to me and pulls a leg up onto the couch. "You think the workmen will be done by tonight?"

I burst out laughing. "No, Mila, of course not. They said it could take weeks."

"But where are we going to sleep?"

"You all can stay here as long as you want," Knox says. "Paisley and I have moved into the attic room, so my old room is free, and there are the four guestrooms..."

I sit up so quickly that Knox breaks off mid-sentence.

"Oh my God," I say.

"What?" Camila asks.

"I've got an idea."

"Oh, no." Knox's forehead sinks into the palm of his hand. "Whenever you say that, it doesn't mean anything good."

"No, no, for real. It's perfect."

Camila crosses her arms. "Spit it out, Wy."

Eyes wide, first I look at my sister, then my best friend. "We'll stay at the B&B."

Neither of them moves. They just stare at me like I'm an alien, but I don't care what they think or say. This is perfect, just *perfect*.

"Wyatt..." Camila begins. She sounds cautious and careful— the tone she's perfected over the years whenever it's got to do with Aria. Helplessly she looks over at Knox, who slides forward in his chair and puts down his coffee.

"Listen, bro." He watches me take a bite of my sandwich, pour myself some coffee, and add two spoons of sugar with a grin. *Man, this coffee is wonderful, and this life! Everything's beginning to fall into place.*

Knox clears his throat. "I can understand that...umm...the idea of moving in with Aria is really attractive to you. But you've got to understand that this is just a knee-jerk reaction and that Aria and you are never..."

"We kissed," I say before he can finish. "Twice."

Camila's face turns gray. "Wy, please tell me you didn't force her and..."

"Que merda, Camila, no!" I glare at her. "What the hell kind of person do you think I am?"

"Well, explain then," she says, laying her hands on her knees. "Aria hates you, Wy."

I swallow the last bit of sandwich and grind my teeth. "Apparently not."

"Was she drunk?" Knox asks. "Or a little messed up?"

"No!" I spring up and begin pacing back and forth behind the couch. "It just happened. And she *wanted* it to, okay? And ever since we've been texting each other every day, every minute, so don't be coming at me with this I-forced-her crap."

"She's texting *you*? Don't you mean she's writing to the lobster?" Knox asks.

"The lobster? O meu Deus. Wy, you can't be serious, right?" Mila adds.

"You have no idea what's going on!" I can feel the rage boiling up in me until I'm just about ready to burst. "Knox, you're with Paisley, and you love each other and are happy, every day. And, Camila, you don't know what it's like to lose someone you love."

All the blood drains out of her face. Knox says, "Duuude," and only then do I realize what I've just said.

Shit. "I didn't mean that. Mom and Dad, I mean, yeah, of course you loved them. I only wanted to say that there hasn't been a guy that you, I mean…"

"It's okay, Wyatt." My sister closes her eyes and takes a deep breath before opening them again. "It's okay. I know what you mean. You're right. I have no idea what being so obsessed with a person is like, what completely losing your shit over a person is like. But to be really honest? I don't think I wanna know."

I feel a heavy weight on my chest as I sit down next to her again. I hesitantly reach out my hand and, when I see that she'll allow me, put it over hers. "I'm sorry for saying what I just did. That was dumb. And I'm sorry for not exactly being the best role model as far as love goes. Actually, it's something beautiful, Mila. And the fact that I'm so messed up just means that the feelings Aria and I shared were on some kind of super-dimensional level where nothing should have ever gone wrong." I squeeze her hand. "Think how great it's going to be when you find someone."

She grunts. "Yeah, before it goes to shit, and I end up in a dark, dirty hole like you."

"That won't happen," Knox grins. "You're smarter than your brother."

I laugh. "A lot."

A faint smile appears on her lips. She looks up and holds my gaze. She must see something, something that softens her heart, for all of a sudden she sighs and says, "Tell me there's a ghost of a chance that you and Aria could get back together, and I'll be okay with it."

"There is." Two words and I feel like I'm in the clouds.

Camila lets out a breath. "Well, good, Wy. Then let's go to the B&B."

Knox groans. "I take back what I just said. Apparently you're both batshit."

"Knox," I say in a businesslike tone while lifting up my coffee and looking my best friend right in the eyes. "If Aria asks why we're not staying with you, I'm going to tell her your relatives are visiting.

And please promise me you're not going to call her to convince her not to put us up."

"As if she'd put you up anyway, Wy. You're her ex, man. That aside, the season just started, and every guesthouse is booked out."

I grin. "We'll see about that."

19

It Hurts Having You in My Life, and It Hurts Not Having You in My Life

ARIA

MY FINGERTIPS ARE FROZEN STIFF. AND I'M NOT JUST saying that. They're red, even a little blue, and literally stiff. I move from one leg to the other and blow on my palms.

Over and over my eyes flit to the shop window with the antique tea service, cutlery, and pastry stand decorated with little flowers. I'm standing in front of the window for the seventh time today already and peeking through the narrow crack of the rose-colored drapes when finally—*finally!*—the back door of the pastry shop opens and Patricia scurries out in her white-and-purple dress with frilled sleeves and her old-fashioned apron. Her watery eyes look to the window and meet my inquisitive gaze. A few seconds later she pulls the curtains to the side before undoing the chain on the door and opening the shop.

"Child," she says as I storm past her into the warmth of the shop. "Every day I tell you to stop staring into my shop."

"And every day I tell *you* to open on time."

"If I didn't know any better, I'd think you were a spy trying to get ahold of my secret butter-tart recipe to put online."

I shake out my numb fingers and wait for them to come back to life before taking an apple turnover from the counter. It's still warm. "I'm not spying," I say in between heavenly bites. "I'm begging for help in the ice-cold night, and you refuse to let me in."

Patricia disappears behind the counter and turns on the coffee machine. "You're not *The Little Match Girl*, Aria."

"How do you know? Have you ever seen my fingers? I bet they're just as cold as hers were."

Patricia gives me a disdainful look before disappearing into the kitchen and returning with a handcart piled high with three boxes of rolls, quark balls, and cinnamon buns.

"You know," I say as I take the handcart from her. "If you don't start opening on time, maybe we'll have to terminate our contract with you."

Patricia erupts in laughter. "I'd just *love* to see your guests when you serve them your homemade pastries."

"I'm not bad at baking."

She bends over the counter, her old-fashioned dress squishing her ample breasts upward, opens her mouth, and takes out her dentures. Just like that, right in front of me! I can hardly believe it. God, is that nasty! Saliva and everything, right here on the counter!

"You see that?" Patricia points to an empty space stretching between her molar and canine. "I lost that three years ago biting into one of your Christmas cookies."

"That really was worth showing me right now, wasn't it?" I make a face. "Now you've got to disinfect the counter."

With another laugh, she puts her dentures back in, grabs a bottle of disinfectant from a shelf, and sprays down the counter. "Get out of here, Aria. I don't want any Little Match Girl in my shop scaring away my guests with her pitiful eyes."

"There you have it! Denying me, the poor, *poor* little creature longing for refuge!"

She *shoo*s me off but smiles. And I return it because I love this woman and know I'll be a wreck the day heaven decides to have her back.

It's just before seven. Not a light in the sky. Finally, the time of year when things turn magical. A few of the city's streetlights, like the ones on our street, are gas-powered and date back to the 1930s. The state of Colorado wanted to get rid of them and replace them with modern stuff, but William fought back as if his life depended on it with I don't know how many PowerPoint presentations, petitions, and even his horses, which he put out to protect every single light… In the end, they were allowed to stay. Will doesn't mind turning every single streetlight on and off two times a day, mornings and evenings, on his stubborn mare Sally. He loves it. Says it keeps him young.

The butter-yellow glow lights up the asphalt as I push the cart across the street and the sound of its wheels travels through the cold morning air. The bell tower chimes seven o'clock. Smoke is coming out of the chimney on our roof—Mom must have started the fire. It's a simple moment, nothing particular, but it awakens so much magic inside me, so much beauty.

The crackling of the fireplace greets me as I step into our B&B. My mother is bustling about in the room behind the stone arch setting up the breakfast buffet.

"We need to fire Patricia," I say, walking over to her and maneuvering the handcart next to the table. "She wanted to let me freeze to death."

Mom begins lifting rolls and quark balls out of the boxes with stiff fingers and dividing them between the baskets. "Daniel would be disappointed."

I nod, bring the cinnamon buns into the kitchen, and come back with the cutlery tray. "And she pulled out her dentures to show me some missing teeth."

Mom opens a package of napkins and puts them next to the rolls. "The ones she lost thanks to your Christmas cookies or Wyatt's elbow?"

"The ones… Wait, what?"

She raises her eyes and laughs when she sees my confused expression. "Patricia used to take care of Wyatt pretty often when his dad was stationed overseas for longer periods of time. When he was two, he had a meltdown, and she got an elbow to the teeth."

The corners of my mouth twitch. "Even when he was little, it was obvious he'd become a hockey player, huh?"

Mom grins. "Wyatt was always a rebel. He got his first pair of skates when he was three and then just shot off across Silver Lake. Fell over a thousand times, sure. But always got up again." Her smile grows warmer. "I can still remember how confused you were in kindergarten by all his energy. 'Mommy,' you said, 'he runs after me every day. It's annoying.'"

"For real? I don't remember that at all."

"Wyatt was in love with you from the moment you joined his red bear group."

I'm filled with a sense of infinite sadness. A large part of me longs to be back in that little group where our biggest problems were who got to have the crayons or whether we'd have those terrible veggie burgers for lunch again. My heart begins to race when I think back to him pulling me behind the bell tower and pushing his weight against me, his hot breath on my skin, the scent of mint and pine right before his lips brushed mine…

"Everything okay, Aria?"

"What? Oh, yeah. All good."

"You sure? You're red."

"It's hot in here, right?" I push the napkins to the left, to the right, left, right, left, and then pick up the bread knife to pretend to inspect it for spots. "The fireplace is really going today."

"It's only got two logs."

An uncomfortable silence springs up while my mother waits for me to explain, when all of a sudden the door opens and guests come in.

"Welcome to Ruth's!" I call out enthusiastically, put the bread knife back down, and go into the next room to the welcome desk. "Aspen is delighted to welcome you. You're in luck, we still have—"

I look up, and the words stick in my throat. A big pair of honey-colored eyes is staring back at me. Liquid amber. Those very same honey-colored eyes I've been rigorously avoiding for fourteen days.

"Wyatt..." Behind him, Camila steps to the side. With pinched lips, she stares past me up the wooden stairs.

Wyatt pulls off his hat, sheepishly runs a hand through his unruly hair, and then puts it back on, backward. *Warning, warning. Déjà vu at its finest.* He used to do that so often that the gesture invariably burned itself into my brain.

"Hi, Ari."

Mom appears in the archway. Blinking continuously, she looks from me to Camila to Wyatt as if this were the most absurd thing she had ever witnessed. But she doesn't say a word. She simply stands there looking at us before TURNING AROUND AND WALKING OFF.

Speechlessly, I watch her go. I mean, hello, this just isn't possible! She's my mom, and my ex has just shown up at our house as if that was something he could do. She knows I can't handle this. She knows that she's got to take over because I've just turned back into a little kid who wants to run off into her corner. I can't cope with this. But she just walks off as if she had to reset the plates, as if that required some kind of sorcery. Come on, THEY'RE JUST PLATES!

I try to clear my throat, for suddenly there seems to be a whole lot of mucus in it. "What do you want?"

Wyatt comes a step closer. His feet are touching the oriental carpet, which means that he's only about two and a half feet away. After making every effort over the last two weeks to make sure that the distance between us was at least half the city, this is too close, definitely too damn close.

"We've got a problem."

Heat crawls up my throat all the way to my ears, and when he notices, he realizes what he's just said.

His cheekbones turn red. "I don't mean you and me. Well, yeah, we do, too, but, no, I didn't phrase that right... I mean, I don't want you to think I've got a problem with you right now or something because, well, what I wanted to say..."

"God, Wy." Camila sighs. "We need a room, Aria."

At first I think I've misunderstood. But when the two look at me with serious expressions, I'm overcome by a feeling of bafflement. The situation is so grotesque I have to laugh.

"You all need a room."

Wyatt nods.

"Here. With us."

Another nod.

In a stiff movement, my head turns sideways to look for Mom, but she's nowhere to be seen. There they are in front of me, looking like two supermodels: Camila slim and tall, fine features, snub nose, slanted eyes. Wyatt tall and broad, even broader than before, well-toned legs, muscular arms hidden under his Hilfiger jacket. And his face, God, that mouth...

"Why do you need one?"

"We've got water damage in our kitchen," Camila says.

It's hard to keep my composure. My nails are scratching beneath the reservation book. "I'm sorry to hear that. I'm sure that Knox..."

"He's got visitors," Wyatt interrupts. "His relatives showed up and they're staying for a while because of the, umm, the..."

"Season," Camila says. "They want to stay longer so Knox can show them how to snowboard."

Wyatt and Camila nod in unison.

"I don't believe you."

"Give him a call," Wyatt says. "He'll confirm."

"No, all good." I lower my eyes and pretend to look through the reservations. In truth, I'm simply holding my breath and trying not to black out. I mean, destiny sure seems to be fucking with me at this very moment, right? I mean, this is an absolute catastrophe. On multiple levels.

One: Wyatt's my ex.

Two: Wyatt cheated on me.

Three: I still love him even though I really, *really* shouldn't.

Four: Paxton and I are just starting to get to know each other, and I actually like him. I can actually feel something inside that I hadn't thought would ever show up again. Even though all we're doing is writing.

Five: If Wyatt's around, it'll be impossible to engage with Paxton.

Six, and worst of all: We actually have a room free. Which shouldn't be the case, as it's high season and everyone knows that something like that in Aspen just doesn't happen. I mean, this is ASPEN IN HIGH SEASON, the most popular ski area in the Rockies, and we have a room free.

Well, ladies and gentlemen, put a red mark on your calendars. Today is one of those days, Maria, in room twelve—that can't be right, that number, *our* number? No, I don't want to believe it. She had to interrupt her vacation. This just isn't happening.

"Aria?" Camila sounds concerned. "Everything okay?"

Suddenly I realize that I've been staring into the reservation book for over a minute. My heart is pounding against my ribs when I look up and meet Wyatt's gaze. It stings, but I don't want to look away. My wrists hurt from leaning against the desk, so I desperately try to adopt an upright posture.

Trembling, I exhale. "Sorry, we don't have anything free. But I can call around and see what can be done."

Wyatt doesn't budge. He just keeps on standing there staring at me, no smile, no disappointment on his face. He assumed I would say that.

"You know just as well as I do that everything's going to be booked out, *Ari*."

Does he have to use my old nickname? My stomach's beginning to tingle and that's not good.

To distract myself, I grab a pen and quickly start clicking it in and out, in and out. *Oh my God, can my head* please *stop thinking about sex?*

"We don't have anything free," I repeat. My throat is scratchy. "You can't stay."

Now a smile appears on Wyatt's face. What's so funny? His eyes skirt across my face, my shoulders, my breasts. I squirm beneath his gaze. From second to second I can feel myself growing warmer. I can feel sweat beginning to form on my neck.

"Your hair's grown long," he says. I look down at myself, at the dark tips of my ponytail resting on the page of the reservation book, spreading out like black ink.

"That can happen in two years."

Camila's eyes dart from me to Wyatt. She moves restlessly, like she's got lobsters in her pants, and keeps on looking toward the door. "Wyatt, come on…"

"Two years… Feels like time's stood still."

I hold his gaze. "Not for me."

He drops his big hockey bag to the floor. It lands with a thud as he takes one, two, three steps forward. I hold my breath. Wyatt's face comes closer. He lays his big hands on the desk, stretches out his arms, and bends down toward me. His lips brush my ear as he tilts his head.

"Liar," he whispers.

Goose bumps break out across my arms. I'd love to say something, something to make him unsure of himself, to puncture his damn self-assurance, but the truth is I can hardly breathe. My fingertips are reacting to the missing oxygen by sending me a warning signal. They start to tingle.

Wyatt's lips move down my jawline before turning back away. The softest of caresses, almost as good as none, but at the same time it's all far, far too much and I can't stop myself from gasping.

Hearing it, his eyes blaze, and that makes me so incredibly angry because he just loves winning, and it's nothing to him. It's just fun, it excites him, even though he hurt me so bad.

"You like that, huh?" My voice begins to quake. "To see what kind of power you have over me?"

Wyatt's face loses all its color. His grin is gone. The fire in his eyes went out. They're a cheerless amber now, no honey at all, just a dull brown, no gold.

"I'm just a fucking game you want to win."

"Aria, no."

He sees that I can't do it anymore. He sees that I'm going to break out in tears at any moment and show him how much I'm suffering.

He wipes his face as if he had to keep from crying himself. "Fuck," he says quietly, hoarsely, and moves to come around the side of the desk to hold me or touch me or run a hand through my hair like he did in the past. *Sssh*, he'd say, *all good. I'm here. We're together. All the heart needs is us.* But before he can do that, before he can give me another reason to miss him, Camila grabs his wrist.

He attempts to shake her off, but his sister hisses and pulls him back. "Wyatt. *Leave her be.*"

Yeah, Wyatt, leave me be.

Leave me be forever.

Never leave me ever again.

For a few moments he stands between the desk and Camila, staring at me. There is so much pain in his eyes, so much bare sadness, that I almost believe he misses me, too. But then his shoulders collapse, and he gives up. He puts both hands to his head, his palms on his hat, and closes his eyes, as if he could hide from the here and now, from all the pain and these terrible stabs in the heart. But, *sorry, Wyatt,* life doesn't work that way. You've got to keep your eyes open. Come on, take a look at yourself, look at what you've done, and take a look at what you did to us.

You destroyed us.

When he does, I see tears. Maybe for just a second, maybe just a tenth of a millisecond, but too *there*, too meaningful for me to miss.

Then the two of them leave. I wait until the door closes, then count to four, seven, nine, eleven, until the tension I've been holding gives way and I collapse. I take a deep breath, but nothing arrives. My limbs are heavy and weak at the same time, like I'm feverish. I lean my head against the wall, pull up my legs, and turn to the ceiling.

"What do you think, Aria?" My mother is standing in the stone archway looking down at me. "You ready to talk about it now?"

I nod. Tears are streaming down my face.

Mom comes over. She groans as she kneels down, but other than that she doesn't let on that I'm demanding everything of her right now. She gives me her hand, and I take it. My safe harbor, my nightlight.

"Come here, sweetheart. Come here."

I struggle to get to my feet. I'm wobbly, real wobbly, but from the corner of my eye notice Mom put the *Be Right Back* card on the counter. The walk to my room feels like a never-ending marathon. Stairs. Hall. Connecting door. Hall. Stairs. Bed.

The mattress bounces as I curl up on it and bury my face in my favorite pillow. I'm only vaguely aware of Mom running her hand through my tear-streaked hair. She is panting with the effort it took to climb the stairs to my room.

"You simply took off," I say, my voice subdued. "You left me alone."

"Aria," she says gently. "Sweetheart, you're not a kid anymore."

"But you're my mother."

"Yeah. And I will protect you my whole life long whenever I have to. But Wyatt and you…" She takes a long pause. "I *can't* help you with that."

I turn onto my side and look at her. "What should I do, Mom? When does it stop hurting so bad?"

A sad smile appears on her face. She catches one of my tears with her thumb. "When you begin to accept it."

"Accept what?"

"That it's over." Seeing my expression, she sighs. "That's what I thought."

"What?"

"It's not over for you, is it?"

The realization comes slowly, creeping up my fingertips all the way to my heart.

"No," I say, and that one single word almost kills me.

My mother doesn't respond. Then she leans back and runs a finger along the line of string lights wrapped around the foot of my bed. "Love is powerful, Aria, and that's why it can hurt. It can hurt so damn much. And I wish I could take that pain away from you somehow, but I can't. You alone can decide whether it should stop or not. Not Wyatt, not me, just you."

"I *want* it to stop." I slowly sit up and scoot back until I'm against the slope of the roof. "But how am I supposed to do that? I mean, how does that work, forgetting someone?"

"You said you were getting to know this Paxton guy. Do you like him?"

"Yeah."

"Does he give you butterflies?"

"Absolutely."

Mom's eyes come to rest on a can of baked beans before she looks back at me and her expression softens. "That's a good start, Aria. That's the right way. Concentrate on him. Let yourself be open to that. Wyatt won't disappear from your life overnight. You can't just cut out a piece of your heart; that's impossible. But when you start to fall for someone again, when you start to *live* again, at some point, everything gets better."

"You think?"

Mom smiles. "Absolutely." She stands up and nudges my foot. "Take the day off. Study a bit. Reflect a bit. I'll be fine."

"Okay, Mom."

Once she's gone, I turn onto my stomach and close my eyes. I'm drained. A leaden feeling of fatigue hangs over me, but I don't want to sleep because I one hundred percent know that I'll dream about Wyatt, and I can't handle that right now. So I pull my phone out of my pocket and write Paxton. I want this feeling in my chest to go away so bad. I want to be able to look at Wyatt and not feel a thing so bad!

> I was wrong. Chocolate brownies for breakfast are NO GUARANTEE that the day's going to go well.

One minute later my phone vibrates.

> Shit. Try banana pancakes.

> I can't bake.

> I don't believe you.

> Patricia lost a few teeth thanks to my cookies.

> Patricia Pastry Shop?

> Yeah.

> She's over two hundred years old or something. You lose your teeth. I bet your cookies are good.

I laugh. Before I can respond, another text shows up.

What happened?

My fingers hover over the screen as I weigh telling him or not. But, well, if this is supposed to be the start of something, honesty's important.

My ex showed up at the B&B.

Typing. Pause. Typing. Pause. Then:

Do you still have feelings for him?

Wow, okay. I wasn't counting on that.

We were together for six years. I'd be lying if I said I didn't care. But I want to look to the future and get to know you, to find out what you like for breakfast, to find out what makes you laugh, to find out whether you talk a lot before falling asleep or if you're out like a light... I want to know what kind of touch makes your heart beat faster, I want to know how you spend your Sundays, whether you wear socks to bed, whether you prefer cheese or salsa on your nachos... I want to find out all that stuff, Paxton, because I think that we could have something good if we let ourselves.

It takes him a long time to answer, but then all I get is the red-cheeked smiley. I guess I overwhelmed him. Or he can't handle that I can't forget Wyatt, or, or, or. Frustrated, I put the phone back down and sink into my pillows before it vibrates again.

Banana pancakes. *The Simpsons* and William. Talking before going to sleep. I bet you'll know how to touch me if we're ever face-to-face. No socks. Depends, but I like walking on Buttermilk Mountain. Cheese dip (who eats salsa??? That's weird). It's okay, Aria, take whatever time you need. Who doesn't need time? Maybe one day you'll manage to get so involved with me that you won't have to let go of the time with your ex but will be able to remember him as a good friend. I think your soul can cope better that way.

His words make me want to cry again. Paxton's right; he's so right it's almost scary. It's all so easy. What's even more frightening, though, is how much he's helping me out of my hole. He's reaching out his hand to me, and I'm grabbing it with all my fingers so that I don't fall one more time.

I even manage to get up and start cleaning my room. I manage to start humming Taylor Swift songs and to re-glue the lights to my ceiling. We spend the whole day texting back and forth, trivial things that make me laugh even though they're not all that funny. We talk about William and Vaughn, how they never stop arguing over Vaughn's music. We write about Patricia and Spirit Susan, who has told just about every one of Aspen's residents at least once a year that, pretty soon, they're going to run into a yeti during a blizzard before their knight in shining armor comes to save them. We text about everything and nothing, and yet every word helps my heart to bloom a little bit more.

In the evening I send him a goodnight text, even adding a kiss-blowing emoji. I've gotten the fireplace in my room going, turned on all my string lights, and have a cup of hot chocolate waiting for me on my nightstand, as I intend to study a bit more in bed. I'm smiling as I walk over to the window to draw the curtains. Thick flakes are falling from the sky. The first of the year. All the house lights and streetlights are in fierce competition to see who the better accompaniment to the flakes' white winter dance will be. I watch the goings-on for a while, warmed by the fire, when my eyes notice something else. There, on the other side of the street, in front of Patricia's Pastry Shop and right in the middle of William's no-parking zone, is Wyatt's Volvo. The light is on, and I see him and Camila in the seats, covered by blankets.

They plan to sleep in the Volvo. They plan to sleep there the whole night long, maybe even longer.

For a while I just stand there with the edge of the curtain in my hand, looking at the car. In the meantime, they're almost completely enveloped by the snow.

Paxton's words come to mind. *"Maybe one day you'll manage to get so involved with me that you won't have to let go of the time with your ex but will be able to remember him as a good friend."* And then Mom's. *"If you want to forget him, you have to accept that it's over."*

The curtain slips out of my hand. The flakes merge into one single storm before my eyes. I take my lined robe off the bedpost, slip into my Birkenstocks, and shuffle downstairs. I take the last key from behind the counter and go outside. Aspen smells of snow, love, and security. The roofs of our town's gingerbread houses are covered with soft white powder. The snow crunches beneath my sandals as I fight my way across the street. It's only a few feet, but by the time I knock on the window, my fingers are already numb.

Wyatt flinches. Seeing me, he puts the window down.

I hold the keys out under his nose. "Room twelve. You know where it is."

He blinks, seems surprised, but just for a second, then he's got himself back under control and grins. That dumb Wyatt grin that always gets me off track without fail.

"Twelve, huh?"

I turn around and go back inside. The two grab their things and follow, but I don't turn around; I just keep on going until I'm back in my room and, with a pounding heart, under my blankets.

For the next few days or even weeks, Wyatt Lopez is going to be just a heartbeat away, and I have no idea where that's going to take me.

20

The Big Sad Part of My Heart Called Aria Moore

WYATT

I CAN'T SLEEP. IT'S PAST MIDNIGHT, BUT MY BODY IS FULL of adrenaline. To be honest, I feel like I've had ten espressos. I'm lying in bed, stiff as a board, my eyes shut, trying to let the meditation coming through my earbuds reach me. Ever since the accident, this elongated, smoky voice that travels to the bottom of the ocean with me and explores my fears has been my most reliable way of getting to sleep. But not today. Today all I'm thinking about is Aria lying in her bed just a few feet away. Her bare thighs and how warm they always were when I'd wake up at night and feel around blindly for her.

I pull out my earbuds and turn onto my side. Camila's heavy breathing fills the room. It's stopped snowing. The moon is casting its gray light through the crack in the curtains onto my sister. She's kicked off her blanket and is lying there with her arms outstretched, mouth open slightly, her dark hair spilling over the pillow. On the white sheets by her waist are four empty chocolate wrappers. She digs her fingers into the faux beaver pelt comforter before she turns onto her side. Right now she looks so much like the little girl from way back when, who, in order to fall asleep, had to cuddle her bald Barbie; I am filled with nostalgia.

So as not to make the floor creak, I tiptoe to the bathroom. Everything here feels so damn familiar. How many times did I help Aria get the rooms ready for guests? How many times did I clean the bathroom knowing how much drains freak her out? How many times did we make the beds together only to be unable to withstand each other and then have to put new sheets on once again?

Too many times for me to be able to forget.

I splash my face with water and look in the mirror. The thing with mirrors is they're terribly honest and ruthless, and right now this one here's showing me how fucking terrible I look. Dark shadows beneath my eyes. Burst veins on my cheek. The gold-brown tone of my skin has turned grayish.

Man, this is all way too much. I just can't do it anymore. What happened last summer is something I've never really gotten over, psychologically or physically. All the pressure on my sister who's got to make enough money to support both of us because I can't. The NHL that's about to kick me back into the minors and, above all, the cherry on the cake, Aria Moore.

My throat begins to tighten. I need fresh air and a distraction; I need to get my head straight. I quietly go back to my room and dig my skates out of my hockey bag. I manage to get my coat on over my bad arm, toss my tied-together skates over my good shoulder, and sneak out into the hallway. Aside from the ticking of the clock over the chest of drawers, it's dead silent. The wooden stairs groan beneath my heavy steps. I feel like an intruder, and that's not a nice feeling, for this house was always like my second home.

Snowflakes whirl inside as I open the door and step out into the frigid night air. My blades tap against my chest and shoulder blade in time to the steady rhythm of my steps. I take the sharp air into my lungs as I make my way through the streets, across market square, and past the bell tower, the bell tower where her lips met mine, her fingers dug into my hair, and her body pressed itself against mine.

Walking past Kate's Diner, my eyes drift up to Gwen's window, no idea why. Maybe because I'm sorry. Maybe because I want her face to appear behind the glass and to smile at me because neither of us is doing all that great (for the same reason), and she understands me. I notice a faint light behind the curtains, and it occurs to me that she hasn't been able to sleep too well for a long time, either.

I keep on going, walking past Will's vintage movie theater and on until I reach Buttermilk Mountain Avenue and head left. At the end of the street, the asphalt beneath the cover of snow turns to earth. I leave the last few houses behind me and take the somewhat steep, faintly lit path past the woods and up Buttermilk Mountain. Shortly before the gondola, I break right and take the narrow path through the trees. Most of the time this path is flat and well-trod, but tonight it's like wading through a blanket of snow. In seconds my jeans are soaked.

I reach the last tree; it's huge and ancient. Its bare branches are covered with white. And behind it, frozen and beautiful, surrounded by rocks and fir trees, the glittering surface of Silver Lake. At the horizon line, Buttermilk Mountain towers into the azure-colored, star-studded sky, even though it's just finished snowing. But that's how it is here in the Rockies; it's magical and special, and the stars like to have a look. In Aspen they feel the essence of their beauty.

Exhaling and turning toward the tree next to me, a white cloud appears before my face. It's dark, and for a moment I have to squint and feel around with my numb fingers before finding what I'm looking for.

A + W.

Her initial first because, for me, she'll always come first. Next to it a misshapen heart that I carved into the bark. My eyes stare at these two letters for so long that, at some point, the bark becomes a single brown spot while everything else around me disappears.

"Wyatt."

I spin around. The trunk scrapes my jacket. Standing in front of me, face half hidden in the dark of the trees, the other illuminated by the stars, is Gwen.

"You scared me," I say, a hand on the left side of my chest, which is rising and falling at a clip. "What are *you* doing here?"

"I could ask you the same."

Shrugging I lean back against the tree. "Couldn't sleep."

"And that's why you were peeping into my window?"

"You saw that?"

"Yeah."

"Oh." I run an embarrassed hand down my neck. "I wasn't stalking you or anything, if that's what you think."

"All good." She pauses before adding, "I didn't know you were here. I mean, just in case you think that...umm..."

"You followed me?" I grin.

She nods. Between the wide stitches of her handmade scarf, I can see her blushing.

"I don't know if I should believe you." With a rough laugh, I push off from the trunk, walk past her, and sit down on a sharp-edged rock overlooking the lake.

"You would if you knew how often I came here at night." She comes over, sits down next to me, and puts her vintage backpack between her legs. With prickly fingers I attempt to undo the laces of my Timberlands and nod at her bag with my chin. "Midnight picnic out on the ice? Great idea. You got sandwiches with you? I'm starving."

Gwen smiles as she unzips her bag, reaches inside, and pulls out her skates, which are so much nicer and more elegant than mine. "Not quite, Lopez."

She says it nonchalantly, with an amused tone, but her smile is delicate, and her jaw is tense as she laces up.

"Gwen. Everything all right?"

She casts me a glance out of the corner of her eye. "Yeah, super."

"Doesn't look like it."

"Wow. Charming, Wyatt, thanks. You look like shit yourself."

I laugh out loud, which at least causes her to grin before our glances meet and my laugh is carried off by the wind.

"So, what's up?"

Her eyes bore into mine for two seconds, three, four, five, and I realize that she's unsure about talking with me about it. Gwen's always been this way. A little like a Labrador that turned into a person. She's nice to everyone and always in a good mood, sometimes a bit too much to be able to hide what's bothering her.

She tightens the bow of her laces with a firm jerk, exhales, and puts her palms down to the ice-cold stone, eyes resting on the glimmering surface of Silver Lake.

"iSkate is considering sending me back to my old club in Breckenridge."

"Shit. Shit, Gwen."

She pulls in her lower lip and flares her nostrils. "I was never good enough, you know? Good, but not good *enough*. Always second place. Started back in elementary school. You remember Mrs. Letterham's theater group? In fourth grade we did *Beauty and the Beast*, and I really wanted to be Belle. But who did I end up playing?"

I remember. Gwen went up and down the halls with the text in her hand for weeks.

"Chip. But you were so good! You always managed that," I stand halfway up, my blades in the snow, and make circles with my waist, "skillful twist of your paper cup. Really aesthetic."

"Ha ha." She pushes my hip to the side, and I plop back onto the rock. She rolls her eyes. "Then in high school I fought for that damn scholarship to UCLA with everything I had."

I remember that, too.

"Penelope Graham got it."

Her eyes grow dark as I say the name.

"Penelope," she repeats, her eyes narrowed into slits. "A whole year long I went on hikes through the Highlands with Aspen's nursing-home residents, and what did she do?" Gwen spins around to face me so quickly that I tumble back onto my rock one more time. "She volunteered at the ski rental place. At the *ski rental*, Wyatt!"

"Well, come on, to be fair, Penelope was always a *terrible* overachiever, Gwen. She deserved it." When I see her face collapse, I quickly add, "But you should be glad you didn't get that scholarship. Otherwise you wouldn't be in Aspen, right?"

She doesn't respond; she just stares at me before shrugging and turning away. "And then there's the thing between you and Aria," she whispers.

All at once I grow so cold, my limbs so stiff, that I could swear I was morphing into the stone. "Gwen…" I struggle to find the words to comfort her, to soothe her, but I realize there aren't any. She *was* my second choice. Not just that, but my unintentional second choice because I had no idea what I was doing, and Aria was always my number one. If I hadn't been fucked up, I would never, *never* have touched Gwen. And she seems to know it because she goes on without waiting for an answer.

"When I got to iSkate, I thought I'd finally made it. That I *finally* belonged to the figure-skating elite. And now they don't want me anymore."

"But that doesn't make any sense." My eyes drift to the sky and focus on the tip of Buttermilk Mountain. It looks like someone's painted it with white paint. "You're so *good*. Harper is crap compared to you."

Gwen casts me a sympathetic smile, but it just looks like she's in pain. "Harper's family's got money. They donate a huge amount to iSkate every year. They'd never give her the boot." She takes a shaky breath. "Paisley's my best friend; she's an extraordinary talent. I wish her all the best, really, from my heart, and I know she's going to make it. But…" Her expression grows tortured. "Does the fact that I am extremely jealous make me a monster?"

A screech pierces the night as a snow owl whisks across the frozen lake.

"No," I say after a while. "Before Pais showed up, you were the star of iSkate. It's human to feel something like that, Gwen."

She takes a deep breath, then drops her head and nods. "That's why I come here at night. I want to train more than everyone else."

"Is there any chance you'll be able to stay?"

A sharp gust of wind blows a blast of snow into our faces.

Gwen wraps her arms around her chest. "Yeah. They've given me the opportunity to skate with a partner. That'd be okay; I mean, the only pair they have is Levi and Aaron, no mixed ones. But, well…That's it. If I stay on my own, I'm out." She looks at me, her mouth twisted. "Sorry. Here I am going on and on; I know you're not doing so hot yourself."

"I'm good."

She tilts her head. "Aria?"

"Sure, there's Aria. There's always Aria." I knock my knee against Gwen's. "What'd be so bad about pair skating?"

A shadow flits across her face. "Nothing. It's just… I don't think I could trust anyone enough."

Her words hover between us for a while before I stand up with a smile and offer her my hand. "It's easy. Come on, I'll show you."

Her eyes grow wide. "*The two of us?*"

"With all due respect, ma'am, I'm a hockey player. I can do this thing with skates and ice, you know?"

Gwen laughs. Her eyes zip to my hand, and she only pauses for a second before grabbing it and letting me help her up. "Well, all right, Lopez. Seeing as it's you."

I go first. I test the ice with my blade to see if it's thick enough before pulling my other leg after me, turning and skating backward out onto the ice, nodding.

She follows. The moment she takes her first step out on the ice, I see her face begin to glow. She stretches her arms out for balance and moves so elegantly, so fluidly, that you could be forgiven for thinking the skates were an extension of her body. In the middle of the lake, she stretches her leg, pulls it up, and bends into an elegant spin. With Buttermilk Mountain in the background and the stars in the sky, it's such an overwhelming image that I take my phone out of my pocket and snap a photo. Not for me. I want to send it to her later so that she never stops believing in herself.

When she comes back up, I stuff my phone back into my jeans, skate over, and move in a half-circle around her. "Okay, Pierce, what are we going to do?"

Moving backward, she skates past me. "Well, what can you do, Lopez?"

Laughing, I spin around my own axis. Not as quick as her, or as elegant, but all the same. Gwen's face is wobbling when I come to a stop and try to focus. "I can do everything."

"I'd forgotten how narcissistic you were, sheesh."

"Hello? You wanna let this broken, bitter guy be proud of what he can still do for a sec?"

Gwen makes a jump whose name I don't know and shoots me a quick side-eye. "I think you see yourself differently from what you actually are."

"Naw." I skate past her, turn around, and look at her. "I *am* broken and bitter, my love."

"No, you're not, Wyatt. You've had a spill, yeah, but you've been doing that your whole life. And did it ever stop you? No. You got back up and kept on going. Maybe you've forgotten how that goes, but you'll get there."

My eyes watch her blades make a fine white line in the ice. "And if I don't?"

Gwen kicks my skate to get me to look up. "Well, I'll be standing next to you to give you my hand. Because we're friends, and friends do that for each other, right?"

"Yeah." With a grin, I give her a soft punch in the shoulder.

"That's what friends do." For a fraction of a second all that's between us is the stillness of the night, then I grab Gwen's hand and quickly pull her behind me across the ice.

"Wyatt!" she gasps. "Wyatt, let go of me! I can't do this turn in two!"

"I'll show you how it goes!"

"How *what* goes?"

"That thing with trust."

I glide confidently and quickly over the ice, while her yell gets louder and louder, but she's laughing; she's laughing *so loud*! Well, at least I can get my friends to laugh, if not myself or the greater part of my heart that's called Aria Moore.

21

But If the World Was Ending You'd Come Over, Right?

ARIA

I'M SLIPPING INTO MY GRAY WOOL SWEATER WHEN MY phone vibrates. A text from Paxton. He's sent a picture. I hastily dig a scrunchie out of the drawer of my bathroom cabinet, put my hair up in a loose bun, and reach for my phone before leaving the bathroom.

Clicking on our chat and enlarging the image, I see a nighttime shot of Silver Lake, ringed by snow, dazzling with thousands of stars.

Oooh, I write and add a smiling face with heart eyes as well as the astonished face emoji. Were you there?

He comes online and writes... Yesterday. And then, But it would have been nicer with you. 🙁

I read his message a hundred times with a huge smile on my face; maybe it was even two hundred times, who knows? In any event, I'm so distracted that I miss the first stair. My heart leaps in fright, and I clutch at the railing. The phone slips out of my hands, my legs buckle, and as I lose my balance, my hand slips off, too. I fall to the side and start tumbling down the steps, a strange situation, because, somehow, I don't notice any of it even though it's happening to me. It all happens so quickly; I can't even think. I just fall, as per my usual, and then suddenly chair legs are scraping across the wooden floorboards in the dining area, there's a collective gasp, children crying, and…Wyatt. He's kneeling in front of me, lips parted, skin soft, and I want to touch it, reach out and stroke it. I don't know why. Maybe I've got a concussion; maybe I'm just disturbed or something in between. I mean, we all know I go all stupid whenever Wyatt's around.

"Everything okay?"

I can't believe it. *Everything okay?* Are you kidding me? Like, how is that even possible? What a joke. What an absolute *joke*. Responding doesn't make any sense. Having said that, what really *does* make a lot of sense at the moment, what seems downright essential, to be honest, is reaching out and touching his face, right here, right now, in front of the guests and a screaming kid.

I run my thumb down Wyatt's face, palm his jaw… His ex-girlfriend's hand is caressing him everywhere, wonderful, totally normal, absolutely. Wyatt flinches as if I'd burned him. Who knows, maybe I did. I mean, that's what it feels like every time we look at each other, every time we share a breath. But he doesn't retreat because it's a good kind of burning, painful maybe, destructive, but too beautiful and too bright and too wonderful to look away.

He swallows. Two times, in fact, because, even though it's nothing, it's all too much.

"Did you hurt yourself, Aria?"

God, how much this voice frazzles me! It's healing; it's so warm, so raw, so absolutely not normal at all. The two of us form a closed unity here at the bottom of the stairs. Everything around us is blurry because we're living in a fifty-millimeter camera lens, both of us in focus, while everything else is not.

It's like we're standing at different ends of a long speaking tube. His words reach me with a lag, one after the other, and I really have to concentrate to understand them because I'm looking straight into those golden-brown eyes I want to disappear into.

"Did I…umm…hurt myself? Yeah. Yeah, I think so."

"Where?"

I slowly let my hand slide off his face and point to the left side of my chest.

Wyatt looks at it before looking back at me. "Did you fall on it?" I shake my head. "My heart."

"Yeah." His forehead is creased, his lids are heavy, and his lashes are thick. "Mine, too."

What's going on? I must have hit my head. I'm starting to feel sick, a little woozy; it's like I've had something to drink, but all I did was look at my phone because Paxton... Oh my God, Paxton. There's a Paxton that you wanted to get to know, that you were starting to adore, Aria. WHAT THE HELL ARE YOU DOING?

"No, all's good, really."

Wyatt's wrapped his wide arms around me and helped me up to keep me from falling. But then all of a sudden he wheezes and lets go, at least with one arm. The kid is still screaming and pointing at me, which is really getting on my nerves. I mean, I'm not dead or anything, just hanging off my ex-boyfriend's arm. What's weird about that?

Then Wyatt carefully puts me down and kneels, and all I can think is, *Wow, is he about to propose or something?* Then I realize I've got to be out of my mind.

He takes the edge of my sweater between his fingers. "May I?"

May I? Back in the day, taking off our clothes was something we did a million times; we could even do it in our sleep, but now everything is different. Nothing of that is left; now it's a *may I?*

I nod, although I want to say no.

Then I say, "Yeah," while shaking my head no.

YEAH-NO-I-DON'T-KNOW. I'm confused, no doubt about it, totally and completely confused.

Wyatt laughs. But it's not a real laugh. It's more like he's just blowing air out of his nose. His fingertips are resting on the skin of my hip as he continues to rub the edge of my sweater. Aware of the fact that our guests are still staring at us, I suddenly become totally uncomfortable, hanging around at the bottom of the stairs like a stranded walrus or something, half in Wyatt's arms, half on the steps.

Be an adult, Aria. At some point Wyatt can't be anything but a friend. Just a friend you share a past with. Let it happen. Accept what it is if you want it to stop.

I take a deep breath, then nod. His touch doesn't feel friendly. It doesn't feel harmless, although he hasn't done anything but lift up my sweater a tiny bit. He's only revealed a *tiny bit* of skin, but I feel like I'm standing in front of him naked.

"What is it?"

"This doesn't look good."

"What do you mean? What's up?"

But before I can get a look myself, he picks me up and presses my body to his; my thigh is against his hip as if I were a baby, as if I weighed nothing, as if I were so light you could carry me just like that. He effortlessly takes the stairs two at a time.

"Where are you taking me?"

He grins. "Don't worry. I'm not kidnapping you."

"Oh, *Wyatt.* I mean, your chances would be so *great* here in my house."

"Yeah, I'm a little disappointed in myself."

We reach the end of the stairs and come onto the landing. My shoes scuff the wooden baseboard. Wyatt looks to the right for a second, as if considering putting me on the old bench at the end of the hall. But then he goes to the left and stops in front of his door. When he starts moving to get the key, I start to panic. I don't want to go inside. I mean, it's number twelve, and that hurts, even though I know it's just a room. But, at the moment, I can't handle any kind of symbolic memories.

"No!" I call out before he can put the key in the door. I start to fidget until he puts me down. "Not in there."

A shadow of hurt flits across Wyatt's face. "Aria, I'm not going to fall on top of you or anything. I mean, sure, if you want me to, but, come on, you're hurt, and you should lie down so that…"

"Let's go to my room."

"Your room?"

"Yeah."

His eyes glide from me down the corridor to the connecting door to our private area. I can feel his muscles grow tense. And I know it's stupid. I know my room will trigger more memories in me than this one does. But just now I wasn't thinking; my panicked mind went into SOS mode and chose the first alternative it could think of.

"It's okay," I say to cover up the fact that I'm about to collapse out of fear and pain. I look away because if I don't, I won't be able to breathe. But when I reach the door, Wyatt's still rooted to his spot. "It's just a room, Wyatt."

He swallows and balls his hands into fists at his sides. Then he shakes them out, as if taking the next few steps was like making it past a wall of hockey players.

But then he starts to move. Not as self-assured as usual, a little hesitant, maybe even nervous. I mean, this is a big deal. For both of us.

We silently walk down the hall, next to each other, until we get to the end and are in front of the ladder up to my room. I've always loved this part of the B&B; it's like it was my own tree house or something. But ever since it's been impossible for Mom to make it up to my room because of her pain, I've hated this ladder. I miss the days she'd randomly come up to see me, what seemed like hundreds of times a day, just to chat. Of course, now that I think about it, she'd always clean up a bit, throwing away old banana skins and Pop-Tarts that I'd forgotten in my wardrobe and putting away scattered pieces of clothing.

She doesn't do any of that anymore. She can't. And now that I think about it, I have absolutely no idea how many Pop-Tarts are rotting in my wardrobe at the moment.

I step to the side and wave my hand at Wyatt to tell him to go first. He looks disappointed, and I'm pretty sure I know why.

You wish, Lopez.

He begins to climb. I curse myself for standing here and staring at his firm ass in those black skinny jeans, and he *knows* that I am because he knows me, the idiot.

He glances over his shoulder and grins. "How *unfair*, Moore."

I blush. Until he's upstairs, I stare at Mom's golden ladle, the one she got at a soup cook-off one year that has been hanging like a medal on the wall next to the kitchen door ever since. Then I climb up after him and manage to bang my head against his legs when attempting to pull myself up.

But Wyatt's just standing there like a tin soldier, his face rigid, his body tense. Only his eyes are moving. They are literally racing all over the place, up, down, right, left, scanning every millimeter of my room.

I manage another step on the ladder before a stabbing pain shoots through my body. Wyatt bends over me, puts his hands under my arms, and lifts me up into my room.

I make a face as the edge of the floor grazes my hip. He quickly steps to the side, helps me up, and leads me to my bed.

"It's not that bad," I mumble, lying down and rolling onto my good side. "I'll be okay in no time."

Wyatt goes to the bathroom. I can hear him opening various drawers, then a cabinet, before coming back with disinfectant, tweezers, and cotton pads.

He clears his throat. "Nothing's changed."

I think, *What on earth are you saying? You blind? We've both changed, Wyatt!*

"Well, you know my OCD."

"Yeah." With slightly trembling fingers, he lifts my sweater up a bit higher to see the full extent of my trip down the stairs. "If the disinfectant hadn't been at the bottom of the cabinet anymore, I'd have been worried."

I rest my cheek on my hand and focus on the window. "Damn straight. Anything else would likely be the work of a demon or something."

Wyatt takes the tweezers to look for splinters. He pulls one out. "You always say that."

"What?"

"That thing about demons." Another splinter. "I have no idea what that's all about. Every time something doesn't go right or isn't normal somehow, you say it's got to do with demons."

"That's not true."

"It is." He puts the tweezers down, unscrews the lid of the disinfectant, and pours some onto the cotton pad. "When Will fell asleep three years ago and opened The Old-Timer late, you were convinced he was possessed."

The skin of my hand tickles as I smile. "Cause that wasn't normal!"

"You bought an exorcism set from some dude online, Ari." Warmth envelops my shoulders as he places his large hand on them, leans his head forward, and looks down at me. "This is going to burn a bit, okay?"

"Okay."

He runs the cotton across my ribs, and I take a sharp breath. Holy shit, it really does burn. I kick my feet, crumple the sheet with my fingers, press my eyes and teeth together, and stifle a cry.

"It'll be better in a sec." Wyatt's voice is soft and comforting. He hesitantly puts his thumbs to my temples and begins to make circles. "Everything's going to be okay."

He repeats his words in a whisper, and though I know he's referring to the wound, lying there, my eyes closed, his hand on my head, his lips close to my ear, I can't help but think he means us.

What a bittersweet illusion. Us. Some things are so broken they can't be repaired. Wyatt and I are one of them. The thought tears me out of my fever, this heat that wants to burn me up, feeling his body against mine.

I freeze. And because Wyatt knows me and can read every gesture, every movement, he knows that it's too much. That *he's* too much. His fingertips leave a burning trace on my scalp when he takes his hand away.

He carefully adjusts my sweater. "You're probably going to have some bruising. It'd be a good idea to let it cool."

"Okay."

"Wait till tomorrow to put cream on it. It's still open in a few places."

"Good."

"Really. Wait until tomorrow, Ari."

"I will! Why wouldn't I?"

"I know you. You're the most impatient person on the planet."

"Whatever."

A tense silence spreads out between us. Wyatt knows that it's time to leave, and I know that it's time to tell him to leave. But I don't say anything. Instead, I listen to a series of banging sounds that seem to be coming from the walls, then a scratching noise that goes up to the roof before the banging starts again.

"Got to be a demon," I say.

Wyatt's eyes shoot to the roof. "Those martens."

"Maybe we're a demon, too."

He looks at me. "What?"

"You and me." I turn onto my back and meet his eyes. "We're not normal. An anomaly. Something's not right with the two of us. Maybe we're a demon that's been cut in two, and that's why we can't let each other go."

"I don't want us to be a demon, Aria."

"I think we're the ones who made it, Wyatt."

"I don't." His voice is husky and soft and, damn it, makes me break out in goose bumps again. When he reaches out to run the tip of his index finger across my collarbone, I hold my breath. In the bright light coming through the window, I can see the hungry look in his eyes. "But even if we were, it's not a big deal. Want to know why?"

"Why?" I whisper.

His index finger moves farther, exploring my jaw, my lips, and then back down my throat again. "Because demons are fallen angels. We were good once, you and me, and we could be again."

I gasp. "Wyatt."

His face moves closer. He looks at me, his gaze lowered, his next word only a whisper. "Yeah?"

My eyelids are flickering. "What are you doing?"

"I don't know." His lips brush mine, wandering farther down as his hand disappears under my sweater and moves across my good side up to my breasts. "We'll find out."

His fingers hook into the cups of my bra. As he slowly pulls down the fabric to stroke my nipple with tip of his thumb, I let out a heavy breath. Instinctively, I dig my hands into the linen. My breath starts to come more quickly. "Wyatt…"

"Huh?"

"God."

"I know."

He leans over me. I feel his breath on my skin just a few seconds before he takes my nipple into his mouth. I toss my head back, close my eyes, and fight against the storm of thoughts in my head that are telling me to put a stop to this while at the same time telling me not to stop it WHATSOEVER.

"I've missed this," Wyatt whispers. "Doing something just for you, something that you really want."

The tips of my ponytail brush the back of my hand as I tilt my head and, between deep breaths, look at him.

"We can't... This... I mean..."

"Tell me to stop, and I'll stop immediately, Moore." His lips kiss a warm path down my ribs before they begin to nibble at the button of my jeans.

"You... Us..."

His hoarse laughter spreads across my skin. "Personal pronouns don't count, Ari."

It's really easy. Just two words and he'll go. Why can't I just say them?

The answer is simple and heavy, undeniable and obvious. Because I don't want to.

Wyatt's mouth moves off my skin. He looks at me while he clasps the waistband of my jeans with both hands, a silent question in his eyes, and I curse myself, curse myself so hard for wanting this, for the fact that my limbs are trembling with desire, for the fact that I'm looking at him and thinking how special this moment is, every touch.

"Lie down," he says, softly, affectionately, just like before. I feel like I'm starting to get a fever. As I let myself fall, I can feel the comforter very clearly against my skin; every single centimeter of it is extremely sensitive.

Wyatt peels my jeans off my legs really slowly. I look at the ceiling, concentrate on the wooden beams, and think about everything in the world just to avoid thinking about how much I like this, how much I need it.

His thumbs run across the lower part of my stomach, moving beneath my panties just a bit. I can feel my pulse beating against his palm, quick, intense, and full of anticipation.

Then his fingers move again, brushing across my panties, right where it's starting to grow moist. Noticing, he breathes in sharply before moaning softly. "And I've missed this, too, Ari."

I dig my fingers into the bed even more and stifle a moan. He's not even really touching me, just the fabric of my panties, and yet

I'm about to lose my mind. Agonizingly slowly, two of his fingers hook into the sides of my underwear and pull them down. When he sees me bare before him, he moans again and moves closer. I can feel his breath on my naked skin. "Just say the word, and I'll stop."

"Not on your life." My breathing grows slow. Everything in me wants this. Squirming with desire, I drive my hips forward, and before I can even think of anything else, his lips move onto my clit.

I explode. It's hot, overwhelming. It's so intense I even manage to ignore the pain I've felt in my ribs up until now. At the moment, I don't feel a thing there. All I feel is Wyatt.

Wyatt, moving his mouth skillfully across the middle of my body. With a moan, I dig my fingers into his hair, looking for something to hold onto because I can barely handle how good this all feels, how *right*. My body reacts to his caresses, making my thighs shudder as his tongue electrifies my nerves and makes me quiver.

"Show me," he whispers. "Show me how badly you want this, Moore."

Everything in me contracts. My leg muscles are trembling with tension as all my desire collects in the middle of my body and starts to pulsate more and more intensely until I hardly have myself under control at all and am cursing, moaning, and begging for *more, more, more.* He bathes the middle of my body with soft kisses, and the sound melts into the excited noises gliding off his lips. It's mesmerizing, and then I feel his warm mouth at the opening to my body, and his tongue slides into me, moving to the rhythm of my thrusts. All of a sudden, I see colored lights, the world tilts on its axis, or maybe it's just my bed, maybe it's just me. In any event, everything grows blurry. And as his lips tenderly suck at me, the waves of desire reach their apex. I can't hold back anymore, and with a loud groan I come against Wyatt's mouth.

My muscles relax. Only vaguely do I check his fingers moving away from my panties and moving the fabric back into place. Breathing heavily, I stare at the ceiling as what just happened slowly becomes clear to me.

Just like that. Completely unplanned. Out of the blue.

Then his broad stature appears in my field of vision as he lies down next to me, turns his head, and grins. "Just like before, huh?"

Better, Wyatt. Better.

The blanket rustles as I turn to look at him.

He reaches out a hand and runs a finger down my nose. "We could have this all the time, Ari."

No. No, we couldn't. Because things aren't like what they were anymore. Things happened that put everything in the shade and ensured that something like what *just* happened should *never* have happened.

I close my eyes for a moment and wipe my hand across my face. "No."

He blinks. His grin disappears to be replaced by a look of uncertainty. "No?"

"Things between us, things... No."

He blinks again as he slowly realizes what I'm telling him. Sitting up, he lets out a dry, joyless laugh.

"Got it. What just happened is okay, but nothing else?"

I put my hands behind my head and take a deep breath. "No. That...shouldn't have happened. I was... I couldn't..."

"Resist." He snorts. "I got it, Moore. Things between us are over. No big deal. I'm cool with that."

His words are like a fist to my stomach, which is paradoxical, because that's exactly what I wanted; that's precisely why I'm, well, rejecting him. But that's not what it feels like. It doesn't feel right.

Wyatt looks at me for a long time. Then he reaches into his pocket and hands me my phone, which I'd lost on the steps. The chat with Paxton is still open. Suddenly I fall, quick, deep, and ruthlessly, and it hurts so bad because he can see that I'm moving on without him and thinks that I *can*. My chest tightens as I take my phone with trembling fingers.

"That's Paxton," I say unnecessarily, as Wyatt can read and it's right there on the display. *PAXTON*. "We, umm, well… We're getting to know each other, and I…like him, you know?"

I don't know *what* kind of reaction I expected, but I definitely didn't expect Wyatt's face to light up and for that glimmer that used to be there when we were a couple to appear in his eyes.

Then it happens. At the very moment I look at him and understand that he *wants* the relationship to happen. He *wants* me to meet someone else. I feel like I've just been punched in the chest by a steel fist, which aggressively and mercilessly shreds my heart (or what's left of it) of everything I've built up to protect it.

"Nice," he says, cool and relieved, as if the mountain of stupid concerns regarding his ex-girlfriend that are only there when you've hurt her had finally been lifted off his shoulders. "*Nice*, Aria. Good to hear. I mean, Paxton, wow. Cool dude, good hockey player."

His cheerfulness kills me. It's terrible. Just now I thought he really wanted me, and *I* was the one rejecting *him* (even though I didn't really want him to turn away from me, of course). But now he is. Suddenly I am fourteen again, opening up my locker and hoping to find his yellow Post-its telling me strange and charming things like how my freckles embody the beauty of concentrated melanized cells, weird stuff like that. But there aren't any Post-its anymore; my locker's just empty.

Wyatt is almost at the ladder when his eyes come to rest on my bookshelf, and he pauses. He moves closer, reading the spines of my college books, then takes one. He slowly turns it over, reads the jacket, and leafs through the pages with a look on his face as if that was precisely what he'd been looking for.

"Can I borrow this?" He turns to me, holding up the book. Yellow letters, blue background. *Myofascial Relief Therapy*. "Umm, just for a few days?"

I nod. I'm not really able to do anything else right now because I still have to process the fact that he wants this book more than me, that he wants *every*thing more than me, and that just sucks because I don't want to have to process that at all. He cheated on me. I want to hate him and to not care about him anymore. I want everything to be gone, just gone. No Wyatt.

He smiles. "Cool. Thanks."

Thanks. Like everything was cool. *Thanks.* I want to tell him to get out. *Get out, you stylish asshole, in your skinny jeans and your Timberlands, and leave the book behind, my friend.* You piss me off. My God, how much you piss me off.

But I just lie back down instead, smile, and say, "No problem."

No problem. As if there wasn't one. But honestly? Wyatt and me, we're not a problem personified; we're A PERFECT CATASTROPHE.

22

Love When It's Easy, Love Harder When It's Not

WYATT

MY BRAIN IS PULSATING. I THINK EVEN MY SKULL IS vibrating. It's *extremely* painful, but I'm convinced that it will help.

I'm lying on the floor of our room, leaning all my weight against a tennis ball. It's pressing directly against a trigger point of my levator scapulae. Aria's book says that you have to do it this way to loosen the nodules that have formed in the muscles, as that's what's behind your pain and limited movement.

Now I know that my flashbacks aren't due to the injury but through being touched by others. Probably some kind of disturbance in my subconscious or something. I mean, someone could find out what *really* happened last summer.

The door opens and Camila comes in. She looks down at me expressionlessly before walking past and throwing her backpack onto the bed. "I didn't know you were learning about the *Kama Sutra*."

"Funny. I'm healing myself."

Camila side-eyes me with a raised eyebrow while digging her Spanish book, notebook, and pencil case out of her bag. "Are you so undersexed that you're expanding your meditative dreams to include what-if sexercises in order to feel better?"

"Man, no." Turning onto my side to look at her, the tennis ball rolls off. "Things didn't work out with those PT folks. I've got to take care of it myself."

"Ah." Her eyes follow the ball and dart to the book on the ground. "That Aria's?"

"Yep." I stand up and begin to stretch in the doorframe. The pain is so bad that little black dots appear, and my neck breaks out in sweat. *Keep up, Wyatt, keep up. Ninety seconds, the book says.*

"I was in her room."

"Wait, what? When?"

At last, I'm done. I exhale but have to close my eyes a second to collect myself. "Earlier this morning. She fell down the steps."

"Oh! Is she okay?"

"Yeah."

My phone starts to vibrate. Both of us look to the ground, where it's lying next to the book.

"You've got a new message from Aria, *Paxton*. I can't believe you're doing this."

"Worry about your own shit."

Camila shrugs and lies down on her stomach to start her homework. "What'd she write?"

"That you stink."

"I know."

Still wheezy, whether from the stretching or seeing Aria's name on display, I open her text. Is this the right person for professional kiss-it-and-make-it-feel-better services?

Grinning, I type, Yeah. But I'm booked out. Special appointments for straight-up kisses only at the moment.

Where?

My grin grows wider. Depends how hurt you are. For little things I accept kisses on the cheek, for bigger ones it's got to be on the lips.

A brief pause, then… It's really big.

I'll be right there.

Ha ha. She sends a laughing emoji. You want to talk?

There it is. The question I knew would come sooner or later. I talked with her at the Halloween party, of course, but my voice was distorted.

"Mila." With a sweeping movement I toss myself onto the bed next to her and put my good arm around her waist. "Intelligent, non-stinky sister who I love more than anything else in the world…"

She jerks her shoulder to get rid of my arm. "What do you want?"

"You've got to help me."

"No."

"Is there an app that'll distort my voice?"

"Great idea, Wy. Go all Darth Vader again. Like the lobster didn't freak her out enough."

"Please."

"Just do a google search."

"I don't know the name of an app that really works." Before she can start writing again, I shove my head onto her notebook and flutter my eyelashes. "Por favor, maninha."

That gets her every time. She sits up and crosses her arms. "Why do you think I'd know something like that?"

"You and your friends do it all the time. I know it. Calling up dudes you all like and hanging up. Calling up dudes you like and acting like the pizza they ordered is going to be late. Calling up dudes…"

"WYATT!" She throws her pencil case against my head. "Come on, man, shit. Give me your phone."

Wriggling my eyebrows, I hand it to her. She types around for a few minutes before holding it back out to me under my nose.

"Here. Say something."

"What."

My phone repeats it back in a deep, manly voice.

"Too creepy. Sounds like a mob boss from the seventies."

"Okay, umm… Try this one. It's Justin Bieber. Hold up… Here."

"Hello."

She's right. My phone repeats my words in the singer's voice. I look at Camila. "All good, right?"

"Totally."

"And that's automatically connected to my phone's mic now?"

"Yep. I set it."

"You're the best, sis." My fingertips are tingling as I stand up and go to sit on my own bed. It's only been a few hours since I last spoke with Aria, and she's in the same house, but this is something different. She doesn't know that it's me, and somehow that means that we're going to have a second getting-to-know-each-other and honeymoon phase.

My sister sticks in her earbuds as I start to type Aria's number. Her phone rings three times before her timid voice responds. "Hello?"

"Hey."

"Hey."

"Hello."

I laugh. "Quite the poem."

"What?"

"You're a poet."

"Oh." Aria chuckles. "Not really. I mean, I never was any good at that kind of thing."

"I know." The words have barely left my lips when I realize the mistake. Damn. Aria doesn't say anything.

"I mean, of course I didn't really know it. I just mean, well…" Sitting cross-legged, I rock back and forth like a hyperactive five-year-old until Camila casts me an annoyed glance, and I stop.

"Okay," she says.

"You sound sad."

"Oh, really?" There's a rustling in the background. She must be lying in bed. "Sorry."

"What? No! You don't need to apologize for that." When she doesn't respond, I add, "What's up?"

After a long pause, she says, "Let's talk about something else, Paxton."

Paxton. *Argh.* I'd almost forgotten that the two of us aren't really the two of us at the moment.

"Why?"

She gives a dry laugh that sounds anything but happy. "I doubt you want to hear about my ex."

I turn onto my side and run my finger over the flowers on the comforter. "You can tell me."

"Why?"

Yeah, why are you interested, *Paxton*, you idiot?

"It seems to be weighing you down, and I want you to be able to talk about things with me."

"But it's dumb."

"Bullshit."

"No, for real. You're going to think, *Man, she's dumb*, and then you won't want to have anything to do with me."

"I swear that that's not going to happen."

Aria sighs. "Well, fine. We broke up because he cheated on me and I should hate him for it and not feel the slightest thing for him anymore, but…"

"But?" My heart begins to race. *Hoooly shit*, just one little word, *but*, and I'm about to implode.

Aria exhales. "But the fact that I am utterly unimportant to him just kills me."

My excitement bursts like a balloon that's too big and miserably sinks to the ground.

"I'm sure you're not unimportant to him," I say a bit too energetically. "Why would you think that?"

Okay, this convo is going in the wrong direction. I mean, what does this sound like? I'm Paxton, her new lover boy, and yet here I am trying to defend her ex—I mean, myself. That's not how these things usually go.

"He knows about us. And it doesn't bother him. He even finds it good. God, I'm so dumb, for real. I can't believe I'm telling you this. I mean, you've got to think I'm totally weird."

I lean back into my pillows and look at the ceiling. "No. We need time to get over people; it's normal. I mean, you two were together for six years and all."

Whoops. There's no way I can know that, either. Man. I close my eyes and press my fingertips into my eyelids.

It feels like an eternity before Aria replies warily, "Did I tell you that?"

I can feel the adrenaline shoot through me. Think, Wyatt, think!

"Umm, no. Sorry. When you're on the same team, you kind of end up hearing about those kinds of things."

"Oh, right." She seems relieved. "I was gonna say."

"What?"

"No idea. That you're a stalker or something."

"Naw." A scratchy sound fills the room as I start to run my fingernails across the comforter. "Listen. I, umm, know… I know that Wyatt isn't over you. Not in the least. I mean, *not at all*. The thing between you and me probably just overwhelmed him, and to cover that, he just acted like everything was cool."

Aria's faltering breaths come through the phone, but, strangely, I can't seem to get enough and press the phone even closer to my ear. *Breathe, breathe, breathe. This is your weirdo ex, and he needs to hear it because he's simply addicted.*

"I don't know…"

"For sure! He was even crying the last time I saw him."

I can't sink any lower. A true sign of how desperately I'm trying not to lose this woman.

"*Crying?* In front of you all? I don't believe it."

Yeah, because you know me and know I'd never do something like that.

Before I can think of a way to get out of this, she takes a deep breath and says, "Why are you even telling me this? It feels like you're trying to make him look good, but why? I mean, you want to get to know me, right?"

"Umm…"

"Is this some kind of fucked-up thing between you and Wyatt to screw with me or something?"

"Wha… No! God, Aria, no, fuck, sorry. I don't know; I got the feeling you weren't quite ready to let him go. And because I don't want to let you go either, I wanted to be there for you, even if it takes another ten years for you to be ready. But I'd be there, you know what I mean? And I will have been by your side all that time, and, umm, no idea, I just want you to be able to trust me and to like me and for me to be the one you talk to when you're not doing that well."

There's a long, torturous pause where all I can hear are Aria's deep breaths and Camila's music wafting over to me from her earbuds in the background.

Eventually Aria gives a bemused grunt. "You're really weird."

"Well, umm, *hello?* I mean, come on, you're talking with a *lobster*, after all. What do you expect?"

And finally she laughs. A sweet, crystal-clear sound that digs into my heart and makes my stomach go weird. With a smile on my lips, I close my eyes to take the sound in and hold onto it tight.

"What are you up to today?"

"Dunno." I can hear her moving around on her bed. A few seconds later, the floor creaks. She must be walking through her room. "There's a movie showing at The Old-Timer that I'd like to see, but my bestie is visiting her brother in Vermont for a few days, and I don't want to go on my own."

"Don't you have any other friends?" As soon as the words are out of my mouth, I realize how dumb they were. I know that she has friends; that's why it sounds so mean. "I mean, even if you didn't, that wouldn't be a big deal."

From the sound of her voice, I can tell that she's grinning. "It's all good, Pax. I've got friends. But Harper's the only one who can go out with me and at the same time worry about whether I'm feeling okay or not. When I'm with the others, Knox and Paisley… They're so happy in love, you know what I mean? Not that that pisses me off or anything. It just makes me get kind of down because I had that once myself and…I miss it."

Oh man… Her words are a weapon of mass destruction for my heart. It's bleeding. It's completely bleeding out, and that hurts, damn it.

"I've got to split," I say, as I can feel a lump in my throat and that kind of shimmer in front of my eyes that's telling me that lump is going to change into tears. And because I don't want that, especially not in front of my sister, I've got to cut this off right here. "Sorry, I'm in a hotel for an away game, and the guys are waiting for me. I'll be in touch later. See you."

"Ah, okay, see—"

I cut her off by hanging up. My heart is racing. I blink a few times, swallow, blink again, and wonder why my luck sucks so bad.

Camila pulls her earbuds out and looks at me. "All good, Mr. Bieber?"

"I don't get it."

"What don't you get?"

"Why this is happening to me."

She frowns. "What do you mean?"

I sit up, wipe a hand across my face, and focus on the rug between the two of us. "Why did Mom and Dad have to die? Why wasn't I in control a bit more? I mean, even just a tiny bit? Then there wouldn't have been that night two years ago. I wouldn't have been blasted, wouldn't have taken shit, wouldn't have lost my mind, and wouldn't have slept with Gwen. Aria and I'd still be together. Aria and I would be…Aria and Wyatt. Instead…" My breath quivers as I exhale. "I fucked it all up."

"Wyatt…" My sister pushes her things to the side, sits up, and comes over to me. "Hey, stop that. Stop putting yourself down. It's unhelpful. What happened happened, and that was a mistake. But, Wyatt, what you were going through back then wasn't normal. From one moment to the next, everything fell apart. At first you were just a kid, without any real problems, just finishing high school, and then all of a sudden you were a hundred years older." She raises her hand and counts her fingers. "A little sister around your neck to take care of and no more parents, but without any real life plan either, or any kind of concept for building a future, or, let's be honest, any idea of what to do. Adult stuff, basically. Things you'd never had to deal with before…"

She puts her hand back down and looks me right in the eyes. "You had a breakdown. That's understandable. And, you know, maybe that's what caused a real big fight between you and Aria. I mean, you got the fire ready, but, to be honest? Aria's the one who got it started. She took off. She didn't want to know your reasons even though she *knew* how screwed up you were, even though she *knew* that there might be some kind of backstory to the whole thing that she should know about. That it all went to shit wasn't just up to you, Wy. She's got a role, too. Don't blame yourself for everything, please. You love Aria, and you're fighting for her, and that means that you never really wanted it to end. That you never really wanted to hurt her or fuck up anything to begin with."

Her words are a wrecking ball, and the dam breaks. I press my fingers against my eyelids, but it doesn't help. The tears come quickly and powerfully. My shoulders quake. I don't know when I last cried like this. Probably when my folks died. But not holding it in anymore, not digging into myself anymore, is a relief.

Camila hugs me. She lays her head on my shoulder without saying a word while I sit next to her and cry to keep my heart from drowning.

23

We Drown Under the Waves of Words We Are Not Saying

ARIA

I'M SITTING IN THE KITCHEN SORTING OUT OUR "NO-point" cups when there's a knock at the dividing door. Mom isn't home. She and Will are bringing the horses back to the stable and preparing things for tomorrow's town hall.

I hang Daniel's cup on a hook and go to the door. I open it a crack and see Wyatt, his hands in his pockets and that grin I fell in love with eternities ago on his face.

"Hi," he says.

Just like that. I open the door a little wider and lean against the frame. Although Wyatt has seen me looking like a slob millions of times, my jogging-pants-and-baggy-white-shirt ensemble makes me blush. "Hi."

"You doing better?"

"Yeah." Pause. "I put ointment on my wound."

Wyatt leans forward on the balls of his feet, his grin dimpled wide. "I was sooo certain of that, Moore."

Everything about his movement electrifies me. I break out in goose bumps and Wyatt notices. Of course he does.

I clear my throat. "Well… What do you want?"

Wyatt takes his hands out of his pockets, balls one into a fist, and begins to punch it into his palm in an easy rhythm. "Camila is talking with her girlfriends on the phone."

"And?"

"I'm bored."

I cross my arms. "That's not my problem." But then I realize what day it is and add, "It's Friday night, Wyatt," as if that said enough.

He tilts his head. "No shit, Sherlock."

"No, I mean… Your game is going to be on ESPN. Snowdogs against the Bullhead Bulls."

He beams. "You knew that?"

I shrug and pick at a knot in the wood. "Wanted to take a peek." When I add, "because of Paxton," I cast him a quick glance from the corner of my eye, accompanied by an apathetic expression, even though my heart is beating double time as I wait to see his reaction.

To my surprise, his face darkens. "You're making me want to punch him, you know that, Aria?"

Oh?

"Just like that?"

Wyatt scratches his collarbone. Three red stripes. "If I was out on the ice today, we'd lose because, instead of going after the other team's center, I'd be going after Paxton."

His words undo a knot in my chest, and within a few seconds a pleasant warmth begins to spread throughout my body. That's no good because that isn't supposed to happen, not at all. With Paxton, yeah. With Wyatt? Not so much. I've got to switch topics to something that doesn't have to do with our emotions and feelings and quick.

"Why aren't you out on the ice?"

If a shadow passed over Wyatt's face before, it was nothing compared to what's there now. His features twist into a tortured expression as if he were in great pain. "Aria. That… I mean, I… I'd like…"

Seeing him like this does something to me. His fragility is tearing my heart out. It's like someone's peeling off my skin. I know that's heavy, but that's what it feels like.

"It's all good," I say quickly because I can't stand to see him like this. I add softly, "You don't have to say it, Wyatt. It's okay."

He lets out a trembling breath before nodding. He's pale. *God. What happened?*

With jittery fingers he takes his hat off and runs a hand through his hair. "I wanted to ask you if you wanted to go to The Old-Timer with me. There's an Iron Man marathon today, and I know how much you dig strong dudes."

He sure does. And, *damn it*, I just can't say no. Not when he's looking broken like this, not when he's looking so hopeless.

"We wouldn't be alone," he adds quickly when he sees me hesitating. "Paisley and Knox will be there. Aaron and Levi, too." My eyes meet his, and he knows immediately, *immediately*, what I'm thinking. "Gwen's working at the diner."

Gwen. Not Gwendolyn. I swallow hard. "How do you know that?"

"I asked Paisley before coming over here."

Friends, Aria. You and Wyatt could be friends, and all this pain would be a thing of the past. You could look at him without having to feel everything.

"Okay." I take a quick scan of the kitchen. "Give me ten minutes."

His eyes twinkle. "Stay like this. I like it."

"Sure. You like licorice, too. Clearly, your sense of taste is screwy."

His expression changes. There's something, well, *horny* in it as he stares at me and lets out a sound when stopping to look at my lips. "My sense of taste is excellent, Aria."

I melt. A prickly warmth that *definitely* shouldn't be there begins to spread out between my thighs. I think of him in my room earlier today, between my legs, catapulting me into another world. Everything within me is longing to pull him toward me and do the whole thing all over again. I couldn't think of anything else all day long. And that's bad. Real bad.

"See you in a sec." I close the door, lean back against it, and take a few moments to breathe and collect myself.

Lopez, Lopez, Lopez. Could you please stop screwing around in my heart as if it were yours? Could you please accept that the two of us are definitively done?

24

Little Do You Know

ARIA

FOR DAYS ASPEN'S BEEN BLANKETED BY SNOW. TODAY IS no exception. Wyatt and I are walking next to each other in silence, nothing but the crunch of the snow beneath our feet.

The bell tower tolls eight o'clock as we cross the street and walk past the open doors of the dance school. A horde of kids dressed up like white swans is whirling around. They bow their heads respectfully when Vaughn steps into the middle. Wyatt and I stop to watch.

"Why is Vaughn wearing a full-body condom?"

"He is so nasty," I say. "Look at him lying there."

"He reminds me of Gregor Samsa. This here is his painful, unsettling metamorphosis into a bug."

"I still don't get how you're so stuck on Kafka, Wyatt."

"He's a true artist."

"He's weird. His books freak me out."

Vaughn curls up like an embryo and starts moving around like a fish out of water. The swan children dance around him with ballet steps while Spirit Susan leads them on with a count of "one, two, three, four, one, two, three, four." But then her eyes drift over to

Wyatt and me, and the children trip over their own feet when Susan interrupts the whole affair.

"You two?" she says. Her voice is dripping with disbelief. Her look is, too, but I can't understand how she finds the sight of the two of us more upsetting than Vaughn rolling around on the ground in that neoprene outfit of his.

Wyatt seems to be thinking the same thing, for he gives Vaughn a quizzical nod. "What's all this about, Susan?"

She fiddles with her stole and looks from him to Vaughn before she gets what Wyatt means. "Oh! We're preparing our Christmas show! It's going to be *magical*."

"And what's the piece?"

"A new version of *Swan Lake*," she says proudly.

Wyatt coughs. "A real unsettling…"

"What did you say?"

"All good." He laughs. "We're looking forward to it, Sue. Have a nice evening."

"You, too."

After a few steps, Wyatt lets out a soft laugh.

"What?"

A snowflake lands on his upper lip. He runs his tongue over it, which makes my stomach warm. "Nothing. Just thought of something."

"Tell me."

He puts his fingers around my elbows as he pulls me to the side and keeps me from walking into one of the gas lanterns. "We were in Susan's dance group once upon a time, too, remember?"

"Oh." I smile. "Vaguely. How old were we?"

"Seven." He casts me a quick glance. "We had to hold hands for a few steps."

"You still remember that?"

Wyatt scratches his throat and nods. "You were the highlight of my year."

Oh, Wy. How much I'd like to tell you that you were the *highlight of my life.*

We reach The Old-Timer. Wyatt opens the door for me. It creaks. The bell echoes through the room. A few seconds later I'm enveloped by the pleasant warmth from the fireplace. I haven't been here in two years, and I didn't realize how much I had missed this place. Whenever I'm here in William's shop at the front of the vintage movie theater with its wobbly walls, colorfully tossed-together furniture, and countless books and records spilling off the shelves, I'm filled with an overwhelming feeling of coming home.

"*Aria*," Will says, a reproving edge to his voice. "The film's about to start."

Wyatt steps up next to me. "Sorry, Will. Susan and her weird Kafkaesque bug show held us up."

William's eyes grow wide. He grabs at the antique popcorn machine from the forties, looking for support. "Susan had to turn in a form, and it said that she would be doing *Swan Lake*; that's WHAT SHE WROTE!"

I have to bite my lips to keep myself from bursting out laughing. "Yeah, well… She's pushed the rules a bit."

William's scalp turns bright purple. He's going to explode at any second, and I wouldn't be surprised to see smoke coming out of his ears. "My rules are straightforward and clear." Droplets of spit fly through the air. "No disturbing content in Christmas productions! That kind of stuff scares me, and everyone in town knows I get nightmares easily."

From behind one of the shelves, Aaron's red hair suddenly appears. "Who's playing the bug?"

Wyatt tilts his head. "Who else?"

"Vaughn," Aaron's boyfriend Levi responds immediately. He's sitting on a worn leather executive chair, a big bowl of chips balancing on his thigh. "Vaughn's the only one interested in embodying Susan's ideas about art."

That was it. The flame that had been lacking to light William's fuse. For years he and Vaughn have been at loggerheads because Vaughn often says he finds William's rules to be crap. William's head is turning redder and redder; I think it's even starting to swell, and I'm sure he'd be proud seeing his old jack-o'-lantern now—they look so similar. Then he smacks his hand down on the popcorn machine and says, "She will *not* get away with this!"

Knox raises his fist into the air. "Go for it, Will."

Will grits his teeth. "I'm going to go see her." He casts his eyes through the room and lands on Paisley. "You'll keep an eye on everything?"

Knox makes an indignant face. "Why is *she* receiving the honor though the rest of us have been longing for it for decades?"

Will narrows his eyes as he shuffles into his insulated Dockers. "Because you all are weird, and Paisley hasn't lived here long enough to be infected."

Levi opens his mouth in shock. "Will, how *dare* you speak about us so!"

"You of all people! I asked you to help out here one time, *just one time*, and what did you do, young man? You didn't even show the film that was on the calendar!"

Levi rolls his eyes and tosses a handful of chips into his mouth. "It was the end-of-the-year party for the ninth grade, Will. No one, and I mean *no one*, wanted to see *Gone with the Wind*."

Enraged, William puffs out his chest. "It is an important film; it's meaningful and…"

"Depressing," Aaron completes his sentence. He comes from around the shelf, a book in his hand, and sits down next to Levi. "We wanted to celebrate our lives and not sit in the corner feeling shitty about how terrible people were in the past."

William raises his brows. "That's exactly why it matters. So we don't forget. So we never forget."

Levi groans. "We didn't forget, dude. We just didn't want to cry over it during cake."

"Don't worry, Will. I'll make sure that everything goes okay," Pais says.

An imaginary boulder slides off William's shoulders. I see them collapse before he says goodbye and steps out into the snowy night.

"You're too nice, Pais." I smile at her as I squeeze past all the furniture and fall onto a beanbag. "Just five more minutes and William would have exploded. That would've been something."

Knox gives a raucous laugh. I can see that he's still wondering why Wyatt and I showed up together. But he skillfully plays it off. He pulls Paisley over to him and she puts her head in his lap, and he begins to stroke her hair.

"She hates PowerPoint and is terribly afraid William will ask her to make a presentation on how to make the town more attractive."

Aaron swings his legs over the back of the chair, leans back, and wiggles his feet. "I can't believe *you* would ever have something selfish in mind, Pais."

"Garlic bread and lemon iced tea, Ari?" Wyatt's head appears behind the counter, highlighted by the light from the fridge.

"Yeah. And…"

"M&Ms." He grins. He manages to get the drinks, garlic bread, and a cheese sandwich with one arm and kicks the refrigerator door closed with his foot. With his other hand, he tosses me a bag of Crunchy Cookie M&Ms, which sails through the room over Paisley's and Knox's heads before landing in my lap.

Yep. He can sure hit a bulls-eye.

He disappears into the kitchen. As I'm opening my bag of M&Ms, I become aware of the fact that Aaron, Levi, Knox, and Paisley are all staring at me.

"What?"

"Explain, A." Aaron stretches out his wool socks and nudges at my ear. "What's going on between you two?"

"Stop, my God. Stop it, you are so… AARON!"

He cackles. I hop up off my beanbag, push it beyond his reach, and train my narrowed eyes on him.

"I can't believe you've still got that laser-like stare, A." Levi nearly falls off his chair as he stretches over to pull a wool blanket off the sofa that's next to him. "When are you going to get that you are *never* going to have superhuman powers?"

Knox takes a bite of his cheese sandwich.

"People." Aaron snaps his fingers. "I *really* want to know what's up between the two of them."

"Nothing's up, Aaron, not a thing." I can feel my throat flush with warmth as I fall back onto my beanbag and grab the M&Ms off the counter next to me. I toss one after the other into my mouth. "And there won't ever be anything between Wyatt and me, okay? Never again. He fucked up, and I mean big time, and I could never forgive him for that, not to mention trust him. Sooo," I take a deep breath. "Sorry not sorry, but the whole Aria–Wyatt love story is over."

Things go quiet. There's only the sound of my chewing. It takes around three seconds for my limbic system to process the fact that it's too quiet, far too quiet. *Look up, Aria, quick, quick. There's a lion around here somewhere that can attack at any moment!*

I look up. I don't see any lions. Just Wyatt.

I can't breathe. The way he's standing there, between the tea wagon and the one-eyed rocking horse, iced tea and Coke in his arms, a plate in his hands, and that beaten look on his face… God. It's as if I'd taken a swing, a real swing, and thrown all the dirt at him that's been trying to drag my heart down for years.

My M&Ms fall to the ground. They roll across the wooden floor until they are stopped by one of the rugs. At this point, anything could happen, and I wouldn't notice. All I see is Wyatt, his eyes full of a silent message. *You see this, Aria? Take a good look; this is what your words just did to me, every one of your syllables a dagger.*

Nevertheless, he manages to move. He comes right up to me

with a smile on his face, and I wonder how much it's costing him. His voice sounds battered, and his grin slips a bit as he hands me my plate, puts the bottle of iced tea down next to me, and says so that only I can hear, "Then stop missing me when you're the one who left."

"Wyatt," I whisper as he pulls back his head and his ear brushes my cheek. He looks at me with a hurt expression, and as he opens his mouth, I think he's going to start talking about everything, about us, about what happened, right here in front of everyone, but all he says is, "I got rid of the mushrooms for you."

My fingers grip the edge of the plate. "Thank you."

And then the moment's gone. His face brightens as we all stand up and shuffle into the theater. The film starts. Wyatt is a champion at hiding his feelings. He fishes a handful of popcorn out of the bag in between him and Levi and begins tossing pieces of them against the back of Knox's head.

"Hey." Paisley nudges him in the side and brushes the popcorn off his hair.

With a tender smile on his face, he takes her ear between his thumb and index finger and pulls softly.

She giggles. "You're terrifying when you try to be sweet, Knox."

"When I *try?*" Now he tugs on both her ears so hard that she pulls back laughing. "I am *always* sweet, Snow Queen, every damn day."

Wyatt and I look at each other. It's automatic; it's something we can't control because Paisley and Knox's love just radiates outward, and whenever our bodies register those kinds of feelings, we automatically turn to those we associate them with.

"You all blubber way too much," Aaron says, stretching out to scratch his boyfriend's neck. Levi in turn reaches his greasy fingers back to stroke Aaron's hand. Once again Wyatt and I look at each other because we're thinking the exact same thing: Camila. Her fingers are always greasy after she eats. The corners of our mouths twitch. I turn away.

With his arm draped over the back of the chair in his row, Knox turns halfway to the right. "This movie sucks. Let's go out to the shop and just chill." We all get up and file back to the fireplace and the variety of chairs and sofas.

Paisley taps his nose. "Well, suggest something, skater boy."

"Don't call me that."

"You call me Snow Queen."

"But that's sweet."

"Skater boy is, too."

"ESPN's showing the Snowdogs versus the Bullheads," Wyatt says, causing everyone to groan.

"Pleeease," Levi says. "I *hate* hockey."

I look at him questioningly. "But you're a figure skater."

"You got it, Moore… *Figure* and *skater* come together to form something rather different from *hockey* and *player*."

"But both take place out on the ice and…"

"Are you *really* trying to compare the two?" Aaron moves to steal the last piece of my baguette.

"All good, all good." I pull up my legs, yank at the elastic band of my right sock, and look out at everyone. The dim light makes our faces shadowy and mysterious, and I like that, somehow, it makes me feel like we're in our own little world. "Let's play Guess Who's on My Mind."

Knox laughs. "We haven't played that since high school, Aria."

"It's cool." Wyatt wiggles his eyebrows. "Nostalgic memories of cheap beer in the gym and bonfires in the Highlands." He puts his empty plate to the side and opens his bottle of Coke to take a swig. My eyes get caught on his lips as they close around the bottle, and I get hot, way too hot—my God, how they move…

"You okay?"

His voice makes me flinch, and the piece of my baguette that I was putting to my mouth falls to the ground. "Yeah…umm…of course."

"Are you having an allergic reaction, Aria?"

"What?"

"Your face is so blotchy."

"It's the light."

Wyatt's grin comes far too quickly, smugly, and seductively for my stomach not to react.

"I'm up for Guess Who as well," Levi says, playing with the buttons of Aaron's cardigan.

Paisley takes a sip of her hot chocolate. "What's that?" She doesn't notice the mustache it leaves. The smile Knox makes as he wipes it off with his thumb is priceless. He says, "It's a game."

"More info, please, skater boy."

He laughs. "Everyone draws a name, thinks of a song that fits the person, and writes it down on a piece of paper. Then they are drawn, one after the other, and we play the song, and everyone has to guess who chose it, who it fits, and why."

"Oooh," she says as her eyes light up. "I'm down with that!"

"Great." Aaron stands up and digs around in the drawer of a huge, dark desk until he finds some pens and paper. He passes them out, makes little pieces of paper with our names on them, and puts out his hand so that each of us can take one.

I draw Paisley. As we think, all we can hear is the film in the background and the rustling of paper. I tap the top of the pen against my lower lip and stare into space. Knox told me that Paisley didn't have the nicest of pasts. He didn't go into details, but Harper said her former trainer had to go to jail for sexual assault, and Knox mentioned that she'd grown up in a Minneapolis trailer park. The tip of my tongue brushes my upper lip as I bend forward and write down "Survivor" by Destiny's Child.

When I look back up, Wyatt's there with his upside down hat in his hands, looking down at me. His eyes are resting on the tip of my tongue, and his expression is almost ravenous. My cheeks burning, I lower my eyes and place my piece of paper inside.

He turns, and his Adam's apple hops. "Okay," he says, swinging up onto the desk and bouncing his legs back and forth. "The first song is…" Levi plays a drumroll on his phone and Wyatt, attempting to make things exciting, digs around in his hat and shifts his eyes back and forth until Knox launches a slipper at his head.

"Dude," Wyatt says, rubbing his temple. "You know how much bacteria is in those things?"

"You're a piece of bacteria," Knox counters.

"Scientifically speaking, that's true," Paisley says. "No offense, Wy."

"Okay, now that that's settled… 'We Found Love' by Rihanna."

Levi plays the song on Spotify.

"Paisley," Aaron says. "For Knox."

Wyatt confirms with a nod. "Because they found each other when the world seemed hopeless for both of them."

Our eyes wander to Paisley, who looks down and grabs hold of her knees. She plays with her fingertips and nods. "Right."

"Babe," Knox says, a soft smile on his lips as he bends forward and plants a kiss on her forehead. Her cheeks still turn red, even after a year of being together. But then I think of Wyatt and me, of our first kiss eight years ago, and then I think of how my body begins to burn whenever he looks at me, and I decide to concentrate on something else.

We keep on playing. We laugh until our face muscles hurt; we make jokes and tease one another, and for the first time in ages, I simply feel *happy*. It's as if the last few years had never happened and we were back in high school.

Carefree thoughts; hearts as light as a feather.

Everyone immediately guesses that "Survivor" refers to Paisley, but Levi thinks Knox chose it, Knox thinks that it was Aaron, and only Paisley guesses it was me.

"Okay, let's move on." Wyatt pulls the next folded piece of paper out of the hat. He swallows as soon as he reads the song, and when his eyes dart over to me, I know immediately, *immediately*, that he must have drawn and chosen a song for me. For a second I toy with the thought of putting my hands over my ears or cutting them off or whatever because I don't know if I'll be able to handle what's to come. I mean, we're talking about his unfiltered thoughts here, thoughts that have probably been going through his head for years, and he can share them with me now without having to speak out loud.

But it's too late. The first notes are already sounding through the tinny speakers of a phone. I know this song. I know this song, and it doesn't make things better cause I know what they're singing about. And then, as the words begin to float above our heads and into our hearts, each and every syllable starts to cause me pain.

The song fades. Everybody is looking at me. Wyatt has balled his hands into fists and is pressing them against his built upper thighs. His knuckles are white. Levi looks like he thinks he made a terrible mistake by playing the song, Paisley's eyes are full of tears as she looks from Wyatt to me to Wyatt, Knox looks like he's expecting me to fall unconscious any second, and Aaron is tugging at a hole in his sock. Everyone's tense and waiting for me to react, like I was a lone suitcase that either had clothes or a bomb inside it.

"Sorry," Wyatt says.

It's hard for me to breathe. It's too much. Wyatt's reveal, those glances and the terrible memories coming up, are too much and have ruined the moment.

I look over at Wyatt. Gold-brown eyes, caramelized sugar in a brown-yellow light.

"You're sorry," I say, but hardly recognize my voice. Whatever. "You're sorry, you say, after all I had to go through, after all I had to feel when I saw you *fuck her*, Wyatt. And you think a few words, a few shitty words are enough to make me forget?"

"Drop it, Aria." Wyatt hops down off the desk. He comes right over to me, and suddenly it's like we're alone, surrounded by a blur of colors, a sea of emotions we don't want to face. "Stop bringing up the past over and over and throwing it in my face. *Here, Wyatt,*

again, and one more time, BAM, BAM, feels good, huh? I know what
I did, okay, Aria? I've known it for two years, and," he gives a dry,
frustrated laugh, "don't you worry, Moore, I'm not going to forget it.
For the rest of my life I'm going to feel like a piece of shit. I'm going
to feel empty inside and simply fucked, yeah. And when I wake up in
the morning, you know what the first thing I feel is? Hate and rage,
sadness and nausea, and the first thing I see are the memories, and
they make it even worse. So believe me when I say that I *know* what I
did, that I *know* what loss and self-hate feel like, and that I'm always
going to feel like a hopeless, beaten dog. Okay?"

He's breathing powerfully and quickly, and I am too because
we're both running, even though we're standing still.

My voice breaks when I speak. "I will never be the person I was."

"Yeah," he says. "Yeah, but I'll love you all the same, A., always,
even if you were someone else every day of the year, three hundred
and sixty-five different Aria Moores. Happy me."

We're both right. We've reached a point where we're turning
around in circles because I can't stop attacking him for what he did
and he can't stop feeling like shit, and it's not going to end if we can't
get away from each other.

"Ari," Wyatt says, real soft and hoarse. "We've got to start accepting what happened and either repairing things or letting them go.
We simply *can't go on like this.*"

His words go right to my heart. My head is spinning as I try to
make sense of it all and put something like the ghost of a thought
together, but everything's moving too quickly, too heavily, too wildly.

And then the door opens.

Surrounded by whirling snow, William walks into The Old-
Timer. "Outdated and dusty," he mumbles, wiping the snow off
his jacket with a gloved hand before snorting. "*Me* and outdated. I
run the town's social media accounts and can fill out an Excel sheet.
Well, Spirit Susan, you'll see how hip I am just yet." He pauses when
he notices all of us. His glance zips to the middle of the room, where

Wyatt and I are standing in between all the furniture, and then to the others in their seats watching us like two protagonists in a gripping drama. And the funny thing is, I completely blocked them out; all I could focus on was Wyatt.

Snow is dripping off William's beard. "Do you have a fever, Aria? You look glassy. If you do, I'm going to have to ask you to leave immediately. My immune system cannot be disturbed in any way until my base tablets with all that zinc are back in stock and…"

"It's all good, Will." I take my bag and push past Wyatt. His elbows brush my breasts, and the sensation makes me shudder so powerfully that I have to take a sharp breath. "I was just about to go anyway."

The cold night air envelops me and begins to speak. *Welcome back, old friend. It's good to see you. And the way we fit each other—so dark, cold, and lonely—still feels good, too.*

Welcome back.

25

Baby, It Was Real, and We Were the Best

WYATT

"CAN I HELP IN ANY WAY?"

Ruth spins around. She's standing at the long mahogany kitchen counter downstairs. This is usually where she prepares breakfast for the guests, but today it smells like pumpkin and apple pie, a sweet scent that tickles my nose and awakens memories of distant days.

She smiles. "Just like old times?"

I nod. I'm standing in the doorway but don't trust myself to step inside. Something's holding me back, a feeling like I was six again and me and Knox were about to play The Floor Is Lava. It seems like forever since Ruth and I would stand in this very kitchen, baking things for Thanksgiving. We had to keep Aria out of it, though, as no one was interested in blackened, stone-hard crumbs.

Ruth rubs her hands together to get rid of the flour, reaches for a second apron, and hands it to me. "Come on in, Wyatt."

"Thanks." It's a pink apron with flowers on it, but I don't care, not right now. "What do you want me to do?"

"Peel and cut the apples." She pushes a bowl across the table, which I stop with my elbow before grabbing a peeler and getting started.

Ruth casts me a quick glance. She looks worn-out. "How are you doing?" she asks.

I put the peeled apple to the side and take another. "Shouldn't I be asking you?"

"Well..." She waves her hand mixer through the air and shakes her head as if her health weren't worth talking about. "Aging, Wyatt. It is what it is."

"You've got rheumatism, Ruth. That's bad. Honestly, I don't know how you manage everything here as well as you do. If you need help, whatever it is, I'm here. I'll take care of everything."

Ruth works on the pumpkin with stiff fingers before smiling warmly at me. "Thanks, Wyatt."

"Goes without saying."

A few seconds go by. Eventually she puts the tip of the mixer in the sink and looks at me from the corner of her eye. "How *are you?*"

I pick up another apple before rubbing my nose with the back of my hand. "Truthfully?"

"Do I look like I'm interested in lies, my son?"

"No." The juice of the apple runs over my thumbs as I quarter it. I clear my throat. "Not all that hot."

Her lips grow small as she puts a pot on the gas stove and pours the pureed pumpkin inside. "Have you spoken with Aria?"

"Not recently." It's been almost two weeks since she stormed out of The Old-Timer. The repairmen are still working on our house. They had to tear down half the wall, which means that we've got to stay in the B&B longer than we intended. No idea if our insurance is even going to cover our stay. We're still waiting for an answer. And although Aria and I are just a few feet away from each other every day, I've hardly caught sight of her. But we're texting and talking on the phone in the evenings about little things but about serious topics, too, like when people are good, why people look like they do, and why they don't like a particular cup or what-have-you. And speaking of cups, we texted about her "no-point" ones, of course, which I was already familiar with, but I like hearing about them because I love that tingling in her voice whenever she talks about things she loves. Aria is talking with me and not talking with me because she thinks I'm someone else.

With a sigh, I put down the bowl of peeled apples and turn to the dough. "I don't get it, Ruth."

Aria's mom is cracking eggs into a bowl and whisking them with milk and cream until there's a smooth consistency. Then she takes the pumpkin off the stove and pours it into a prebaked pie crust. "What don't you get?"

"Why you're still so nice to me."

Ruth gives me an almost sympathetic look as she opens the oven and shoves the pie inside. "We live in Aspen, Wyatt. You think what *really happened* hasn't made the rounds?"

My heart skips a beat. "Does Aria know?"

"No." She slides another prebaked crust over the counter to me and, with two fingers, signals me to pour in the filling. I do what she says, then we place the apples in a circular form on top. "She was gone so quick and just shut up whenever your name came up. She avoids talking about the night because…it hurt her so bad, son. *So bad.*"

"Me, too."

"I know. It's not fair. For you or for her. You made a serious error. Aria probably did, too, by refusing to listen to you. It's not that I condone what happened, Wyatt. You made a big mistake. Unconsciously, perhaps, but nevertheless." A sad smile appears on her face. "It wanted to test you. Life."

"And we failed across the board."

"I don't know, Wyatt." Ruth turns to slide the pie onto the lowest rack of the oven. Then she turns around again, puts both hands down on the counter, bends forward, and looks right at me. "You and Aria, you were…" She sighs, takes a dishcloth, and wipes the work surface down. "Whenever one of you would enter the

room, you could see the other tremble, as if you two could sense each
other, like two magnets that are impossible to separate. It was wild."
She hangs the cloth over the faucet in the sink and then shakes her
head. "It was just...different. Like magic. And magic can't lose out
against life."

Her words make my nerves tingle. "Thanks, Ruth."

For a while both of us are silent, each caught in our own
thoughts, between us just the ticking of the egg timer, when all of
a sudden I feel my phone begin to vibrate in my pocket. A message
from Caden.

Yo, bro. You coming to the game today?

Sometimes I go and sit next to Coach Jefferson to cheer on my
team. And every time I'm torn by not knowing when I'll be back
out on the ice. When my arm may be better. And with every day
that passes, the end of the transfer deadline gets closer. The deadline
Zayne graciously gave me after I blew it at the press conference and
the exhibition game afterward. Today they're playing Vancouver. I
consider it for a second but don't have anything else going on, so I
accept.

Sweet, Caden responds. There's gonna be a MAD PARTY at
Paxton's after.

To be honest, I'm not really interested. Ever since I've stopped
being the heavy drinker I was before—in other words, ever since
the accident—I've become more and more aware of how stressful
parties really are and how quickly I get tired. But maybe the relaxed
atmosphere around the team will help distract me, and so I decide to
go to the party, too.

I look up. "You still need help, Ruth?"

She waves her hand. "Not until tomorrow. You going to the
rink?"

"Yeah."

"Soon enough Aspen's going to be admiring you in your first NHL game," she says and smiles. "Your parents would be so proud of you."

Her words bore into my chest and plant seeds of healing, a fresh start on dry land, and suddenly I feel that tiny, stubborn percentage of hope that just doesn't want to let me go. At least it believes in me.

The stadium is freaking out. The stands are full of our brown-and-green jerseys, and everyone's yelling at the top of their lungs. Shortly before the end of the third period, it's 2–1 for Vancouver.

"Come on, Owen! Shoot the puck home!" Coach Jefferson is pulling at his hair. He's been doing that since the start of the game. I'm afraid that if he keeps on going, there won't be any left. "Come on, kid, just skate on by, come on! Ah, FUCK!"

A collective "NOOO!" explodes through the hall. It was the perfect chance. Owen was face-to-face with the opposing team's goalie, but right before he could take a shot, the defenseman stole the puck. Jefferson smacks his palm against the plexiglass. He spins around, wipes his hand across his face, and points at me. "*You* would never have missed that chance, kid."

I stretch out my legs, lean back against the wall, and grin. "Yeah, Coach, there's only one Wyatt Lopez."

He rolls his eyes. "Yeah, and I really hope that this Wyatt Lopez gets his ass back out on the ice soon."

On the one hand, watching my team play feels great, inspiring even, like standing in front of your big love. But on the other hand, it hurts like hell. Having reached what I'd been working my whole life to achieve only to end up physically unable to play and sitting on this fucking bench next to the subs pisses me off.

Gray, the substitute winger, has the puck. He races across the ice but gets surrounded by two defensemen and passes off to Paxton. It only takes a couple of seconds for him to get free and sprint toward the goal, but Paxton doesn't pass the puck back. He's afraid Gray will screw it up. As soon as I realize this, I grow so angry that I'm close to grabbing the skates off the guy next to me and telling Coach to let me play. I mean, goddamn, hockey's a *team* sport, and being able to count on your crew to know what to do as soon as their sticks meet the puck is more important than anything else.

I've got to get better. Gray's got to go or the Aspen Snowdogs are going to have a terrible season. I'm so lost in my thoughts that I only become aware of what's happening when I feel the hall quaking. Cheering fans, feet stomping the ground, hands clapping, and Coach Jefferson hitting the plexiglass like a madman, yelling "YEAH! YEAH! YEAH! YEAH!" My boys dart across the ice and pounce on Paxton: it's 2–2.

"Okay, people, okay." Jefferson rubs his hands together and stares at his team as they reposition. "You got this. Make papa proud, come on."

The puck gets hit and, man, just those two sounds—the sounds of blades slicing across the ice and the puck sliding—kill me. I feel naked and overwhelmed by longing. This really hurts. I mean, I love this sport; it's my life, but now I feel like a hungry dog being teased by someone holding a big bone out in front of its nose.

Soon, I tell myself, *soon*.

We're in the last two minutes. Paxton passes the puck to Owen. The way that Gray's being excluded by the others would be funny if the situation wasn't so serious. Owen storms past the other team's two wingers, which is risky enough to cause him to almost lose his balance. I can tell by their aggressive movements and their impulsive edgework that Vancouver's guys are pissed. Owen has no choice but to pass off to Gray, who is immediately surrounded by Vancouver's massive players and loses the puck. Coach Jefferson freaks. He curses. Drops of spit fly from his mouth as he lays into Gray with words I didn't even know existed. And that, ladies and gentlemen, must mean something.

Thirty seconds. My stomach contracts. I don't know if I can watch as Paxton chases after them but doesn't get any opportunity to break through Vancouver's wall. It's like a horror movie; everything's dark, and you just know that any second something's going to happen. But then Owen traps the winger, who has no choice but to pass, and what happens next is exactly what the boys have practiced over and over: the puck skids across the ice, Vancouver's center sprints ahead, but Caden and Xander rush out of their defensive positions and cut him off just as Paxton gets the puck. I jump up off the bench and yell at the top of my lungs. Pax races into the attacking zone, completely free, not a soul around to stop him, raises his stick, shoots, and scores. Time. The third period ends 3–2.

Aspen's fans go out of their minds. Everyone starts chanting Paxton's name like he's a saint—some people are crying, and others are just shaking their heads. Coach Jefferson grabs me and pulls me to him; he stinks, but whatever, I'm grinning from ear to ear. After losing our last game, we just had to win this one, and although things weren't looking so good, the boys were able to turn it around. I happily watch them throw themselves at one another, a mess of people tugging jerseys and slapping helmets. And yet, I still feel a stab of pain around my stomach.

I want to be the one out on the ice. *I* want to be the one to have my team's arms around me when I've made the winning goal. *I* want to show everyone what I can do and what I fought so hard for.

Coach Jefferson hurries past me to the rink-board door to high-five the guys as they come off the ice and disappear toward the locker room. I see our spokesperson Carl moving off behind them, trying to catch hold of what I'm guessing is Paxton to have someone ready to give an interview. I watch them go and remember how, when we were kids, Knox and I used to imagine this moment. We'd play hockey out on Silver Lake with our tiny legs and tiny feet, already acting like hotshot NHL players. Afterward, we'd interview each other. Man, we felt like gods.

The vibrations of my phone bring me back to the now.

Aria: OMG! I watched the game on TV. WHAT A GOAL, PAXTON!

My throat fills with a sickening burn. Aria's watching hockey games for him now, not for me, even though I was her number one, even though she was in the front row at every one of my games, her petite body in my oversized jersey, the number twelve finger-painted on her cheeks. But now? Now she's stanning *him*. Now she's eagerly anticipating *his* moves toward the goal, and it's *his* name on her lips even though he doesn't even really know her.

Man, what an asshole I am. What a *fuckhead* I am for making her fall in love with an illusion that will only lead to her having her heart broken one more time.

I know I should stop. I know I am selfish and inconsiderate and terrible, but what can I do? I need her. I need her so bad, and she doesn't see the Wyatt I used to be anymore.

I have no idea what I'm doing, no idea if this is kickstarting a new catastrophe or if it's destiny winking at me, but as I'm writing my response, I know that Aria Moore just makes me absolutely overconfident.

Thanks, babe. Party at my place. I want to see you.

26

You Hold My Hand, and I Want You to Hold My Heart

ARIA

"I'D FORGOTTEN HOW BIG THIS INFLATABLE SNOWMAN was. And how creepy."

Harp nods. We're standing next to each other in the snow, risking frostbite, and staring at Paxton's house. The bass is booming so loud down the entire street that I feel like I'm about to take off.

"You wanna go in?"

My teeth are chattering, and there's nothing I'd like more than to finally get my bare legs into this darn house and start moving, but my body doesn't react. "I can't."

"Why not?"

"I'm too nervous."

Harp sighs, places both hands on my shoulders, and turns me toward her. "Listen, A. I don't know how you put this together, but you look totally hot in this wool-sweater-schoolgirl-skirt-and-Converse combo thing you've got going on. But if we stay out here any longer, our legs are probably going to have to be amputated, and that wouldn't be...pleasant. Okay?"

I take a deep breath. "Okay, let's go, or okay, amputation?"

"Okay, let's go."

The snowman's looking impassively down as we make our way past and step inside. Back in high school I used to come to Paxton's parties frequently. We thought we were pretty damn cool with all the beer we weren't legally allowed to drink, our games, and the good whisky from the Hilcons' cabinet. *Man, awesome stuff,* we used to say, although, to be honest, we really would've preferred to spit the stuff out than have it burn our throats. We thought we were super bad, but, man, was that kiddie stuff compared to today's party. A real NHL party—the phrase alone makes you imagine tall, half-naked, and perfectly built supermodels with so much makeup on that you don't know whether the girl you're talking to has a bad fever or is simply wearing too much blush.

Strobe lights are flashing, everything's filled with colors, everything's loud, and everything's absolutely unreal. The first thing I notice is the DJ, who has set up his mixer on the kitchen island, nodding along with the beat. He's sucking on a straw that's sticking out of a bucket. I don't even want to know what's inside it.

"Now I remember why I didn't want to come!" I shout over the bass.

Harper turns away from a brunette who's feeling up one of the players, Xander, I think. My best friend looks at me quizzically, so I add, "Hockey parties are too much!"

Her eyes blaze. "Welcome to Aspen, A.!"

I let my gaze wander and notice that the majority of those present are, in fact, women showing off their bodies on the dance floor, pressing themselves against guys' chests. Some are riding them while making out on the sofa in the corner, next to the big potted plant.

Harper looks toward the ceiling and over the mezzanine with the glass railing, behind which an obviously very drunk woman is riding a broomstick up and down the hall for some unknown reason, cackling.

"I *really* don't want to know what she's on," Harper mumbles, turning away and pushing through the crowd.

"Harp!" I reach out my hand and tug at the delicate fabric of her silk dress. She tosses her smooth hair over her shoulder and turns. "What are we doing here?"

"What do you mean?"

"This!" Extending my arms, I take in the whole room. "I've been here, done it, Harp, and what did it bring me?" She is about to interrupt, but I shake my head. "I don't need this a second time!"

"Aria! Wait!" Harper cries and gets in my way. "Don't get sidetracked. This is a party, and it's really going off, true, but think about the texts he sent you and your calls. You really think he's just some weirdo who wants to lay puck bunnies and *nothing else?*"

I take a look around. "Are we at the same party, or are you in some parallel universe?"

"Man, Aria, come on!" Harper rolls her eyes, grabs my wrist, and pulls me past the couches to the makeshift beer stand. "Have a Bud Light. If you still want to go afterward, I won't object, promise."

I skeptically accept a red cup. "Just one?"

She nods. "Just one."

For a little while I watch the foam before I raise my eyes again. "Okay. But I'm going to be mad if you don't stick to it. Seriously. I'm going to go to your house and put *Pinocchio* stickers all over your walls so that every morning when you see his nose, you're going to know that…"

"There he is."

"Pinocchio?"

"No, you dope."

"Who?"

"Paxton."

"Where?"

"In the Whirlpool."

"*In the Whirlpool?*"

And, indeed, through the glass door to the terrace, I see Paxton sitting alone in the hot tub with a red cup in his hand.

"No women licking his chest, I see."

Harper nods. "They tried, I'm sure, but he fought them off, waiting for you."

"Good, Harp." I take another deep breath. "I'm going over there."

"You ready?"

"No."

She gives me a thumbs-up. "*Awesome*. Good luck."

The red cup's dented on both sides. I'm gripping it so tight. It's been so long since I last flirted. Eight years, to be precise. I don't even know how to do it anymore. What if the rules have changed? What if I'm making a fool of myself, and he thinks I'm some kind of freak?

I set off and manage a few steps before it becomes clear that the space between the sofa area and the open kitchen isn't a dance floor but an oversized air-hockey field where I'm the puck. There's no other explanation because everyone, and I mean *every*one, bumps into me with their shoulders, with their hips, and oh, here's some hair whipping into my face, and, how nice, a peach-colored butt twerking against my hand, *great*. My Bud Light spills over, covering my hand and leg with sticky beer.

The field is reluctant to let me go, but eventually I'm standing next to the Jacuzzi staring at Paxton's chiseled and very naked chest. Reaching the terrace, I could have sworn I saw someone next to him. But in the next second I realize it's just the gloomy tree trunk on the lawn next to him.

I'm holding onto the red cup like a trophy because, well, we made it through the battlefield together. I feel a little strange standing there, half of my face illuminated by the spotlights under the roof, the other half shrouded in darkness.

Paxton turns halfway to the left to grab a beer out of the cooler but starts so violently at seeing me that he spills it over his arm.

"Just happened to me, too."

He blinks. "What?"

My eyes dart to his arm. "That." I try to put on a smile that doesn't seem forced. "Funny, huh?"

"Umm." He looks around as if trying to find someone. Maybe the joke. "You're here?"

Is he serious? "Why shouldn't I be?"

"Well…" He runs a hand through the wet hair. "Wyatt is here, too, somewhere, and…"

Oh. *Oh.* That might be a little problem.

"And you're afraid of him catching the two of us together?"

Paxton is holding onto his cup, eyes wide, mouth open, staring at me. He looks like he truly has *no idea* what's going on here.

"I'd be stupid not to." He gives a dry laugh. "Shit, Aria. You were at the exhibition game, and Wyatt lost his shit when the others simply asked who you were."

I lower my eyes and shift my weight from one leg to the other. "Then why did you invite me?"

"I… Wait, what?"

"You invited me."

"I definitely did not…" he groans.

I blink. "Everything all right?"

"Yeah, I…" Another groan. The cup slides out of his fingers and falls into the water. Lips pressed together, he digs his fingers into the edge of the hot tub and closes his eyes. Then, opening his mouth, he releases a whole volley of moans until he bends back, throws back his head, and says, "Fuck yeah!"

My brain is working in slow motion. And then I realize what's going on. I see the silhouette under the water, the bubbles as the woman emerges, a lascivious grin on her lips, her wet blond hair sticking to her face. She brushes it aside as she straddles Paxton's lap and shoves her tongue down his throat.

My cup falls to the ground, but neither of them is paying any attention to me. Suddenly I realize that what I saw was her, not the tree. When I was coming outside, she was going underwater. How can anyone hold their breath for that long? Having said that… Our exchange was fairly short. Maybe a minute, tops, and…

God, Aria, stop! This can't possibly be happening right now. *He* invited me. *He* wanted to see me. *He's* the one who's been texting me all these weeks, talking to me on the phone, making me feel special and unique, just to get me over here to this over-the-top party and *get a blow job in front of me?*

"PAX!" One of his teammates appears in the open door, a hockey stick and puck in his hand. It's Caden. "Yo, Pax. Wanna go shoot some goals out on Silver Lake? Jennet and his girls want to watch." He wiggles his eyebrows. "Owen and Samu are in."

Paxton tears himself away from the blond and bends forward to peer around his teammate into the house. "And Xander?"

Caden waves his beer bottle through the air. "Upstairs. With the brunette."

Paxton's eyes dart back to me, but not in a good way, not with a look like he didn't want to leave me alone or explain or, no idea. No, it's like I'm some kind of uncomfortable factor he'd like to get rid of as soon as possible.

"Cool, I'll be right there." He pushes the blond off his lap and swings up over the side. He grabs a towel off the back of a lounge chair, wipes himself off, and tosses it back onto the table. Walking past me to follow Caden, he actually raises his eyebrows at me. One time. Up-down. *See you, Aria.* It *was nice. Now hit the road.*

The cold has made my limbs numb. I plod back inside to find Harper. I am so shocked that it feels like the ground beneath my feet is shifting. Strangely, though, I don't feel hurt. Not a stab of pain in my heart. Not even close to what I felt when I saw Wyatt and Gwendolyn together, not at all; I am just perplexed. But I'm angry, really angry! Harp, where *are* you? I make my way around the edge of the dance floor—a.k.a. the air-hockey playing field—to avoid becoming a living puck again. I walk straight into a wardrobe, hard as a rock. It's broad and… Wow, does it smell good! I press my nose deeper into the warm fabric and…

Wait a sec. Since when have wardrobes smelled of fresh pine, mint, and lemon?

They don't.

There's only one person who smells like that.

"Wyatt."

"Look alive, Aria." He's staring down at me. His hands are on my upper arm, probably to keep me from falling. "Everything okay?"

I nod. "Yeah. I was just on my way out."

He looks at me. His eyes wander down my body, stop for a moment on the soft curve of my breasts beneath my sweater, move on to my hips, my skirt, and my bare legs. I am really close to him; when he swallows I can count the dark hairs on his face, the somewhat darker line of his lower lip standing out from the rest of the pale red.

"Listen." The bass is thumping, the electro sounds are echoing throughout the house, but Wyatt's voice rings clear, just as deep and husky as when I fell in love with it way back when. "What happened recently…" He bites his lower lip, pulls it in, and lets it back out. The sight of it makes my nerves start to tingle. Just a minute ago I was out in the cold, freezing, and now I'm starting to get hot, so hot that I feel like I'm standing in the middle of a flame. "That was stupid of me."

I swallow. "What do you mean exactly?"

Wyatt's eyes hurry to his finger that suddenly grows a bit too bold and traces a soft line across my shoulder. I hold my breath.

"Playing that song. In front of everybody else. That was too much."

"True." My throat feels scratchy. Maybe I was outside too long and am getting the flu already. I should go home. Right away.

Almost starting to panic, I start looking around for Harper. I look toward the DJ, toward the crowd, and toward the snowman outside blowing back and forth in the wind and knocking against the window. I look everywhere just so I don't have to look Wyatt in the face.

"Aria," his finger reaches the bare skin of my collarbone. "Aria, look at me."

I take a deep breath and do as he says. Why am I still standing here? Why don't I just go? I should just turn around and leave him behind. And I even try, but it's as if my feet were sticking to the floor. My God, how he's looking at me, with his backward baseball hat and those ripped black jeans. *How he's looking at me*, the colored lights spinning across his body, his nose red, his hoodie green... Something's happening. Suddenly I'm fourteen again, back in math class with old Ms. Clearwater, Wyatt directly to my left. He's tilting his chair, all relaxed and natural, though it had to be tough for him to keep his balance. I can still remember looking at him and thinking that he had talent. And so I tried to mimic him. He'd drawn his brows together and was chewing on his pencil. Ms. Clearwater was saying something about pi, and then it happened; he gave that deep laugh, and my heart immediately responded. I really thought something was wrong with me, maybe my circulation, maybe something worse, but it was simply Wyatt. How deep, how *magical* that sound was. And then he made a joke, something corny about *pirates* and *pi* and laughed, and I fell off my chair.

Wyatt jumped up—a few others did, too—and ran over to me. But only Wyatt asked if I was okay. He looked at me, so close, just like now, with the exact same look on his face, and that's when it happened. At that very second, I fell in love with Wyatt Lopez. I fell in love—and I got lost.

And now it's happening again. I'm falling in love again, although I never stopped loving him, and that's unreal. I mean, how does that even work? Were the last two years just some kind of warm-up for something even more intense?

Wyatt runs his thumb down my jaw. I gasp.

"Let's go for a walk, Ari."

"A walk?"

The corner of his mouth twitches. "That means, use our legs." While his fingers continue to inflame every single one of my nerves, he moves the index and middle fingers of his other hand so that they look like two little legs.

"I can't walk."

"It's not that tough, you know?"

"No, I mean…" I look around for Harper one more time, hoping she'll *finally* show up. "I've got to go."

Wyatt bends down toward me. My pulse begins to pound as his nose brushes my cheek and then shoots up to a hundred and eighty when his breath brushes my ear.

"It's just a little walk."

"I can't," I repeat, wondering how it is I can even speak anymore, for his fingers have reached the soft skin along my temples before he tucks a strand of my hair behind my ear. "My legs… My legs are bare."

Oops. That word out of my mouth, *bare*, is the socket, and Wyatt is the cord. His entire body lights up when I say it, but can something like that really happen, or is it just the strobes? He's glowing. And all I can think is how fine he looks in this light. Suddenly I start to become afraid that it could stop, and I don't want it to, not at all, and so I say it again.

"Bare. My legs are bare. And because they're bare, I can't go outside. I mean, all that cold and snow and bare legs? No, that won't work, so…"

"If you say that one more time, I'm going to throw you over my shoulder and disappear with you, Moore. Right upstairs." He moves closer. Tilts his head. His forehead is almost touching mine, and we are both radiating a heat that has nothing to do with the stuffy air. "Don't say that word. Or do, yeah, say it." He moves even closer. His lower lip brushes my top lip, just a delicate touch, barely perceptible, but it's the spark in gasoline-soaked wood setting off an explosion in my body.

Without being able to control it, I gasp and stretch my arms out toward him, clawing at his hoodie, one hand in the fabric under his chest, the other on his hip. His muscles tighten under my touch, and I hear him draw a sharp breath. I have to stop this. It's all too much. My feelings, my emotions, Wyatt, right in front of me, the two of us tearing our clothes off right here in front of everyone in this bass-filled, stinking, pulsating party cave. I don't trust myself not to do it, because the word is just waiting for me to nudge it so that it can roll off my lips. I want him to touch me, want him to do things the way he did back in my room, even though it went against all my principles. I keep thinking that we don't work, that it just can't be, not after what happened—but I want him so badly. Every spare second I think about him there between my legs and how everything felt like it used to feel. My mind screams *NO*. My heart says *YES*. WHAT SHOULD I DO?

My fingers rebel; they are stiff and clumsy as I let go of him. It's an immense effort. In my head sirens are going off: *ERROR, ERROR, ERROR*. I have to struggle not to immediately throw all self-respect overboard and jump on top of him, place my center on his crotch, and allow myself to do what my body has been craving for years. Even more so since that kiss in the rink. The kiss behind the bell tower. The thing in my room. I want to distance myself *so*, so badly, but instead I'm drawn to him again and again and can't resist.

"I can't," I say, meaning the walk but obviously something completely different, too. My breath is trembling as I take a step back.

Wyatt's hand, which had gotten lost in my hair, sinks back down.

"It's too cold."

He *knows* that that's not why. He *knows* that I would have made my way through the snow in a bathing suit for him once upon a time. But now it's because of what he did. He shudders but, instead of stepping away, instead of giving up, says, "Then tomorrow."

That's Wyatt. He never gives up. He's a hockey player. They fight for their passion, even if it's the last thing they do.

"Tomorrow's Thanksgiving."

"Then afterward."

"Why are you doing this?" I raise my arms in the air only to let them fall back down. "Why won't you let us go?"

Wyatt jerks as if I had hit him. This guy can withstand huge bodies throwing themselves at him to knock him to the ground and can withstand a puck hitting his helmet at full speed, but these words, just these six words, are too much.

One of the blond puck bunnies walks over to us from the dance floor with a toothy smile and a delicate film of sweat across her skin. "Wyatt Lopez," she says, placing her long fingers around his biceps and snuggling up to him. Watching her do that, listening to the way she says his name, *my* Lopez, and not being able to do anything about it is bad. It hurts. She blinks up at him from below, her sticky eyelashes touching the brow bone above her eyelid. "You want to get a drink?"

He slowly turns to look at her, as if he has just been woken up and needs to understand what is happening. My stomach rebels. I can't look at the way the woman is glued to him as if he belongs to her. She has the right to do it, sure. He's a free man, but… Wow. This just won't do. It's not just bad; it hurts *like hell*.

I gather up the last of my strength to put on a shaky smile. "From what I can gather, you're needed here."

The groupie shoots me a grin as if I were her accomplice and had just wished her a lot of fun with him.

"And how," she says, winking at me. The feeling of wanting to grab her by the hair and tear her away is powerful. "*And how* he's needed."

"Okay, that's enough. I'm out of here."

"Wha…?" Only now does Wyatt seem to realize what's going on. "Wait, Aria, no."

I turn around and push through all the guests. I can feel an enormous pressure building behind my eyes, but I don't want to cry, not here. Heading for the door, I quicken my pace. Wherever Harper is, she'll just have to deal with the fact that I've taken off.

My fingers are pulling open the front door when I feel a hand on my waist, spinning me around. Wyatt's eyes are boring into mine. He flares his nostrils and puts his other hand on the door to push it shut.

"*I'm not letting us go* because I want us to work again. If not together, then as people who have accepted what once was. Because I know it's over. I *know* it." He turns his head and scans the room as if he were looking for words before turning back to me with a haunted look. "We need to look forward but don't kid yourself, we can't. Neither you nor me."

He is saying exactly what everyone else is saying—Mom, Paxton, Harper, Knox—and I know he's right. So I nod. Maybe that's mature, or maybe it's just a desperate gesture because I'm not ready to let him go. I don't know. But I really, really want to find out.

"Okay. We'll go for a walk, Wyatt. Tomorrow evening, after Thanksgiving."

And there it is again, that glow in his face. I'm still admiring the deep dimple in his cheek when I feel a vibration go through my thigh. At first I think, *That's it, now my body does its own shit*, until I realize that it's my phone. I reach into my pocket and look. Harper. I slide the green receiver icon to the right, stick a finger into my left ear, and the phone to the other.

"The missing princess. How lovely."

"Get up here, Aria." Her voice is anything but relaxed. She sounds panicked. "Right now. Something *really bad* is going down."

"What do you mean?"

A brief pause. There's a clanging sound in the background. She gasps for breath. "Camila."

Then she hangs up.

27

That's Where My Demons Hide

WYATT

ARIA'S EYES ARE WIDE IN FRIGHT AS SHE STUFFS HER PHONE back into her skirt pocket. I'm immediately alarmed. "What is it?"

"Your sister. Upstairs. We've got…"

Before she can finish, I'm bounding up the stairs with her behind me. My ears start to ring and the world around me blurs as I take two steps at a time. Arriving upstairs, I see Harper pulling at a doorknob with one hand and banging against the door with the other. As I move closer, she takes a step back.

"Camila's in there. With some…"

Her sentence is drowned out by the deafening noise the door makes as I kick it in. I hold out an arm to protect Aria from the splinters of wood flying through the air before I rush into the room.

What I see stops me cold.

Camila is lying on the bed in her underwear, her dark hair spilling out over the white sheet. Her cheek is resting on a spot of yellowish orange; one arm is draped above her head, and her lips are open just a crack, dripping with vomit. She's completely gone, and someone's bent over her, pulling out his penis and moving to pull down her panties.

"Fuck off!" he growls in a real dirty voice, and that's when I see his face.

It's Gray.

And I see red. I completely lose it. Something inside me explodes, and I'm at him. I tear the motherfucker off my sister with such force that he crashes against the heavy wooden wardrobe along the wall.

"What the fuck, man?"

I dig my fingers into his curly hair and pull until he howls in pain. He squirms and tries to hit me on the chin. I reflexively fend off the blow with my left arm, which is a mistake. Pain shoots through my body, making my head throb, catapulting me back to that summer day—the day I never want to think about again. Nevertheless, with a jerk, I manage to pull him toward the adjacent wall and jam my forearm against his neck. But the pain doesn't stop. It just grows. I can't see straight; everything's swirling. There's a sharp smell of gas and iron, and then I let out a bloodcurdling scream.

"Wyatt!" It's Aria. It's a miracle that I can hear her, that she manages to get through to me. I'm overcome by a strange feeling. It's like my mind's wavering between the present and that summer day, unable to decide where to stay. I feel dizzy. Bile is burning my throat, and I'm only vaguely aware of my forearm still pressing against the guy's throat.

Then I hear her a second time, and that's the decisive moment my mind needed. With great effort, I fight my way back to the here and now—drenched in sweat, panting, my entire body trembling, and Gray still writhing beneath my arm. I can't look at him because everything is shaking and blurring, and there's agonizing pressure on my temples. Then I puke. My stomach cramps; I get hot, cold, hot again, everything shakes, before my eyesight slowly clears.

I've barfed all over Gray. It's running down the front of his shirt, trickling off his sweater onto that pitiful dick of his that he was going to force upon my sister. The thought makes me retch a second time, and I increase the pressure against his throat before Aria appears next to me and tries to pull me away.

"Wyatt, stop, that's enough. YOU'RE GOING TO KILL HIM!"

The sound of her voice against my ear, her sweet scent, her hair tickling my cheek as she tries to tear me away from him—they pull me back from my frenzy, from being about to rip this filthy motherfucker's soul from his body and dismembering him for what he wanted to do to Camila.

And *thank God* Aria has this effect on me, thank God, for when I come back to myself, I see what I'm doing. I see his reddened face, his eyes popping out of his skull.

I let go of him with a jolt. My pulse skips a beat. Sweat's dripping off my forehead. It takes all the strength I can muster not to throw myself straight back at him.

Aria knows it. Aria knows *me*. And that's exactly why she puts her warm hand on mine and wraps her fingers around mine.

Breathing heavily, I look at Gray. He's gasping for breath, coughing, and pulling up his pants to cover up his vomit-covered balls all at the same time.

"If you ever get close to her again, I'm going to castrate you with my bare hands, motherfucker." I spit in his face. "Get the fuck out of here."

Still coughing, he rushes past me. Aria squeezes my hand. Normally I'd be freaking out with joy, but right now I can't think about anything but my sister. I whirl around, bound across the room, and take a seat next to her. Harper tries to get her to sit up, but Camila just keeps slumping down like a newborn with no tension in her limbs. She's completely gone.

"I'll take her," I say. Harper carefully places her into my arms while I look around the room for her clothes.

"Here." Aria has gathered up her leggings, UGGs, and knit midriff sweater. Sitting down next to me, Harper's eyes dart back and forth between my sister and me. She begins to nervously slide around on the mattress before she gets up and leaves the room to stand in front of the door to keep anyone from coming in.

It's quiet. Neither of us says a word as I hold Camila and Aria pulls the sweater over her head. Aria's fingers brush my chest before disappearing into my sister's collar to pull her hair out. The smell of Aria's hand cream streams into my nose. Along with beer. And yet I can still catch the scent of vanilla, which will remind me of Aria forever and ever and a little bit longer, too.

I lay my sister down on the bed so Aria can pull Camila's leggings up for her while I bend forward to tuck her feet into her boots. She's wearing reindeer socks. My chest tightens.

"It's my fault."

Aria looks at me. "That's not true, and you know it, Wyatt."

"It is." I lean against the soft king-sized mattress with my temple, my eyes focused on Camila's knee, on the hole in her leggings. "I'm responsible for her. I should have been paying attention. I should have made sure nothing like this could happen."

"Wyatt." Her sympathetic tone makes me look up. Aria is sitting cross-legged on top of the comforter while stroking Camila's hair. "You're a good older brother. Always have been. But you can't be looking around everywhere at the same time. Camila's seventeen. She's starting to want her own life."

"She is so *delicate*, Aria. Seventeen and yet so done with the world. That's just not right."

Aria lowers her eyes. "She's been through a lot. First your dad, then your mom, and then…"

"You." I swallow hard. "And then you."

Only a faint glimmer of light comes in from the hallway, but when the shadow on the wall moves, I know Aria's nodding. For a while neither of us says a word until, eventually, she sighs.

"I should have called. Camila was… She didn't deserve me leaving her, too."

"No. She didn't."

"Anything happen recently to explain why she's so drunk?"

"Not really. No idea. Mila's been difficult lately."

"How so?"

"I don't know. She's got secrets. Only gets home real late at night. Well, in the morning, actually. Whenever I ask her about it, we fight. I just can't get through to her."

Aria takes the edge of her sweater to wipe the last bit of vomit away from the corner of Camila's mouth. "Should I try to talk to her?"

I consider her suggestion for a long time. Not because I don't think it's a good idea, but because it makes me remember things. Like how Camila always wanted to talk to her when something happened in her life. That first crush? Aria. That first fight with her friends? Aria. When Mom was no longer there? Aria. And that was all before Aria left me. Her leaving changed a lot of things. It tore open wounds and left scars.

"You can give it a try. But…"

"It won't be like it was. I know that."

Her words leave an oppressive silence between us, while the bass booms in from outside and the electronic beeps creep toward us over the walls.

Eventually I stand up. "Let's take her to the hospital."

Aria nods. "You here with your car?"

"No. I…" My heart rate increases. "No."

"No?"

"No."

She stares at me with a look I don't like. A mixture of curiosity and sympathy. But I don't want to explain that my arm's screwed up or have her pity me because of it. I want to be Wyatt, just Wyatt, the guy who can do everything and overcomes any challenge with a smile.

I expect her to inquire further, but she doesn't. Instead, she puts her arm under my sister's neck, lifts her up, and says, "Okay. Then we'll go in mine."

I bet Aria's wondering why I'm carrying Camila over my shoulder instead of in my arms. But she doesn't say anything, just gives me far too sad a smile and follows me out of this god-awful room. Harper silently joins us by the door.

The Mitsubishi's leather seats are cold as hell. I carefully place Camila in the back and get in next to her so I can rest her head in my lap. Aria turns on the car and sets the heated seats on max. We make our way through Aspen's narrow streets and drop Harper off at her house by Snowmass Mountain. Ten minutes later, Aria's parking her car in front of the hospital, and I put Camila back over my shoulder. I'd love to carry her in my arms, but my injury just won't let me. Aria follows.

The hospital's sterile smell bites my nose as our footsteps echo off the walls of the hallway. We take her to the ER and wait for what feels like an eternity out front. Aria repeatedly strokes my thigh with her hand to calm me down. I hate this place. Ever since Mom's death, I haven't wanted to step foot in here, but, ironically enough, I end up having to come here pretty often. Most of the time because of Camila. Sometimes because of me. And always because of drugs.

I have no idea when we got here. Meanwhile, we've seen a kid with a bad cut, an older woman with ingrown toenails, and four aggressive dudes smelling of booze come and go. But now it's quiet, and I really wish someone would show up just so I wouldn't have to listen to my own thoughts.

"Wyatt," Aria whispers. She reaches her hand out slowly, almost cautiously, to run it through my short hair. "Everything's going to be okay. I'm here."

"But you're not going to stay," I say softly and close my eyes. "You're here the whole time, and somehow not. I've got you next to me, and somehow I don't. This is almost worse than all the time you were away."

I hear Aria take a breath. Her fingers stop moving through my hair. She opens her mouth to say something but stops. Then she opens it again. "I've got to talk to you, Wyatt. About us. It's…"

The door to the waiting room opens and interrupts her. The doctor comes in; he has a tired yet alert look on his face. He closes the door and looks at me. "It's not as bad as we thought. Any suspicion of date-rape drugs was ruled out by the blood and urine tests. It seems that your sister became incapacitated not simply because of alcohol but also from being exhausted. I am afraid she just *really* needs to rest. Could that be?"

His words are like a knife to my chest. My limbs are cold as ice as I nod.

The doctor writes something down on his clipboard and then sticks his pen back into his white coat.

"But she vomited," Aria says. "She was lying in it."

"Her blood-sugar levels were rather low. It looks like she did not have anything to eat before she went to the party. It is not uncommon for someone with an empty stomach and that blood-alcohol level to react with nausea or vomiting." He hands me a letter. "I have written down everything here. We do not think keeping your sister here is necessary. I think Ms. Lopez will feel better when she wakes up in her own bed tomorrow morning."

As if in a trance, I nod as Aria and I stand up. I hardly notice that she's holding my hand.

Back in the car, I don't say a word. I just stare out the window and stroke Camila's hair.

"I'm a fucking terrible older brother," I mumble when we reach downtown. My throat feels uncomfortably sore.

Aria looks back at me in the rearview mirror. "That's not true, Wyatt. You're doing your best."

"No, I'm not. Camila hardly eats a thing and is getting thinner and thinner. She spends all her nights stripping somewhere after working at the ski hut. Just to drag herself to school afterward. And what am I doing? Nothing. Nothing at all."

"Well…" Aria turns on her blinker and takes a right. "You can't lock her in, can you? And I'm sure that you've talked to her. Have brought up other options." She interprets my silence as agreement. "Camila's got her own mind. Of course we've got to help her. Of course we've got to think about how to make it clear to her that she can't go on like this. But you haven't failed, Wyatt. You're completely overwhelmed with the father role in your current life situation, sure. But that doesn't mean that you haven't taken care of her. That you haven't constantly tried to approach her."

"But it wasn't enough."

"We'll manage, Wyatt." Aria stops in front of the B&B, switches off the motor, and turns to look at me with a sad smile. "We always have."

For the first time in a long time, I feel it again. The hope for some kind of improvement. The feeling of warmth spreads pleasantly through my chest, chasing off the cold and enveloping me in a feeling of security.

We bring Camila up to our room. After putting her in bed, I kiss her forehead. As I'm tucking her in, Aria arrives with a bucket to put next to Camila. Her glance falls on the book she lent me, *Myofascial Relief Therapy*, and the ball next to it.

"Can we still talk for a second, Wyatt?"

An emotional, irrational part of me thinks she wants to talk about us, about me and her, about trying again, but another, much more intelligent side of me laughs, saying, *Man, Wyatt, are you dumb? As if.*

I know what she wants to talk about. What I don't know is that I'm prepared. All the same, I nod. "But not here. Camila needs quiet."

She nods and I follow her down to the ground floor. Apart from the string lights, the guest lounge is dark. The last bit of wood is glowing in the fireplace. Outside it's snowing, and the wind is whistling.

Aria goes past the couches to the bay window, her favorite place down here. She'd often nestle up in the cushions reading a book with a cup of tea on the serving trolley and the silent snow coming down outside. Just like now.

She kicks off her Chucks, crawls up into the bay window, and leans back. I follow her lead and sit down across from her. Our toes touch.

"Wyatt…" She looks at me, pulls in her lower lip, and runs her tongue across it as if considering how to approach the topic. "Recently, at the exhibition game, something happened with you."

My heart pounding, I take a cushion and focus on the button at its center.

"And earlier, when you blocked the guy's punch with your arm, it was there again. You wailed as if you weren't here at all, as if you were somewhere else completely."

The fact that she expresses exactly what is going on inside me makes me shudder. It's like I can finally talk about it, but without really having to say anything.

"And then the book you borrowed." She shifts to sitting cross-legged when her cat, Hershey, hops into her lap, and she absent-mindedly scratches his head before looking back up at me. "What happened, Wyatt?"

There it is. The question I didn't want to hear. The question that scares me more than anything.

What happened?

The soft, dark-red velvet curtains brush the back of my hand. Pushing them to the side, I see big white flakes coming down in the light of the gas-powered streetlights, making the world brighter than it really is.

"You don't have to tell me." Aria's soft words mix with the relaxing purring of the cat. "It's just…" She leans her head back into the cushions and looks at me searchingly. "I'm worried about you."

My head is a whirl of words that I can't seem to catch. Everything is a mess.

Aria sighs. She pushes the cat off her lap and stands up. "Maybe you'll manage to talk about it at some point. Sleep well, Wy."

Wy. She just called me Wy. The sound does something to me.

"Aria, wait."

She turns, her hand already on the railing, her foot on the first step. She looks at me expectantly.

I expel the air I've been holding in, wipe my palms across my jeans, and try to say what I want to say, but don't succeed. Again and again, I open my mouth to speak, but every time my voice fails me. An unpleasant tingling reaches my hands, which is the form the panic always takes as soon as the memories wake it back up.

"Wy." Aria comes back and sits down, one leg on the floor, the other pulled up in the bay window. She puts her gentle fingers on my hand, and the cold is immediately driven off. "It's okay. I'm here, you know? You don't have to go through it alone."

Everything within me concentrates on her touch, the soft circles her thumbs make on my skin. It might be the last time I ever feel her, the last time I can ever enjoy her closeness. I slowly raise my eyes to look into hers, those big, bright green almond eyes, and get lost. Whenever Aria is with me, I feel safe. I feel better, almost like I wasn't a monster but just some poor dude with a bit of bad luck. But as soon as I'm by myself, as soon as the warmth that she alone can make me feel is gone, everything comes crashing down, and I slide toward the abyss, filled with fear.

I take a deep breath, ignore my heart that's throwing itself against my ribs in protest, and begin to tell her what has turned the last few months into a living hell.

"It was the last hockey game of the season. After the game, my coach told me that he'd received an offer for me and that I'd be going to the NHL. The feeling that exploded inside me was...indescribable. That was my dream, Aria. My whole life long, that had been my dream, and suddenly there it was, right in front of me. I'd made it… And then there was the post-game party. One of the guys, Jake, said we just had to go; he said it'd be killer."

"Jake? Jake Frazer?"

Her question tears at my insides and presses down until there isn't any air. Nodding slowly, I look to the window. I can see my face in the glass. I look like a ghost. "He didn't want to stay long. 'One, two beers,' he'd said. He and his wife had to be at the pediatrician's early in the morning. But we went for it anyway; the other guys weren't letting us off that easy to begin with. I mean, things were really going off. At some point, his wife called and told him to come home because their child couldn't fall asleep without him and was crying. I was ready to leave, so I told him I'd give him a lift."

"But…" she stops, as if finding the error in the equation. "But hadn't you been drinking?"

Everything inside me collapses. I just can't anymore. I reflexively press my face against my upper arm. A whimper escapes, and as I catch my breath, I realize why: I'm biting myself.

"Wyatt, hey, *hey*, stop that. Don't hurt yourself." She pulls on my arm with one hand, gently but firmly, while drawing soothing circles over my back with the other. "Shh… Everything's okay, Wy. Everything's okay. You're here with me. You don't have to talk about it if you don't want to."

I shake.

"I was drunk. And high. But I didn't think anything of it. *You've done this so often, and nothing's ever happened,* I thought. We took off, and everything was fine, but it had rained, the streets were slippery, and I could hardly see a thing… It wasn't that far from the party in Breckenridge to the highway, just down the main drag, and everything would've been fine; nothing… Nothing would've happened. But there was that cross street where a car was turning, everything was dark, and suddenly… Suddenly…" My voice breaks. I can't say it. My body automatically goes into defensive mode. I start bobbing back and forth, squirming, fighting against the memories, trying to keep them from touching me, but of course they do, of course they're stronger. Frantic, I press my knuckles against my closed lids and grimace in pain.

Aria puts her arms around me as I start to fall.

"Jake didn't survive." Her voice is just a whisper, but I flinch so violently it's like she screamed.

I want to answer, to say something, to talk about it so that I don't have to be alone with this weight anymore, this endless barrier, but it doesn't work. Instead, I cover my ears with my hands, my eyes and lips shut tight while, for the hundredth time, I feel the brutal pain of that fateful day.

"Wyatt. Hey, Wy." Aria slides up next to me and carefully pulls my hands down off my ears and presses them to her chest. "Wyatt, look at me."

An uncontrollable trembling causes my lips to quake as I open my eyes. I can feel them darting back and forth in a panic and can feel myself breaking out in a sweat.

"The other car, coming from the cross street? It hit you?"

My nostrils flare and my eyes fill with tears as I swallow and nod.

"Then it's the other person's fault, Wy. They're guilty. Were they convicted?"

I nod again.

"And you?"

I shake my head.

"Okay." She takes a deep breath and reaches for my other hand before looking me straight in the eye. "Now, listen to me very carefully. I want you to internalize what I'm about to tell you, okay?" I look at her, waiting, agreeing. "You'd been drinking. You got behind the wheel drunk that night. That's not good, and I'm not going to defend that because that kind of thing is indefensible. But—and this is what you've got to keep in mind—even if it's hard for you, even if you don't want to believe it, you have to internalize it, over and over: you are not to blame. You could just as easily have driven past that cross street sober. Jake could have gone past it in a cab or with anyone else at that second. It hit you because you were there, drunk or not. You were simply *there*. It was a case of terrible, terrible luck, yes, but *not your fault*. Do you hear me?"

I look at her for what feels like an eternity. But then, I can hardly believe it—I nod.

"Come here," she says, and puts her arms back around me. "Come on."

And then she holds me in a way no one has ever held me. She puts her head on my shoulder. Hershey casts me a warning glance as if he knew what she'd gone through thanks to me.

I don't know how long we sit there, listening to our heartbeats. The sweet smell of her hair tickles my nose as we watch the dancing snow. It's like it wants to prove to us that everything's not so bad. As if it were saying, *"Look at me dancing. Look at how beautiful I am and how, in my own way, I'm changing the world, doing something big."*

They fall in order to shine. And maybe we can do that, too, Aria and I.

Maybe.

28

Like Strawberries on a Summer Evening

ARIA

WHEN I OPEN MY EYES, I'M LYING IN MY BED. I CAN'T
remember how I got here. My eyelids are crusty; I roll onto my
back, stare up into the warm golden dots of my string lights, and
think back to yesterday. About how I went to the party to see Paxton
and wound up meeting Wyatt instead. I wait for the familiar pain
that always arrives when his name pops up, but this time it doesn't.
Something has changed. And there's another feeling inside me. A
growing sadness, and suddenly I know why.

Camila.

I jump out of bed all at once, rush into the bathroom, quickly
brush my teeth, comb my hair, and get dressed—quick, quick,
quick. I jump down into the hall instead of using the ladder and tie
my hair in a bun on the way to her room. I tap my knuckles against
the rough wood of the door. Camila's exhausted voice calls me in. I
peer cautiously through the crack. "Hey. Can I come in?"

Camila nods. She's sitting cross-legged on her bed, her phone in
her hand, her hair still wet from a shower. As I sit down next to her,
she starts winding it around her finger nervously. "Wyatt's already
told me what happened yesterday."

"How do you feel?"

She shrugs. "Okay, I guess. A bit tired, and I've got a headache, but otherwise…"

I react with a distracted nod while considering the olive-green titmice on the wallpaper and what the best way to begin might be.

"Listen, Cam… Is there anything you'd like to talk to me about?"

Her fingernails scratch at a glitter sticker on the back of her phone. Without looking up, she shakes her head.

"You're seventeen," I say, my voice gentle and understanding. "Seven*teen*, Camila. You shouldn't even be drinking beer, but you've been hitting much harder stuff than that." The wet strands of her hair leave damp traces on the back of my hand as I stroke her shoulder. "What's going on in that lovely little head of yours? What can't you handle?"

There's a long pause in which Camila just taps her phone against her ankle. Eventually she takes a deep breath as if ready to say something. But at the last second, she swallows and shakes her head. "Nothing. I'm just trying things out."

"We tried things out, too, eh? But I'm talking two, three beers, Camila. Now and again a shot of something stronger, but that was it, and the next day we'd be hungover enough to last the next half year of school."

Camila puts her phone down in her lap and looks up at me. "Those were different times, Aria. Everyone else in my grade drinks every weekend. At least."

"Good for them. Really cool. I'm sure they'll be overjoyed when they get cirrhosis. Must be as cool as it sounds, huh? I mean, cirrhosis, wow, exotic. Who wouldn't want that?"

She acknowledges my sarcasm with a disparaging glance.

"Well, Cam, what do you want me to tell you? Lie? You're going to do yourself in if you keep up like this."

All of a sudden, there's a knock at the door, then Mom's voice rings in from the hall. "Housekeeping!"

"Not now, Mom!"

A few seconds go by. I can see my mother standing behind the door, wondering what I'm doing here in Wyatt's room, even though he's not even here—but of course she can't know that. Finally, she starts moving again. I hear her footsteps and the room service trolley rolling down the hall before her voice rings out again outside our neighbor's door. By the time I turn back to Camila, she's turned away. She's looking at her red nail polish, her head tilted. "Last night, that was... No idea," she says, timidly and quietly. "I didn't drink all that much. Paxton was at the party, and, seeing as I wanted to talk to him, I drank a few beers at the ski hut after work first." She shrugs. "That's it."

"Paxton?!"

She blushes.

I frown. "What's up between you and Paxton?"

"Nothing."

"You have a crush on him?" When she doesn't answer, I add, "Are you in contact?"

The red spots on her face get bigger and move down to her neck. She slides around restlessly on the mattress. Suddenly she grabs her phone and jumps up. "No. He, umm... Friends of mine have told me that he's into you, so... Yeah." Her eyes hurry to the door. "Your mom asked me yesterday if I could help her out with the stuffing, so I better be getting downstairs." A short and quite obviously fake laugh crosses her lips before she adds, "Need to make sure Ruth doesn't fill it with raisins instead of bread again."

What a lame excuse. Mom just walked by.

Camila goes toward the door.

"Wait. Cam, wait. I wanted to ask you if, well, I mean, Knox... He's studying psychology, right? And, well, seeing as he's something like a second brother to you, maybe the two of you could talk about everything that's happened sometime and... Hey!"

The door clicks shut. No chance. Camila's locked up tight. I think she has *a lot* to say, but she's too distant for my questions to ever reach her.

The button on my jeans is tight. My tummy is so full that it protests loudly against the restriction. Mom wants to load me up with another piece of turkey, but I wave my hands and shake my head while the sweet potatoes melt in my mouth. "I'm stuffed."

She simply dumps it on William's plate instead, which is next to mine. He immediately digs in as if he hadn't already eaten two fully loaded plates. Cranberry sauce is dripping from the depths of his gray beard. My eyes meet Wyatt's. He grins, and it looks so beautiful that I choke on a bean.

The corners of Wyatt's mouth grow even wider before he turns away and briefly puts his hand on my mom's shoulder. "That was really good, Ruth. Thanks for inviting me."

"Oh, Wyatt." She ruffles his hair just like she always used to when, for a change, he wasn't wearing his hat. "Of course." Then she looks around the table. "So, who'd like to begin?"

Right, almost forgot. Time for giving thanks. I nervously stick my hands under my thighs and lower my gaze. All day long I've been wondering what to say. Indeed, what am I thankful for at the moment?

But before I can think of anything, Mom starts speaking again. "I am thankful for having my daughter back."

I look up. She's smiling faintly, and the glow in her eyes is warm and loving. "And for having gone to the naturopath." She outright begins to beam as she raises her hands and looks at them as if they were new. "After I talked it through with my doctor, we adjusted the meds—less cortisone, more support. Thanks to that and the right supplements, the swelling is going down, and the pain is getting more manageable by the day. I wouldn't have thought that a mix of injections, vitamins and just doing things differently could help that much. And no, I haven't thrown out my prescriptions, just found out something that helps on top of them."

William pats his chest. "That's what I always told you, Ruth. Life can be painful, but nature heals. That's what *I'm* thankful for. For nature. And that I live in this wonderful town with all its wonderful people."

Mom gives him a glorious smile. She's looking at William like he was the most beautiful creature on earth, with his cranberry-sauce beard and suspenders. He smiles back, a bit awkwardly, but with an expression I've never seen on him before, and suddenly I get the shock of my life—I realize what's been going on here all this time.

It's not just that William likes my mom; it's that she likes him, too.

OH. MY. GOD.

My head automatically whirls around, my widened eyes bore into Wyatt's, who immediately knows what I'm thinking and has to make an effort to suppress a laugh attack. Holy Mary, Mother of God. This situation has got to finish, like, now.

"I am thankful for this, umm, pumpkin pie." I poke it with the fork, without having cut it into pieces beforehand, and leave a large crater behind. I shove one fork after the other into my mouth. "Wow. I mean, *wow*. This is just sooo good, really."

Camila wriggles her nose. "I'm sorry, but I'm not going to be having any of that now."

"What?" Crumbs spill over my lips. "You of all people are saying that?"

"I am thankful for being healthy," she says. "And, in case you've forgotten, you had herpes once, and I am not interested in that at all."

Wyatt spits his wine back into his glass, sprinkling the edges with red. "I remember that."

"That was seven years ago!"

She shrugs. "Once herpes, always herpes."

My chin drops. "You *monster*! Take it back. Oh, and by the way, your insurance statement came yesterday; they're covering your stay. But take a guess what caused the water damage."

Wyatt raises his head; Camila sinks hers.

"What? No one's told me a thing yet."

I point at his sister with my fork. A piece of pie falls into my wine glass. "The pipes were eaten away. Presumably from too much Drano. Not accusing anyone of anything, of course, but I wouldn't be surprised at all to learn that our chaos queen here never cleaned her drain when her thick strands of hair blocked it and simply poured too much cleaner down it afterward." Camila turns bright red. A confident grin sneaks onto my face. "Tell me again to my face I've got herpes."

Everyone breaks out in laughter, even Camila, until William looks at his watch. Sizing up the situation, he tilts his head from left to right before saying, "I'm afraid I have to leave you all."

"Already? I'd hoped you would be able to stay longer," my mom says with a sad look.

Ugh, no, this is something I don't want to hear, not at all.

"Sorry, Ruth, but I can't." He rigorously shakes his head, pushes back his chair, and stands up with his chin out and hands behind his back as if he'd just gotten orders from a superior. "In seven minutes and thirty-five seconds, the moon will enter its highest phase of the cycle, which will make me unbearable, utterly grating."

Camila coughs. "Only then?"

He turns to her. Cranberry sauce drips onto his odd, colorful, knee-high wool boots. "You should see a doctor, Camila. Your bronchitis doesn't sound too good. I'll make you a special mixture."

"I don't need any..."

"Oh!" His eyes grow wide as he looks back at his watch. "Six minutes and fourteen seconds! From here I need five minutes and three seconds to get home, so... Oh, Aria! Sorry, excuse me, sorry."

I think I've been blinded. His elbow just hit me in the face.

Wyatt laughs. "Quick, Will, quick! Hurry up, you're already getting unbearable!"

Will starts to panic. He trips over Hershey, who hisses, and we all break out laughing again and are laughing still when the door shuts.

Mom is sitting there looking outside, a dreamy smile on her lips, shaking her head. "William Gifford, you are incomparable."

She is still smiling as she stands up and begins to clear the table. Wyatt, Camila, and I help, but when she moves to empty the dishwasher, we send her upstairs. Despite the conversation Camila and I had, things are relaxed as we clean up, and, once we're done, we all sit down in front of the TV together to watch a documentary on the pack behavior of elk. At some point Camila begins to snore. Her grunts are only partially muffled by the pillow she is lying on. Wyatt looks at me with a wry smile that makes my heart sink into my pants. He slowly stretches out his arm, puts it over my shoulder, and pulls me closer. My stomach tingles. His lips are very close to mine, and I feel the softest of touches as his rough voice rings out. "So, *Moore.*" He cocks an eyebrow. "I seem to remember you owing me a walk."

My hand finds his thigh without my being able to control it, and this closeness, this longing within me, makes me close my eyes to try and collect myself. "What luck," I whisper at his lips, "that I stick to agreements, *Lopez.*"

Kiss me. Kiss me. Kiss me, please.

He doesn't. He grins instead. "Yeah." A gap-toothed smile. My heart leaps. "What luck."

29

Three Words Can Warm
the Coldest Storm

ARIA

FOR THE FIRST TIME SINCE I'VE BEEN BACK, I HAVEN'T avoided Wyatt's street. There's no pain inside me, no stinging sensation, no drilling in my chest as I steer the car onto Buttermilk Mountain Avenue. Ever since we got going, Wyatt's been tapping the button on the center console at regular ten-second intervals to find a good song on the radio. I'd almost forgotten that he always does this, but suddenly this gesture is so familiar, so completely normal to me, that it feels like the past two years had never happened. He makes me not care about what Paxton did at all, and that's pretty incredible. When Wyatt's around, there's just Wyatt, nobody else. There isn't a second I think about Paxton whatsoever. But as soon as I'm alone, I get angry. *Really* angry. I want to call Paxton up and make *him* angry, shout at him, and even go over to his house just to shout at him even more.

"That's a good song." James Arthur's "Quite Miss Home" comes on. "Leave it."

Wyatt leans back and grins. "I'd almost forgotten how much you dig these melancholy tunes."

I'd love to sing along, but that'd be too much, so I just hum instead. "I used to listen to him at Brown all the time."

He stretches out his finger and taps the miniature cup dangling from a ribbon on the rearview mirror. The handle is green, just like the turtle that's on it. It's holding a little heart in its hand with a grim look on its face, and underneath it's labeled, *YOU'RE MY FAVORITE IDIOT.*

"You kept it."

We pass his house. Nothing in me makes a sound. It's just his house, just like it was before, but with such happy and heavenly memories attached to it that I'm filled with a warm feeling of bliss.

"*Hello?* That's a no-point cup!" I park the car at the start of the path that leads to Buttermilk Mountain. "You don't throw those away."

"But it's from me."

With a sigh, I push the button for the handbrake and turn off the car. "Mom held onto it. I probably would've thrown it off our ledge on Ute Trail."

"Ouch."

We get out. The cold immediately digs into my limbs even though I'm wearing my whole set of cap, scarf, and gloves. Wyatt has traded his baseball hat for a red-and-black bobble hat. As he comes around the car, his face buried up to his mouth in the fur of his Canada Goose jacket, I feel like I'm hallucinating or something because I'm floating. Seriously, it feels like my feet are being lifted off the ground. It only lasts a few seconds, but it's a feeling you don't ever forget.

Wyatt is pulling on his gloves when he stops. "Why are you looking at me like that?"

"Like what?"

"Like I was a piece of cheesecake from Patricia's. The good one with grated lemon peel."

"I could *never* look at anyone like that."

Laughing, he nods in the direction of the mountain. "Come on, Ari. Let's go."

"Any idea where we're headed?"

"No. Just walking."

"Just walking?"

"Yep." He casts me an amused glance from the corner of his eye. "Why is this all so strange? We always used to do this."

He's right. We did. Lately, there just hasn't been any other man who wanted to go for a walk with me who could have reminded me.

To our left, the snow-covered firs start to clear, and we can see the icy lake in the distance. "You want to go to Silver Lake?"

Wyatt shakes his head. He nods into the distance. "Let's keep on walking straight."

"But all that's there are mountains."

He laughs. "You just don't want to go because it's uphill."

Wyatt knows I love to hike. All the same, I go along with him.

"Yeah, no doubt. You ever see me playing any kind of sports?"

He thinks for a moment. "Not after that volleyball tournament in ninth grade, no."

"Oh God, *that*." I cover my eyes with my gloves. "I dove into the net by accident when trying to get the ball." My shoe gets caught on a piece of rock beneath the snow. Wyatt grabs my arm and keeps me upright.

"Yeeeah. That aside, you weren't *that* bad." His eyes blaze. "I dug your hotpants."

The ascent gets steeper and steeper. By now, I'm getting side stitches and wheezing at every other step. I used to be able to hike forever without getting exhausted. But two years off and you can kiss all that goodbye.

"I don't need to play sports to wear hotpants."

"Is that a promise, Moore?"

Man, how can his penetrating gaze make me so hot even though it's *cold as hell* out here?

"Just an observation, Lopez."

He laughs again, real soft, real husky, a magical sound that drifts off over the snow.

"Just a little bit more till we reach the ledge," Wyatt says after a while. He sounds so relaxed compared to me. Naturally, as a hockey player, he's in much better shape; nevertheless, my burning cheeks are embarrassing.

When we finally make it, I fall to my knees and cool my overheated face with snow. Breathing heavily, I roll onto my back and look up at the mountains, their peaks disappearing into the black-blue veil of the sky.

Wyatt drops down beside me. Snow lands on his lips as he turns his head to look at me. He licks it off with his tongue. The sight triggers a strong pulsing between my legs.

"We going to make a snow angel?" I ask.

"You and your love of snow angels."

"They're nice."

"You're nice."

Three blinks of the eye. Two heart-stopping seconds. One thought.

Kiss me.

His face approaches mine—above us the sky and around us nothing but freedom. Cold lips graze my cheekbones, the corners of my mouth, and my jaw. I gasp, but not from exertion this time. *Kiss me*, I think, *Just kiss me.*

But once again his touches leave my mouth out. Instead, he puts a finger on my chin, pressing lightly so that I tilt my head forward. Snow spreads across my temple as he places a hand there, leans forward, and lowers his lips to my forehead.

I keep my eyes open. I am too surprised. Too overwhelmed. This moment is so intense, so explosive, it's as if his touch has made the sun shine. In these few seconds, I perceive everything twice and three times over. The smell of snow that surrounds us. The echoing cry of the falcon swooping past the mountains. His scent of fir and mint, most of which comes from the soft skin on his neck where he has applied cologne. My own pulse thundering in my ears.

And finally, the sound of his lips as they peel away from my cool forehead.

His eyes are bright and clear as he looks at me. "Let's take a photo."

I can't say anything in response because I'm still stuck in the moment that just passed. He takes his phone out of his jacket pocket, and we look into the camera, the backs of our heads in the snow, he with a broad smile on his face, me with a quiet one—I still haven't quite arrived in the here and now. He presses the camera symbol with his thumb, and it's only when I look at the picture that my head slowly clears. It's a beautiful photo. Our pupils are small from the flash, our irises just big blobs of color; his eyes are a nice honey-brown, a little golden, and mine are that bright, piercing green he loves so much. The first thing I think when I look at our faces is, *Oh, Aria, you two, you are just so in love with each other.*

"And now let's make that snow angel of yours." Wyatt tucks his phone back into his pants, rolls onto his side to make space, and starts moving his arms and legs. I have to laugh. The way he's lying there is just too funny; he looks like a little wooden doll whose limbs start to move as soon as you pull a string.

When he sees me, he indignantly opens his mouth. "Are you laughing at… Stop laughing at me!"

"I can't. You look so funny!"

"Funny, Moore? *Funny?* Come on over here. I'll show you what funny looks like." He digs into the snow, makes a ball, and lets it fly. It lands right next to my nose. I laugh even more, stumble to my feet, trudge through the snow, and tackle him.

"You're going to pay for that!"

He squirms beneath me as I try to soap his face, but he's got to laugh, too—it's so loud that it gets carried into the air, all the way to the mountains. And then he gets snow in his mouth and almost chokes, but he keeps on laughing anyway, and so do I, because the moment is just too beautiful. He stops resisting, and my gloved fingers brush his cheeks as our laughter dies down; all that's left is our quick breaths as we stare at each other, his hand around my waist, mine in the snow at either side of his head. It would be the perfect moment to kiss, really, like in the movies where there's music and laughter and fun until all of a sudden everything gets more serious and the melody quiets down. And if that's how it happens in the movies, then that's what's got to happen now, right?

Wrong. Wyatt picks us up and the moment is gone. I don't want to admit it, but the disappointment hits me so unexpectedly hard that I can no longer pretend that I don't want this again. His closeness. His lips. His smell. His touches. His jokes. His heart. *Him.*

"Look," he says, pointing past me into the distance. His other arm is still around my waist as I sit on his lap. I turn my back to him, my shoulders against his chest, to see what he means.

Beneath us—surrounded by the wooded, snow-covered mountains and spanned by the azure, star-studded night sky—our little town is glowing warmly. The downtown is the brightest, like a real sun, with multiple small, widely spaced patches spreading outward from it.

"Wild, huh? That's our home, Aria. *Our home.*"

I nod. My cap rubs his jacket. "Aspen is magic in every breath."

Wyatt's lips graze my ear. "Just like you."

My emotions are on a roller-coaster ride because I don't know what this is all about. Wyatt wants to spend time with me. Does he want to be more than friends? But he won't kiss me on the lips, even though he's never, ever been able to keep his hands off me. Maybe he just wants to be friends? But there are touches. Like just now, or, I don't know, always, if I'm being honest. The little teases, these most definitely ambiguous statements… More than friends?

Ugh. Can someone please come and stop these thoughts?

The worst thing is my own thoughts, which keep on telling me that I shouldn't care. That all we are is friends and nothing more. But deep down I know that this friendzone thing between me and him is the biggest bullshit of the century. I want him. With my heart and mind and feelings and everything. Period.

Some moments are timeless. Like this one. I don't know how long we've been sitting like this, with our pants completely soaked. I mean, all we really wanted to do was make snow angels. But now my whole body is shaking, and we can no longer ignore the snowflakes swirling around us.

So at some point I crawl off Wyatt's lap and stand up. Then we start on back.

"Am I going blind, or do you see next to nothing, too?" Wyatt asks after a while.

"I was just wondering the same thing. Just now I thought I was about to fall into some crevasse or something, but... Shit. I'm caught again."

"How do you manage to do that all the time?" It takes Wyatt a second to find me; in the meantime, it's started to snow so heavily, but then he helps me. I dig my fingers into his arm because now I really *am* afraid of falling into a crevasse.

"I've got small feet."

"Yeah, and?"

"You and your clown feet make it everywhere. I can't."

"I'm afraid of clowns."

"I know." The snow has developed into a real blizzard, pulling at every inch of my body, and the wind is blowing so hard that we hardly make any progress. "Do you know where we are?"

Wyatt squints. "Near Silver Lake, I think. It's not that far now."

"I feel like a ghost."

"Why?"

"Everything's numb. Every centimeter. I can't feel a thing."

Wyatt drags me on. Without his incredible strength, I wouldn't make it. I'd simply sink into the snow and freeze to death. Colorado's snowstorms are no joke. They're dangerous.

"You think that's the way it is? I mean, that ghosts don't feel anything?"

"They don't have a body to feel with." My teeth chatter as I try to speak. "I want to go straight into the bath, Wyatt. And then a hot-water bottle. And tea. Man, I would kill for some tea."

The path down the mountain just keeps getting steeper and steeper. Wyatt holds onto me when our feet slip. It's so dark we can hardly see our hands in front of us.

"When we get to the B&B, I'll get you your electric blanket from the basement. The one on the top shelf you can never reach, and... Stop. Right now."

His tone is so alarming that I dig my feet into the snow and stiffen. Now I can feel myself again; I'm not a ghost, because my heart is in my throat.

"What is it?"

Wyatt is looking into the distance. I follow his eyes but can't recognize a *thing* in this darkness.

"Fuck!" Wyatt's voice is hardly more than a tiny whisper torn away by the storm, but I can hear the fear within it. "Aria, there's a *grizzly!*"

30

Sky Above Us, Earth Below Us, a Fire Within Us

ARIA

AN IMAGINARY HOOK PULLS AT MY NAVEL AND CATAPULTS me through the air at breakneck speed. A dizzying whirlpool swirls in my head. It takes a while for my mind to switch to emergency mode and stop the merry-go-round.

"What should we do?" I ask as quietly as the storm will allow. "I don't want to die."

"You're not going to die."

"Oh God, Wyatt. It's going to eat us. It's going to rip through our organs with its teeth and tear our bodies apart with its claws and…"

"Speak louder, Aria."

"*What?*"

Wyatt lets go of me and begins to move his right arm in circles. He's lost it. That's the only explanation. Absolutely loony tunes. "Speak louder. It needs to hear us; otherwise, it will get spooked."

"But then it really will go after us!"

"No." First he stretches out one leg, then the other. "Have you forgotten what old Clearwater taught us every time she organized one of our high school camping trips?"

"I'm fairly certain she didn't tell us to jump around like idiots!"

"Don't run. Speak normally. Move your arms and legs at a normal pace. Then the bear won't see you as a threat or a meal. Its hunting instinct will only be awakened if we run."

"No doubt it's hungry. I'm sure it's not thinking that, just because we're moving around, we're no longer a tasty treat." Beginning to panic, I start to whimper. "I don't want to *die*, Wyatt."

"Slowly move to the right. Arms up."

I do what he says. Adrenaline is coursing through my body in such huge waves that it's even chased the cold out of my limbs. "Where do you want to go?"

"You'll see. We're not far."

"I wish I had a snowsuit on."

"Me, too."

"And some long underwear."

"Yeah."

"How much longer do we have to walk?"

"Just down the slope here."

In despair, I see the mass of snow in which my legs are sinking. Making progress is difficult. And suddenly I think of Wyatt's father, who died in the mountains under an avalanche. I wonder if he must be thinking about that, too. I'm sure he is. I'm overcome by the urgent need to distract him, even though a damn grizzly wants to eat us.

"Is it still there?"

"It's come a little closer."

"*What?*"

"But it's not running. All good, Aria. It's just standing there. Keep going. A little more quickly."

"I thought we were supposed to go slowly?"

"Yeah, but now I'm kinda freaked, too."

I'm just about to ask how much farther it is when I bang into a huge tree with my shoulder. Wyatt runs into me. His quick breath brushes my cheek, and I can feel him lifting his head to look upward.

"All good. We're there."

"Where?"

"Come on." He takes my hand. No idea how it's even possible with a grizzly nearby, but I actually feel a kind of euphoric fireworks inside, pushing away the fear. What a mix. "We're there."

I blink against the darkness but can't see a thing. "Wy, I am absolutely losing my shit right now. We're being followed by *a bear!* What's going…"

Before I can finish my sentence, I feel his arm around my butt. "I'm gonna lift you up now; reach for the rope ladder."

"Rope ladder?"

He doesn't respond. Instead, I feel my feet leaving the ground. My arms outstretched, I try to reach for a ladder, but my fingers don't encounter a thing. The violent storm continues to batter us. Wyatt staggers. I'm about to tell him that he must have made a mistake; there's no rope ladder here when my gloved fingers close around a crossbar. Relief floods my body. "Got it."

"Good. Hold on tight. I'm going to give you a push, and you pull yourself up until you find your footing, okay?"

"Okay." I sound skeptical, and I think of the volleyball tournament, of the moment when I jumped into the net, and that there's no way I can do this; I'll never make it. But the adrenaline seems to awaken unexpected abilities in me because when Wyatt catapults me into the air, my left foot lands unsteadily on the lowest strut.

It's damn wobbly. The storm is blowing me in all directions, and I've got to use all my strength to pull myself up, but then my knees hit solid ground. I almost howl out loud with joy with the only thought that's in my head: *I'm not going to die.*

My limbs are numb. My whole body is shaking. I can hear him groaning beneath me. Normally the jump wouldn't be a problem for him because he's tall—almost six two—and strong, but he can only hold on with one arm.

And then he's next to me. He's been swallowed by the dark, but

I can hear him breathing. Then his iPhone flashlight illuminates everything.

We're sitting on a small ledge; behind us there's a crooked and crudely built cabin, held up by a group of ancient tree trunks.

"The cabin tree house. *Of course*. But, Wyatt, we need a…"

"Key?" The light from his phone glints off the key he holds up and temporarily deprives me of sight. "I wanted to come here with you yesterday, remember? And today I forgot to give it back to William."

"God, Wy. You just saved us from a bear; you realize that, right?"

He helps me up with a grin. "I'd strike it off my bucket list, but that won't work."

"Why not?"

"Because that would mean that there really *was* a grizzly and not just something I made up to get you here."

I blink. "There wasn't any bear?" When he shakes his head, I throw my arms into the air. The snow whips into my face. I have to keep wiping it away to see Wyatt at all. "Shit, do you realize how scared I was?!" He laughs and goes to the door. I follow him. "We could have just walked back up the hill and taken the stairs that lead here from the other side!"

Wyatt opens the door and glances back over his shoulder. "But then it wouldn't have been as exciting, Ari."

"I hate you."

"Never."

The door swings inward with a soft squeak, and the wooden floorboards creak as we enter. The cabin tree house is fifteen minutes from Silver Lake, on the side of Buttermilk Mountain. It belongs to William. He built it a few years ago for tourists, and when I say he built it, that's exactly what I mean. I used to be afraid it would collapse as soon as the tip of my shoe touched the ground, but it's actually stable…and gorgeous, damn gorgeous.

Wyatt places the phone on the back of a worn, olive-green

leather armchair. I bend down to untie my boots while he walks to the fireplace next to the window. "Ha," he says, "matches."

We take a look around. Rustic eighteenth-century-style iron lanterns hang from the broad wooden trunks that form the supporting structure, and thick candle stumps are scattered around the room on decorated saucers. Wyatt lights every single one of them before starting the fire, and suddenly the hut is filled with candlelight and warm flames flickering along the wood.

"I am...sooo...cold!" My teeth are chattering as I continue to stand by the door in my wet clothes, arms wrapped around my chest.

It's a mystery to me why he hasn't done the same. His movements even seem somewhat graceful as he strides across the room to the wooden chest by the bay window. "Blanket, blanket, potholder, who-knows-what, blanket... Ah, jackpot." He pulls out a long, brown wool parka.

Wyatt laughs as I eye it greedily. He keeps on digging through the chest and finds a thick knit sweater, which I think used to belong to William, and a pair of wide gray faux-fur pants. We turn away from each other as we change, my fingers itching. I realize that he is naked. So am I. Our underwear is soaking wet from the snow. I inconspicuously take a glance over my shoulder. What I see takes my breath away. He's already wearing his pants, but his broad, well-defined back is facing me. The flames in the fireplace cast faint cones of light on his skin, and there, along his left shoulder and across his entire shoulder blade, is a long, white scar. Trying to push his arm into his sleeve, he makes a series of soft groaning sounds. Shocked, I turn to pull my parka over my head, but the lump in my throat doesn't go away.

When we turn back around, his eyes wander down my body. The corners of his mouth twitch. "You look...stylish"

"And you look like a yeti."

With an amused expression, he walks over to the basket next to the big couch, whose cover seems to be made of woven patches. He digs about in the basket. "Sweet potatoes, pumpkin, zucchini, carrots…" His head pops back up, and he looks to the side. "And what do we have here? Some oil. Spices. Wow. It's like William had prepared for any emergency."

"There's no *way* Will brought all that stuff up here."

Wyatt grins, in one hand a zucchini, in the other a carrot. "Busted. I brought it all."

Something is stirring inside me. I think about how Wyatt bought all these things for us and then brought them up here. Warmth seeps through my body. I walk past the coffee table and explore the compartments of a wooden shelf. "Oh, there's a loaf of bread under the dish towel." I press a finger into it. "It's soft." My eyes wander over to Wyatt. "Also from you?"

Wyatt carries the basket with the vegetables over in front of the fireplace. He nods and points to two tin jugs by the shelf. "Take a look."

I lift the lids and look inside. "Water. Perfect."

In the light of the fire, his caramel-warm eyes shine. "Wanna make a soup?"

As if in answer, my stomach growls. "I can't believe that after all that food I'm going to say yes. Absolutely. The path through the mountains wore me out."

In another box we find knives and put them in the fire for a second to disinfect the blades before sitting down on the floor and chopping the vegetables. I get a weird medieval feeling, barefoot on the floor in our robes and throwing vegetables into the cast-iron cauldron as we are. I add water, oil, and spices, and Wyatt attaches the handle with a fireplace glove to the hook in the fireplace so that the pot can hang over the fire.

"I still haven't defrosted," I say, sitting down and holding my hands out in front of the fire.

"How much you wanna bet it'll go quicker if you come over to me?" The flames light up the devilish glint in his eyes. He pats the space on the rug between his legs. "Just like old times, Ari."

I hesitate. But I can't act like that wasn't exactly what I've been thinking the whole time, as if the image of me between his legs—*oh-my-God-oh-my-God*—wasn't exactly what I've wanted.

"Well, okay. But just because your yeti pants look so soft."

"Of course. Why else?"

With a pounding heart, I crawl over and move between his legs, then lean back against his tight chest. Every time he inhales, I can feel it in my shoulder blades; every time he exhales, his warm breath brushes my neck.

"Back at Thanksgiving dinner I didn't want to say it."

I lean my head back a little to look up at him. "Say what?"

"What I'm thankful for." He looks down at me, meeting my eyes. He smiles. "For you, Aria. That you're doing well. That I didn't lose you. Not completely, at least. Even when it's not... Even when we're not...like we were, I am so thankful. For every conversation. For every touch. Every smile. Everything."

I can't look away. His eyes pull me in like two magnets. And I don't know what to say. I don't know how to explain what his words are doing to me. The butterflies in my stomach are doing loops.

"I'm thankful, too," I whisper eventually, turning back to the fire. "Above all, for the fact that you're doing well. That this accident... That it didn't take you. I wouldn't have been able to handle that. No idea what would've happened to me."

His warm chest nestles a little closer to my back. I am highly sensitive to every single one of his touches. We sit in silence for a while, listening to the crackling fire, the bubbling of the pot, and the violent storm blowing against the wooden walls, enjoying every minute we're touching thanks to the simple excuse of being cold. Again and again his hand brushes mine, seemingly at random, as he pretends to want to pick a piece of lint off my clothes, trace the pattern of the rug, scratch my leg, whatever. And I like it. I like it so much.

But at a certain point, neither of us can ignore the fact that we've been sitting way too long. The veggies have got to be completely soft.

Suddenly Wyatt gets up to stir the pot. "It's ready."

He carefully lifts it out of the fire and places it on a crocheted coaster. We toast the bread over the fire and eat it by dipping it into the pot and sliding the vegetables on top. It's one of those simple moments where nothing's really happening, and yet it has an overwhelming, almost magical effect. I could sit here forever, in this tree house, outside the storm and life and everything that makes it difficult. In here, it's just him and me and our hearts beating for each other.

Unforgettable. Timeless.

My dish is almost empty when Wyatt points his piece of bread at the corner next to the door. "Look." He plops the last bit into his mouth, gets up, and comes back with a Tetra Pak carton. "Red wine."

"What luck," I say as I push my dish to the side. "Rotgut Tetra Pak."

Wyatt laughs. "You want some?"

"You bet."

"One sec." He takes two clay bowls off the fireplace and hands me one. "We've got to slurp it."

"Nice. Like the Neanderthals."

"Your parka fits the bill."

"I know. I feel really attractive, let me tell you."

He pours some wine into my bowl, and I take a sip. The furry taste spreads across my tongue.

Wyatt takes a sip of his own and wiggles his naked toes before the fire. He looks at me. Tenderness smooths his features as he slides his finger from my right cheek across my nose to my left. "I love this."

My stomach tingles. His touch makes me nervous. Just to have something to do, I take another sip. I run my fingernails over the hardened clay. My bowl is almost empty, and a pleasant airiness spreads through my head like billowing mist.

"What do you love?" I ask and sink down onto the rug.

A grin creeps onto his face as he moves the utensils to one side to lie down next to me. He stretches out on the woven carpet and crosses his arms behind his head. The sweater stretches taut over his biceps. I see him take a deep breath, as if trying to taste this moment on his tongue and not let it melt away. Then he opens his eyes again and looks at me. "The way your freckles dance every time the fire casts light across your face."

I stare at him, in my Neanderthal dress, with the now-empty Neanderthal bowl, and catch thoughts swirling around my veiled mind, telling me Wyatt is everything, Wyatt is spring sunshine and autumn whispers, warm tingles on my skin, and the delicate crackle of golden-brown leaves.

"Your wound," I whisper, driven by the wine that's starting to make my limbs heavy. I take a deep breath. "Can I... Can I see it?"

There they are again. Those two weird little words.

CAN I.

Wyatt blinks. He hadn't expected that. But then he nods, straightens up, and pulls his sweater over his head. His hair is standing up straight, but I can only stare at that for a fraction of a millisecond because, sorry, there's a naked body here, *his* naked body not even seven inches away. The light of the flames is coloring him with golden flecks. And, my God, *those muscles*! Wyatt was always well-built. That's how hockey players are; they're broad and strong and sexy and hard (in many ways, let me tell you), but he wasn't *this* buff, not *this* well-defined.

Wyatt is aware of his effect on me. His eyes are sparkling. "You like what you see."

Clearing my throat, I ignore this and point to his left arm instead. "That one, right?"

Just a single question, a single gesture, and Wyatt's confident grin gives way to a look of fear. He nods carefully.

"Don't worry," I whisper, gingerly laying my hand on his

shoulder, where I begin to identify the hurt muscle groups with my thumb. "I'll be really gentle."

Tiny drops of sweat begin to form on Wyatt's neck. My thumb runs along the levator muscle up to the shoulder blade, and when he draws in a sharp breath and gasps, I know immediately that the hardening there is the crux of all the trouble. I stroke the muscle with slow movements; over and over I massage the clearly noticeable trigger points. With every passing minute, he breathes harder.

"You're the first," he says at some point, as I make my way up from his shoulder blade to the tender muscles of his neck. I span his head by placing the tips of my thumbs on his temples and lightly tilt it to the side. Then with the outer edge of my hand, I move down the sterno-cleidomastoid muscle of his neck and the scalene muscles on each side.

"The first?"

"The first that can touch me there."

Realizing what that means, I hold my breath. "No therapist was able to help you?"

He shakes his head. "That's why I started trying to treat myself."

"*That's* why you couldn't play."

Wyatt nods. I tell him to tilt his head forward and begin to stroke the muscles at the back of his neck along his spine with firm pressure. "I can help you. If you want me to. I've had a ton of practical seminars and exams."

My fingers slide off when he abruptly turns his head. He looks at me wide-eyed. "Really?"

I nod.

Wyatt's shoulders slump.

"Thanks, Ari." He lets his forehead sink onto my shoulder in relief, his warm breath tickling my neck. And as I take in his scent, I wonder for the very first time whether I might have made a mistake not listening to him back then. Maybe there really was a reason for what he did to me. Maybe I could have prevented his alcohol and drug escapades if I'd listened.

The harshness of these thoughts hits me violently and over-whelms me. For the very first time I think about the fact that it might not be his fault we broke up, but *mine*.

This feeling is destructive. It's destructive, and it's ugly, so ugly that I can't stand it a second longer.

My hands rest on his shoulders. I release him with gentle pres-sure, sit down in front of him, and look him in the eyes. "What *hap*pened? Between you and Gwendolyn, I mean."

Shock crosses his face. Now I know that any sense of ease is gone. When he exhales, his chin shakes. He's going to tell me. Of course he will. For two years he's been waiting to do just that.

"Jared came up. From the minor league. He took me to a party where I ended up drinking a lot, a *hell* of a lot. I was out of it. At some point, I'd smoked some weed because I simply didn't want to think or feel anything anymore. And then, at some other point, Jared talked about having some E if I wanted it."

"E?"

"Ecstasy. At that point I was so messed up, he could have talked me into anything. And after that, I have absolutely no idea. I mean, the alcohol, the weed, the E—we're talking a pretty heavy cocktail. From then on, the night's a blank." He feels for my hands before interlacing his fingers with mine. His eyes bore into mine, not honey in green now, but fire in fire. "I had no idea what I was doing. None. When I think about that night, there's just nothing. You left me, and I knew why, because there was that video, but to be honest, there's not a single memory in my head."

The floorboards beneath my knees begin to shake; it's like the storm outside will tear the cabin away, and we'll fall and die. Or maybe we'll survive, but then a bear will come, and we'll die anyway… Until I realize that all of this is just in my head.

I was wrong. I was wrong the whole time. I should have listened to his reasons. If I'd been a good friend—a sensible one, a rational one—I wouldn't have left him hanging like that. And with him, I wouldn't have abandoned the six years we shared, which now hover between us, expecting an answer to this damned whatever-it-is we have.

"It's... If I wasn't... If I had... We're..."

"Shh." Wyatt places a finger on my lips. He's so close, the tips of our noses are almost touching. "Don't say it. That wasn't you. Not you, not me. It was life wanting to test us. But now we're sitting here, right? We're sitting here, you and me, and it's all in your hands." His finger slides from my lips and is replaced by his mouth, which brushes them tenderly, only briefly, barely noticeable, but the first flame within me, the one that had just been waiting to light up, erupts. "What do you want, Aria? Tell me, show me, and I *swear* I'll be yours."

My hand moves. Slowly, I stretch my fingers out toward him. Touch his cheek. He closes his eyes, his eyelids flicker, only briefly, but long enough for me to see what this touch triggers in him. I move on, put my hand on the back of his neck, stroke his short hair, and enjoy the feeling of it tickling me.

"I want *everything* from you, Wyatt."

This is the spark our bodies have been waiting for. The spark that was missing to turn the waiting embers into a sea of flames.

His lips meet mine. I feel desire and taste snow, cheap wine, lust, and *Wyatt*. This kiss is more than just a kiss. It's a homecoming. A let's-give-all-of-ourselves moment. A shining forget-me-not that blooms as soon as hope germinates.

That's how things are between Wyatt and me. When we touch, the world shakes. When we touch, our hearts go up in flames. Wyatt and I, we burn. We're a raging inferno that needs our love to live.

"Aria." Just my name, just a whisper, but the way he says it, what he means, goes right through me. I climb onto his lap, place my hands on his neck, and kiss him, slowly at first, gently, then more and more quickly, demandingly. In between two caresses he gasps for breath, as if he had been waiting for this moment forever, as if he had been imagining it forever, and now here it was. But better. So much better.

Our bodies know each other. They know how all this works, how we can drive each other crazy, how we can cloud our minds and feel the touch of our lips everywhere, deeper still, much deeper. I pull in his lower lip, nibble on it, and he lets out a husky moan. His fingers disappear into my hair, pull out the braid, and lose themselves in the individual strands. He wraps one arm around my waist while our tongues touch, our lips meet wildly. He pulls me even closer. The edge of my parka rides up; I'm not wearing any panties, of course not, and suddenly I feel his erection beneath me, nothing between us but the fabric of his pants.

My moan gets lost in his mouth as I rub against him, our lips uncontrolled, teeth bumping. I increase the pressure, want to feel him, want these pants to disappear—less fabric and more of him, *more, more, more.* Then he lifts me up, just briefly, before my back sinks to the floor. He turns my head to the side, toward the fire; the space behind my eyelids becomes light, my face warm. Then his breath touches my ear—the tip of his tongue, his lips—and goose bumps appear up and down my entire body. I dig my toes and fingers into the carpet, gasp, moan, and hold my breath as his hand disappears beneath my parka. Electrifying flashes send pulses through my nerves at every point along the path his fingertips travel.

As he strokes my nipple with his thumb, lights explode behind my eyes. Suppressing a moan, I arch my back and stretch out toward him, craving his touch. But then he pulls away. I let out a whimper, which Wyatt acknowledges with a barely perceptible laugh.

"No worries, Moore." His fingers clasp my woolen parka. He undoes the zipper and pulls on my sleeves, and I stretch my arms, and then I'm lying underneath him, naked, exposed, just right. I can see how much he wants me. The expression with which he examines me, from top to bottom and back up again, is full of lust, full of desire, *hungry.* He emits a low growl, then he's over me again, taking my nipple in his mouth while stroking my waist, my thigh, and moving on to the space between my legs. The desire inside me is boundless. Panting, I squirm beneath him, expectant, trembling, and then it's there, the tip of his thumb on my pulsating, wet clit, and I moan out, louder now, much louder, not a single clear thought left in my head, just Wyatt. He gently moves his thumb in circles because he knows I need it that way, because he knows that the gentlest touches there ignite the biggest explosion in me.

"Wy... I... *Please.*"

An agonizing emptiness reaches me as he detaches himself. I open my eyes and look into his. Liquid honey. Golden-brown skin over firm, hard muscles. His hands are next to my head as he looks at me, breathing heavily, his full lips parted. The thick lash line touches his cheekbones as he lowers his eyelids.

"You have no *idea* how many times I've imagined this, Aria."

"So, you want me?"

"More than everything else."

"Then show me."

Just a brief movement of his hand, and suddenly I see everything. *Everything.* And it's...like it was before. But different. New somehow, though it isn't new. More, though it isn't more.

And then I can't take it any longer. My hands grab his hips and pull him onto me. He fumbles around for his jacket and pulls it over. Again, he moves away, and I squirm while he takes a condom out of his wallet and tears it open. Just two seconds, then his knee pushes between my legs, a silent plea. I put my feet up and open myself as I look deep into his eyes. I need to see this. I need to see how he reacts to me. I need to feel how much he wants me.

His eyes widen as he looks me over. And then, as if unable to wait another second, he pushes himself between my legs, one hand in my hair, skin to skin, both of us trembling, shuddering, and suddenly his tip is touching my opening. Almost reflexively I claw my fingers into his back while I arch my own and gasp. His lips graze my jaw as he supports himself on the floor with his healthy arm, and there are so many sensations blazing inside me, so many emotions, my abdomen is contracting in supplication, the space between my legs pulsing hotly, our hearts literally beating against each other. Full of burning desire, I squirm beneath him, stretch my hips forward, wanting him to continue, to go deeper, but he doesn't move; he just smiles against my lips. No more movement, nothing.

"Tell me what you feel, Aria."

"I... Wyatt."

"My name is not a feeling." The throaty sound of his voice vibrates upon my mouth. I can feel him slowly circling the tip of his penis forward, right where the nerves are the most sensitive. "Do you love me, Aria?"

Our eyes meet. The fire warms our skin, flares in our eyes. We both know how heavy the question is. We both know the moment depends on my answer, and not just that, but the two of us together.

"Yes." A purr. "I love you, Wyatt."

The trembling that moves through his body represents a liberation for which his heart has fought for so long.

His lips meet mine, and he slides into me, fills me up, and makes me whole.

His moan meets mine as he penetrates me, and we begin to move, his fingers in my hair, my hands seeking support on his back. Then his hand wanders down, finds my nipple, tugs at it as he begins to thrust into me faster and faster, finds the hidden point that only he knows, kissing me wildly now. Everything is chaos. Everything is love. We lose control, and then there is this tremor that comes in waves, but not those of water—they're fire. They go higher and higher until the wave of fire breaks in a thunderous explosion, everything bright, everything glowing, everything shining.

He thrusts into me one last time; our moans fill the air and join the crackling of the fire. "Aria," he says, as if my name was the answer to everything, then empties himself into me with a passionate groan.

Our sweaty upper bodies meet, my belly touching his as we breathe frantically and fast, arms and legs exhausted and heavy.

I feel Wyatt's damp lips at my collarbone say, "That thing between us, it was everything."

"That thing between us," I say, digging my fingers into his dark, silky hair, "that thing between us *is* everything."

31
Just Like Back Then

WYATT

ASPEN'S MARKET SQUARE IS OVERFLOWING WITH MAKE-shift tables. Today's the yearly flea market that William brought to life years ago in order to rid himself of his "crap."

Aria is strolling along next to me, one hand occupied with a bag full of churros, the other...wrapped up in mine.

It's wild. So wild that I have to keep looking to make sure this is really happening. Ever since that snowstorm ten days ago, we haven't been apart. I even got a new SIM card so I could give her my number. I mean, the other belonged to the fake Paxton after all.

"There's Will!" Aria points out William with her churro. He's standing behind his table bundled up in his snowsuit. "Let's see what kind of weird shit he's selling this year."

"You remember when the mayor of Breckenridge was visiting, and William lost it over his not wanting to buy his toothpick art?"

"Yeah! You know, sometimes I have nightmares about Will getting all blue in the face."

We stop in front of his table. When Aria starts examining something that looks like a shrunken finger, William thumps his chest.

"A pipe. You interested?"

"There is no *way* that's a pipe."

"You bet it is." William puts his fists on his hips and eyeballs me with his smart-ass look. "All Aria has to do is try it."

"Will, you know how susceptible to herpes Aria is."

"Hey!" She attempts to cast me an angry glance but ends up grinning instead. "You have any no-point cups, Will?"

"Umm. I don't think so." Her fingers become entangled with mine again as we move to walk on.

William eyes us skeptically. "Next week there's an important town hall."

"And?" I ask.

"It's the most important one of the year. We're planning the Christmas party and allocating tasks."

"We're aware of that, Will."

He crosses his arms. "You'd better be there."

"Why wouldn't we be?"

"Because one never knows with you two. Back when you and Aria first got together, you started to skip every single one and didn't think I realized your excuses were bunk."

Aria turns red. "That's not true."

William snorts. Ever since we got back together, he's looked at us with narrow eyes. He clearly doesn't trust the situation. Doesn't trust *me*. Most other people have taken it in stride and are happy for us, especially Knox and crew. But William is really protective of Aria. He puts his hands around his mouth to form a megaphone and shouts, "HEY, SUSAN, ARIA AND WYATT ALWAYS USED TO SKIP MY TOWN HALLS, RIGHT?"

"I DON'T HAVE A THING TO SAY TO YOU SINCE YOU BLOCKED MY SHOW!"

"BUT IT'S UNSETTLING, SUSAN, UN-SET-TLING!"

"YOU'RE UNSETTLING!"

"ONLY DURING A THREE-QUARTER MOON, BUT IT'S PAST, SUE!" His head turns red. "PAST!"

Aria and I move on. William has long forgotten us, but his exchange with Susan continues to echo across the square. I put my left arm over Aria's shoulder and pull her toward me as we saunter over to Vaughn's table.

Over the past two weeks, Aria has worked on my wound three times a day. I never believed I'd be pain-free again, but she managed to do it. There's still work ahead, of course, but not that much. I'm doing well. So well that Coach Jefferson is going to let me onto the ice for my first NHL game tonight. Home game against Ohio.

Am I nervous? You bet.

Am I going to tuck in my tail? Hell no.

Vaughn is sitting behind his table restringing his guitar. I pick up a cup with a turquoise-colored llama with red cheeks. It's labeled *No ProbLLAMA*.

"Oooh," Aria squeaks. "Cute!"

"Hey, how much?"

Vaughn looks up. "A churro."

"You can have two!" Eyes shining, she holds out her bag to him as she bounces up and down with joy. His locks bounce up and down as he stands up, too, and, in addition to the churros, he nabs two cinnamon sticks.

And then we move on again, but now Aria's hands are wrapped around the cup.

"You're holding onto it like you're in love."

"Maybe I am."

"Well, I'm afraid I'm going to have to break the cup then."

"Touch it and you lose a finger, Lopez."

"Doesn't matter." I raise my hand to say hey to Knox, who's getting into his car with Paisley on the other side of the street. "I'm just going to buy Will's weird pipe and stick it to me."

"Sexy."

"I know what you're into, babe."

"Well now! You sure you feel ready for the game tonight?"

"You bet."

"You happy?"

"Happy isn't the word." I use her distraction to steal the cup out of her hand and put my fingers back where they belong. "Hockey's my passion, and when it's taken away from me, it's like being locked up in a big cage. There's enough room, yeah, but it's limited, and you never have the chance to spread your wings."

"Well said."

I accompany her to the door of the B&B. My bag is already in the car. The game doesn't start for a few hours, but we have to be at the training center early. During the season, Zayne has us meditate and do some yoga, followed by a long player analysis with extensive commentary from Coach Jefferson based on recorded matches of the opposing team. Then we warm up and go over our own tactics again.

Aria leans back against the wall next to the door. I move in front of her, her hands in mine, her shoes between mine, and rub my nose against hers. "You have the tickets I gave you?"

She nods. "Four of them. Camila, William, Mom, and me."

"I still can't believe that your mom and Will…"

"Don't. I don't want to think about it, or I'll start imagining them… Ugh. Too late. Thanks!"

I laugh and give her a kiss, which makes her shudder. "Well, later, Moore."

"Later, Lopez."

"I love it when you say my name."

"Me, too."

"You know what I'd love even more?"

"What's that?"

I kiss her knuckles. "Me being able to say it."

"You being able to say what?"

"Later, Lopez. How handsome you are, Lopez. Hard to believe, Lopez."

The bell-like sound that leaves her lips at this moment, this soul-happy laughter, completely open, completely in love, tugs at my heart and awakens a voice in me that says, *Wyatt, man, you are so* lucky.

"Okay, guys." Coach Jefferson takes the remote control off the table and switches off the screen. "We've just analyzed five games, focusing on every one of your opponents. You know what you've got to do tonight." He turns to Xander, who's running his fingers through his hair. "Don't forget, the left winger always swerves at the last minute. That's his MO. You've got to keep him in check early, got it?"

"Yep."

"Good." Jefferson puts one hand over the other and looks around the room until his eyes land on mine. "As you heard at the press conference the other day, Gray got the boot."

"Got the boot?" Owen frowns. "They said he left voluntarily."

"That's what they always say to avoid a scandal," Caden says. "What was really going on, Jeff?"

The memories his question triggers make me feel sick. Coach hesitantly looks at me while scratching his cheek.

"He tried to assault my sister."

The team collectively gasps.

"That motherfucker," Paxton spits. His face is distorted by rage, and he balls his hands into fists. "If I'd known, I would've killed him."

"I couldn't stand the guy from the beginning," Samuel says. "Your sis okay?"

I nod. "It's all good. We pressed charges. Let's be happy that the piece of shit is gone, and we can really shine tonight!"

The boys give a collective cheer as we stand and leave the conference room. I'm glad to be back. I don't see my team much outside of training and games. I mean, sometimes we go out to eat or whatever.

But we spend so much time together in this training center that we've almost become family. Of course they know what happened to Camila and me. I'm touched that they reacted so angrily to the thing with Gray.

Together we walk through one of the glass doors on the upper floor to take the stairs down to the catacombs. Before a game, it's impossible to take the regular route through the training center. We would be overrun by fans and never make it out onto the ice.

"Hey, Lopez." Paxton catches up to me and punches me in the shoulder. "I wanted to talk to you about something."

We take the left hall through the cold basement. A dim glow lights the way.

"What's up?"

"Something weird went down between your ex and me at my party."

"What do you mean?"

Behind us Xander and Caden are making fun of Owen for his gas. When he can't manage to get it under control, they push him to the side, laughing.

Paxton looks at me. "No idea, man, suddenly there she was at the hot tub saying that I'd invited her or something."

I almost choke as I vigorously try to suppress the wheezing sound that's creeping up my throat. "And what did you say?"

"Nothing." We turn to the right and go through a door that leads to our changing room. "Before I could tell her that that definitely was not the case, Caden showed up and we took off. Just wanted you to know."

I'm flooded by a feeling of relief. I was wondering why suddenly there were no more messages from her to the number. Of course, a very optimistic part of me convinced myself that it was because we were getting closer. And maybe it was. Maybe everything just fell into place, one thing led to another, Pax was just weird, and she couldn't resist our attraction anymore. No idea, but it doesn't matter. Aria and I are together again, and that's all that matters.

Smiling ear to ear I take my jersey out of the locker. I let the smooth polyester glide through my fingers, run them over the number twelve, and just enjoy the moment. Until a bottle hits me in the side of the head.

"If you need a minute alone with your jersey, all you gotta do is say so, rookie."

Laughing, I take the bottle and throw it back at Caden. "Shut it."

Owen sighs. "I wish I had a girlfriend who looked at me like Wyatt's looking at his pads."

"And I wish you'd finally stop farting, man," Xander says.

"I *can't*; it just happens."

The guys keep messing around, throwing crap at one another, just because we hockey players are predestined to do that for some reason, but I opt out. I'm thinking about Aria, in the good seats, waiting to see me play.

Eventually, I'm suited up and standing with the others in the players' entrance. As soon as the opening music starts to boom through the stadium, my heart begins to race. We take off, bumping into one another, body check here, body check there. Caden taps Samuel against the helmet with his stick, and Owen farts—the usual pre-game rituals. Then our names are called. A projector plays a highlights reel of our games accompanied by epic music and lights, and our names appear in bright neon together with some really impressive bass. One by one, we hit the ice, and the fans go wild, as does my heart. It's mind-blowing; there are so many people, the bass is booming above our heads, there's a blue pulsating light like we're in a huge club, and all the stands are aglow because everyone's holding their phones and taking videos. We do our laps, and I'm covered in goose bumps. The way the crowd is yelling, I feel like the coolest guy ever.

NHL openings are the absolute shit. I've dreamed about this ever since I was a little kid beneath my NHL blanket.

We move into position. I know that, somewhere, Aria's watching me, and that makes me feel like I'm on cloud nine. With my gloves on my stick, I skate to the middle of the ice. Fans are chanting my name. It's all so surreal.

The game starts, and it's immediately clear that Ohio has no intention of playing fair. They're aggressive and don't even attempt to make their checks and high-sticking look like mistakes. Their center tries to hit me a bunch of times, which I only manage to avoid because I'm *really* quick and *really* good, but Caden takes a bad one and has to be helped off the ice. Right before the end of the first period, it's 1–1, and that's only because I was able to free up the goal line for Paxton through a cheap trick. I got busted, of course, and had to sit it out for two minutes, causing Coach Jefferson to give me a lecture about how I've got to stay out on the ice no matter what.

By the last third our opponents have grown even more aggressive, either because the coach has throttled his team or because they're getting tired, I don't know, but the chants are getting rougher. When Samuel blocks a seemingly perfect shot and Xander passes off to Owen, who manages to dodge a check, his opponent yells across the ice, "You, fucker, I'm going to plant my stick in your nuts!"

But Owen doesn't get distracted for a second. This is hockey. It's how it is. You ignore it and move on. All that matters are the goals.

The opposing defender sets up in front of him and blocks his path to the goal. Owen pretends to break out to the right and instead passes the puck to the left—toward me. The center forward and I rush ahead at the same time, and, hoping to throw me off by playing dirty, he yanks on my arm, my injured one, the fucker. It still hurts. I can definitely feel it, but Aria's done a good job of getting me back in shape. Or well enough for me to play, at least. I jerk away from his grip, shift my weight forward, and speed up. The fans collectively suck in their breath as I take control of the puck at the last second. But it bounces and slides off my stick. A huge "NOOO!" rings out. I don't give up and rush forward once more, check the opposing left winger who's trying to get in my way, and grab control of the puck again. The fans let out a collective breath. Behind me the boys are scrapping with Ohio's team; I hear insults and blades on ice coming after me as I press into the attack zone, raise my stick, shoot and…

Goal.

My first ever goal in the NHL. Single-handed. The second the stadium clock announces the end of the third period, I feel the mass of my teammates' well-trained bodies throwing themselves at me. A real dogpile—everyone screaming in my ear and hitting my helmet. And then there are all the people in the stands in their green fan jerseys completely losing their shit and all the reporters' camera lights flashing. But I only have one thought.

I get away from my team and shoot across the ice to the VIP seats right behind our bench.

Then I see her. Aria's standing behind the plexiglass next to her mom, William, and Camila; she's in my jersey with number twelve painted on her cheeks.

She's laughing.

I laugh.

And it's all like it used to be, just a little bit more.

32

Like I Was Never a Reason to Stay

Aria

"You've got to help me!"

Harper recoils when I plop down next to her on the red chair.

"God, Aria!" She tightens the bow of one skate before turning to the other. "What are you doing here?"

"I already told you." Wrinkling my forehead, I pull a piece of lint off her tightly wound bun. "I need your help."

"And that's why you're here at iSkate? Couldn't it have waited?"

"No. It's almost an emergency."

She looks at the digital clock on the other side of the ice. "I've still got ten minutes."

"Super." I absently tuck my long hair behind my ears while Harper takes off her skates. "It's got to do with Wyatt."

"No way."

I let her sarcasm slide. "It's his birthday today, but he'll only be coming back to the B&B later on because he's got training. So, what I was thinking was…"

"Oh, hey, Aria."

I spin around. In the entrance corridor between the stands, I see Paisley and, next to her, in a blue training dress and two French braids, Gwendolyn. Suddenly my mouth is so dry that not a single word makes it over my lips.

Paisley follows my glance. She nervously looks from me to Gwendolyn and back before her expression makes it clear that she's remembered we don't speak to each other. "It's so nice to see you." She doesn't sound as easy-going now. More happy-shaky. She attempts to ignore the awkward vibe. "How are you doing?"

"Good, thanks." It takes everything I've got to ignore Gwendolyn and concentrate on Paisley. But I'm not entirely successful, as the background isn't as blurry as I'd like. "You?"

"Me, too."

I nod, she nods, head up, head down, but the cringe factor just grows because neither of us knows what to say to end this.

Wait. Harper. Turning around to look at her, she clicks her tongue. "This is unbearable. Come on, A., let's go."

"But you've only got ten minutes."

Harper slips into her sneakers. "Eight, to be exact. And I'm not going to spend them in the middle of y'all's force field."

She begins to dig through her sports bag until she pulls out her wallet. "You coming?"

I nod. Paisley smiles as I walk past. I do my best to return it, but I'm afraid it comes out more like a grimace.

Harper bends over to pull up her tights so that her boot covers don't drag across the ground. "Can you imagine what it's like having to train with those two every day?"

"Paisley's nice."

My best friend stands back up and wrinkles her nose. "I just don't think I can human."

"You're friends with me."

"Yeah. You."

"What, *me*?"

"You're...*you*."

"Huh. That hadn't crossed my mind."

"I can handle you."

"And no one else?" I smile at the server in the lounge as we approach the counter. "Two cappuccinos, please."

Harper leans against the wall, smearing the daily special off the board in the process. "You know what I'm like."

"Yeah, I do indeed." I slide two singles over the counter and take the cups before looking at Harper again. "You're sweet. No, really. Helpful. Unselfish. You want me to go on? I've got a few more adjectives for you…"

"It's all good, thanks." She pushes off the wall, takes one of the cups, and points to two empty chairs far away from the balcony-side that overlooks the ice. She knows that I'd just end up staring at Gwendolyn—watching the movement of her legs across the ice and imagining Wyatt between them. An ice-cold shudder goes through me.

We sit down. Harper crosses her legs and takes a sip of her cappuccino. "So, what do you need my help for?"

"Back in high school, you knew this one guy…"

"I knew a *few* guys back in high school."

"I can't remember his name." I thoughtfully snap my fingers. "Big. Lots of hair."

"Lots of hair? You serious?"

"Man." I laugh. "That guy who was always making all the school videos. The guy who touched up your picture for the yearbook. You know, when you had that big zit."

"Oh, man! Hyong!"

"Exactly! You still in contact?"

"*He retouched my pimple*, A. You think we're still in contact?"

"So that means you're not?"

"Of course not!"

"Damn. I need him."

"What for?"

Harper patiently listens to my plan before heaving a sigh.

"There's one chance," she says.

"Really?"

"Yeah." She empties her coffee and stands up. "It's been a moment, but at one point he sent me his number via Insta. I mean, it will be *super awkward* getting in touch with him now because of you, but I will."

"Perfect!" I jump up and euphorically wrap my arms around her and keep on bouncing up and down as we make our way to the stairs. "Will you let me know by this afternoon?"

"I will."

"You're the best!"

Harper makes a face when I kiss her on the cheek, but she lets me. I think I'm the only person who can get this close to her. Harper's my best friend; I know almost everything about her. But for some reason, I've never learned why she's so *terrified* of any kind of human closeness.

"It's all good," she says, pressing me away softly but definitively, then looking into the rink. "I've got to get back out on the ice; I'm already too late. Later, A."

"Later."

It's a quarter past five. I'm sitting on the swing over the cliff edge off Ute Trail. Our place. Wyatt's and mine. The sun's slowly going down. In the snow in front of me are the two lanterns I brought, right next to my backpack with the bottles of champagne and glasses. I'm softly swinging back and forth, tracing a pattern with my boots.

He's not coming. And yet I planned everything down to the last detail. There was no way anything could go wrong. Just like every day over the last two weeks, he was supposed to get back to the B&B around four, and there, on his bed, he would find the Post-it telling him that he'd find me at the place we first kissed, at the same time as he was born, 4:44. Well, actually, our first kiss was somewhat unromantic, behind the barn during a town hall that we'd skipped.

But later, when we took a school trip up here to the cliff, Wyatt went around telling everyone that he would marry me here. His friends just laughed and said, "Ha ha, well, if you're serious, kiss her." Boy stuff, just kidding around. But then, all of a sudden, there he was: Wyatt, in his carrot-colored pants and that blue-and-white-striped T-shirt, planting a kiss on my cheek.

Wyatt knows that this is the place I mean. But he's not here. I tried calling him, but he didn't pick up.

In the meantime, the snow beneath my feet has gathered into two little mounds when I come to a stop and get off the swing. I can't keep on waiting. The sun's going down, it's ice-cold, and I really have no interest in getting caught in another snowstorm. Or running into another grizzly. Alone.

I'm so fucking disappointed. The weight of my backpack is slowing me down. It's getting darker. I have to relight the candle in my lantern multiple times before switching to the flashlight on my phone. The longer I make my way between the trees, the colder I get. Snow's dripping off the leaves. Every couple of seconds I flinch because of some unknown sound.

It feels like forever until I'm back in my car. I turn on the seat warmers and drive downtown with cold limbs and cold thoughts, everything simply empty because I don't know what I should think because I don't know how I should feel. Am I disappointed? Angry? Am I sad or concerned? I mean, what if something's happened? And then my heart really begins to race. If something's happened to him, I'm going to die, and all of a sudden my head is full of thousands of thoughts. I even consider driving to the hospital.

My heart pounding, I pull up to the B&B. I turn off the motor, hurry across the street, and run into the house. Mom says hello, but all I offer her is a weak smile in return as I rush up the stairs.

I stop in front of room twelve. I knock, but no one answers. I hesitantly turn the knob, counting on the door being locked. But surprisingly, it opens.

The room is empty. Wyatt's hockey bag is lying on the bed. Next to his phone.

"Wyatt?" Maybe he's in the bathroom. But he doesn't respond. Did he forget his phone? And if he did, where is he? On the way to our place at the end of the trail? Maybe I missed him. Maybe I came back too soon.

I cross the room and stop at his bedside. The sports bag is on my Post-it. It's hard to say whether he even noticed it before he threw his bag down. I hesitantly pick up his phone. I turn it between my fingers, unsure whether I should do what I want to do. Never in the six years we were together did I ever feel like I couldn't trust him. I never felt the urge to look at his cell phone. Right now I'm feeling the enormity of what his betrayal has done to me. The stable trust I had back then is nothing more than a destroyed wall.

Nevertheless, I don't want to be like that. I want to at least try to build it up again. Give it a chance. I toss the phone onto the mattress, but it's unlocked by my touch across the screen. And then I stare at it like it's a bomb, unable to move, unable to exhale.

I don't see a home screen but a WhatsApp chat.

My heart can't take this. I can't breathe. My hand is trembling as I reach for the phone a second time.

Gwen: Happy birthday, Lopez!
Wyatt: Thanks, Pierce. 😊
Gwen: You coming to the diner?
Wyatt: When?
Gwen: Now. I've got a surprise for you.
Wyatt: What?
Gwen: It wouldn't be a surprise if I told you, ha ha. At Silver Lake the other night, you showed me that I can trust you. Now you've got to trust me.
Wyatt: On my way.

I can literally feel all the blood draining from my face. I stare at the chat while my lips silently repeat that one sentence.

"At Silver Lake the other night, you showed me that I can trust you. Now you've got to trust me."

What happened at Silver Lake? Why did they meet up there in the middle of the night? Shit, I'm losing it. I scroll up. There's a lot. All this time. Every day. Oh my God. I scroll past most of it; I just want to know what happened at fucking Silver Lake. And then I see a picture Wyatt sent her.

It's of Gwendolyn. She's making a spin on the ice; Buttermilk Mountain is behind her; the stars are twinkling above her. Under the photo, he wrote, *Awesome, Pierce!!! Believe in yourself.*

I'm ice-cold. I want to cry, but I'm empty. Simply empty. The phone slips out of my hand. Everything blurs before my eyes, while something stirs inside me, something too ugly, too dark for me to welcome. It whispers to me things that I've suspected all along—that I can't trust Wyatt, not when it comes to Gwendolyn.

The door opens. I flinch.

But it's just Camila. She walks in and smiles. "Hey, Aria. You waiting for Wyatt?" When I don't respond but just look at her open-mouthed, she adds, "You okay?" Her eyes wander to Wyatt's phone. "Did something happen?"

"No. All good. It's just…nothing. Later, Cam."

The furrows in her forehead deepen. Camila looks like she wants to stop me, but I'm too quick and already out the door.

I literally run out of the B&B, across the street, past passersby, past William, who's sitting on Sally and lighting one of his street-lights, until I arrive in front of the big window to Kate's, out of breath. Anyone seeing me would think I'm not normal, but I can't help it.

Wyatt is sitting in a booth. Across from him is Gwendolyn. She's saying something. He's laughing, a bit shy, a bit reticent. Then she takes his hand and tilts her head, says something else, smiling as if he were the most handsome man in the world. And all hers.

A car honks behind me. Wyatt and Gwendolyn both turn their heads to look at the same time. Seeing me looking in through the window, Gwendolyn starts and lets go of Wyatt as if he'd burned her. He looks thunderstruck.

And I feel numb. My legs are wobbly, maybe from the hike, maybe not. Strangely enough, I am completely calm, and that worries me. The calm before the storm, so to speak.

Wyatt rushes out the door before I can come in. "Aria," he says, taking my hands. I pull them away. His face fills with pain. "Aria, let me explain."

I slowly reach into my jacket pocket and pull out the USB stick. I press it into his hand. Wyatt looks puzzledly from the stick to me.

"Aria, wha—"

"Happy birthday, Wyatt." No tears. No tremor in my voice. Everything is just steady and secure and far too composed for this to be me. I left him a message. He knew I was waiting for him in the snow. Nevertheless, he calmly went out to eat with her. And spent a night with her at Silver Lake. Took photos of her. Once again, he prefers her to me. And I realize that I can't stand it. That this situation alone is already throwing me off, that things with us can never be as they once were.

We aren't the Wyatt and Aria from before anymore. We're Wyatt and Aria and Gwendolyn.

"I saw the photo," I say, my voice totally flat. "Of Gwendolyn on Silver Lake. You were there with her. And now you're here with her, although I was waiting for you with a stupid picnic and stupid champagne. You saw the message. You knew that I was waiting for you, but Gwendolyn was more important. Gwendolyn needed your trust, and, sure, when *Gwendolyn* needs it, you've got to be there. Although I was waiting for you in the fucking cold, up on the fucking mountain. We're through."

I turn around. He follows. He reaches for my hand, but I keep on going. He calls my name, but I don't turn around. I am not listening. I do nothing, nothing at all, except think about how ironic it all is, how *ironic* life is, this pain. It gets better and better, only for it to get worse again. And still you hope, collect shards, cut yourself, and carry on, only to see the next piece of glass fall, and another and another, and then all that's left are shards, and you want to gather them up, but you know you can't; you just can't—it's over.

And then you let yourself fall, hopeless, deaf to the wounds, deaf to the pain, because you know they'll heal. Of course they will, but how ugly will it be? How many scars will there be before there are fewer shards?

It's too ugly. There are just too many.

That's how love is.

That's how it is.

33
My Always

WYATT

It's been two days. Camila and I left the B&B yesterday. The workmen finished up at home, so there was no reason to stay.

Aria's disappeared. She's blocked my number and wasn't at the town hall. Whenever I'm not at training, I sit on the couch and stare at the little black spot on the wall next to the window that used to be a mosquito. I sit there and play with the USB stick that's labeled *My Song for You.*

Right now is one of those moments. It's Saturday night. Two hours ago we played Philadelphia—and won. Caden's throwing a wild party. The first ridiculously large payments from the Aspen Snowdogs are finally making their way to my account, and what am I doing?

I'm staring at the remains of a dead mosquito.

The stairs creak, and a moment later my sister's small face appears in the archway. She puts her hands on the brick and moves back and forth. Seeing her at home on a weekend night, in leggings and one of my training hoodies that reaches to her knees, is rare.

"Hi," she says.

"Hi."

"What are you doing?"

"Nothing."

"Will you take a look at my Spanish homework later?"

"If you clean your room."

Camila lets out a sigh like I'd asked her to give me one of her kidneys. She tiptoes across the room to the bay window, sits down, and puts her arms around her knees. She looks at me blankly.

"What?"

She nods at my hands. "That thing's controlling you."

The USB stick blurs before my eyes as I let it glide through my fingers. "That's not true."

"No, I know."

"I'd be willing to see what's on it whenever, Mila. Just not right now."

"As if. You're chicken."

"Bullshit."

"Okay, you big bad hockey star." Before I realize what she's up to, she's already hopped over and snapped the USB stick out of my hand. "Let's have a look at this damn thing."

My heart sinks, and I jump up. "Mila, no! Wait, give it here!"

But she's already stuck it into the USB port in the TV and grabbed the remote.

"This has got to end. For two days I've been having nightmares about this thing."

She's not the only one. I'm rooted to the spot in front of the coffee table and stare at the fading display.

At first there isn't anything, just the hood of a green jacket on a pair of thighs, and in the background, an excited humming.

"Quick, come on," someone says. "It doesn't matter what he'll say; this is great material for the end-of-the-year speech."

Out of the corner of my eye I can see that Camila is just as confused as I am. But then someone picks up the camera.

I gasp when I realize what kind of video this is. And then it comes. A punch to my solar plexus, just like that. Even though no one has touched me, and there's no one here except my sister, it hurts so much that I choke. I struggle to catch my breath as I'm catapulted through time. Really, it's a simple formula: today minus eight equals then equals *shit*.

Seeing fifteen-year-old me is a shock. I watch myself take the microphone from the commentator and glide across the ice in my green and white jersey. I know what's next. That moment is forever etched in my brain. The spectators in the stands are as quiet as mice, and I remember the charge to the air. Suddenly my mischievous face appears on the square screen above my head where the game is normally shown, and I push up my visor with a self-confident grin. "That was the goal, Moore." Then a quick laugh. "So, you gonna go out with me?"

My teenage voice is so different. And I'm not talking about the shortness of breath from the game. No. It's the carefree sound, the relaxed tone, as if nothing in life was causing me any problems—there was no pressure on my shoulders, no worries in my head. As if everything was so easy. Realizing this, my hair stands up all over my body. What's happened to me? I hardly recognize the boy on the ice laughing so self-confidently, wiping the sweat from his right cheekbone with the ball of his hand.

Aria is superimposed. Her heart-shaped face appears on the screens in the stadium. She's painted a twelve under her right eye and, on the left, in white, a large W. When she realizes she's on the screen, she shakes her head and laughs, buries her face in her hands, only to reappear, putting her hands to the corners of her mouth, and shouting, "Yes!"

If I thought I was choking just a second ago, that was nothing, *nothing* compared to what I feel now. An unpleasant tingling spreads through the back of my head as I breathe in, but there's this blockage, this pain when I see how happy we were, how unbroken. There were no ghosts buzzing around us, no demons—we were just present, every moment a serotonin boost, every breath euphoria.

The video ends, but it's not quite over. The black screen plays a song, and I know which one it is from the very first sounds. Francois Klark's "Always." A slideshow starts, one picture after another, countless memories from six years together, while she tries to tell me in her voice that I will always live in her heart, always be in her dreams, that I am the one who has never left her; no matter how hard she tries to hide, I am the one who makes her heart beat faster, faster than light, and I will be her always forever.

The slideshow stops. My breath catches in my throat.

"Wyatt. I know I'm just seventeen and all, and maybe I don't have any idea about love, but, damn, you and Aria *belong together!*"

I sink back onto the couch, my limbs numb. "She doesn't want me anymore."

"She doesn't want you because she's trying to protect herself!"

"Impossible, Mila. When Aria gets something into her head, you need a miracle to convince her of the opposite."

"My God, Wy, then give her that miracle!"

"HOW?"

Camila fires the remote against my shoulder. "By fighting for her, idiot!"

"She's hiding, Mila. She doesn't want to hear from me. She turns away anyone I ask to speak with her. And she's blocked my number."

"Then use the other one!"

"The other one?"

"You can't be serious. You dressed up like a *lobster* and texted with her for months, but it hasn't occurred to you to pretend to be Paxton?"

"Paxton," I murmur, and the scales fall from my eyes. "Of course. I can reach her as Paxton!"

"You're a genius," she says sarcastically.

Within milliseconds I'm on my feet and digging through the

chest of drawers for the little SIM card. As soon as I've found it and stuck it into my phone, I open the chat with Aria. She's online. Just seeing that, just feeling that tiny bit of her, makes my pulse race. Camila looks over my shoulder as I type.

Hi.

It takes about a minute for Aria to answer.

?

Next to me, Camila lets out an annoyed sigh. "Come on, man, just ask her if you all can meet!"

Funny to see you writing all of a sudden.

It takes me a second to remember what Paxton told me about the party.

Could we see each other?

Why?

Let me explain why I was such a jerk at the party.

It doesn't matter, Paxton. I'm sorry, but I couldn't meet anyone right now anyway.

My lost enthusiasm gets a new boost. Camila excitedly taps my shoulder. "Oooh, you see? You're the only one she wants!"
As I respond, I begin to smile.

Please. Let's clear that up at least.

Fine. When and where?

Camila shrieks. "Yes, baby!"

Silver Lake. In an hour.

34

Hardest Lesson I Ever Had to Learn

ARIA

THE AIR IS ICE-COLD. MY ARMS ARE WRAPPED AROUND MY upper body, and I'm shifting my weight from one foot to the other. A bluethroat shoots out of the fir tree next to me, stretches its delicate wings, and flies across Silver Lake. Snow trickles down and lands gently on my shoulder before I hear footsteps behind me. They fade as the person next to me stops.

The aura is so familiar to me, the smell—I don't even have to look.

"What do you want, Wyatt?"

"I saw the video."

I vacantly contemplate the frozen lake, whose surface is reflecting the stars. "That's no longer important."

"It will always be important, Aria."

To keep perspective, I'm concentrating on the cutting feeling of the cold on my skin. We're standing next to each other but staring straight ahead. From the corner of my eye, I can see that he's buried his hands in his jacket, and every time he exhales, I see his breath.

"I'm meeting someone. You might want to get going."

"I can't."

"Why not?"

He takes a deep breath and turns to me. An owl hoots in the distance. "Have I ever stood you up?"

"We don't have a date."

"We do."

A few feet to my right, the starlight illuminates the head of a baby elk peeking out from between two firs. It ventures forward cautiously, but when it stretches out its still fragile little leg and touches the ice with one hoof, it quickly pulls back again and disappears into the shelter of the trees.

I turn away. "I'm meeting Paxton, Wyatt."

"I *am* Paxton."

Now I turn to face him. And it hurts. Seeing his face, so striking and beautiful, so loved, and just so *Wyatt*, breaks my heart.

"What?"

He briefly looks out onto the lake, to the mountains in the distance, before turning back to look at me. "You never texted with Paxton, Aria. It was me. The whole time."

For a while, all I can do is hold his stare as I try to understand what he's just said. His words only filter through to me in bits and pieces, and when I finally realize it, I can only shake my head.

"Bullshit."

"It's not bullshit." Wyatt pulls his hand out of his pocket and with it his phone. He unlocks it, and the display lights up. With trembling fingers, he holds it out to me. I focus on the image until I realize that it's a chat. Ours.

As if in a trance, I reach out my finger, touch the display, and scroll.

There they are. All of our texts. Beginning with the one I wrote telling him I'd like to get to know him.

"Impossible. That's… You stole his phone."

Wyatt laughs drily as he puts it back in his pocket. "You really believe that, Aria?"

"We talked on the phone. And I know his voice."

"That wasn't my voice or Paxton's. Camila downloaded an app that made me sound like Justin Bieber. Ask her if you don't believe me."

I blink. Quickly. This can't be. He's full of crap. "You're telling me that it was *you* in that lobster outfit?"

He nods.

"And that you texted with me all that time I was trashing you?"

He nods again. And suddenly it dawns on me. The strange attraction between us as we sat in the dark at the party. The tingling in my stomach the whole time we were texting, talking on the phone, whenever I was thinking about him. His strange behavior at his party. The sudden silence when I'd had enough of him after the thing with the woman in the pool... When I stopped messaging him after we got closer again...

My throat constricts, squeezes the air out of me, and at the same time forms a lump that is far too big for me to bear. The time with him was my only hope, my only proof that I could leave Wyatt behind. That my heart was capable of beating for someone else. But it was never anyone else. It was Wyatt the whole time.

Everything collapses. The full extent of what the wreckage of our past is doing to me. I gasp. I can't stop the lump inside me from bursting. I can't stop the hopelessness from turning into tears.

"You destroyed me, Wyatt. You destroyed me and won't stop."

"Aria, I never wanted..."

"Why don't you just stop?" I yell. "You won, Wyatt, okay? You won. You're the only one for me, and I'll probably never manage to get away from you. I'll probably always have to think about how I thought liking someone else was possible, but it was you. YOU. WON. Okay?" With every word I hit him in the chest, and there are tears dripping off my upper lip, salt on the tip of my tongue, and somewhere inside me there's a butterfly that's forgotten how to laugh, that's forgotten how this whole flying thing works.

That's forgotten what sunshine tastes like.

"Ari." Wyatt takes hold of my fists. His touch causes a burning sensation on my skin, right where his fingers close around my wrists. "There wasn't anything going on between Gwen and me. She's a friend and invited me to the diner for my birthday. We ran into each other at Silver Lake by accident. The picture, that was… I took that for her because she'd stopped believing in herself. I even told her about us, and she was happy. *Believe me.*"

My breath is heavy. I can feel my chin trembling as I swallow again and again to hold back the tears. Unsuccessfully. All it takes is the smallest movement from my end, and he lets go of my hands immediately.

"Whether I believe you or not doesn't play any role." I slowly step back and wipe my arm across my face. "It doesn't play any role because I don't trust you anymore, and that's why all this here hurts so goddamn bad. For the first time, I'm realizing that it's really over, that the last bit of hope has died."

His face goes completely white. He looks like a ghost. "Don't say that. Please don't say that."

I ball my hands back into fists, but instead of punching them into his chest again, I press them against my thighs. "What's a relationship without trust, Wyatt?"

He doesn't respond. He's frozen, panic etched into his features, his eyes, everywhere, because now he sees it, too, and he's feeling the pain, more than just pain, because we loved that hope so much.

"Exactly. Nothing."

The butterfly inside me sinks to the ground. Its wings tremble a few more times—those wings it would so much like to use to fly, to taste the clouds, the sky, life, love.

I turn around and go. This time Wyatt doesn't call after me. This time he doesn't try to stop me.

The butterfly no longer moves.

35

We Are the Pages, the Words, the Poem

ARIA

THE WARM GOLDEN LIGHTS OF THE DECORATED FIR TREES blur before my eyes. The longer I look at them, the more I feel them tingling on my skin.

Christmas is a week away. I've never felt lonelier. Not even in Rhode Island.

"Hey, Aria."

I start. Gwendolyn appears next to me, her hands wrapped around a steaming cup. Her black corkscrew curls are spilling over her large, blue down jacket. She looks at me with a somewhat insecure, careful smile.

"What do you want?"

"I can't hold your reaction against you."

"Of course you can't. You slept with my boyfriend. Well, ex-boyfriend."

I ignore her by focusing on Paisley and Knox instead. They are standing next to one of Will's giant reindeer, drinking mulled wine and talking with Levi and Aaron. Paisley is laughing. I wish I could laugh with her.

"Yeah. I did. And I think it's time we talked about it."

"Sorry, but that video was enough for me. Hearing all the gory details straight from you isn't at the top of my list." I make a move to go and join Harper on Silver Lake when all of a sudden Gwendolyn's fingers close around my wrist. Her touch burns like fire. Not a good one. A painful one.

"Wait, Aria. Just listen to me. Please. We have to talk. We used to be such good friends, before…"

"Before you fucked my boyfriend. Yeah. Unexpected plot twist."

"I wasn't myself."

"You don't say. You going to tell me you were drunk now, Gwendolyn? Sorry, that doesn't count. Drunk or not, you check to see what's going on when suddenly your good friend's boyfriend's dick is in your face. Sirens go off, Gwendolyn, and they're pretty hard to ignore. So don't tell me it was a little mistake or whatever because you were smashed because…"

"I wasn't drunk."

Now I'm confused. "That doesn't make things more positive. I mean, are you trying to tell me you decided to sleep with my boyfriend when you were sober?"

"Yeah. No. Aria, honestly, I don't know. If I knew what was wrong with me, I could tell you. All I know is that, at that moment, something happened with me that I don't understand myself. It…" She turns away. Her breath is shaky, and I can see her trying to swallow.

Whether I want to or not, I can't help but see her desperation is real. She seems completely exhausted. This isn't an act. She bites her lower lip and looks at the lake. "Something happened to me, Aria. Something that terrifies me. You're the first person I'm talking about this to, and you're probably going to think I'm bizarre or something, but I think I was possessed."

I can't stop staring at her. "Possessed? Like, by demons or whatever?"

Gwendolyn shrugs. She looks pained. "No idea. Not really. I

mean, that's not possible. But my memory of that evening and the days beforehand… I wasn't in control of myself. It was like I was being controlled by someone else. No one knows that because they wouldn't take me seriously. Everyone would just think I'm bonkers. But the fear it could happen again paralyzes me every day." Only now does she look at me. Her caramel-colored eyes meet my perplexed gaze.

I don't know what to say. What to think. Never in my life would I have expected to hear something like that, and the worst thing is…I believe her. The way she's standing here telling me, the fear in her eyes, the panic in her face… You just don't make this kind of thing up.

"You don't have to believe me," she says, her soft voice fading into the Christmas song filling the air. "I probably wouldn't if I were in your shoes. But telling you was important to me. I owed you an explanation, and you needed to know that I would never have done that thing with Wyatt if…if I'd been myself."

I blink. Quickly. I know I should say something, but instead, all I do is stare, which probably makes her feel that I think she's bonkers. Gwendolyn smiles sadly before she shrugs one more time and turns away. It's only when she's moving off in the direction of the woods that I come to my senses. "Gwen!" I run after her, and this time it's me grabbing her wrist.

She turns and looks at me. And I can't believe I actually say the following, but I do.

"I believe you."

Her lips part in surprise. "You… What?"

"I believe you," I say, this time more forcefully. "And I'm sorry that you have to go through feeling so afraid. And I'm sorry you did something I'm judging you for even though you didn't want to. But all the same…"

"All the same, you can't forgive me."

"No, it's not that. I mean, I want to. But it's hard. Wyatt was…*is* everything for me. And these images are always in my head. I so want everything to be okay again, Gwen. So much. But you're always there, beneath him, and all this time I have blamed you both for everything. Believing you is one thing, you know? But forgetting everything is…"

"Next to impossible." Gwen's eyes dart to a fir tree, its branches dripping with snow. She sighs, then turns back to look at me. "I get it, Aria. And no doubt things will never be the same between us ever again, but I give you a lot of credit for listening to me."

Only now do I let go of her wrist and knit my brows. "I'm going to try to forgive you. I promise to do my best. I can't tell you when that'll be. I can't tell you *if* it will ever be. But I'm going to try, Gwen, because I think I need it as much as you do."

Gwen nods. "Maybe someday."

I smile. "Maybe someday."

For a moment, all we do is look at each other. Eventually, Gwen lowers her eyes and walks past me, back to the square. I watch her go back to Paisley and the others and how they immediately turn toward her. Levi says something, and Gwen laughs reservedly.

"Just like you always were."

And I wince yet another time this evening.

Suddenly Mom's standing next to me. She hands me a cup of mulled wine with a soft smile on her face.

For a brief moment, my mother closes her eyes, and I can see her taking in all the sweet smells. Toasted almonds and doughnuts, buttered waffles and gingerbread, powdered sugar, chocolate— everything heavenly, everything sumptuous.

"Whenever you were sad or had to be stronger than you could be at the moment, you'd withdraw. Looking deep inside yourself, delicately, wistfully."

I look at her for a spell before taking a sip of my mulled wine and looking out over the square in its Christmas best. Sinatra's "Jingle Bells" is playing in the background while Aspen's residents are laughing and happily making their way past all the makeshift tables. I take another sip and watch the people, their hearts, and the joy in their eyes.

"It hurts."

"Yes, it does." She glances over to William, who's in conversation with Spirit Susan again. She's waving her arms wildly while, behind her, in a careless half-circle, stand twelve nervous kids in swan outfits. "And that's okay, Aria. Be sad, but don't forget that you're also more than that. More than your memories. There is so much about you that's worth loving, and you should. With or without Wyatt."

"I know." And I really mean that. It's strange, completely unreal, because I would have thought that after our last meeting, the last stone would finally break away, that I would finally lose my grip and fall into the depths. But while my feet were still dragging me through the night—through our messy little town, my home—I realized that nothing of the sort was happening. There was no abyss. Everything was solid, every step, every movement, but it still hurt. A fire was burning inside me that could not be extinguished, even in the hidden places of my soul. Sure, I mean, of course. I love Wyatt, the boy with the gap in his teeth and the dimples. I love that star hockey player whose eyes would shine with moonlight in the deepest nights when our lips touched, when we wordlessly spoke of love. I will always love him.

But pain wasn't the only thing that came with saying goodbye. There was something else. Something that I only discovered now, even though it had been blooming for a long time. It was as if the dense fog inside me had finally lifted, as if I had grown, even though I thought I'd lost it. I realized how strong I am. How strong the pain had made me.

"It hurts; it's tearing me apart, and anything else would be inhuman. I mean, he was a part of me. Naturally, I'm an individual. Naturally, life will go on without him because I'm valuable, with or without Wyatt. I know that, but nevertheless I can't give up. The hope that we *still* could manage to be something someday is there. Someday, he and I could be he and I again. Like before."

Mom nods. A satisfied smile appears on her lips as she takes hold of my arm. Together we walk across the square. Passing by William, Mom shoots him an oh-come-on-already-Will glance that causes him to sigh.

"Fine," he says. "You win. Do your darn show, Sue."

Susan's squeaks are followed by the heartwarming laughter of children. We stroll on to Silver Lake. Harper's out on the ice, ready to practice one of her programs for Skate America.

"That's all I wanted," Mom says.

The Christmas music is replaced by Duncan Laurence's "Arcade." Harper's music. She begins to skate. I take another sip of wine and follow her elegant movements with my eyes. "What do you think?"

My mother puts an arm around my shoulder, pulls me to her, and places a kiss on my cap. "I want you to finally see how valuable you are—just you, on your own, no matter what's going on around you, or who you're with or not."

"Thanks, Mom."

She lets go. "But there's just one problem."

"What's that?"

"You miss him. The last few days you've been nothing but a heap of sadness. Whenever I saw you, you had bags underneath your eyes and baked-bean stains around your mouth. Aria, dear. If you really want to be together again so bad one day, why not now? Why wait, sweetheart? Life is too short when you're sure."

Harper looks toward the sky and goes into a spin. The sight makes my heart skip a beat.

"No idea. Maybe to give the two of us a little time. I don't know how I'm going to manage. To trust him, I mean. After everything that happened. At the moment, it just seems impossible."

"Do you think it has to be this way? Don't you think it's time to let go of your fear? He'll help you to build that trust back up. You'd be much better at it together than time could ever be on its own."

In one graceful movement, Harper pushes off her skate edge and leaps. Her landing is a bit wobbly, but she lands it all the same. But the way her eyes light up at this little thing, how happy it makes her, knocks me out. How *simple* it can be.

"I don't know. What I *do* know is that letting him go doesn't feel right. It feels like I'm giving up. As if I were taking the easy way out, not wanting to fight. As if I was thinking that I was just too weak, even though I know I'm strong."

Mom cranes her neck back to follow Harper's movements as she makes another jump.

"That's what I thought."

"Things could go on without Wyatt. Up until now, I was afraid to say that; I was afraid to even admit it, but…isn't owning the fact that I want to fight for what I love a sign of strength?"

"Not just strength, Aria, but courage. Resolve. And that your heart is too big to keep for yourself alone."

A lot happens in this second; it's a charged moment of life, one of the rare kind that allows my senses to perceive so much. All at once. I feel all my hair standing on end. It's so intense. It's like I can sense every single one of them. Scents in my nose—double and triple strong—of snow and Christmas, magic and fir trees, and home. The taste of mulled wine in my mouth—tart but sweet, cinnamon and vanilla, and sugar and orange. There is the melody of the song, the sounds that get under my skin, the astonished sounds of others admiring my best friend, and the cheerful sounds of people chatting. And finally there's Harper, gripping her skate with her fingers, stretching her leg and spinning fast, fast, faster, a cream-colored blur accompanied by golden lights reflecting off the ice beneath her, a sight that embodies the beauty of this moment.

A new feeling tingles inside me, a strange one I am unfamiliar with. I think it's *acceptance*. I have accepted that Wyatt and I are no longer who we used to be; I have accepted that what happened happened and that nothing can change the past. We don't have to pick up where we left off. We can start again without knowing where it will take us. How we want to shape the present and what we want to feel in the here and now is up to us—happiness or sadness, ecstasy or darkness. Whatever the future holds, wherever my decisions will take me...

I am Aria Moore. Chaotic, loving, my cupboards full of no-point cups, and a predilection for cake.

I am Aria Moore, and I love who I am, an individual in the world, happy and full of life. But to be honest?

This life should be with Wyatt. It's more beautiful with him in it. More worth living. Warmer. More loving. More exciting. Funnier. More *poetic.*

I alone have the power to decide how I want to shape my life, and I want to make my life with Wyatt. I want to do everything with him.

Harper lands. She opens her eyes. Sees me. Sees that I'm there, that I believe in her, that I saw how she believed in herself right before attempting this jump that's so tough for her.

She laughs. A quiet laugh, true, but to me it's loud because it's the only thing I hear. Pure and bright and free, and that takes away the last bit of doubt, the last bit of uncertainty. Because it reminds me of how I sound every time Wyatt makes me laugh, whenever he says something that doesn't make any sense at all but still makes me smile; he makes sure that the butterfly flies.

I hand Mom her cup back. "I've got to find him."

Mom's eyes dig into mine, green on green. "Then get going, Aria. *Go.*"

I nod. I frantically search the square, but not for him. I knew he wasn't here upon arriving.

He's not here, but his sister is. Camila is munching on some almonds while watching Vaughn roll through the snow in his full-body costume, surrounded by dancing snowflake children.

"Camila!" Huffing and puffing, I tap her on the shoulder. A few almonds hit the snow as she starts.

"God, Aria. You scared me."

"Where's Wyatt?"

"Wyatt?"

"Yeah!"

"Why?"

I become impatient, inhale haltingly, but the air doesn't reach my lungs quickly enough, so I end up breathing even *more* frantically. "I've got to tell him something."

"Aria." Her face turns sympathetic. "He got the point."

"What point?" She doesn't answer, so I repeat my question—this time hysterically—because of course I know what she means. I just don't want to hear it. But I have to because our heads are weird sometimes—really weird.

"That it's over. He made a mistake, unconsciously, sure. But he sees that now. Wyatt has understood that he needs to let you go. He regrets what he did, regrets it hard, but he can live with it now. He's moving on, Aria; he's accepted that at this point. I still love you like a sister, but, please, *please* leave him alone. I can't handle seeing him suffering like this."

"Where is he?"

"I don't get it. You don't want him but won't leave him alone."

"*Where is he?*"

When she presses her lips together and her expression takes on a harder tone, I see that I won't be getting any farther. I rub my gloved hand across my face and blink so as to be able to look into her eyes better. "Listen. I know that you don't believe me, but I want to save what we had. Really. And this time conclusively, me and him like before, but new, and everything."

Camila holds her breath before shakily letting it back out. "If you hurt him again, I'm never going to forgive you."

"I wouldn't forgive myself, Cam."

She hesitates. She looks at me for a moment, then turns and watches the dancing children.

And then she sighs. "He's at the airport."

"*At the airport?*"

"He got an offer from the Seattle Kraken. They want him. He's flying out there to sign the contract."

Her words break over me like an avalanche.

"*What?*"

Camila doesn't respond; she just looks at me, and that makes everything worse, more real. "But... What about...your house? You?"

"He's looking for something new for the two of us out there."

"*Something new?*" My head simply will not accept the idea of Wyatt leaving Aspen, of starting over somewhere new. Aspen without the Lopezes is like... I don't know. It just doesn't work. It doesn't *fit.*

Camila digs her hands into the pockets of her jacket. "If you want to talk to him, you better do it now. Drive out to the airport. Otherwise it'll be too late."

My mouth moves to speak, but no sound comes out; my eyes are like saucers. I blink.

Once.

Twice.

And then I start running.

I run like I've never run before, past Vaughn, past the children, past Paisley, Gwendolyn, Levi, Aaron, and Knox, who look at me confusedly, on and on, more and more quickly.

My breath's a rattle by the time I make it to my car, rip open the door, and get moving. The snow whirls as I make a sudden turn past Wyatt's house. I take Buttermilk Mountain Avenue far too quickly—right, left, left, right. My fingers hurt because I'm using my blinker more than I need to. Wyatt's no-point cup is spinning around on its string like it's cheering me on, *Quicker, Aria! Quicker!*

If I take the highway, I'll be at the airport in ten minutes— another benefit to living in our little town. Racing down the road,

I tap my index finger against the steering wheel continually. The radio's making me nervous. I turn it off, and then, finally, I park.

I run through the carpeted lobby, dodging tourists—some just arriving and some leaving. "Sorry, sorry, thanks," stretching out my neck on the lookout for a big guy, quite possibly in a baseball hat.

I look around everywhere, turn in circles, and search every inch of the lobby, glance at every one of the countless heads, but he's not there. Cursing, I dig my phone out of my pocket; it takes me three attempts to unlock it. My fingers are shaking so much, but then I look for his number, unblock it, call…

Voicemail. The veins in my jugular are pounding. I look at the departures board. And there it is. White type against a blue background.

Seattle—boarding.

One second—doubt.

Two seconds—too late.

Three seconds—I'm going to lose him.

Four seconds—I'm not going to let that happen.

Five seconds—the butterfly's wings are moving. I'm not giving up. There's got to be a way. There's *got to.*

And then I see her. There, behind the counter in the departures hall, eyes staring at the computer screen. Emma Jones, an old high school friend. My face burns as I run across the lobby toward her. I edge past the long line, getting angry stares, but I don't care. I push my way to the head of the line and step in front of the person who's just about to go to her.

"Hey!" a guy in a chic Burberry coat hisses.

I shoot him an apologetic glance before my hands land on the countertop more powerfully than intended. "Emma!"

She starts so violently that she puts a hand to her chest. "God, Aria! Did you ever scare me!"

"I need your help."

"Calm down a sec. Did something happen?"

"Yeah. No. I mean, Wyatt."

"What about him?"

"He's… He's about to get on a plane. To Seattle."

"And?"

"That won't do."

She looks at me like I've lost it. "Aria, what kind of weird crap are you saying?"

"He's… We… I need a ticket, Emma."

"To Seattle?" Now she *really* thinks I've lost it. "They're *boarding*, Aria. You can't buy a ticket."

I swallow hard. I hate to do this, but desperate times call for desperate measures and all that. I take a deep breath. "In seventh grade you pooped your pants, Emma, when William had to step out to buy some more popcorn and the guys turned on an old horror movie. I gave you my pants. I gave you my pants, Emma, and I spent the rest of the night in my reindeer leggings without batting an eyelash because you needed my help. And now I need yours."

"My pants?"

"Your help!"

She presses her lips together and looks at me, and then she looks from right to left, once, twice, three times, then heaves a sigh. "But there's no way. You simply cannot buy a ticket anymore."

"Emma…"

"But I can let you make an announcement."

Relief. Pure, unfiltered relief. My shoulders slump. I nod. "That works. Just a few seconds. That's all I need."

"My boss is gonna kill me," Emma mumbles. She looks anything but convinced as she waves me behind the counter and nods at the thin microphone next to her computer.

The line behind me lets out a collective sigh. Some of them throw their arms up in frustration. With the absolute certainty that I have never been so nervous in my life, I bend over the microphone. My heart throws itself against my chest with strong, racing beats.

Every nerve pathway in my body transmits a thousand charged sparks of tension, making me tingle, pulsate, hope, and fear all at once. I am a nervous wreck. My field of vision blurs.

"Aria." It's Emma. "You okay?"

The fog slowly clears. I am only vaguely aware of a buzzing babble of voices as I nod. I try to stand on my shaky legs. He's here somewhere, somewhere. My gaze flits over the many heads, but I'm too nervous, completely beside myself. Oh God. Help, help, help! I don't see any baseball caps.

Get going, a voice whispers in my head. *You don't have any more time.* I take a deep breath.

"You know, Lopez, we were courageous," I begin, my voice shaky but there. "The way we fought for each other the whole time, knowing we didn't want to give up despite how much we had hurt each other. You me and me you—that was really courageous. I mean, shit, just try fighting for something that hurts so bad that you can't even breathe, that wants to knock you down and keep you there—how masochistic is that? But, to be really honest, Wy, it was worth it. All of it. The tears. The hopelessness. The empty feeling in my chest when I slowly began to feel like I just couldn't do it anymore... What did it think it was doing, nesting in me as if I'd allowed it in, as if I'd wanted it?"

The whole time I keep rubbing my chest and try to ignore how everyone in the lobby is staring at me. "But if someone were to ask me, 'Aria, you can have all that time back, with all your love and everything, but you have to go through all the pain again—you interested?' I would say *yes* right away. Because it's so easy to love you, Wyatt, and it's so hard to try not to. Sure, sometimes I'm afraid. The thing we have is so big and real and powerful, and I was never good at anything, not really, not at baking, not at volleyball. But you know what? I love you, and that's one thing I can do really well, and I don't want to give that up. Wyatt, please, don't let me give up on that. I want us to work. I want you. I want everything. But the one thing I don't want is for you to go. Because, come on, Wyatt, a Kraken? You're a Snowdog!"

I stand there out of breath. And I wait. No one says a thing. We're talking that famous silence where you can hear a pin drop. The guy in the Burberry jacket is wearing a sympathetic look now.

"I think that thing we had was right," I continue just because I don't want it to be over. I want to continue thinking that he can hear me, that I didn't come here in vain. "It's just that time didn't understand, and this here is our reunion; that's the challenge. I want this, really. I would give everything for us, every day and forever, because if you're by my side, then I'll never be lost and… I know I thought I couldn't love anymore—but I was just too afraid of losing myself, but that's not a danger anymore because I know who I am, because I love who I am. So, Wyatt, please, let's give it another try, you and me, like before, with nothing between us anymore."

Breathing quickly, I scan the lobby and wait. I've said everything. But no one moves. There's no Wyatt running down a corridor to meet me. Nothing happens.

Why isn't anything happening?

And then it comes. Panic. He's not here. It *was* all in vain. He took an earlier flight. Or he is on a later one. Here I am, my soul bare, speechless, having said everything in just two minutes, but for nothing.

In this hopeless, desperate moment, suddenly I see him. He was here the whole time, sitting on that gray stool just ten feet away, but I didn't notice him because all I was doing was feeling.

He was here the whole time.

He stands up. Walks over to me.

"You're here," I say.

"Sure." He shrugs. "Where else?"

"In Seattle."

"Aria." He gives me his hand. I take it. Electric shocks run through my body as he leads me around the counter.

And then I'm standing right in front of him, looking up into his face. His fingertips skim my freckles, a faint smile on his face. "How could I fly to Seattle while leaving my heart behind?"

"Your heart?"

"You, Aria. You're my heart." There's his face, right in front of me, his forehead touching mine. "I want you. Forever."

"Me, too. And I want you to call me Lopez at some point because I love that name, just like you, just like us."

His lips brush mine. "Do you know what I'd say?"

"What?"

"We're total chaos, Lopez."

"And I would agree with you," I whisper, my eyelids lowered, mouth parted. "You got that right, Lopez, one hundred percent."

A brief, husky laugh against my lips. "We're lucky that I *love* chaos."

Dimples, honey-colored eyes, a heart-stopping moment.

So, here we are, just three of the things that connect me to Wyatt. But they are all that lies ahead of me, all that I want.

Look at how beautiful this butterfly is: it knows how to fly again.

How beautiful.

Playlist

Noah Cyrus—"July"
Jeremy Zucker, Chelsea Cutler—"You Were Good to Me"
Francois Klark—"Always" (acoustic)
Kodaline—"High Hopes"
Katelyn Tarver—"Love Me Again"
James Arthur—"Quite Miss Home"
Jaymes Young—"Happiest Year"
JP Saxe, Julia Michaels—"If the World Was Ending"
Lewis Capaldi—"Before You Go"
Anson Seabra—"That's Us"
Michael Schulte—"You Said You'd Grow Old with Me"
Calum Scott—"You Are the Reason"
Alex & Sierra—"Little Do You Know"
Lewis Capaldi—"Don't Get Me Wrong"
Dean Lewis—"Lose My Mind"
Anna Clendening—"Boys Like You"
Duncan Laurence—"Arcade"
Sody—"Reason to Stay"
Maisie Peters—"Favourite Ex"
We the Kings, Elena Coats—"Sad Song"

Acknowledgments

What a wonderful experience writing this book has been. What profound moments my heart experienced as my thoughts filled these pages. And, for this, there are several people I would like to thank.

First and foremost, my affectionate, wonderful, and strong mama. You taught me that fear is not an option and introduced me to many life paths while pushing me to choose my own, whatever it might be. From the beginning, you believed in me and still do, never doubting me for a moment, and for that I will be forever thankful.

I would like to thank my agent, Kathrin, from Agentur Schlück, for making my dream come true. Without you, this series would not exist—thank you from the bottom of my heart.

Thanks to Gesche Wendebourg for finding a home for this series in English at Sourcebooks. Further thanks, of course, are due to my editor, Laura. Your immeasurable commitment to this series means so much to me. Thank you!

And the deepest thanks to my husband, Jannik, for supporting me heart and soul. I don't know how many times I would have fallen were it not for you holding my hand and showing me how beautiful it is to believe in yourself.

I would like to thank my siblings for having my back and showing me how wonderful, how *right*, it is to follow your dreams.

Dearest Lexie, thank you for the countless hours we wrote together via Skype. For your motivation, your zest for doing, your large heart, and your friendship. I am so thankful we got to know each other!

And Mirka, thank you for the many conversations about writing and life and all the motivational words. From the very beginning, huh?

Sandra, thank you for always being there and for always lending an ear. And you, dear Toni, for so many years of authorial friendship and all the steps we've taken together. Thank you!

And not to forget my dear test readers, Nadine and Janine. What would I have done without you? Nadine, I can't even count how many times your familiarity with hockey saved me, and Janine—how quickly you read everything through right when I needed you! Thank you both.

Finally, and above all, I'd like to thank my readers for reading my stories, for giving me courage, and for showing me that my love of writing manages to spark a little bit of poetry in your hearts.

About the Author

Bestselling author Ayla Dade was born in 1994 and lives with her family in northern Germany. She has won the hearts of her readers with her new adult romances, each of them a *Der Spiegel* bestseller that remains in the top ranks for weeks. She studied law but spends every spare minute she has writing. She is a popular book blogger and fills the pages of her novels with tumultuous feelings, secrets and intrigue, and love and spice. When she isn't dreaming about the world of her books, she spends her time playing sports and snuggling up in front of the fireplace with a good book.

Instagram: @ayladade
TikTok: @ayladade.author

LIKE SNOW WE FALL

She knows she should stay away from him...but
how can she when they're living together?

All figure skater Paisley Harris wants is to leave behind her troubled past for something more. So when she's given a way out of her Minnesota trailer park by applying for iSkate, a prestigious skating school in Aspen, Colorado, she takes it, seeking a fresh start in the picturesque winter landscape.

Knox Winterbottom stands on the precipice of a new level in his snowboarding career. When Paisley and Knox meet, their worlds collide: she, the disciplined and determined newbie, and he, the arrogant, unpredictable, and charismatic risk-taker. Despite his strict rule against dating figure skaters, their attraction slowly pulls them together.

Paisley gets a job at the Winterbottoms' chalet, unaware that Knox lives there. She needs the money and lodging, so she stays. But with Paisley and Knox under the same roof, it's only a matter of time before they can't keep their hands off each other.

"A gripping story and an irresistible setting!"
—Anna Todd, *New York Times* bestselling author,
for *Blackwell Palace*